Ultimate Lesbian Erotica 2006

Edited by Nicole Foster

alyson books
NEW YORK
Celebrating Twenty-Five Years

MANUFACTURED IN THE UNITED STATES OF AMERICA.

THIS TRADE PAPERBACK ORIGINAL IS PUBLISHED BY ALYSON BOOKS,
P.O. BOX 1253, OLD CHELSEA STATION, NEW YORK, NEW YORK 10113-1251.
DISTRIBUTION IN THE UNITED KINGDOM BY TURNAROUND PUBLISHER SERVICES LTD.,
UNIT 3 OLYMPIA TRADING ESTATE, COBURG ROAD, WOOD GREEN,
LONDON N22 6TZ ENGLAND.

FIRST EDITION: DECEMBER 2005

05 06 07 08 09 a 10 9 8 7 6 5 4 3 2 1

ISBN 1-55583-917-7
ISBN-13 978-1-55583-917-8

CREDITS
COVER PHOTOGRAPHY BY ANDREAS KUEHN/IMAGE BANK/GETTY IMAGES.
COVER DESIGN BY MATT SAMS.

Contents

Introduction

Girls, your fantasies are never going to be the same after reading this new collection of the sexiest erotica of 2005, by the hottest writers out there. When I call these stories the ultimate in lesbian erotica, I'm not just teasing you with empty promises. These stories are hot, hot, hot.

Find out how Kim makes her girlfriend's fantasies come true with some delicious birthday spankings in Rachel Kramer Bussel's "Having Her Birthday Cake, and Eating It, Too." In Diana Chase's "In the Closet," our hero only has so much time to see what her friend Eva's boi is hiding in those jeans before Eva comes home. In Kristina Wright's "Unrequited," learn more about how to make a friend feel much, much better after she goes through a painful break-up. Enter a dilapidated farmhouse and see what happens between two women—one young, one mature—when a tornado approaches in Jean Roberta's "A Full Moon for Lammas." Spend "Another Night at Daddy's," the sexiest dyke bar, with a girl who can flutter her tongue 216 beats per minute. I'd like to meet her.

And that's just the beginning. Okay, sweeties, come a little closer, and take a look for yourself. Peek behind the curtain of these pages to read never-before-seen stories that I selected from the sexiest out there.

—Nicole Foster

Juke Joint

JANET WILLIAMS

Catfish was on the Thursday night menu at the juke joint for those who arrived early. Fried on the grill with flour, corn meal, and a heavy dash of seasoned salt, it was fresh as the day, succulent, hot, and juicy. Jasmine and her youngest sister, Iris, caught the tail end of it, so to speak. Sharing the last plate, it was barely enough to satisfy. Jasmine's hunger was such that she could have polished off a tall serving all by herself, but after finishing her half, she settled for a beignet followed by a longneck from the bar.

At the side entrance, the open double doors strained against a pair of sand-filled copper spittoons. Every now and again a little breeze made its way inside, breaking up the wispy blue streaks of cigarette smoke. The October air was heavy with moisture, the kind of evening when it's hard to tell just how warm or cold it really is.

Jasmine and her sister took delight in live music, especially swing and bebop, the kind of jumping sound that makes your feet do things they wouldn't ordinarily do. The two danced together on the crowded wooden floor, and later with men who whirled them about for a song or two. But now it was late in the evening and the crowd thinned enough to reveal a few empty tables. They expected Iris's beau, Charlie, to roll in well after dark, which he did.

"Charlie!" Iris shouted over the music. "Over here!" She waved with enthusiasm, causing Jasmine to grab her beer and steady the table. Iris latched on to her man like the clamped jaws of an alligator. They exchanged a round of pleasantries and the couple soon excused themselves from further conversation, leaving Jasmine to wait out the evening just as she had done so many times during the summer months.

Sitting alone, Jasmine rested her chin in the pocket of her upturned hand. String Bean was at the stand-up bass and would be playing well into the night. Come quitting time he'd walk Jasmine home, give her a kiss, and hope for more. He was a patient man, tall and gangly with a prominent nose. The girls didn't exactly throw themselves at his feet. Like Jasmine, he was getting up in years for a single person. Not having a day job didn't seem to bother him much except when it came to thinking about settling down. Anyway, he'd inherited the old bass from the man they say was his daddy. String Bean took to it early; he started playing when the bass was a good length taller than he was. He'd since grown into the instrument and exhibited an amusing personal style. His long fingers and sinewy arms bounced around as if they were made of some kind of newfangled rubber. On soulful numbers he caressed the long neck and body, sliding his fingers up and down the thick strings with sensitive deliberation. The possibility existed, she supposed, that he might be good in bed, but she wasn't eager to test the theory.

As his hands slid along the strings, she recalled the last man she bedded, Floyd—lying as one, his face dark as night, his large, even teeth reflecting the faintest glimmer of whatever light there was. Something was never right being with him, feeling his desire, trying desperately to find her own. Complicating matters, the rubber had broken and she had worried about it for two weeks until "the curse" showed up and became a blessing. Once patient, Floyd realized they had different ideas about life. Rather quickly he went off and married Maybelle, and now they have twin girls who sit between them on the church pew. Jasmine hadn't seen him at the juke joint for years. She hadn't made love in years. After Floyd she took up with String Bean, in part because it kept the others away, giving her time for the right person to appear.

The waiter dropped off another beer and picked up two empties. She placed the cool bottle next to her temple and felt the moisture from the glass mingle with her own sweat, little beads lined up next to her hairline. Then, holding the longneck, she took a drink.

The bottle was dark brown, much darker than her skin, which was the color of coffee when you poured in too much milk. There were times when she could have passed, could have nonchalantly ignored the "coloreds only" sections around town, but it wasn't a high priority. Some folks just assumed, and she never corrected them. She understood the element of danger for those who deliberately tried to pass, and admired the ones who made a successful go of it. If it worked for them, well, that was their business.

Her face, though tired around the eyes and soft at the jaw line, was unmarked, unlike her sister's, whose blotchy skin tones were hard to blend out without harsh products or a lot of makeup. Jasmine didn't care much for makeup, nor did she feel she needed it. It certainly wasn't a requirement at the dress shop where she put in a full day. The dress she had worn to work was still on her back, a yellow cotton print adorned with a ruffle at the neckline, armholes, and hem. It flattered her figure and was good for dancing. The material had a nice weight to it. It moved with her, at least until sweat, like static electricity, made the material cling to her body. Her feet ached from standing, yet it was dancing that made the world go away.

The evening was winding down, and being a patient sort, she waited. Her sister had literally become entangled with Charlie in a dark corner booth, and it looked like they wouldn't be leaving for a while either. One of Iris's legs was crossed over Charlie's, and their heads were joined in a dance that would likely lead to ecstatic electricity beneath the oilcloth table cover.

Feeling restless, she sighed and let her eyes wander about the room. In another corner at the far end of the curved bar she saw a young fellow taking her in. She caught his glance and wished she could throw it back. It was too late. He slid off his bar stool, laid a bill on the counter and sauntered her way.

He came right up, nodded a greeting, and took the empty chair next to her, swinging it around so he sat in it backward with his legs spread to each side. He looked barely a man, certainly younger than she, a fact he likely realized now that he was up close. If he fig-

ured her for older, he didn't pay it no never mind, for he took his
long graceful index finger and boldly traced a line down her arm
from just beneath her ruffled sleeve to her elbow. She gazed at his
face, smooth and hairless with a hint of a smile showing through
his closed lips. She noticed his fingernails were clean and short, as
if he had paid for a manicure that very afternoon. His black hair
was nappy, no pomade, cut closer on the sides than the top, and his
clothes hung on him a little big, as if he had just lost about twenty
pounds or so.

Grasping her arm ever so lightly, the gentleman signaled his
desire to dance. Jasmine checked on String Bean, who was
absorbed in the final bars of the musical number, and decided to
go with the moment. Dancing seemed a better alternative than
shouting a meaningless preliminary conversation. The band
immediately started in on a hopping number featuring a clarinet.
Already she could feel her energy level lift as she rose from the
chair.

He was a graceful dancer, respectful of their first meeting, not
holding her too close, twirling her round, moving her in, then out,
leading with direction and style. His hand swept around her waist
and released. Moves were easy with him and she acknowledged it
with her smile. It was the way he touched her, definite, yet not
rough, that pleased her and stirred her feminine nature. Now she
was glad the fellow had come to her table. Breathing deeply, she
clasped his hands at the end of the long dance while turning away
from String Bean in case he might see her joy.

Rather than return to the table, he escorted her outside, not an
altogether unpleasant prospect. They walked in silence, veering
down the less-used dirt path—that is, away from the juke joint and
not toward town—her hand fixed in the crease of his jacketed
elbow. He mopped his brow with a white handkerchief and she
could hear his breathing slow. Warm air currents gently dropped
down from the hills, swirling with the cool moistness of the hollow; and because it was late in the year, they walked on with no
bother from mosquitoes. After a spell, they had strolled far enough

away that the music was faint in the distance. No one was around, and Jasmine wondered if they should be heading back, or at least exchanging names and other formalities.

As they crossed onto a low wooden footbridge, the dull noise of their steps interrupted a chorus of nearby frogs. She hesitated and glanced over her shoulder. He stopped walking. Jasmine reached for the round hewn bridge railing, and in the filtered light of a gibbous moon looked the quiet fellow in the eyes, trying to make out his intent. She thought she had seen him once before, maybe last Thursday. The nice woven shirt, cotton pants, heavy leather shoes—he could be one of those new fellows they brought in at the bank, she thought. Probably doesn't know anybody.

Dampness wafting up from the bog chilled her skin, sending a flush of goose bumps over her exposed arms. She tried to rub off the feeling, but stopped when he took off his jacket and placed it lightly around her shoulders.

"Thanks." Jasmine's voice seemed loud in her head.

When his jacket was square on, he placed his index finger under her chin, dropped his head just a little and planted a soft kiss on her lips. She felt the softness of his chest meet her bosom and knew immediately—this was no man—this was a woman!

Jasmine pulled back at this unexpected development and felt the knobby bridge rail hard against her spine. The tempo of the moment was set by the quickened heartbeat in her ears and her vision sharpened in the darkness. Her body tightened and tussled with her reeling thoughts, but it was curiosity that came up from behind to win. She stroked the woman's face with the flat of her hand and was rewarded with the sight of broad full lips that curled into a knowing smile. In wonderment, Jasmine twirled her fingers through the woman's untreated hair, and fingered the masculine stiffness of her pressed collar.

"How can this be?" Jasmine asked. "I thought…"

"I'll take you back." Her voice was midrange, ambiguous.

"No, wait, it's…it's just not what I thought." Jasmine touched the woman's lips as she took in this one who passed for a man. Her mind broke free and spun away, landing somewhere it would not ordinarily go. "Do it again."

Jasmine stood tall and allowed another kiss. The woman paused. Jasmine stood strong, eyes half closed, breathing audibly in measured bars as she drew the young woman near. Another kiss followed, a long sensuous kiss that sent renewed chills through her body—chills that were welcome. The sensation of those generous lips pressed against her own imparted a luscious desire that made her feel alive! Unabashed by her greedy hunger for this strange fruit, she shared the saliva generated from her renewed appetite.

Reclaiming her tongue, the woman released and passed her mouth along Jasmine's neck to the hollow at the base of her throat, down to the neckline of her scoop-cut dress. Jasmine leaned back and wrapped her arms around the rail, allowing her seductress the liberty she had denied others—had denied even herself. Her heart pounded against the woman's hands as they lightly passed over her dress. She visualized the shapeliness of her own figure as the stranger tenderly, unhurriedly, wound her hands around and around in an exotic choreographed dance designed to take in the curves of Jasmine's small waist, pronounced hips, mature bottom and heaving breasts. *This was the dance that made the days worth living,* she thought. *And, my dance partner, I never…*

The woman squatted low and eased her long fingers up Jasmine's skirt, tracing lines up and down, up and down, going a little higher each time until she gently placed her hand on Jasmine's cotton-covered mound. Without letting go, the woman rose and pressed her mouth to Jasmine's, extending her tongue to reach in deeply.

Oh, it had been a long time, such a long time, and never like this, never so wildly delicious.

And, being so otherwise occupied in her musings, she couldn't quite tell how that hand moved inside her panties. Jasmine gasped, and though no one was near, she dared not utter the rhythmic composition building within her, leaving her mounting tension unannounced to the frogs that had resumed bellowing out their love songs in the steaming bog beneath the footbridge. That same long delicate finger slipped inside her, up and down, up and down, causing a bass line beat that a body could not resist, nor should it try. The jacket fell off her shoulders and draped carelessly over the rail. Not feeling the cool of the air against her, she held this woman who thrilled her core. Jasmine let her fingers flick haphazardly through the woman's cropped hair, over her small ears and the soft skin of her face and neck where it met the resistance of her starched collar.

The woman dropped to her knees, and Jasmine looped one arm around the railing to steady herself. Plump kisses on her inner thigh accompanied by the smooth tongue of an experienced lover brought a melodic sigh to her breath, a pleasant tone that set the key for the music to follow. As she felt her panties slide down her legs and over one foot, Jasmine closed her eyes, and without further prompting spread her stance. Clutching the ruffled dress hem with her free hand, she brought it up near her waist.

At first, the sensation was so light, so delicate, she could hardly detect the wetness she knew was already there. Her lover's unseen tongue parted her finely coiled hairs, eventually finding their way into the stream that ran from the confluence of her stiffened limbs. She gloried in the staccato yet constant search for pleasure—wet, probing, finding, filling her with excitement, a thrill not found on any juke joint dance floor. An unexpected move sent lightning through her body and she heard what sounded like distant thunder emanating from deep inside her chest that echoed faintly into the nearby hills. The throbbing measure of her met desire pressed against the woman's still tongue. Jasmine fluffed the fuzzy wool of her lover's short hair until the night music playing within her body rolled and faded into the softening beat of her heart.

Slowly, the woman straightened up to her full height. Jasmine's knees buckled, but her lover was strong and embraced her until she once again steadied herself against the bridge rail. Sharing a gentle kiss, she tasted the musky earthiness of her own body, salt and sea.

Jasmine recovered during a long silent refrain as the frogs had quieted at the sound of the one who had found her lover. The music at the juke joint also had stopped, having been replaced by a muffled din. She slipped her panties back on, and holding her lover, focused on the wooden building illuminated in the distance. String Bean, patient as ever, would be waiting to walk her home. String Bean could wait.

Having Her Birthday Cake, and Eating It, Too

RACHEL KRAMER BUSSEL

Last Saturday started out just like any other. My girlfriend and I shared a nice, quiet, cozy dinner that I cooked for her, and then made out on the couch as we pretended to watch a movie. But I knew that something more had to be in store. After all, it was my thirtieth birthday. But Kim is sly, and while she'd wished me a happy birthday earlier in the day and had organized the cards I'd received across our coffee table, that had been, thus far, the only acknowledgement of my turning one year older.

It wasn't until we were in the bedroom that Kim started to give me a hint of what was to come. Even though it's always her topping me, never the reverse, it doesn't happen every time we fuck. Sometimes she wants something soft and sensual, other times she wants to go full out and take us to those deep, dark places that we can only visit once in a while. I like leaving things up to her; she seems to have a sixth sense about when to rein me in and when to let me go flying off into a world where pain becomes pleasure, where the everyday gets distorted and changed, where I'm Alice and my sexual psyche is a wonderland she can manipulate at will. If we did it every day, it would get old fast, but I could tell from the way she looked at me, her gaze traveling up and down, and the way that look made me feel—safe and scared, calm and nervous, aroused and on edge all at the same time—that we still had it.

I was leaning over the bed, waiting for her next move. My hands automatically went behind my back, a reaction that told me that I not only wanted to submit to her, but that I needed to. "Can I spread my legs?" The minute I asked the question, I felt my pussy twinge. It didn't matter what she said, but asking her permission further established our boundaries, roles now so firmly cemented I couldn't imagine not lying before her, my ass thrust out, waiting. I felt her start to wind something soft around my wrists. When I tried to look, she gave my ass a hard smack, across the outer curve, where it still felt good but didn't give my pussy that special tingle. "If you want the good kind of spankings, you won't peek at what I'm doing. Keep your mouth shut and your eyes closed, you brat," she instructed.

But then, instead of taking me to task or even touching me sensuously, she lifted me up and dragged me into the kitchen, then plopped me into one of our basic wooden chairs. I looked up at her and she laughed. "It's your birthday, honey. What do you think I'd do for my girl on her birthday? I'm going to make you a cake, and you're going to get to eat it." I was a little confused at this point, but simply nodded. "But since you're such a slutty pig, I want to make sure you keep your hands and mouth where they belong, so I'm going to tie you down tight to this chair and make you watch me, then I'll feed you when it's all ready. How does that sound?" She kissed me then, her tongue plunging into my mouth, filling me up, as her fingers dove into my cunt and she pushed into my already wet, aching hole. Kim had a way of making me lose track of everything except the feel of her lips and hands, and I was absolute putty at her disposal. She quickly pulled her fingers out, then offered them to me to suck on. I did, hungrily, and she wrapped two digits around my teeth, giving a little tug before inching away. Then out came something stronger than what was wrapped around my wrists. She spread my legs and secured each ankle to the chair, adding a few wisps of a soft material underneath so they didn't chafe. She tied my already bound wrists to the chair as well, then pulled my hair so I could look up at her. "I think that'll do nicely, and I'll leave you right here so you can watch me as I make you your cake. Be good," she said, and with a quick peck on the lips, walked away and began rummaging through the drawers for all the ingredients she'd need. I sat there, feeling my cunt continue to spasm.

It was amazing that we'd been living together for three years, and yet I could still feel slightly embarrassed to be sitting in that chair, absolutely naked, my pussy on display. Not that it had never been before, but being tied down in our kitchen, where we've entertained guests, where when the light is right our neighbors can see in, made me squirm all the more. I clenched my pussy tightly and arched my back, trying to push my breasts upward; these were really the only movements I could make from where I sat.

She must have planned on doing this, because in no time at all, her cake-baking ingredients were assembled in front of her. She stepped carefully out of her clothing, stood before me naked for just a moment, and then tied a little yellow flowered apron across her waist—folding the yellow string bow so it fell along the crack of her pert ass. I wanted to reach out and grab it, to sink to my knees behind her and lick her pussy, test her and see if that would have any effect on her kitchen skills. Or even stay in the chair and arch one foot upward, lifting the skirt to get an unobstructed view of her ass. But I couldn't move, and having to sit there and wait for her, knowing that my cunt was surely about to leak my juices all over, if it wasn't already, was both maddening and arousing.

She was humming to herself, acting like she didn't have a care in the world, or a girlfriend bound to a chair behind her, as she merrily went about making a cake. You'd have thought she was a housewife with the dedication she showed to perfecting that cake—beating the batter until it was smooth and creamy, pouring it into well-greased pans, carefully setting them in the oven, continually checking the temperature, mixing the ingredients for the frosting. I could only whimper to get her attention, and occasionally she'd come by and give me a kiss, or feed me a chocolate chip or two, giving my nipples a tug or two, but studiously ignoring the one spot I most urgently needed her to touch. I was sure the cake would be delicious, but I didn't really care; I wanted my birthday fuck, not my birthday cake.

"Be patient, my sweet," she said in her gentlest, cruelest voice. Kim had managed to perfect this trick where she'd tell me the meanest, most humiliating things possible, but say them in such a sickly gooey way that I wouldn't be quite so bothered. Just when I thought I couldn't stand being ignored any more, she whirled around with a wooden spoon full of frosting in her hand. "Were you feeling left out, baby?" she asked. Before I could take a breath, she slathered the sticky pink frosting all over my breasts, then my stomach and my thighs. The smell of sugar hung in the air. The heat from the stove made the kitchen warm, and I was starting to sweat. The frosting quickly oozed down my skin, collapsing into messy blobs. She held the spoon up to my mouth and I opened as wide as I could, while she slid the spoon in. I sucked every last drop of frosting off of it. "Hungry, aren't you?" she asked, a slight sneer creeping across her lips. Then she continued to press the spoon into my mouth, no longer feeding me but fucking me with it. I made sure to relax my mouth's muscles and found that every time the smooth wet wood slid across my tongue, my pussy gave another twitch. Tears were starting to well up in my eyes from the strain of being bound, being under her gaze, and being fucked in my mouth with the spoon while she watched me like a hawk.

Her eyes noticed everything, and she soon took the spoon out. She held it up in the air between us, twirling it around and around, examining it. "Do you think this is totally clean now?" she asked me.

"I guess so."

"You *guess* so?" She wasn't happy with my answer.

"Yes, Kim, there's no frosting left on it anywhere," I said, my voice shaking slightly. She had morphed from joking around to deadly serious.

"Good," she replied, her voice clipped and short. She knelt down and examined my pussy, splayed wide open for her. She tapped the spoon lightly against my clit, smiling for a second when I responded with a groan of pleasure. Then she turned it around, taunting me by inserting just the thin handle, teasing me as she rotated it around and around in my needy cunt. She licked her thumb and pressed it against my clit, which was now hard, bulging out from under its hood. "You better hurry up, birthday girl. Your cake's going to be ready in five minutes, and you'll only get to have your cake if you come before then." Involuntarily, my pussy tightened around the spoon's handle, and when she slipped a finger in beside the wood, I bucked against her, half afraid that I might tip the chair over, but she had it under control.

Kim finally removed the spoon and knelt down in front of me, licking my pussy the way only she can, while her fingers pinched and prodded my clit, knowing just when to ramp up the pressure by pinching my nub. Then she switched, sliding four slim fingers inside me while her tongue and teeth attacked my clit. Not being able to move made every sensation all the more thrilling, and the tremors that started to run down my legs felt like they were racing back up, creating a spiral of arousal—the center of it, my cunt. I lost all track of time as I closed my eyes and reveled in the warmth of her tongue and urgent, seeking fingers, which didn't stop until they found that special spot that always gets me. She stayed there, pressing and arching her fingers, sliding them in and out until I barely knew where I was. When I finally came, it was in one huge explosion, which left me light-headed. I had to shut my eyes because the kitchen light suddenly seemed much too bright.

Once she was done with my pussy, Kim gently untied me, lavishing me with kisses as she lifted me up and carried me to the couch. She helped me into my purple silk robe and plumped up my pillows. And then, just in time, she rescued the cake. I rested my eyes, marveling at how I could still feel the ghost of her fingers inside me, and then the lights went out and she was walking toward me with a candle-topped cake singing "Happy Birthday." It would've been amazing even without the cake, or the chair. Kim is my favorite birthday present, but this time, she'd truly outdone herself. I smiled as my robe fell open while I took a bite of her sweet, delicious cake. She was already jumping on top of me, her leg sliding between mine, hungry for more. I put down the plate and kissed her. She grabbed my ass, and I knew what was next: my birthday spankings. Anyone who says you can't have it all just doesn't know where to look. I don't even have to leave my own apartment to have my cake and get eaten too. Who could ask for a better birthday present than that?

In the Closet

Diana Chase

I was supposed to meet Eva at her house when she got home from work. The tentative plan was to get something to eat and then check out this women's spoken word event that was becoming a regular thing in the San Diego dyke scene. I was running really early, but I didn't have anything better do to, so I just showed up.

Eva and I had been friends since college. When we met I fell madly in love with her—she was one of the most beautiful girls I had ever seen. She had long dark hair and soft skin. She was beautiful, but not in a showy way. Everything that she was proud of about herself came from within, and she just let it show. She didn't have to create an image of herself to present to the world.

She was the reader in one of my lit classes, and I would joke with my friends about sleeping with her to raise my grade. When I finally got the balls to ask her out on a date, the course was almost over, so it didn't help anyway. We ended up fucking on our first date—which was a rarity for me because in previous relationships I was so sexually reserved.

Anyway, although the sex was all right and we really cared about each other, we couldn't get it to work. I think it was because we have vastly different ideas about what an emotional relationship looks like, but that's a long story. I like being friends better. I like flirting and begging her to sleep with me again better than actually doing it, if I'm going to be totally honest.

Anyway, I got to her house and let myself in with the key she had given me "in case of emergency"—I figured this counted; I was bored as fuck and an hour's worth of traffic away from home.

When I walked inside, I saw Chris, Eva's boi, standing in the kitchen. "Hey, what's up, man?" I said, not really paying attention or waiting for a response. I went to the couch and sunk down, tired from a long day of trying to teach apathetic teenagers to appreciate good literature.

"What time is it?" Chris asked, walking into the living room.

I looked at my watch. "'Bout six thirty."

"You're late."

"Uh, actually, I'm early. Eva said seven fifteen."

"Okay," Chris answered evenly, taking a seat in the chair opposite me.

When he sat I noticed the telltale bulge. He was packing hard. Pants a little loose, but nowhere near baggy. It was fucking sexy, and I could feel a little trickle of excitement building in me. He must have seen me staring.

He smiled and said, "What you looking at, baby?"

"Do you always pack like that, or were you planning on fucking Eva before we all go out tonight?" I almost couldn't believe my own boldness. Most of the time I am too inhibited to say what I am really thinking, but every once in a while my brain lapses and the words just tumble on out before I can stop them. I could feel the hot-pink blush building in my cheeks. I looked down at my denim-covered knees. My feet. The carpet. Chris's shoes. Aw, fuck, there it was again. I couldn't help myself, and I couldn't ignore the pull that I felt. I twitched. Looked up at Chris's face for a second.

He was smiling in an almost sweet way. Like he didn't always go out of his way to make me blush "because it's cute." Like he didn't know what I was thinking right then. Like he wasn't thinking the same thing.

"Something like that." Chris suddenly got up and walked to the back of the apartment. How rude. I sat there on that couch getting all squirmy, picturing what exactly Chris was hiding in those jeans, when I heard him call to me from the back bedroom.

I got up and wandered back, cognizant of the slippery sensation that had developed between my legs.

I saw Chris standing in the closet, holding up a pair of jeans that looked almost identical to the ones he was wearing. "Do you think I should change?" He asked.

"Uh, no," I said, a little annoyed by his almost constant vain self-obsessions. "Those look exactly the same as the ones you got on."

I was about to turn around and leave when he said quickly, "Wait. Don't you think you should see them on before making a decision?" In a flash he had tossed the jeans away and was working his belt and then the button. I paused and felt my feet sewn to the soft, cushy carpet.

Slowly, teasingly, he pulled out a blue cock made of iridescent silicone. He was stroking it ever so slightly with an air of confidence that made me melt. As he did this, he never took his eyes off me. Those clear, gray eyes that could sparkle with wit and exuberance one minute and look almost lascivious the next.

"Let's stop fucking around here, okay?"

"Sure," I said.

I scooted over toward him with just a thread of reluctance remaining. When I got close enough, he grabbed my crotch and pulled me closer. My jeans were tight, and the friction against my increasingly wet pussy was intense; it made me gasp.

He paused for a moment, looking down at me, then he kissed me, sweetly, on the lips. We kissed like teenagers, letting our tongues loll around, just feeling the soft fullness of each other's mouths. Sometimes, I feel like I can get off from a really great kiss. Makes me feel tingly all over my body, makes my nipples harden.

Slowly he pulled away from me and looked into my eyes, giving me a mischievous smile. He rubbed his fingertips delicately, up and down my arms, getting me tingly again. He rubbed his finger gently against my lips and then kissed me again, then gently helped me sink to my knees.

I took his silicone cock into my mouth, licking the head and shaft all over before taking it deep into my throat. You could hear the wet sucking noises that I was making, working his cock, which elicited an equally erotic sound from deep in his throat. He leaned against the bare wall, and I closed my eyes and listened to the delicious sounds he was making, rubbing and squeezing his ass with both my hands.

As I continued, he began to move his hips with me, his breathing got faster, and I felt like we would spontaneously combust. We built this rhythm until he was almost thrusting against me, then I felt him shudder, and I held onto him tightly so he wouldn't knock me down. As his breathing slowed he caught my arms and pulled me up, then spun me around so my back was to him. He pushed me against the corner, which was already cramped with clothes and shoes. The cramped space and lack of mobility only made me wetter.

Chris pressed his body into me. He kissed my neck lightly, sweetly, and then bit me hard. His hands reached for the warm, soft skin of my stomach, moving upwards toward my ribs, my breasts. He slid my tank top and bra off over my head and took both my tits in his hands, rolling and tugging my nipples until I was rubbing my hips and ass against him, begging, "Fuck me. Please."

He grabbed my hands and put them on my breasts, then slid down to the buttons of my jeans. He only undid the top two buttons and scooted them down to the bottom of my ass, creating an unbearable tension and sense of longing in me.

Chris kissed and licked my back and my neck, softly licked my ears, and gave me the sweetest kisses on my cheek. As his hands explored my hips and ass, he traced the outline of the fleur-de-lis tat I have on my very lower back, just above the crack of my ass.

"I don't remember this." He spoke softly, in a voice a little huskier that usual.

"Oh, I just got that one a couple of weeks ago. It's new." It was difficult for me to get all the words out between my panting breaths.

Lazily kissing my shoulder, Chris undid the rest of the buttons of my jeans, and pushed them down to my ankles. I was literally dripping wet and I didn't think that I would be able to take any more of his torture; I might spontaneously come and pass out.

He kicked my feet apart as far as they would go with my denim ankle restraints in place, and then took his big, sparkly blue cock in his hand and began sliding it all over my sopping wet pussy, getting everything juiced up. He was making little grunting moan sounds. I bent over a little and braced myself against the wall with both arms, my whole body beginning to shake.

"Please, fuck me," I pleaded once again.

"Where," he asked innocently.

"You know where," I breathed. After a few more moments of exquisite torture, he slid that beautiful, blue cock into my ass. I gasped as I felt it filling me up, blurring my vision, dizzying me. He fucked me deep, steady, and slow, giving me something I could count on.

He took his hand off my hips and began stroking my clit, taking his other hand to grab both of my small breasts. I thought I was going to pass out, all those different, beautiful sensations competing for my attention, overwhelming me.

"Is it good, girl?" He asked.

"Yes," I moaned.

I didn't really feel like I was me, inside my own body. I didn't feel Chris against me. All I could feel was the exquisite fuck that we were creating together. The beautiful feeling that the whole is greater than the sum of the parts—that together in this moment we were more than what we were before or what we would be after. The feeling that only the right balance of chemicals can evoke.

He rubbed my swollen clit, at random intervals dipping a couple of fingers into my pussy. I bobbed against his strong, muscular hips as I felt myself start to come. My eyes squeezed tight. As I rolled over the edge into the waves of orgasmic bliss, I lost control of my arms, and Chris had to hold me up. I let him hold me.

He stuck two fingers, the ones that had been inside me, in my mouth, stifling my screams. I bit down on them.

He softly grunted, "fuck, yeah."

After another moment, he spun me around and held me next to him. I let the full weight of my body fall against him, relaxing totally.

After a moment or two, he pushed me off and said, "Get dressed. It's like ten past seven already. Eva's going to be here."

"Oh, fuck." With that he disappeared into the bathroom and shut the door, leaving me alone to put myself back together.

As I was putting my bra back on, I heard Eva's high heels (she always wears them) clicking on the driveway, so I scurried back into the living room and sunk back down, just as she opened the door.

"Hey," she said, smiling. "I hope you haven't been waiting long. I know I'm a little late."

"Naw, it's all right." I could feel my face was still flushed, which wasn't entirely strange—I'm really Irish and therefore pink most of the time. I tried to will my face to return to its normal color, my heart to return to its normal tempo.

Where's Chris? He's supposed to be here."

"Oh, I think he's still in the bathroom."

She put her purse down and I got up to give her a hug. As we kissed each other on the cheek, I realized that my mouth tasted like my pussy. I hoped she couldn't smell it. Chris walked out of the back, no more bulge in the pants. He leaned in and gave Eva a kiss.

"Hey baby, I'm going to go change. I'll be right back."

"Hurry up, all right? I'm starving," Chris replied.

I sat down. Chris sat in the chair opposite me. I felt a rash of awkwardness creep up on me, like when you hear a secret about a friend from someone else, and then you have to sit there as your friend tells you her secret and pretend like you didn't already know.

"I really like that tat," Chris said softly. "It makes your ass…" He made a popping noise with his lips and held his hands up in a wide circle.

"Thanks," I smiled.

Eva came back into the room wearing a supershort skirt and tall boots, looking like the vixen that she is. Chris whistled, and I said something about how hot she looked. Sometimes I thought about giving Eva and me a second try, you know, just to see if anything had changed.

I got up and said, "Well, we'd better go. I don't want Chris to starve to death or anything."

We all stood there for a moment in silence. Then Eva looked at Chris and asked, "Did you tell her?" Then, turning to me she said, "I was going to tell you yesterday, but Chris wanted to see your face. We're moving in together!" She held Chris tightly around the waist and smiled her sugar-sweet smile.

I stood there with a puzzled, pensive look on my face. Then I realized. The fucking closet was full of Chris's clothes.

"Yeah," I said. "He told me."

Exotic Hands

TARA ALTON

I loved hands. Anything to do with them. I had dozens of books on the mysteries of palmistry, and I owned handfuls of costume jewelry rings from antique stories. On my fridge I had pictures of mehndi tattoos with tapered fingers decorated with henna. I wanted designs on the inside of my palms so badly. I daydreamed how exotic and sexy it would be.

One afternoon I stopped at an Indian store to get some chutney. I loved the place. It made me feel as if I was in another world with its unfamiliar smells and shelves of spices and food. I saw the business card on the counter for mehndi. I asked the clerk if he knew who Sarita was. He said she was his cousin. She was very good, and she was a certified artist. The business card said PRIVATE APPOINTMENTS OR PARTIES, SPECIALIZING IN INDIAN AND MIDDLE-EASTERN DESIGNS. I saw an article in a magazine about the fine line floral Indian designs—that was the style I wanted.

But I only had a week off work. I hadn't been getting along with my boss, Judy. She overlooked me for a promotion after three years of hard work at the collectibles store. She gave the position to her niece who had only been there six months. I told her I'd done everything she

asked. She said blood was thicker, so I demanded my first vacation a week before she left for her annual Florida holiday. She grudgingly agreed. That was when I decided to get the mehndi. Judy fired another girl for getting a nostril ring, but I figured by the time she got back it would be faded, or I could wear white gloves and say I was being 1950s retro-fashionable.

I called Sarita and made an appointment for the next day. She sounded younger than I had imagined. I wondered what she looked like. When I was in New Orleans on vacation, I had a crush on a palm reader in Jackson Square. I kept going back every evening. Eventually she ran out of things to say. I told her just to hold my hand, and I imagined she thought it was beautiful and never wanted to let go.

Sarita told me to meet her at the grocery store the day of the appointment. I was so nervous. In the store, I found a young woman behind the counter.

"I was looking for Sarita," I said.

"That's me. You're Mary?"

I nodded. She called someone else to the counter and motioned me out the back door. I thought she would be wearing a sari or something exotic, but she wore a T-shirt and jeans with tennis shoes. She had long, thick, wavy dark hair that went to the middle of her back, and her skin was light colored. Except for her looks, everything about her was so American. She had no accent and told me she was second generation. Her grandmother had taught her the mehndi.

Behind the store was a small strip motel that I hadn't noticed.

"My family lives in the last three," she said. "We rent out the rest. My cousin owns the store, and my sister owns the sari shop across the street."

Sweeping her hair into a ponytail, she secured it with a strand of her own hair. Glancing over her shoulder at me, she flashed me a smile.

In the motel room she asked me to sit in front of a coffee table on the floor. She gave me lots of pillows to support my back. The room was warm. On the table, she had cones that looked like mini pastry bags laid out along with other things.

"So what were you thinking about in terms of a design for your palms?" she asked, sitting across from me.

"Something Indian," I said. "I want something that celebrates the beauty of hands."

She looked thoughtful.

"I can do a peacock feather on the right palm and lotus blossom on the other."

"That would be lovely," I said.

She reached for my hand. I felt a nervous butterfly tickle my stomach.

"Before we start," I said, pulling my camera from my purse. "I wanted to get before and after pictures."

Sarita said okay. She snapped a picture of my bare palms and put the camera on the coffee table. I didn't tell her I wanted proof that my hands could be turned into something exotic.

"I've been meaning to start a portfolio," she said. "Maybe you could get double prints?"

"Sure," I said.

Now she took my hand. The sudden warmth of her fingers made me feel giddy, but I wondered what she thought. Did she like what she saw? I knew I had my doubts about the beauty of my own hands. I didn't think my fingers were long and tapered enough. My nails were too frail. My skin was too pale. I thought the contrast between Sarita and I was startling. She had lovely hands with one gold ring around her pinky. I wished I looked like her.

"I just love hands," I said. "Anything to do with them. Really. You should see how obsessed I can get. I bought a ton of palmistry books since my vacation to New Orleans, and I met a palm reader. I'm pretty sure I can read palms now."

"Maybe you could read mine sometime," she said.

I smiled and nodded. Sarita began the peacock feather. It got quiet. I looked around the room and spotted a framed picture of a beautiful young woman in a sari. The picture looked old.

"She's beautiful," I said.

"She's my grandmother," she said.

"I can see the resemblance."

There was a pause. I wanted her to keep talking to me.

"On the phone, you said you're an art student," I said. "What mediums are you studying?"

"Mostly drawing," she said. "I like eyes the best. I'll show you my sketch books when this hand is done."

As the last line of the feather was completed, I felt as if my hand was transformed. There it was! Beautiful black henna against my skin, and Sarita had done it all freehand. I loved it. I couldn't wait to see it dry. My other hand looked so bare now in comparison. How could I ever go back to that?

"Your work is amazing," I said.

Sarita smiled and got out her sketchbooks. She did love eyes.

"I use a lot of magazine ads to draw from because they show a woman's face so close. I'd like to do more mehndi and art classes, and not work in the store so much, but it's hard. It sounds cliché, but my parents wanted me married by now. They are visiting India indefinitely with some family. I told them that by bringing me to the U.S. they chose to raise me as an American. I haven't had much time for a social life with work, school, and this."

She put aside her sketchbook and sat back down. She started the lotus flower on my other palm. I was glad she was holding my hand again. Her skin was breathtaking, her nails short and clean.

"Do you have any mehndi?" I asked.

"Just on my toes right now," she said.

She paused.

"How did you find my card?" she asked.

"In the store. I love chutney."

"You do? That's sweet." She smiled shyly. "I have a confession to make. I saw you before."

"When?"

"About a month ago. Before my cards were printed. You were buying chutney. I was in the store room with the door open. I liked what you were wearing. You looked like a naughty Catholic school-girl with your plaid skirt and white shirt and your funky black shoes. Your blouse was unbuttoned."

She blushed.

"So I was glad to see you today," she said.

I was so flattered that she remembered me. The lotus flower was almost finished. I didn't want it to be over…her holding my hand, drawing this exquisite art on me.

"How long until it's dry?" I asked.

"It can take anywhere from three minutes to half an hour, depending on the temperature and the skin. When it's dry enough, it will take on a matte finish instead of the shiny one. You can get some truly deep red colors because of the skin of the palm."

She put on the last line. I was so happy to see it done, and yet I felt a keen disappointment that the contact between us was gone. For a moment I thought I might blurt out how I felt.

"Photo op," I said.

"Wait," she said. " I've got an idea."

She went into the closet and brought out handfuls of beautiful fabric.

"These are saris from my cousin's store. We could drape them around you for the photos, and then I could use them for my portfolio. Maybe even an advertisement, if you don't mind."

How could I mind? She showed and explained each sari to me. The top one was a cold pale shade of blue with a watercolor-effect floral print. It was a Georgette fabric, very light. The next one was a crepe silk in dark green with a small floral print in navy blue.

I sat on the sofa, and she wrapped the sari over my shoulders like a scarf. It was bliss to have her touch me again. She was so close I could smell her skin. The contrast was beautiful between my palms and the fabric. She took several pictures with me in different poses, telling me how to hold my hands and how to look out the side of my eyes for an erotic look. Like a photographer, she pretended to tease me into more seductive poses.

"You're beautiful. You're an Indian princess. Flirt with me," she said.

She hesitated.

"It would be prettier, more natural, more exotic, if your blouse wasn't showing, just bare skin. We could fold it down and back."

I held up my hands.

"I can't do it," I said.

She put down the camera and came close. I opened my legs and she crouched between them. She pushed off the sari off of my head and shoulders. With her exquisite fingers, she unbuttoned my blouse. I could feel her warm hands on my skin as she folded the blouse to expose my breast bone. She looked me in the eyes as if asking for permission and hesitated at the button on my cleavage.

"You can go a little lower if you need to," I said.

My bra was revealed. She edged the blouse off my shoulders and rested her fingers on the curves of my breasts peaking out at the top.

"You have beautiful skin," she said.

"I like having your hands on me," I confessed.

"You do?" she asked. "Why?"

I hesitated, unsure how to say it. She looked at me expectantly. Her gaze was so penetrating. Was she really looking at me this way? I felt as if her fingertips were waiting on my skin like question marks. I decided to say it.

"You're arousing me."

She let out a small sigh of relief.

"I was hoping you were feeling the same as me," she said. "I want to touch you all over, Mary."

I nodded. My heart beginning to race with the thought of it.

Slowly, she ran her hands up to my collarbone, up to my chin, where she lifted it. Her body was pressed against mine. She kissed my chin, then ran her nose over my lips to my nose, where they met. She kissed me, her lips like butter. Feeling her nibble my lower lip, I opened my mouth in surprise. Her tongue slid inside, exploring my teeth and the roof of my mouth. I was reeling with desire.

She started kissing down my throat to my sternum, where she unhooked my bra and exposed my breasts. Her tongue explored each nipple as she finished opening my blouse. At my waist she flipped up my skirt and tugged off my tights, along with my underwear. I felt like I was tied up with the mehndi on my hands. I couldn't touch her. She planted kisses on my skin, exploring my body. She was really feeling me—not just casual caresses, but getting to know the texture of my body.

"I want to make you quiver," she said.

Her hands caressed the inside of my thighs. She made a V with her fingers, holding me open while she fucked me with her tongue. Just when I thought I would go mad with arousal, she tugged me down and opened me up more. Her mouth clamped down on my clit, and she began sucking on it. Her hands reached up and fondled my breasts. The sucking sent me over the edge.

She knew it. I came in her mouth.

"You're sweeter than chutney," she said.

After my orgasm, she told me to lie down on the sofa and close my eyes. My pussy was still throbbing. I heard her take something off the coffee table, and I felt her lean over my body.

"What are you doing?" I asked.

"Shh," she said.

I felt something cool and damp tickle my lower abdomen and thighs.

"Open your eyes," she said.

I did. She had decorated my skin.

"Now you can't move at all. You are my mehndi prisoner."

Sarita put down the cone and came to the end of the sofa where my head was. She kissed me. I reveled in the texture of her tongue against mine. I could taste myself on her. With one quick movement, she pulled off her T-shirt and bra and wiggled out of her jeans and panties. Like a cat, she climbed over me so her breasts were over my face. I sucked her nipples. She let out a small moan of pleasure.

I let go of a nipple. She climbed down further, her tongue meeting my belly button. My mouth found hers. I was surprised to find a piercing. I took the ring in my mouth and flicked it with my tongue.

Like an erotic picture in a pillow book, she poised her body over my mehndi designs, her fingers spreading open my pussy lips like a flower. Slowly, she lowered her pussy over my mouth. I arched up my head, my arms wrapped around her thighs, my newly decorated hands poised in the air. She finger-fucked me as I licked her delicious pearl.

One finger inside me. Then two. I wanted them all. She began to rock back and forth over my face. As she pulled away, I playfully bit her. She groaned. In and out of my mouth her pussy popped. The rhythm between us picked up, until she was just fucking my mouth. I was lost in her wetness, her clit of a precious gem swimming around on my tongue. A third finger went inside me to the second knuckle. Her whole hand could slide inside me. My pussy hit the high note of a second orgasm, throbbing, ear-ringing, toe-curling, out-of-body bliss.

Sarita's cries reached a new level as she came and shuddered above me.

She climbed off me. I saw her lovely terrain in reverse, her tummy, her piercing, her breasts, her neck, chin, mouth, and then those eyes. She untied her hair. It cascaded over her shoulders. Kneeling by the sofa, she took my hands in hers and looked at the mehndi. She smiled.

"I can't wait to feel your exotic hands on me," she said.

"You think my hands are exotic?" I asked.

She smiled.

"Yes," she said. "Even without mehndi. That day I saw you in the store for the first time, I watched you brush a strand of hair off your forehead. It took my breath away."

"Are you sure?" I asked.

Her kisses on my fingertips were her answers.

Finally

WENDY CASTER

You wonder: *Is a miracle about to occur?*

She smiles at you with that smile. Not her regular smile, which is devastating enough, God knows, but with that extraordinarily radiant smile, the one that makes you want to devote your entire life to keeping her happy, just so she'll keep smiling.

You remember the first time you saw her. As soon as she walked into the room, every molecule in your body wanted her. And when she turned out to be sweet and charming and funny, every piece of your heart knew you would love her. Then she mentioned her girl-friend…of eight years.

Now she throws you sideways glances as you walk toward your apartment, and you know that it means "yes," but you can hardly take it in. For a year you've put your feelings aside, back-burnered them, stuffed them, buried them, categorized them as fantasy, as wishes, as the ever-out-of-reach payoff for a lost lottery ticket.

You remember the day she told you that she and her girlfriend had broken up. Like the good girl you are, you reacted with sympathy and concern, and it was genuine. You knew from experience the cost of a major breakup, the lost person, the lost way of life, the lost confidence, the total unmooring of reality. You'll never forget when it happened to you, and you felt like a living shock wave, stumbling from day to day.

Now she leans against you the tiniest bit as you wait for the light to change. Neither of you has said a word, but the air is thick with communication. And you begin to think of what else you felt when she told you her relationship had ended. A guilty shock of hope.

Now you're at your apartment. As you go to unlock the door, your eyes meet hers, and you stop moving, key halfway to the lock, and look at her. And look at her. The air undulates between you, and that little part of your left brain that never rests starts to ponder: *What makes the air ripple like that? Can we be actually heating the atoms between us? Is it chemistry? Physics? Magic?* The rest of you doesn't want to wait for your mind to figure it all out.

And you remember that period after her breakup. You weren't really friends; you weren't really not friends. You were pretty sure she knew that you were interested, but there was no proper time to just say so. And you had no way of knowing if she was interested in you. Her life was pain; getting a new apartment, pain; splitting the CD collection, pain; divvying up the furniture, pain; and forcing herself to get out of bed every day—or at least most days. Neither of you could guess who she would be or what she would want when the grieving period was through—or how long that grieving period would be.

Now you manage somehow to look away from her long enough to put the key in the lock and open the door. The apartment is sparkling clean, which is unusual, but you had a feeling that tonight would be the night, and you dusted and swept and vacuumed and scrubbed with a sense of ritual preparation for a holy event. You laughed at yourself for that feeling but didn't try to fight it.

Now she excuses herself to go to the bathroom, and you put logs into the fireplace, and kindling, and light a twelve-inch match, and coax embers into flames.

And you remember—was it only a month ago? Yes, about eleven months after the breakup she mentioned in passing that she might be sort of ready to kind of start dating again. The news was so unexpected that the expression on your face screamed out your feelings. She looked at you for a long time and finally said, "Oh." She looked at you for a long time more and smiled. That extraordinary smile.

Now she comes out of the bathroom. She sits down next to you on the floor in front of the fireplace. You lean gently shoulder to shoulder, watching the flames.

You remember your early dates, her anxiety over dating again, your fear that you might not be able to contain yourself. How difficult it was to dam the torrents of your desire behind careful conversation and gentle flirting.

Now she reaches out to you. Forget Blake's grain of sand, your left brain thinks—you can see eternity in holding her hand. And you remember that night last week when she gave you a look, a glance, a sideways nothing that let you know that the answer would be yes. And your body jolted from first to fifth gear, speeding into rapture, while you did nothing but glance back your own promise.

And now, a week later, you and she are sitting and holding hands in front of the fireplace, and you want to be in bed, exploding into each other, but you also want to make every moment last an eternity.

She pulls her hand away from yours, just slightly, and strokes her middle finger diagonally across your palm, coaxing embers into flames. While looking into her eyes, you lift her hand to your mouth and kiss her palm gently, slowly, thoughtfully. She smiles that smile, then leans in to kiss your mouth. It is a moment of clarity. You see, really see, the color of her eyes. Each individual eyelash is a miracle. Her mouth reaches your mouth.

At first you kiss with your eyes open, looking at each other with wonder. Then you close your eyes and taste her, hear her, smell her, feel her. The kiss is all you could have imagined, and that is saying a lot. Having spent the better part of a year doing little more than imagining the feel of her mouth against yours, the darting tongues, the lingering caress of lip against lip? But this is better than fantasy. This is real. You open your eyes for a second, just to check. It's her. Finally. She opens her eyes too, and you moan in unison.

The two of you stretch out next to the fireplace, on your sides, face to face. With one finger you outline her beauty, tracing her forehead, the slope of her jaw, her chin. You outline her lips. She sucks your finger into her mouth and wraps her tongue around it. The sensation is shocking. Your nipples harden as they reach out to her. You feel swollen with potential ecstasy.

Yet you still have a lingering doubt: can this really be *real?* She flutters her hands across your breasts, barely touching them, and the intensity of your response is all the proof you need. She wants you. She's touching you. You're touching her. Soon the two of you will be naked…but you choose not to think ahead. Feel this moment. Feel how the spirals she is drawing around your breasts with her fingers make your nipples feel like rock, warm, living rock.

You reach out and make the same motions around her breasts. She smiles at you. This is a new smile. Not as devastating or as radiant but deeper somehow, with an underlying sadness. You remember that this is the first time in years she is having sex with someone other than her ex. You put the palm of your hand against her cheek and nod at her. She nods back. You realize that you are both frightened to go where you are going—and eager too, and grateful.

You gently roll her onto her back and lie on top of her. The full-body contact is so intense through your clothing that you wonder if you will survive once it's skin to skin. You hold each other tightly, limbs entwined. As your lips meet again, you lose a few seconds somehow, and the next thing you realize you are humping against each other, kissing as though your lives depended on it.

How long do you kiss? There's no way to know. Time has no relevance or meaning. Nothing does, really, other than your bodies pushing into each other. And the fact that it is her. Your eyes sting with tears of wonder. You quiet down and cling to each other, feeling the rise and fall of each other's chests. She whispers, "I want to feel your skin against mine."

After a few moments of hesitation, you roll apart. Disengaging from her feels like instant starvation. She stands up and faces you and kicks off her shoes. You kick off yours.

She unbuttons her blouse, button by button, then drops it on the floor. You pull your shirt over your head and drop it on the floor. She takes off her socks. So do you. Her skirt and your jeans follow. She reaches behind her back and unfastens her bra. You mirror her movements exactly. You both let your bras fall to the floor. She holds her breasts in her hands and caresses them. You forget to echo her movement as you watch her nipples harden between her fingers. Your mouth waters with the desire to have them in your mouth. She slides her hand into her underpants and cups herself between her legs. You move to her and tug her underpants down, off of her body, then shuck your own.

You look at each other for a long moment, like the instant before jumping off a diving board.

Then you are in each other's arms, mouth to mouth, breasts to breasts, bush to bush. You stroke each other hard, kiss each other hard, press together hard. She pushes you to the futon, not roughly but not gently either. Urgently. She covers your neck with kisses then bites your shoulder. Her teeth are surprisingly sharp, and you love the sensation. You run your nails down her back, returning sharpness for sharpness.

She moves down to your breasts and holds her mouth over your nipple, breathing moist wetness without actually touching you. You try to wait until she chooses to lick you, but you can't. You arch your back and push yourself into her mouth. She moans and sucks on your nipple. You feel it bloom into her mouth. A year of desire is in your response, and your body goes crazy. Your legs rub together frantically. Your hips rock back and forth. You fling your arms across your forehead and whimper with need.

She continues sucking one nipple and starts fingering the other. Still pleasuring your nipples, she puts a leg between your legs and rides you like a cowgirl on a magnificent filly. You open up against her leg, your wet swollen labia embracing her strong thigh. You rock together, each movement pushing you that much closer to critical mass. You want to slow yourself down, but you don't know how.

She lifts her head so that she can watch you. She plays with both of your nipples, rolling and pulling them while she continues to rock her thigh against you. You feel the triangle of heat and light from nipple to nipple to clit and back again, and you know it is only a matter of time. You manage to open your eyes for a moment and you see her watching you, and again you know. This is real, this miracle is real. You feel your sensations gather and focus. Gather and focus. Gather and focus. Almost there. You forget that you wanted to slow down.

And then you see the bolts of lightning and you know the thunder will follow in a moment.

Your muscles tighten. Your nipples pulse. Your toes curl. Your blood pounds. You push into her as hard as you can. And then you let go, the emotions of a year spilling into your veins and arteries like golden ore. And again. And again.

You hear yourself saying, "I love you, I love you, I love you." Your left brain says, *Too soon, too soon,* but the rest of you knows that you cannot wait another second to tell the truth you have waited so long to tell. Your muscles relax. Pure contentment suffuses every part of your body. She kisses your breasts, your neck, your mouth, then collapses on top of you.

She whispers in your ear, "I love you too."

And you realize that the miracle is just beginning.

Fantasy

Amie M. Evans

Chelsea breathes in deeply. In her mind forms a sharp image of two women—one of them her—engaging in animal-driven sex. The women are dressed in proper Victorian clothes and the sex is taking place in a church. Not just any church, but the Catholic cathedral where Chelsea had attended Mass with her family every Sunday when she was a little girl. The same cathedral she stops by once a month now as an adult to photograph the stained glass, carved wood, and stone statues. The images in Chelsea's mind are in black and white. She is at the front of the church and the other woman is forcing her to bend over and rest her upper body on the altar. Behind her she knows the heroic-sized Jesus is hanging on the cross above the elaborately carved priest's seat. Tiny drops of blood are dripping from his spear wound, head, and the metal spikes used to attach him to the cross. To her left is the statue of the Virgin Mother surrounded by flowers. She holds the infant Savior while her bare foot pins a snake by the neck. To Chelsea's right is the tabernacle. It shines in the multicolored sun strained through the stained glass windows—gleaming gold and intricately carved. Inside, encased in velvet, a gold chalice holds the consecrated host—the body of Christ himself. She imagines looking out at the empty wooden pews and the massive carved marble pillars that extend upward as the other woman pulls Chelsea's skirt up, exposing her bottom. The expression *fucking like rabbits* pops, unfiltered, into her fantasy, and is closely followed by the expression *holy fuck*, and she laughs out loud, her voice echoing through the unnatural quiet of the library.

The well-dressed woman with the tight bun and expensive tailored suit sitting across from her at the large, wooden table looks up with only her eyes—over the horn-rimmed glasses perched on her nose, across the open books spread out in front of her—and frowns directly at Chelsea when their eyes meet. The woman raises one perfectly straight finger across her lips and makes a loud "shh" sound, then returns her hand to her lap.

Chelsea runs her fingers through her stubbly hair. She feels the red creeping into her face, and she mouths the words "I'm sorry." The well-dressed woman's face is solid, still, and her eyes bore into Chelsea without mercy for a few more seconds, causing her to squirm a little in her seat. Without acknowledging Chelsea's apology, the woman's eyes return to the text in front of her. Chelsea shifts in her seat, holding in her hand the chain that links her wallet to her belt loop, ensuring it doesn't make a clanking sound against the wood. She rolls her eyes to herself at how uptight her neighbor is and looks at the open book in front of her.

The page depicts a picture of a schoolgirl during the 1800s, her butt exposed to the class, and her teacher, wooden paddle in hand, ready to administer the punishment. A public spanking—the material of school days gone by. When Chelsea had been at Catholic school, tales of older brothers and sisters who had been publicly spanked by nuns at the head of the classroom had circulated. All Chelsea ever saw was the occasional hair pulling or knuckle wrapping, and even that stopped after the third grade. Until she entered St. Edmund's Junior High School, the tales persisted that Sister Such-and-such had pulled So-and-so's sister's skirt up and paddled her with a ruler fifteen times for not doing her homework or for passing a note in class. Chelsea never found any proof that these public paddlings, at the hands of the Sisters of Christian Charity, were anything except myth. She never actually met anyone who had been publicly, or privately, for that matter, spanked by a nun. Nonetheless, she masturbated to these images as a junior high school student. It only seemed fitting that her MA analytical work in photography be on public spanking pornography from the 1800s to the early 1900s.

What was I thinking? Doing my term paper on the history of erot-

ic photography? Why did I think that would be a good idea? Chelsea asked herself. The words her instructor had written on her proposal came back to her, "Wonderful! Very creative idea. Original!"

The reference book in front of her held yellowed pages of erotic pictures from 1800 to 1920. Chelsea had a weak spot for spanking photos. Her panties were wet under her jeans, and she'd spent most of the morning engaged in long fantasies involving the acts depicted in the old pornography she was studying for style. Her notes on lighting, techniques, and poses consisted of one line: "Pick up a copy of *On Our Backs.*" A note that was as self-motivated as it was academically driven. Chelsea justified it as research; she wanted to compare the modern-day spanking photos to those she was studying from the 1800s.

The well-dressed woman turns the page of her text without looking up. Chelsea, however, finds herself staring. She has on a brown suit made of wool. The jacket is perfectly tailored to her body and buttons snugly under her breasts. A white, freshly pressed shirt with a tasteful ruffle is buttoned to the neck and visible in the scoop of the jacket. Her brown hair is pulled back away from her face in a tight, perfect bun. Brown horn-rimmed reading glasses sit forward on her small nose. The well-dressed woman had neatly placed a small brown felt hat with one tiny but perfectly intact feather and a hatpin of plain gold with a single pearl on the table when she sat down. Her wool overcoat, in the exact same shade of brown as the hat, was folded and draped over the back of the chair next to her. There was a faint scent of lavender in the air. *She looks like a 1940s schoolmistress with her back completely straight and away from the chair as she reads her reference books,* Chelsea thinks to herself.

Chelsea shifts in her chair again, glancing at the next photo of two girls in bloomers with their butts exposed for the teacher to punish them, then back at the well-dressed woman. Chelsea wants to fuck her, the well-dressed woman with the perfect hair and tight lips. More precisely, Chelsea wants to be fucked by her. Chelsea wants the well-dressed woman to be *her* headmistress.

Her wallet chain clanks against the chair as she shifts restlessly, and before the woman can look up to scold her again, Chelsea looks down at the photo in front of her. Two young women in prairie dresses with white cotton slips and aprons were bent over at the waist. Their rear ends were facing the camera and their bloomers were spread open. The headmistress stands to the left side looking at the camera as if it was the class. In her hand a long, thin stick poised to impact on both of the offending girls' exposed bottoms.

Chelsea glances up again at the well-dressed woman, then back at the picture.

In her mind, the library shifts to the one-room school depicted in the photos in the book. Chelsea envisions herself dressed in the 1820s schoolgirl's cotton dress with the white bloomers and black stockings. The well-dressed woman looks exactly the same but without the jacket and with a long skirt and hook-and-eye boots. The stiff white blouse still covers her full breasts, but the ruffle is gone. Chelsea closes her eyes to sharpen the image in her mind.

Chelsea is standing at the front of the room, facing a blackboard. The teacher stands rigid next to her. In her hand Chelsea holds a long thick wooden paddle. She stands as straight as possible holding the paddle by the handle pointing it upwards. Chelsea is in trouble for laughing aloud in class.

Chelsea opens her eyes and stares directly at the well-dressed woman. She examines her features, the way her nose curves up slightly at the end, the way her glasses seem to be perched on that nose. The way her eyebrows are tweezed into harsh thin lines, not so thin as to look odd, but thin enough to look sharp to the touch. The well-dressed woman's hair seems to grow out of her scalp and up towards the tight bun, centered at the back of her head. Not one hair is out of place, not one single wisp falls into her face to add softness. Her mouth is thin and although it is not taunt or pulled, her lips are pressed tightly together. The idea that the woman hasn't had sex in a long, long time floats into Chelsea's mind and she leans in her direction as she begins to imagine the details of the woman's private life.

The well-dressed woman looks up at Chelsea with just her eyes, catching her leaning forward and staring intensely at her. Chelsea looks quickly back at her photography book, then closes her eyes allowing the daydream to sooth the red flush out of her cheeks, to enfold her, and consume her. The made-up details and the physical features heighten her schoolroom fantasy.

"You are a very bad girl," the teacher says as she places a stool in front of Chelsea and taps her index finger on the seat.

Chelsea does as she is instructed: placing her stomach on the stool, leaning her upper body forward causing her ass to stick out. "But, Madam, I am sorry."

"I have had enough of your attitude, girl." The teacher takes the paddle from Chelsea's hands and positions herself behind her. "Class, let this be a lesson to all of you about inappropriate outburst and behavior."

Chelsea feels the cotton material of her skirt being lifted up, then the rear opening of her white pressed bloomers being pulled open to expose her bare bottom. She hears the thick paddle slice through the air on its way to making contact with her skin.

Whack! Whack! Whack!

"We will have to start over, Chelsea. You didn't count the strokes. Begin."

The paddle impacts again on her already red bottom.

Whack!

"One."

Whack!

"Two."

It continues until she shouts out "five."

The teacher rubs her hand over the red-hot flesh of Chelsea's bottom, then leans down close to her face. Chelsea imagines herself crying. "You'll have to stay after class to finish this," the teacher whispers into her ear. Chelsea turns to look into her eyes. What color are they?

Chelsea opens her eyes and leans forward to look at the well-dressed woman's eyes. The woman is reading, her eyelids cast downward. Chelsea stares, caught up in her fantasy. She must know the color. The well-dressed woman looks up, again, with only her eyes. Green! Chelsea smiles. The woman lifts her head and leans toward the smiling Chelsea.

"What is it you want?" Her voice is stern but not harsh.

Chelsea's mouth drops open involuntarily.

"You must want something. You keep staring at me." The woman's voice is even, almost familiar in tone, as if she knows Chelsea.

"I, I…"

"Don't just sit there, staring with your mouth open like a child. Tell me what it is you want." The well-dressed woman removes her glasses as she maintains eye contact with Chelsea.

The blood surges into Chelsea's face causing it to turn red. She knows the woman has no idea what she has been doing across the table from her, yet Chelsea feels as if her sexual fantasy has been projected onto the wall for everyone to see. All she can think of is the color green. She has no idea how to answer the question, and she cannot seem to get her mouth to close. The sweat that started to form on her nose and upper lip when the woman first spoke to her is now sliding down her face.

"Well?" The woman raises one eyebrow as she speaks.

"I'm sorry, Madam." Chelsea grabs her backpack and coat as she runs from the table into the hall towards the public restroom.

Her whole body is burning as she opens the door to the empty ladies room. She enters the last stall, drops her stuff on the tile floor, undoes her jeans, and sits on the toilet. She cannot move quickly enough as she slides one finger of her left hand deep into her very wet cunt. She starts to work her clit with her right hand in small tight circles. Images of her fantasy encounters and her very real interactions with the well-dressed woman flash in her mind. The woman with her perfectly packaged presentation—every hair in place, her uptight attitude, controlled mannerisms—seemed like a prude to Chelsea, and that excited her. She wants to peel back the prude and unleash the sex-starved woman. And in her fantasy that woman is the headmistress punishing her for her wrongs. Chelsea strokes her clit in harder, faster circles—spreading her legs, pushing her hips towards her hand, and coming hard as she plunges two of her fingers deep inside her cunt—her mouth opening in a silent gasp.

Chelsea wipes her fingers and cunt with some toilet paper then pulls her jeans up. At the sink she splashes some water on her face, then puts her coat on and opens her backpack for her gloves.

"My notebook," she says aloud to her own reflection in the mirror, realizing she's left it on the table in her haste to get away from the well-dressed woman's questions. Chelsea contemplates leaving it, but realizes her class notes, as well as her useless project notes, are in that book. She takes a deep breath, then heads back to the table.

The well-dressed woman is gone. Chelsea's notebook is there next to her still-open reference book of old nudes. Relieved, she walks over to the table. As she grabs her notebook, she sees unfamiliar handwriting on the center of the project notes page. In neat even script are the words "You will never get what you want if you do not ask for it." It is signed "Meredith A. Brown."

Chelsea rereads it then looks around for the well-dressed woman. For a moment the red starts to return to her face. "There is no way she could have known," Chelsea says aloud.

Chelsea's reference book is still open to the classroom picture. She looks at it again, then at the now-closed books the woman was reading. She leans across the table and grabs the texts. The titles on the spines read: *The Complete Guide to Disciplining Schoolboys in England 1780–1890* and *Schoolhouse Discipline: 1700 to 1890.*

There is a small rectangle of white paper sticking out of the first text and Chelsea opens the book to that page. On the top is the word *caning,* and pencil illustrations show correct forms for holding the cane at various moments in the strike with text on technique. In the same script as in Chelsea's notebook on the small piece of paper used to mark the page is written, "I am doing research on disciplining little girls who laugh in public libraries." Chelsea turned the paper over and the logo and name of the university she attends along with the name "Meredith A. Brown, Assistant Professor of History," and a phone number were printed on it.

Chelsea laughs aloud as she puts the book down and pockets the card.

Cowgirls and Science

CATHERINE LUNDOFF

Rodeo. Just thinking about it made me quiver all over, just like it had ever since I was a little girl. And I even got a day off from the archaeology dig to enjoy it, every last little bit from Grand Entry to roping. Rodeos meant hot women on gorgeous horses. Women with sun-browned, leather-tough faces, with long strong hands and confident walks. Women with ropes in their hands or hanging from their belts—ropes that could be used for all kinds of things besides livestock. Not that I'd ever gotten up the nerve to ask, mind you, but I sure liked thinking about it on those lonely nights in my little tent. A big grin spread across my face as I drove into the lot.

I had just stepped out of my truck when I heard her. Hell, all of downtown Dallas most likely heard her. "What the hell is a 'cowgirl of science' anyway?" I pulled on my dusty jean jacket and considered ignoring the voice. It wasn't like I had to explain my choice of bumper stickers to anyone. But I could feel her, whoever she was, grinning at my back, so I finally gave up and turned around.

The two women sitting by the rail looked like they'd taken one fall too many. Not that it slowed down the comments they were making at my expense. "I mean, can you even ride, girl? You look like you been mucking out stalls for sure." She and her friend exploded in laughter.

My shiny, happy mood was beginning to fade. "What's it to you? Seems to me all the good riders are up by the arena, not hanging out in the parking lot." I straightened up and tilted my head back so I could meet her eyes from under the brim of my baseball cap. Sure enough, she was bigger than me—broad shoulders and blue eyes living in a nest of wrinkles. Just the kind of gal I knew I'd be lusting over later that night.

And it was just my luck that she and her buddy were about ready to fall off the bench laughing at me. I knew there was no point in standing there gaping at them. By the time she finished having her laugh, I was headed toward the arena in search of greener, more hospitable pastures. That was when she stood up and I could see the large gleaming prize buckle she was wearing. The words were out of my mouth in a second. "You sure won't win any prize money busting my chops in the parking lot."

She grinned at me again, this time stepping close enough that I could see that she had a sexy gap between her front teeth and that she was a bit younger than all those crow's-feet suggested. "Okay, now I'm being serious. What's the sticker about?" She gestured with a surprisingly long thumb toward my truck, then tucked it back into her belt. It was a something I assumed she did often.

I met her eyes for a couple of breaths and got a little wet. Damn rodeo cowgirls. They always did this to me. But she looked like the lights were on upstairs, and I decided she might be able to handle big words. "I'm an archaeologist. The boys started calling themselves 'cowboys of science' years back. Since I'm not a boy, I made some changes when I had the sticker made."

"I can see that." She looked me over until I surprised myself by blushing. She grinned again. "Archeologist, huh? Like in *National Geographic*?" I nodded and she kept going. "What are you doing here in lovely North Texas? Caddo stuff?"

The lights were officially on. "I'm working on a reservoir project. They have us come in and dig to see if anything's there before they flood it all out. We'll take what we can get as far as what turns up." I was talking fast, the way I always did when I got nervous. Normally, I could talk about digging big square holes all day long without a second thought. I could describe the thrill of making a good find on a beautiful day or the fun of wrestling with line levels and cord to get your excavation just right. Just not to this woman right here and right now.

Instead I looked at her hands, wondering if I'd get the chance to see them on the reins. I knew I'd be dreaming about them in a few other places once in bed. Everything below my waist heated up with the thought, and I tried not to squirm.

It looked like she could read my mind. "You like rodeos? C'mon, we'll give you the tour. Unless you got something better to do?" I shook my head, trying not to look too eager. Part of my brain was wondering if she did roping, and if I'd make a good substitute calf. I tried to squish that persistent, warped little fantasy down deep where no one else would see its seamy little face.

"You got a name, cowgirl of science?" The friend was trailing along with us, her snub nose wrinkling as she stepped out of the shade. She smelled like horses and had a long scar running from her mouth down her chin. Must've been one hell of a fall. Otherwise, she was as curvy as her friend was long and lean, but her dark eyes had a look to them that made it impossible to call her "cuddly."

I added a second player to my roping fantasy and wondered if they were an item. "Molly. You?" I could see the arena from where I stood. A lone clown was whooping it up for the small crowd. The real action wouldn't get going for a while.

The shorter one answered for them both. "Patty. This is Hank. Short for Henrietta." Patty came up to my shoulder, while Hank didn't look like she'd ever been taken as short for much of anything. They both had a slightly bowlegged walk that suggested hours in the saddle. I got a little wetter and wondered if they'd notice if I pulled my underwear into a more comfortable position. Deciding against it, I followed them down the aisle between the stalls, taking it all in. I loved the sight and smell of stables, almost as much as I loved rodeo cowgirls.

Hank asked the question I'd been dreading. "So, you ride?" I shook my head, not wanting to talk about all the times I tried. Truth was, I loved horses when we were both on the ground but they scared the crap out of me when I was on one. So I made up for it by falling for damn near every woman I ever saw on a horse.

"C'mon," Patty volunteered. "You might as well check out Grandmaster Flash." My eyes must've bulged at the suggestion because they both laughed. Flash had his own fan club—horse-struck gals like me who thought he was the prettiest thing on four feet. He'd earned the "Grandmaster" too, winning just about every time those dainty hooves touched an arena.

"Patty's Flash's trainer, you know." Hank said in a way that suggested it was no big deal, all the while making it clear that it was.

"Really?" I squealed, done with playing it cool. Flash was one of the horses I'd been hoping to see do his thing today. Not that his rider was any slouch, just a bit too straight for even my idol worship.

"Got a crush on the rider too, or just the horse?" Hank grinned, elbowing Patty.

"Just the horse. And it's not a crush." I growled.

Patty gave me a wry smile that twisted the scar on her chin as she steered me around the corner. "Good thing. Beatríz only likes guys, so you'd be outta luck there. Well, here we are. Flash, Molly. Molly, Flash. Give my baby a carrot." She dropped a couple of carrots in my outstretched palm.

Flash was just as gorgeous up close as he was from a distance, all pure gold hide and silver-white mane and tail. He lipped the carrots out of my hand, and I rubbed his nose in cautious adoration. There was something else on my mind, though. "So how come you think I don't like guys too?" I don't know why I asked; I usually trip anybody's gaydar that's worth the name.

Apparently that was an invitation. Hank stepped up so close to me that her breasts pressed into my back, then leaned in to blow very gently against the bare skin of my neck. "Lucky guess," she purred, her lips just barely brushing my skin. I flinched, breathing fast like a startled horse. A quick glance down revealed my nipples showing hard through my T-shirt. The horse caught my mood and pulled away with a snort and a vehement shake of his head. Hank backed away more slowly and I could feel her grin at the back of my head.

That got me, though I can't really say why. I was probably just horny; it'd been a while. All I know is that I turned around and grabbed her, pulling her in for a long kiss. She tasted like pepper-mint and Coke with just a hint of tobacco. Her arms closed around me like wire and bound me to her, holding me fast. I could feel Patty watching us and scared myself by wanting her to go away and at the same time wanting her to join in.

As if she could read my mind, Hank broke the kiss and spun me around in her arms to face Patty. She held me close while she ran her tongue down the back of my neck until I moaned as softly as I could. Out in the arena I could hear cheering and stomping, so at least I knew that whatever sounds I made would be drowned out. Patty reached over and grabbed one of my tits in her hand, her thumb rubbing it through the T-shirt while she watched me, as if trying to assess what I'd be good for. That was when Hank shoved her leg between mine and dragged my shirt out of my pants. "Not now," Patty said firmly, jerking her head at the arena.

"Shit! I gotta ride in the next event," Hank snarled, looking from her watch to the arena like a hunting dog on point. "Hate to let a good thing go to waste." She flipped me around and kissed me hard, smothering any protests I was inclined to make.

When she was done, Patty chimed in. "I got an idea." Hank let me go and I turned around so I could see the length of rope in the trainer's hands. I shivered all over, soaking my way through my jeans.

"Yeah," Hank murmured. She reached out to stick one of her big hands under my shirt, stroking and pinching until I thought I'd scream if I didn't get something between my legs soon. "You ever been tied up, Molly?" I shook my head, the words failing to come to me. Patty stepped forward so that she was looking into my eyes from an inch or two away. She stuck a hand between my legs and laughed when I jumped and yelped. Hank laughed too and went on murmuring into my ear. "Think you might like it? I'm getting the feeling you've been dreaming about this for a while. Am I right?"

I struggled with my common sense for a minute or two. What the hell was I doing? I didn't know these women, and for all I knew

I'd be tied up naked until I starved or found the whole crowd from the arena looking at me. I stared back at Patty, trying to figure out how crazy she was. She gave me an unreadable stare right back. "I think we better wait till you're done with your ride, Hank."

Hank sighed deeply and kissed my neck before releasing me. "Maybe later then, darling. If you decide to stick around." I grabbed the wall to keep from falling over and turned around to give her a look of pure amazement. *If I stuck around?* What did she think I was going to do in soaking wet jeans, aching like a woman's tongue and fingers had never been inside me? Hump a cowboy? She saw my expression and laughed. "Take her out to the good seats, will you, Pats?" With that, she planted a loud kiss on Patty's lips and sauntered off toward the other side of the barn like the last fifteen minutes or so had never happened.

I gaped after her until Patty tugged at my arm. When she finally got my attention, she turned and headed for the arena without a word. I staggered after her, my legs still not quite my own. Somewhere along the line she'd put the rope back down. I couldn't say whether I was relieved or disappointed. Patty led me to a seat down front in the bleachers next to a couple of other women and a guy. One of the women looked me over and laughed. "Got another greenhorn, Pats? Dunno about you."

Great, I was one in a series; that made me feel swell. Patty curled one lip in a snarl as I flushed. But I sat next to her anyway, even though I didn't catch what she said back. At least the other one didn't say anything more, just gave me a knowing look and went back to watching the arena. Patty leaned forward so her leg touched mine, sending my nerves back to sparking. From the corner of my mouth, I asked, "Would you really have tied me up?"

"Do you want me to?"

My stomach two-stepped when I caught her eyes. *Oh, yes,* I thought, but couldn't get the words past my lips. I'm such a chicken shit. She just looked me in the eye and gave me a smile that started the goose bumps going up my arms. That was the moment when the announcer said Hank's name over the speakers, and I used it as an excuse to look away, hot and sticky all over. All I had to do was wait till after the event, and then something I thought about at every rodeo was going to happen. All I had to do was wait.

I was imagining so hard I almost missed Hank's ride around the barrels. She whipped through them in a small dust storm, the big bay between her thighs spinning on his haunches to give her the speed she was asking for. Hank herself was leaning forward, one hand on the pommel, the other on the reins like she and the horse were one big animal. Her long face was set in total concentration as she urged the horse on with her legs and hands, like she had no memory of what had almost happened before her ride.

Like she had no memory of me. I bit back a whimper, wanting with all my heart to be that horse if only for a few seconds. Wanting to have every ounce of speed and strength pulled out of me by those big hands, those long legs. Clearly, I was going to wait for as long as it took.

Hank charged out of the arena, only to be replaced by another rider, then another. I saw them all in a blur of hands and hooves, taut faces glimpsed under cowboy hats. My pussy clenched, guessing at what it would be like to be full of Hank's fingers, Patty's tongue. What it would be like to be tied down and made to like whatever they liked.

I'd never had the nerve to try something like that before, and even now the thought made me shake in my work boots. I tried to put some distance between me and my fantasies, imagining the pain of rope burn, the humiliation if someone saw me like that. It didn't help.

Patty leaned in and murmured against my ear, "Still game?" I nodded and got to my feet to follow her out. The woman who made the greenhorn comment gave me a look of pure contempt and whispered something to her friend. I stopped in front of her, desire and anger surging inside me until I didn't know whether I wanted to fuck or fight.

She looked up at me, squinting a little at the sun at my back, and I smiled down at her. I knew the look I was wearing; more than anything it said, "C'mon, try something." I wore it a lot on the site when the boys were giving me a hard time. Usually they backed off, and it looked like she would too. Her eyes slid away from mine, and she smiled a little. It made her look queasy and Patty laughed. I swaggered away, feeling her watch my back as I followed Patty into the barn.

Hank walked up, leading the bay. "Nice," Patty remarked. "Should've seen our girl here stare down Bitchy Barb, Hank. Maybe the little shit'll actually keep her mouth closed for an hour or two." I was watching Hank, aware of her every breath like it came from my own lungs. She smiled at me, and I smiled back.

"Well, I see you're not scared any more." She reached out and ran a finger along my cheek, then down my neck. She trailed it over my breast, lingering until the breath caught in my throat. "I need to put my horse up and collect my prize," she added. "Why don't you see if you can find a nice private hitching post, Patty?"

I chewed my lower lip as Patty rolled her eyes and Hank slipped an arm around my shoulders. She pulled me along with her as she walked the horse back to his stall, one long hand casually brushing itself over my nipple until I squirmed against her. She nodded to a couple of guys who yelled "Nice ride!" after her, then steered both me and the horse into a box stall.

"I'm hoping they mean you." She pulled a knotted cord loose from the side of the stall and shoved my legs apart with her hand. Then she ran the rope through my belt and between my legs so that the knot rested against my crotch. She spun me around to tie it off at my belt in back, then turned me to face her and yanked it tight so that I yelped at the friction. Damn, she was fast! I hardly knew what had happened when she pushed me back against the wall and kissed me hard, making my hips rock against the cord harness. "Don't lose interest now."

By now I was gasping for air, my pussy gaping empty, hot and wet inside my jeans. I wanted her so bad. "I think I'd like you to play with that little bit of rope while I put the Sheriff here up. I like to have a little distraction when I work."

Her tone didn't leave a lot of room for disagreement. I knew I wasn't going to get what I wanted unless I was a good little girl. With that in mind, I put my hand down on the rope and wiggled against it a little. The knot sent sparks through my clit, even through denim, and I unbuttoned my jeans to get a little closer. She didn't miss much. "Uh-uh. I didn't say you could play with yourself that much, darling. Not yet, anyway."

Guiltily, I pulled my fingers out of my jeans and rubbed against the rope instead. Hank tugged off her saddle as I moaned. "You gotta try harder than that, little girl. I got women beating down my door, all wantin' the same thing you want right now. What makes you so special?" She pulled off the bridle, rubbing the horse behind the ears until he snorted happily.

Her eyes didn't leave mine, though. I suddenly knew how mice feel when there's a snake in front of them. I forced myself not to freeze. Instead I rubbed the cord against myself with one hand and reached up to play with my nipples with the other. I was chewing my bottom lip by now, barely holding back the moans that were working their way out of me. Hank smiled and grabbed an armload of hay for the horse.

I decided to try a little harder and pulled my shirt up, then tugged my bra down so she could see how hard my nipples were. By then, I didn't much care if I had more of an audience than her or not. Patty opened the stall door a crack and stepped inside. "I think the old trailer out in the lot would work. Got her nice and warmed up yet?" She stepped close to me and ran her fingers over the rope harness. A groan found its way out of me and she leaned down to plant her mouth on my nipple. She sucked hard, tonguing it against her teeth until I dug my fingers into her hair and let out a yelp.

"Let's get over there before you wear her out, Pats." Hank's voice almost suggested that she was jealous, and I grinned when I realized it. Patty gave my nipple one last bite and pulled my bra up and my shirt down. She herded me out the stall door, the harness still rubbing against me until I didn't think I could walk any farther.

From the corner of my eye, I could see the length of rope in Patty's hands again, and this time I knew I'd say "yes." Hell, by now, I'd beg for it.

The walk to the old trailer seemed to be the long way round and I was stumbling over every pebble by the time we got there. Only Hank's iron grip on my arm kept me standing while Patty slipped the bolts, and they hustled me inside. Clean hay crunched underfoot and I could see a couple of hitching rings on the wall in the dim light. Patty pulled out a clasp knife, and before I even had time to gasp both the rope harness and the blade were gone. I surprised myself by sighing with relief. Some things still scared me.

Hank laughed. "So, Pats, how fast do you think we could have her stripped down and tied up?" She pulled a stopwatch out of one pocket. "What's the matter, darling? Practice makes perfect and all that. How about you give us a word to let us know that you've had enough? That make you feel better?"

I nodded and choked out "archaeology." I wouldn't be dropping that by accident, no matter what they did. I mean, I loved my work, but there was a time and place for everything.

"Not science? Well, whatever you like, darling." She pulled a bandanna out of her pocket and walked toward me with an evil grin. "I'll just get this tied over your eyes and then I think we'll take it from here." Before I could say a word, she had me blindfolded and was starting on my belt buckle.

"Hold it. We haven't set the timer yet, Hank. No cheating." I could hear Patty's thumb click down on the button like it came from inside a big metal drum. I imagined the strip and hog-tie as a new event, held in an arena filled with cheering women. Patty yelled, "go!" and I could feel one set of hands at my buckle, the other tugging my shirt off. The bra followed and I could hear the hiss of breath from my imaginary audience when my nipples met the air. The crowd in my head echoed the one in the real arena when they yanked my jeans off, even louder when my underwear followed.

The ropes were next, just like I hoped they'd be. Someone

pulled my arms above my head, and I squawked as the coarse fiber met my bare skin. The wire-tight grip on my wrists loosened slightly and there was another loud click. "45.62. Not bad. Not as good as our last team event, though. I think we can better our time." I squirmed, my thighs slick and hot, the scent of pussy filling the narrow trailer. "Besides, we tied her legs together. Not much fun in that." I whimpered my agreement and someone laughed. The ropes slipped away from my wrists and ankles and I imagined the crowd in my head holding their breath.

The repeat performance was even faster, ending with me trussed up in the hay, heart racing. Before today, if you'd asked why I wanted this, I would have laughed it off. Now I knew that it was about being possessed, about yielding to a superior force. About giving myself completely to the two women I could feel wanting me, wanting each other from inches away.

The ropes dropped away, and I got pulled to my feet. Without being asked, I spread my legs wide and held my arms over my head again. "I do like a cooperative gal, don't you, Hank?" Two fingers shoved their way up into my wet cunt, one callused thumb finding my clit. A hot mouth closed on one of my nipples while someone else came up behind me and held me tight. I started to lower my arms only to have them pulled behind me and tied together. The rope felt smoother this time on my grateful wrists as I squirmed against the two bodies that pressed against mine.

I was tugged backward, stumbling until I could feel the cold metal of the trailer against my back. The hitching ring rattled as the rope on my hands got pulled through and tied off. I wondered what they'd do next, but it turned out I didn't have long to wait long for an answer. A jean-clad knee ruthlessly forced my legs apart and I stretched as wide as I could. "I bet I could get my whole fist in there. What do you think, Pats?" The crowds in my head let out a primal howl. I heard the telltale snap of latex and tried to open just a little wider.

One finger thrust its way into me, making me gasp. A second one made me groan and chew my lip. The third and fourth had me panting and rocking back against the wall, thrusting my hips forward to take in anything they could give me. I was dimly aware that there was a finger at my asshole, a tongue caressing the sensitive skin of my neck and shoulders. The fifth finger went inside my pussy just as my virgin asshole closed around the other finger. The fingers inside me began to curl up and pound in and out of my soaking flesh. I could feel my knees begin to buckle as I started to come, sounds I'd never made before stampeding their way past my lips.

A hand braced my shoulder and pinched my nipples until I shook all over, my body shuddering its surrender as the imaginary arena went wild. I knew that every woman there wanted to be me just then, except for the few who wanted to be Patty and Hank. I gave them everything I had, arching my back and howling as those hands worked their.

Anything after that would be just a tease. I could hear Patty and Hank kissing, smell the sweat and desire from their bodies and my own. I could hear them moan as someone's tongue, someone's fingers found their way home. I tugged at the ropes binding my hands, wishing more than anything that I could reach them, feel their bodies press against mine. Or reach myself, satisfy the aching that was spreading its way through my pussy, but it was no use. Instead, I squatted on my heels, legs spread and clit burning while I listened to them make love a few feet away.

When they were done, they untied me and removed the blindfold. Patty kissed me while I stood there, blinking in the stripes of sunlight, her tongue and mouth both fiercer and gentler than Hank's. I kissed her back as hard as I could, eagerness and longing in every movement of my lips and tongue. That was what I got for hoping for an encore. Instead, Hank leaned over and grabbed my naked ass. "Nice ride," she growled and kissed me hard.

Then they were gone, leaving me in a horse trailer on the edge of the rodeo grounds with a pile of my clothes in front of me. I got dressed, stopping to breathe in the warm scent of sex and sweat every few moments. I couldn't help sticking my hands down my pants and rubbing my way to an orgasm that I knew wouldn't be worth the effort. Then I headed out past the arena and back to my truck, skipping the rest of the rodeo.

I knew I wouldn't see them again, that I would never have the nerve to give myself to strangers a second time. It filled me with a warm sadness that started up at my chest and worked it way down to my tired pussy and rope-burned wrists and ankles. On the other hand, riding a horse was looking like a piece of cake now.

Another Night at Daddy's

Crystal Sincoff

Ricky spread a handful of grease through her jet-black hair and combed it into a practiced ducktail. She thought it made her look tough, and she liked that. Curling her lips around a cigarette, she blew smoke at her reflection. She tucked the tails of her shirt into her faded Levi's, leaving the front unbuttoned. The silver buckle on her studded belt read DICK, circled with a slash through it.

"Hurry up, slut," was the call from down the hall. Her room-mate, Sam, appeared behind her in the crooked mirror. "Fuck," she drawled, eyeing the show of cleavage in the V-neck of Ricky's shirt. "If I knew my old lady wouldn't kick my ass, I'd ball you right now."

"As if I'd let you," Ricky mumbled from behind her cigarette. "Hey!" she protested as Sam came up behind her, laughing, and humped her ass. "Shit, will you grow up?" She pushed Sam off and picked up the cigarette from where it had fallen into the sink.

One last look in the mirror and Ricky headed down the hallway to the living room. She took her black leather jacket from the back of the recliner, zipping it to her throat and turning up the collar. She was looking to get some hot tail tonight, and the sooner she got to Daddy's, the sooner she'd get her rocks off.

"Come on," she hollered as she left the house. "Your old lady's gonna be pissed." The screen door bounced shut behind her.

At the end of the driveway Ricky swung her leg up over her hog, feeling the familiar thrill of her crotch settling into the leather. It increased as she started the engine, sending the vibrations through her body. She ground herself into the seat for that extra buzz and gunned the engine. Looking over her shoulder, she saw Sam lock the door and run to her own bike. With one last drag of her cigarette, Ricky tossed the butt to the ground and revved the engine.

The earth flew by beneath her, and the wheels of her bike ate up the asphalt. Ricky was smiling from ear to ear as the wind rushed past her face.

Daddy's was not the most popular dyke bar in town, but it was Ricky's favorite. She felt right at home in the dark corners and crappy lighting. The floor was sticky with spilt drinks and unnamed bodily fluids. There was no air conditioning, and danger hung in the air along with the strong scent of Marlboros. It was an acquired taste, one that she felt suited her.

Daddy's was the only place in town with pool tables, so that was an added draw. It was a typically busy Saturday night, and wherever Ricky looked she saw eager chicks waiting to get some action.

"Hey, Maggie," she called, unzipping her jacket. The layer of smoke at eye level made her squint across the bar.

"What's your pleasure, sugar?" Maggie shouted over the din. She leaned across the bar so that Ricky could get a good look at her double D's. They were impressive.

"You still have Pete's Wicked Ale on tap?" Maggie went to get her order while Ricky leaned back against the bar. She let a little cleavage show as she checked out the possibilities. Without being picky, she did have a penchant for redheads, who, in her experience, usually had tempers. She liked her women feisty, to give her a wild ride. It seemed she wasn't happy unless someone was throwing things at her.

"Tabatha was in here looking for you," Maggie said, setting the beer on the bar. Ricky cringed, wondering what her psycho ex wanted.

"She say why?" Ricky asked. She pulled her billfold from her back pocket and dished out some cash onto the bar.

"To give you hell." Maggie laughed, pocketed the money, and went off to help another customer. *Hell*, Ricky thought. *Well, that's what Tabatha is…hell on wheels.* She hoped against hope that she wouldn't run into her.

Bringing another cigarette to her lips, she let it dangle there, unlit, while her eyes feasted on the hottest ass she'd seen in a while. It was at the pool table, bending over to make a shot. A very short black leather skirt barely covered it, a skirt so short that Ricky had a wonderful view of a clean-shaven pussy. The woman straightened up, bringing into view a long mane of russet colored hair falling in a sheet down her back, gold and red glistening under the beer lights. Ricky brought her lighter up and lit her cigarette, slowly exhaling a stream of smoke.

"Hey, Maggie," she called. Maggie walked over, tucking another tip into her bra. "You know what she's drinking?" Ricky asked, gesturing toward the redhead at the pool table.

"I don't know why *I* can't interest you in some fun," Maggie crooned, leaning close enough for Ricky to taste the mint on her breath. "I played the flute in high school," she confided. Ricky raised her eyebrows. "I can flutter my tongue 216 beats per minute." Ricky laughed and raised her glass in salute.

"What's she drinking?" Ricky asked again.

With a practiced sigh, Maggie went to make the mystery woman a fuzzy navel. Scanning the bar, Ricky noticed that Sam was already off in the corner with her old lady. They were making out like high-schoolers. She smiled, putting out her cigarette in the ash tray. Sam was lucky. She had found love early.

"Heard you like fuzzy navels," Ricky said, shrugging off her jacket and hanging it on one of the wooden hooks that lined the wall by the pool tables. The redhead was even more striking close up. Her eyes were a surprising dark brown and framed by thick lashes. Her body was all soft curves, hips full and wide, waist a gentle indention leading to her decidedly perfect breasts. She could see every curve through the sheer fabric of the woman's shirt. Her tits were full and her nipples dark, pleading for attention.

Her dainty pout stretched into a smile at Ricky's approach. "Do you have one?" the redhead asked. She took the drink, and set it next in line with another half dozen similar offerings.

"Why don't you find out?" Ricky asked. Her new friend laughed, leaning back against the table and crossing her arms beneath her breasts so that they rose to flirt playfully with Ricky's eyes.

"You see the woman behind me, racking up the balls?"

Ricky took in the aggressive-looking butch dyke slapping the balls into the triangle. She had a black flattop, thick black framed glasses, and a nose ring. The sleeves on her plaid shirt had been ripped off, revealing rather impressive biceps. Not as tall as the redhead, but thick and muscular. "You need to get permission from her. I'm her bitch." She giggled, taking the first of her fuzzy navels. More than one person had thought of the drink idea, but none of them were playing at that table.

The question is, does Butch like to pass her bitch around, or does she want to share in the pleasure? Ricky walked around the table to Butch's side and leaned in close, letting her thigh touch the other woman. "Whatcha drinking?"

"Whatcha offering?" Butch growled suggestively. Ricky felt heat rise in her body as her eyes met Butch's. They were open to play. Ricky grabbed the waitress and ordered a Budweiser.

A good hour later, Ricky leaned over Bitch, pressing her bush into the redhead's ass through their clothes. She was helping Bitch with her stroke on the pool table, and she had more than a good buzz going. Her new buddies were very friendly; it was only a matter of time before they went outside to cool off.

"Ouch," she yelped as Butch walked by, slapping her on the ass. Bitch giggled beneath her, driving her wild. Ricky closed her eyes, fighting off the urge to take her right there on the pool table. She needed more than teasing and innuendos. She ground herself suggestively against Bitch as they took the shot and asked, "You two want to get serious?"

The redhead's eyes met Butch's and she nodded, leaning her pool cue against the wall.

"Nice soft-tail, man," Butch said when they got outside, running her hand along the handlebars. Bitch hopped right on, making motor noises and pretending to rev the engine. Ricky lifted her eyebrows, but said nothing, focusing on the ass bouncing on the leather seat.

"And totally customized," Ricky bragged. She pulled out what looked like a strap-on from the saddle bag. It resembled your basic belted dildo but the strap was longer than most would need. She bent across the seat, between Bitch and the handlebars, and buckled it tightly around the frame of the bike. The large black rubber prick rose into the air. Strapping it onto the bike was preferable to a woman sometimes. Ricky could ride for miles with the vibrations of the bike ripping through her body, bringing on amazing orgasms. "I call it my pommel," she shared, straightening and winking at Butch.

"Fuck, no!" Bitch immediately pulled up her skirt and positioned herself over the dildo, then lowered herself down onto the cold rubber, warming it slowly with her juicy lips. She gasped and giggled cautiously, taking in its entire impressive length. Butch smiled, her arms crossed over her chest. She was softly whistling "Back in the Saddle Again."

"Start the engine!" Bitch pleaded. Ricky mounted behind her and turned on the ignition. Bitch's giggles became groans. Ricky reached around to massage Bitch's nipples, pleased to find them like long erasers. She kneaded the full breasts, letting their weight fill her palm. Her other hand slid around Bitch's waist, fingers coming to play in the folds of the clean-shaven pussy she had admired earlier. It was wet and slick, smelling of hot sex and warm seat leather.

"Butch...Butch," Bitch chanted, until Butch came up beside her, just in time to kiss her as her orgasm peaked.

Ricky jumped when a car door slammed nearby. A couple walked into the bar, arms around shoulder and waist, paying no attention to them.

Butch lifted Bitch off of the toy and set her on the ground. Her smile was wide with satisfaction. *Yep, that is the coolest thing*, Ricky thought, getting off of the bike, unstrapping the appendage from the seat, and putting it away.

Butch was leading her woman down the alley on the side of the bar. Her arm was around Bitch's waist and they were nibbling on each other. Ricky lit a cigarette and followed. The lighting was bad and the smell was less than thrilling, but she knew the back of the bar opened into a field followed by what seemed like endless mountains. The moon was bright and there was plenty of room to play.

They walked around the corner and there was a large black van, straight out of every horror flick Ricky had ever seen; the windows dark, the bumpers rusted. Butch pulled out a key and unlocked the side door, which opened with a squeal. The interior light came on and brought a shag carpet and a bed into view. Ricky raised her eyebrow and took another drag of her cigarette.

Bitch crawled in and Butch pushed against her ass, making her fall across the bed in a fit of laughter. Ricky chuckled too and put out her cigarette in the gravel.

"Come on," Butch called. Ricky looked up, met Butch's heat-filled eyes, and climbed aboard.

"Fuck!" Bitch cried out as Ricky's hand opened her box.

"Yes," ordered Butch, twisting a nipple roughly. Ricky was sweating, twisting her hand in Bitch's love juice. She could not believe how far into this woman's snatch her hand was. The muscles squeezed her wrist. She slowly opened her fingers, causing Bitch to groan. Ricky twisted her hand and Bitch's hips rose into the air, seeking. Smiling maliciously, she pulled her hand out with a loud sucking noise.

"No!" Bitch protested, and Ricky didn't disappoint her. She dove in again and picked up a steady rhythm. Butch had removed her clothes and was now squatting over Bitch's head. Ricky's eyes were drawn to the ropes of muscle in Butch's thighs as she held herself over her lover's face. Bitch's eager tongue was like an arrow finding its target. Her eyes glazed over and she began cursing, calling Bitch a nasty whore, a fucking slut, a dirty cunt sucker. She was moaning and bouncing, her small breasts jiggling. Her abs were tightening and quivering, the sight making Ricky even wetter.

Suddenly Butch screamed and her come came flying out in a

stream. Bitch was swallowing, her tongue searching for more. Butch dropped back on her hands and her juice sprayed straight into Ricky's face. "Fuck!" Ricky laughed, wiping her face. Her hand was mangled by the vice of Bitch's trap as she came in turn.

"You want your twat sucked? That fuckhole of yours filled?" Butch asked as she approached Ricky. She took a fistful of greasy locks and pulled her up so that Ricky's nose was in her pussy. The smell made Ricky's mouth water. "Eat me," Butch commanded, and Ricky didn't hesitate. Her mouth latched onto Butch's lips. Her tongue dove between the folds, finding her hole wet and salty. Ricky's nose bobbed against her clit in an eagerness to please. Butch pulled Ricky's hair, and yanked her face harder into her lower lips. Ricky brought her hand to her own cunt and began frigging herself.

She jumped as she felt Bitch's long-nailed fingers join her own, gently pulling the soft hair of her pussy. "Let me take care of that," Bitch whispered. She licked her ear and bit it playfully as she slid into Ricky's wet folds with skilled fingers. Ricky could feel Bitch's nipples pressing into her back, and something hard and wet sliding along the crack of her ass. "Feel that, honey?" Bitch cooed. Ricky couldn't answer. "That's my cock. It's special." She nudged Ricky's hole. "Feel how big it is?" Bitch poked her again, teasing her entrance. Ricky shoved back eagerly, wanting that fullness. Bitch laughed and began to push into her cunt. Ricky groaned, finding her pussy protesting. Whatever Bitch was shoving into her was huge. She felt the walls of her cunt expanding, inch by inch, the width of the cock stretching her wide.

Butch pulled Ricky's face from her snatch and leaned over to kiss her. She licked Ricky's lips and cheeks, sucking every last drop of come from her face. Ricky then felt Bitch force her "special" cock inside. It would be painful had it not felt so good. It hit every wall. It filled every bit of space. Ricky took hold of the shag, pushing back against Bitch as she began pumping into her. Groans echoed in the small space.

"Oh, fuck, Daddy," Bitch said, and Ricky turned her head to see that Butch had strapped on her own bit of fun. It was heavily greased. Bitch froze inside as Butch began fucking her ass hard. They knelt in a row, fucking and cursing.

Ricky's hand found her clit and she pulled and pushed it the way she liked it, while her pussy took in the biggest rubber cock she had ever known. They moved in unison. The only sounds were their nasty words and the suction of their juices mingling.

Ricky found her spot. The air around her seemed to vibrate. It felt as though she were on bike and they were speeding up a winding road, faster and faster, until she toppled over a cliff, falling into sensation, needing oxygen. She collapsed against the shag wall, trying to breathe. The air was heavy with the sweet smell of their come and stale unwashed carpet.

Bitch eased out of her. The absence of her colossal dick caused Ricky's muscles to contract in protest. Bitch giggled and crawled in front of her, squeezing in next to the wall. Her special dildo projected out of her nest like some obscene growth. Ricky was drawn to it. She took it in her hands, twisting it in Bitch's twat. Her lather bubbled around the circumference. "Come here, honey," Bitch invited, her voice hoarse. She put her hands around Ricky's waist and pulled her closer, sliding her massive gap-stopper back where it belonged. Bitch began nibbling her lips as Ricky swayed slowly into her body.

"Ricky!" They all jumped. "Ricky! You fucking slut!" Someone was hitting the side of the van. "Ricky! I know you're in there!"

"What the fuck?" Butch said as she opened the door, wet cock swinging into Tabatha's outraged face. Tabatha wiped her cheek in disgust and forced her key into the side of the van. Before she could go more than a foot, she was on the ground, with Butch's knee in her back.

"Ricky, I loved you," she sobbed into the ground.

"You gonna join us, or leave like a good little girl?" Butch asked, removing the keys from Tabatha's hand.

"I'm only leaving if Ricky comes with me." Ricky and Bitch were still joined at their fuck centers and the very thought of leaving this party caused Ricky's quim to quiver unhappily.

"Sorry, honey," Ricky said, ignoring her ex and rocking her hips against Bitch, who moaned dramatically for Tabatha's benefit. Butch took her knee off Tabatha's back. As she started to clamber upward, her rosebud pout came directly in line with Butch's rubber hard-on. She looked up at Butch with weepy eyes, her tongue sweeping across her lips invitingly.

"Suck it, brat!" Butch demanded. As Tabatha leaned in, Ricky smiled. It was just another night at Daddy's.

Unrequited

KRISTINA WRIGHT

What I remember most about that weekend with Julie was the couch. Even when I refuse to let myself remember the other stuff, because remembering the good also makes me remember how I got my heart broken, I still remember that damned couch. It was bright orange vinyl, a glossy, saggy relic left over from the seventies and destined to finish out its life as the crash pad for Julie's friends. I spent one brief night in Julie's bed before we (meaning she) decided nothing more could happen between us, and I spent one long, agonizing night on that orange couch.

"It came with the apartment," Julie told me as she showed me around her small one-bedroom place. "Is it okay?"

I tried to smile, but the couch didn't look very comfortable. Still, it was the best, the only, choice I had. "Groovy. Thanks."

Julie had been the first one I'd called when I hit Tampa. Truth was, Julie was the only one I'd thought to call. I was twenty-two and running south—nine hundred miles away from a nasty family situation to the one place I felt safe—Julie's arms. She didn't know how I felt. As far as she was concerned, we were best friends.

Only friends.

"I'd let you share my room, but Kevin moved back in last night." She gave me a lascivious little wink that made my stomach flip-flop.

Kevin was her on-again, off-again boyfriend. Things were on again, apparently.

"The couch is great," I said, eyeing the orange monstrosity dubiously. "I won't stay long."

That last part cost me a lot to say. I wanted to stay forever. I wanted her to want me to stay forever.

"Oh, please. You can stay as long as you want." She handed me a pillow and blanket and grinned. "I'd better get to bed. Kevin wants to make up."

I tossed all night, the vinyl couch squeaking with every restless movement. Behind the closed bedroom door, I heard Julie and Kevin. The walls were as thin as my flimsy cotton T-shirt, so I heard every whimper. Every giggle. Every moan. I pulled the pillow over my head, pressing my cheek against the cool vinyl couch. God, I was tired, but the sounds coming from the next room—and the continuous loop of images playing in my fevered imagination— wouldn't let me rest.

It was a long time before I fell asleep to the soft sound of Julie's breathy moans. I dreamed I was trapped inside my own heart, pounding out the rhythm of my heartbeat as I tried to escape. My heart was made out of orange vinyl.

I woke at dawn, blinking away the panic of not knowing where I was. Then I remembered. Julie. A moment later, I felt like I'd been sucker-punched in the gut. Kevin. I lay there on the couch, my sweaty cheek still pressed against the hideous vinyl, pillow flung halfway across the room. I rolled onto my back and groaned as my neck and back protested.

I heard a soft sound, little more than a catch of breath. For a moment, I thought they were fucking again. My stomach clenched until I realized what I was hearing. Crying.

I didn't know what to do. My first instinct was to go to Julie, but I knew better than to get into the middle of a lovers' quarrel. A couple of minutes passed, those soft crying sounds tearing me to shreds. I couldn't sit on the couch and wait for them to come out, so I padded to the bathroom and started the shower. The water did little to soothe me. I needed to know if Julie was all right.

I finished my shower and pulled back the curtain. Julie was standing in the open doorway, staring at me. She quickly looked away as I reached for my towel and wrapped it around me.

"Damn, girl. You scared me."

Her eyes were red-rimmed and puffy, her hair pulled back into a tight ponytail that made her look younger. She forced a weak smile. "Sorry." She balled up the hem of her faded black Journey concert T-shirt in her hand, then smoothed it out again. "I didn't mean to scare you."

I could feel her gaze on me as I stood in front of the sink. "Forget about it. Everything okay?"

She met my eyes in the mirror as I combed the tangles out of my long hair. "Kevin's gone. He never intended to stay. He just wanted to get laid."

The breath whooshed from my lungs, but the relief was bittersweet as I watched Julie's reflection crumble. I turned to say something comforting. What, I didn't know. Thankfully it didn't matter.

She reached for me and I pulled her into my arms, my wet hair trailing down her shoulder as she sobbed against my neck. I hugged her awkwardly, unused to the feeling of her body against mine. We'd been friends for five years, but neither of us was a touchy-feely kind of person. She clung to me like she was drowning and I was a life preserver. I held on, feeling the soft press of her small breasts, the sharp angle of her hipbone where it pressed against me.

"Come on, you need to sit down," I whispered softly when her wracking sobs threatened to shake the fillings loose from my teeth.

She whimpered and shook her head against the crook of my neck.

"It's okay," I said. "I won't let go. Okay?"

She just nodded.

Wrapped around me the way she was, it took some maneuvering to get us out of the bathroom and across the hall to her bedroom. The sheets were tangled and the room smelled of male and sex, but I'd be damned if I was going to haul her out to that hideous orange couch. I sat on the edge of the bed and half dragged her across my lap, cradling her against my chest as she cried.

"Shh, it's all right," I soothed, making gentle circles on her bony back. "It'll be okay."

She shook her head against me and I realized my towel had slipped below my breasts. "No," she breathed against my skin. "It'll never be okay."

There was no way to adjust my towel without moving her, and I wouldn't move her until she didn't need me anymore. So we sat there, her face against the swell of my breast, her arms wrapped tight around my waist. I rocked her like a child, even though she was four inches taller than me, as if I could give her something she needed.

Sobs gave way to soft tears as I stroked her hair and whispered nonsensical things. My skin had become desensitized to her touch to the point that I didn't know where she stopped and I began. It was only when I felt the gentle, insistent tugging on my nipple that I realized Julie had stopped crying.

A quick intake of breath, my hand stilling on her back, as I tried to figure out what the hell had just happened.

She released my nipple and looked up at me, wide-eyed, tears filling her eyes and spilling over to slide down her blotchy cheeks. "I'm sorry. I don't know why. I just—"

I pressed her head gently to my chest so she wouldn't see I was crying too. "It's okay. I'm here. Whatever you need." I meant it.

Silently, her mouth closed around my nipple. I sighed, holding her closer, my hand making gentle circles on her back. She tugged harder and I whimpered, feeling a corresponding tingle in my clit as her lips and tongue coaxed me to feel things I shouldn't feel.

Somehow, we ended up stretched out on the bed, my damp towel balled up in the small of my back, Julie's leg thrown over mine. She let my nipple slide out of her mouth with a wet slurp and covered my breast with her hand. I twisted toward her, our legs tangled, my cunt throbbing.

Julie's T-shirt rode up and I reached out to tentatively stroke the curve of her hip, aroused beyond measure by the contrast of her olive complexion against my pale skin. I stroked her hip, then slid my hand up under her T-shirt and let my fingertips glide over the swell of her breast. Unsure of her response, I pulled back, my hand settling in the curve of her waist.

"Don't stop," she murmured into the hollow of my throat. "Touch me. Make me forget him."

It was all the encouragement I needed.

Dappled sunlight fell across the bed, across our bodies, as I reached under her T-shirt and caressed her breasts. Her nipples were hard and I sucked them through the fabric of her T-shirt until she whimpered and arched against me. I tugged her shirt up, over her breasts with their tight brown nipples and sucked them hard, cupping and squeezing her breasts as I did. I could have lain there all day doing just that, but she reached for my hand and guided it under the waistband of her panties. I will never forget how hot and wet she was. So fucking wet.

"For me," I whispered softly, trailing kisses down her body, wanting to tattoo her skin with my lips. "For me."

I hooked my fingers in the sides of her white panties and tugged them down her legs. I settled between her thighs, breathing in her scent, a combination of arousal and latex. I blocked that last part from my mind as I stared at her cunt. Her pretty, pretty cunt, opening for me, swelling and darkening for me.

"For me."

I reached out and traced the lips of her cunt—from where they met at her clit, down to her perineum and back up the other side. My finger trembled on her clit, my breath coming in quick little pants. It was part arousal, part fear. So afraid she would make me stop, change her mind. She didn't.

Her mouth opened wordlessly when I closed my lips around her swollen clit and licked. Gently at first, then harder, until my entire world was this succulent bit of flesh against my tongue.

"Mine, " I breathed against her clit, as if saying it could make true.

She arched against me, trapping my head between her legs as she clawed at the sheets. Wrapping my arm around her thigh to anchor her to my mouth, I plunged my tongue into her cunt to draw her juices back up to her clit. I thrust two fingers inside her and fucked her hard while I licked and sucked her clit. When I whimpered, she trembled at the vibrations of my mouth.

Her body quivered beneath me. Her hands fisted in my hair as she moaned, pulling me closer, not pushing me away. Almost unconsciously, I was grinding my cunt against the sheets wadded up between my legs, my clit as hard and sensitive as hers. I came, my mouth all but devouring her.

She went still then. Silent. I panted, my body throbbing, as I licked her with quick, firm strokes until her cunt contracted on my fingers and her juices flowed over my tongue.

She moaned something as she came. One word. One name.

Not mine.

"Kevin."

A Full Moon for Lammas

JEAN ROBERTA

Terra liked to drive with one arm around Faith's shoulders. Faith had tried to talk her out of it, and Terra had responded with reassuring squeezes. One-handed driving in a solid truck on almost-deserted roads seemed safer to Faith than such bravado in a two-door in town. This pleasure-drive was Terra's offer of a compromise.

"Look up, babe," Terra told her. A full silver moon was perfectly framed by the paired telephone poles that rose steadfastly from the ground at regular intervals.

"Oh-h-h," sighed Faith, suddenly feeling small. She felt as if she could hear the land breathing all around as the moon beamed down on a flat landscape that was both serene and unsettling. Unlike most environments, urban or rural, this one had no visible boundaries. At ten o'clock at night, the sky was still not dark enough to show stars. A flock of slate-gray clouds, tinged with lavender, hovered near the horizon.

"Where are we going?" asked Faith cautiously.

Terra grinned in the summer twilight. It reminded Faith of the Atlantic Ocean that she left behind when she moved west in stages: first from the wave-battered quaintness of Nova Scotia to the city of Toronto to get an education, and then to a town on the prairie in the Canadian heartland to accept a job in advertising.

"A little further on, honey," Terra assured her. The asphalt under the wheels abruptly gave way to gravel and potholes. Terra's breasts bounced heartily as Faith tried to hold herself still in the vain hope of adjusting to the rough ride. Not that it was ever really smooth, she thought; even the major highways of Saskatchewan were torn and unevenly patched like farm overalls.

In the dim light Terra's tanned face, dark eyes, and plump body looked sly, as though she embodied some of nature's most protected secrets. The smell of the lush weeds in the ditches beside the road seemed as seductive to Faith as the aromas of marijuana and sandalwood incense in a student apartment shared by four womyn-loving womyn.

Young Faith felt like a mermaid out of water. She had a slim, urban pallor that dramatized her tattoos, her nose ring and her short indigo hair; she defined her taste in everything as "alternative." She had a quick, defensive wit, which made her sound hip to many in the local queer bar. But something about the open prairie made sarcasm seem childish.

Faith's ass jiggled and grew clammy in her cotton pants. She felt as though the road were bucking her on its lap like an obscene playmate—causing her clit to vibrate and shaking her perky breasts just for a reaction. "Enjoying the ride, honey?" snickered the driver.

"Oh, sure," groaned Faith, embarrassed by the truth of her answer. She wondered if little Terra, growing up on a farm in the area, had thought of a ride to town in the family truck as a treat, like a roller coaster ride at the fair.

"We're almost there, honey," soothed Terra. "We might see the tornado that's supposed to be headed for Folle Avoine. I want to show you an old farmhouse that's been deserted since the Dirty Thirties."

A pleasurable chill of fear ran down Faith's spine as she wondered if she might be whisked away by a tornado like Dorothy in *The Wizard of Oz*. She also tried to imagine living on an isolated farm during the drought and the Great Depression, when dust covered the land and money was scarce. She wondered what hungry, demanding spirits might still be lurking in the old shack.

Terra also believed in ghosts; she had seen too much to be a skeptic. She thought of them as fellow inhabitants of the generous earth, and she couldn't blame them for lingering in the places where they had worked, hoped, rejoiced, and cried. Terra honestly loved the land that had bred her.

She pulled onto a shoulder of the gravel road. The truck shuddered to a stop. "Here we are," Terra told her date. She and Faith opened their doors and jumped to the ground. Little gusts of air brought the smell of plant life to them in waves as crickets and other night insects created background music. Faith looked up and was dazzled by the clarity of the moon and stars in the darkened sky.

"No mosquitoes," Terra pointed out. "We're lucky this summer." Still tingling from the ride, she took deep breaths of fragrant summer air. She wanted to tear off her tank top and cutoff shorts, pull Faith down with her, and roll on the ground at the edge of the wheat field.

Faith was gazing out over the acres of green plants that rippled like waves in the breeze. "That's a lot of food," explained Terra, feeling like a tour guide. "Number 1 Hard. Imagine all the flour that's going to make."

Faith couldn't really imagine it, but the wheat looked like a promise to her. She could imagine each little wheat stalk bursting with ripeness, waiting for the blades of a combine harvester, and this image seemed bizarrely sexy to her. She felt a laugh tickling her stomach.

Terra pulled Faith into her arms and pressed a long, hot kiss on her mouth. Faith reached up to run a hand through Terra's honey-brown hair, and felt the heat radiating from her. Terra wore her hair shoulder-length in all seasons, and it reminded Faith of country weeds not intended for cutting. Terra's tongue in Faith's mouth made the younger woman weak in the knees, but Terra was determined not to satisfy her yet.

"Mm, babe," laughed the seducer. Faith could feel Terra's breasts and hips shaking. "You have to see the house. Look." Faith followed the direction of Terra's eyes and the twitch of her mouth toward an old, wooden, two-story house.

The steepness of the caved-in roof and the unmistakable tilt of the whole structure made the house look like a sinister drunk, threatening to tumble to the ground. But the moonlight mellowed the gray wood with silver highlights. Faith wondered how far the boards had been transported before they were hammered into a human dwelling place in a treeless landscape.

"Come on," urged Terra, pulling Faith by the hand. The visitor had dreaded those words, but she didn't resist. This visit to the farmland beyond the town was turning into an adventure.

The house was about a block away from where they were standing, as distance was measured in town. Terra kept a warm hand on Faith's lower back as they walked through the tall weeds and over a patch of bare ground that showed recent tire tracks. Faith wondered about these, but Terra's hand distracted her from inquiring. It had slipped down to rest on Faith's girlish behind.

The house still had a front door that led to an enclosed verandah. Faith hesitated, as though there were still people inside who would be offended if she entered without knocking.

Terra gave her a light slap on the bottom. "Go on, honey," she ordered. "You're doomed anyway. There's no one to hear you scream. Except me." She faked a demented laugh.

The door stood ajar because it hung unevenly, like everything else between the shifting foundation and the ruined roof. Faith pushed the door, and it creaked open. The verandah was dark, but another door that had once been painted a cheerful robin's-egg blue led to a spacious ground floor which was sprinkled with moonlight from the holes in the roof. Most of the walls between rooms were half destroyed, so everything could be seen at a glance. A cast-iron stove still stood in the kitchen, and miraculously, a splintered wooden table stood nearby. The house whispered and creaked in a way that made Faith nervous, but everything she heard could be explained away without the benefit of ghostly voices or footsteps.

"I wonder how many kids there were in the family," speculated Terra, trying to keep Faith's courage up. "They must have had chores to do, and if they didn't do them, or they mouthed off to their parents, they got a taste of the strap or dad's belt…on the bum." She pushed Faith into the kitchen and gently bent her forward over the edge of the table. Terra stood behind the smaller woman, and squeezed her protruding cheeks as though they were fruit in a market. "What do you have to say for yourself, young lady?" she demanded.

"I haven't done anything," laughed Faith. "I'm a good girl."

"Really?" sneered Terra, remaining in character. "That's hard to believe. I know you too well for that, honey. If you haven't done anything bad this time, though, I'll just give you a few licks to keep you in line."

Terra swatted Faith's rear-end, and the tremors rushed into Faith's cunt. Terra noted that her victim wasn't fighting her off, and she shimmied slightly in a way that looked provoking. Terra followed up with two harder swats. Faith gasped quietly, but didn't try to change her vulnerable position.

"Good girl," Terra commented. She was tickled by her new girlfriend's cooperation. She though about how every soul is a mystery, and that she and Faith still had a lot to learn about each other. Terra pressed herself against Faith's back, holding her in place.

Faith was quivering, but not with rebellion. Ignoring her common sense, Terra held the girl with one hand and backed off enough to give her a satisfying whack, then another. The temptation was irresistible, and Terra gave in to it. *Whack!* For being young, talented, and confident. *Whack!* For being so ignorant about the hard times before the birth of lesbian chic. *Whack!* For having so much time and experience ahead of her. Terra pulled sweet country air deep into her lungs and tried not to notice the orgasm that seemed to be building all through her lower belly.

A sniff tinged with fear came out of Faith despite her efforts to contain it. Hot shame rushed through Terra like a brushfire. "Aw, honey," she crooned to Faith, pulling her upright with an arm around her waist. When Faith turned to face her, Terra was startled by the tearful gleam of her eyes. "I didn't mean to hurt you," the bigger woman mumbled. "You can stop me when I'm too rough." At such moments, Terra felt hopelessly uncouth.

Faith held Terra with a strength born of resolve. Not really wanting to be heard, Faith muttered something that sounded like "sallright."

Terra slid her hand down to rest on Faith's lower cheeks, which seemed to be giving off a mild heat, even through her pants. Something about Faith's innocent young bottom moved Terra beyond words. For an instant, the older woman indulged in an image of Faith as a patient or a suspect, naked and spread face-down over the lap of someone in a uniform who was sinking a gloved finger steadily deeper between her butt cheeks, which seemed to be blushing.

"Want me?" Terra asked cautiously, not really expecting her date to accept ass-fucking—not yet, anyway. First things first.

"No," joked Faith in a bratty tone. "Not a bit. If I'd known you were a lez-bi-an, I wouldn't have come out here with you."

Terra reminded herself that Faith couldn't possibly know how painfully those words could remind a prairie woman of her high school years, when being even slightly unfeminine or indifferent to boys was the fast track to being cast into the wilderness.

Faith was taken aback by the look on Terra's face, so she ran her hands down the bigger woman's firm, comforting back to her generous buttocks packed into tight denim. "You didn't bring me out here to seduce me, did you?" she joked.

Terra growled, and her eyes held a dangerous glow. "Watch out," she warned, "little tease." She unzipped Faith's pants, which prompted a giggle. "What do you think?" asked Terra rhetorically. She slid a hand down her date's panting abdomen and entered her with two fingers.

Faith squealed and squirmed. "Not here, standing up," she protested.

Terra stroked the younger woman's clit, making her jump. Faith forgot everything she had ever believed about her inability to respond to such an abrupt, inconsiderate move. "Why?" asked the seducer. "Can't you come standing up?" She pressed on, feeling for Faith's G spot.

"Oh!" answered Faith, squirming almost enough to dislodge Terra's fingers. She was very wet. Terra used her other hand to hold Faith in place.

"Can't come this way? You sure?" persisted Terra, wiggling her fingers in Faith's welcoming cunt. Just when Faith thought she couldn't stand any more stimulation, Terra bent down to suck and nibble her nipples through her halter top. For a moment, Faith lost her footing and was impaled on Terra's fingers. Her breathing sounded like a wild prairie wind.

"If you can't come," Terra threatened slyly, "I'll stop."

"No!" wailed the excited young woman. Her pants were now bunched around her knees. Terra stroked her with a steady beckoning motion. "The wall," gasped Faith.

Terra pushed Faith against the nearest wall, and felt the first convulsion of Faith's muscles around her fingers as the friction increased. Terra inserted a third finger, and twitched the first two almost hard enough to be heard through the sound of wet swishing. Faith gripped Terra by the shoulders and let out the full shriek of a starlet performing in her first horror film. It was a shriek to wake the dead.

The two living, sweating women didn't care. "Ahh," they sighed together, coming down from their peak.

"Ah-hah," affirmed Terra, unwilling to pull her fingers out of their warm, slippery home. "So you *can* come that way. You can scream too. Are you practicing for the opera, honey?"

"No one can hear us," muttered Faith.

"Is that something you always wanted to do?" Terra felt tickled to her core.

"Mm-hmm." Faith was trying to sound nonchalant.

Terra withdrew from Faith's eager wetness, holding her up with one arm. Like an attentive mother, she pulled up her girl's pants and zipped them closed. "It's time to go upstairs to the bedrooms," she remarked.

"Uh," Faith gasped. "I don't trust the stairs. How do you know they can hold our weight?"

"They can," insisted Terra. "You scared to go up there?"

"Yeah," admitted Faith. "This place is creepy."

"But it excites you," gloated the seducer. Faith realized that a family that had gambled on the land and lost had once occupied this house. She wondered if being with Terra was just as much of a gamble. "Come on, baby," urged her guide. "You can't come all this way and not see the whole house."

Faith went first, and Terra kept an encouraging hand on her bottom. Moonlight flooded the upper floor through broken windows and the broken roof. Terra followed the light into a large square room and looked out the window at the horizon. The sky was much darker in the west, and the woman thought she could make out a familiar funnel shape. "Look," she urged Faith, "there's the tornado."

Faith squinted out the window. "I don't see anything," she complained. "Just dark clouds."

Terra grinned, seeing her chance. "It's coming. I might get you all naked and then the tornado will come tearing through here like a train, and carry you up in the sky, then drop you down in some all-night party. With bikers. Or guys playing poker, and you can be the prize."

Faith groaned.

Terra changed mode. "We'll probably just get the storm, honey," she explained. "Rain and maybe some hail, that's all." Terra turned Faith's attention to the room they were in. "Look at this. Big rooms but no closets. They used wardrobes in those days." Something scurried behind the wall, and Faith looked uneasy.

The guide pulled her visitor into an even bigger room with a fireplace. "I bet this was the master bedroom." She paused for effect. "Where the master got the mistress pregnant. After all that farm work, I bet they both needed some recreation. You can almost hear the bedsprings squeaking." Terra imitated the squeak of dry metal coils. She wrapped her arms around Faith, who was still trembling with a mixture of feelings. Like a couple on the cover of a paperback lesbian romance, the two women kissed in the moonlight. "Do you want to make a baby up here?" Terra demanded, eyes glowing.

Faith didn't point out the obvious flaw in this proposal. "Not on the dirty floor, Terra," she complained. "There's nothing else to lie on." She mentally surveyed her surroundings. "It's still nice outside. Can we go out there?"

"Okay," agreed the genial hostess. "One condition, though...you have to take off all your clothes up here."

Faith realized that she still felt like a trespasser, and she was afraid to strip to her skin in the presence of—what? "Why?" she pleaded. She shrank away from a large spider that was strolling across the floor.

"Why not, eh? It's bright enough up here for me to see all of you." Terra grinned lecherously. "And the atmosphere kicks you up a little. You know it, honey. Do it for me. And anyone else who might be watching."

Faith had heard, read, and watched enough scary stories to know that the dead were supposed to want living flesh more than anything else. Any flesh in any shape, as long as human energy ran through it like electricity. She couldn't help wondering if being dead was an endless tease, a state of unrelieved desire with no limits or conclusion. *Even if it is*, she thought, *that would be better than an endless sleep*. It occurred to her that she was afraid of ghosts because she wanted them to exist.

Terra reached around Faith's neck to untie the knot that held up her top. In an instant her small breasts were revealed. The tattoo of a red heart in the general area of Faith's actual heart looked purplish in the watery light.

Gaining confidence, the exhibitionist wiggled as Terra pulled her pants down, bringing a damp little scrap of fabric along with it. Faith concentrated on her balance as she kicked off her sandals and stood on one foot, then the other, to pull her clothing completely off. Terra took it all for safekeeping.

"Oh, girlfriend," sighed Terra at the sight of the pale sapling of a body that glowed before her in the moonlight. "You have to give me something here." The bigger woman pulled off her shorts in one smooth motion.

Faith knelt on the floor and held Terra's solid hips. Steadying herself, the kneeling woman used both hands to separate Terra's lower lips, revealing her slick folds and her swollen clit. Faith stretched out her tongue and gave Terra a few shy, catlike licks. An encouraging moan floated down to her.

Faith shivered at the gossamer touch of something running down her back. The phantom fingers rushed down one arm and tingled her scalp. She remembered her grandmother's terms for these feelings: "fairy kisses."

Terra spread her legs and greedily pushed her cunt in Faith's face. Terra felt her date breathing against her wetness as an enthusiastic tongue teased and probed the clit that throbbed like a heartbeat or the ticking of a bomb. "Wanna get fucked?" taunted the brat. This was her version of whistling past a graveyard.

"Yes," responded the older woman as she climbed surely toward a long, shuddering climax. Faith slid two fingers easily into a wet cave as she sucked Terra's clit into her mouth.

Terra felt herself grazed by careful teeth as she erupted, clutching her tormentor with her thighs and her hands. The discomfort at Faith's anus rippled inside her and ended with a pinprick in her bowels. Her anal muscles squeezed closed.

"Uh!" gasped both women.

Faith was so tense with fear that she didn't notice how wet her face was. "Terra, something touched me," she whispered, afraid of being ridiculed.

The older woman laughed with pleasure. "It was me, honey," she bragged.

"No," Faith insisted, "it was in my…bum. You weren't doing it."

"But I will, baby," Terra promised. "You felt my dirty mind."

Faith noticed a frayed length of dirty rope on the floor in a shaft of moonlight. She wondered if she had simply not seen it before, or if it had appeared suddenly. Her teeth chattered. "Terra, we have to leave here now."

"Okay, honey." Terra pulled her shorts off her legs without letting go of Faith, who was covered in cold sweat.

The two women ran down the warped, noisy stairs. Terra's hands on Faith's waist

helped to relieve her fear of falling, but Faith couldn't wait to get out of the house. The possibility of being exposed to passing drivers and an approaching storm troubled her less than the thought of being trapped inside that house all night.

Faith burst out of the front door to meet the night air, which was still warm, but breezier than it had been. It felt like a subtle warning. "Let's fertilize the field," Terra suggested, wrestling her top over her head.

"I want something underneath me," the naked woman pointed out. She liked Terra's ideas, but she wanted her to know that imposing a little human comfort on rough nature was essential. "We need the blanket from the truck."

"Sure," replied Terra in her role as tour guide. "I've brought a few other things too, so we can honor the goddess. This is the full moon closest to Lammas on the first of August, festival of the first harvest. I thought we could offer our energy to the land, you know, instead of just fucking for the hell of it." She showed her teeth in the moonlight. "Come on." Terra led Faith by the hand, pulling her toward the truck.

"Good idea," responded Faith primly, wondering why she hadn't foreseen that Terra would want to perform some variation of a fertility ritual that had probably comforted her ancient ancestors in various old countries. "I feel closer to the goddess out here than in town," the young woman assured her guide. *She's a moody bitch too*, thought Faith.

Terra's supplies included a bottle of merlot, a corkscrew, two fresh buns, a little ceramic Venus of Willendorf, and a fat candle in a bowl-shaped holder that refused to stay lit in the rising wind. After invoking the spirits of the four directions—north, east, south and west—Terra addressed the goddess directly. "We give thanks for your bounty," she intoned, opening the bottle and passing it to

Faith.

Guzzling directly from a bottle of liquid that looked like blood in the dim light made Faith feel like some kind of redneck vampire, but the uncouth simplicity of it satisfied her. The buns complemented the wine nicely.

"We honor those who have gone before us," Terra continued, "as well as those yet to come." Both women were aware of the need for haste.

As the wind moaned louder, they wanted to devour each other while they could still do so in some degree of comfort. "As we honor the goddess," continued Terra, "so too do we honor the god." She grinned as she strapped on the harness that held her prized silicone dildo from the sex shop in town. Faith had never seen it before, and her little gasp of surprise delighted its owner.

Terra reached out to find and tease Faith's clit, which was still swollen. "Do we accept the god?" she asked softly.

"Oh, yes," answered Faith, spreading her legs. Terra guided her instrument into its home, and the two women moved together like a bucking horse and a stubborn rider. At some point, they discovered that they could roll over in unison without missing a beat. They both wanted to tickle each other's souls while showing some smart new tricks to the moon. They filled the air with shrieks and wails as though they wanted to be heard in the farthest gas stations and farmhouses.

When they finally lay quietly in each other's arms, listening to their breathing under the song of the wind, they knew they would really have to leave soon. There was a chill in the air, and the shadow of the house looked longer and darker than before. "We thank all those who have blessed us here," concluded Terra, and opened the circle. Faith shuddered.

"Do you think we left a crop circle?" Terra asked her date to cheer her up.

"We'll have to look," answered Faith without conviction.

"You be the scout," taunted Terra. "Maybe the aliens have landed. They're probably waiting for you with their long anal probes."

Faith didn't answer, and she looked uncomfortable. She really wanted the thrilling invasion that Terra had hinted at, but she wanted it from Terra, the prairie woman she was coming to know. Terra tackled her, pinning her to the ground and tickling her without mercy.

"Stop, stop! I can't breathe," gasped the younger woman, shaking all over with laughter.

Terra relented. "Breathe," she ordered. "Then we have to go."

Terra wrapped Faith in the blanket and held it close, as though to persuade her that the goddess provides, while they walked back to the truck together. Both women dressed quickly and climbed into the truck with regret wrapped in relief. The wind had strengthened until it sounded like a grieving woman. Terra started the truck as if to drown out the eerie wailing. Like a trusty farm animal, the truck headed forth on the gravel road to the highway.

Terra waited until the house was out of sight before she launched into its history. "I wanted to show you the Lupichuk house before the new owners tear it down," she explained. Faith felt reassured by this rational explanation for the tire tracks she had seen. Terra passed the wine bottle to her, and this was comforting too. "The barn was torn down right after—about the time the Lupichuks moved away."

Terra took the bottle from Faith and took a swig before passing it back. Faith caressed the cool glass, waiting for the rest of the story.

"Do you want to know why it was torn down?"

"Tell me," responded her patient listener.

"Mr. Lupichuk was found hanging from the loft. It was in the fall, after he'd brought in a bad crop. It wasn't enough to support his family, and I guess he couldn't see any other way out. The wife and kids moved away after that. I think they moved back east to live with relatives." Terra took her eyes off the road to glance at Faith. "I didn't want to tell you that story before."

Faith touched Terra's shoulder. "I'm glad."

Both women felt pleasantly tired as the truck reached the end of the gravel and turned onto smoother asphalt. Terra speeded up as the lights of town appeared in the distance.

A warm silence filled the truck as the driver and her passenger passed the wine bottle back and forth. They considered the immense pleasure to be found in simple things and the awful, unpredictable nature of loss.

Rain was pelting the truck when Terra pulled into the parking lot behind Faith's apartment building. The sting of cold water on the women's skin felt like the excitement of a new relationship. They kissed and ran to the front door, squealing like schoolgirls.

They each smelled like growing plants, and the smell gave them hope that something might ripen between them. They were already treasuring their shared memory of sex in the wheat, and they resolved never to forget the taste of life at this moment.

Summer Firsts

PAIGE GRIFFIN

Each month one woman from the Westside Book Club would choose a book for the group to read and then host the gathering. And once in a great while someone would decide to take a break from the Nobel Prize winners and go for a guilty pleasure she'd wanted not only to read but also to chat about. This month's selection was *Summer Sisters* by Judy Blume.

It did the job getting the ladies so worked up that they skipped chatting about the sexual coming-of-age of the two main characters and instead waxed poetic about their own first summer flings. As eight of my closest straight acquaintances gushed about the pecks of hot lifeguards and the way one minor-league ballplayer's cock curved to one side, I found myself, the token lesbian of the group, feeling relieved. They were so wrapped up in manly biceps and tight asses that I was sure I wouldn't have to recount the one summer that had been playing in my head every time I masturbated for the last twelve years.

My relief was short-lived as I realized that the chatter had died down to a single longing sigh from June, an accomplished producer who occasionally hired her first summer fling to fix the plumbing in her 2.2-million-dollar Palisades home. Everyone agreed it sounded like porn in the making.

"So what about you, Mel?" June said with a grin. I tried to act nonchalant as I noticed that all heads were turned to me. Sixteen eyes dissected me with morbid curiosity. Had I been a lesbian from the get-go? Had I experimented with men before realizing that women were what did it for me? I was the only lesbian in the group, and apparently I was going to earn my position by offering a little vicarious diversity to their understanding of fucking.

"Yeah, I had a summer thing once. It was great. It lasted two months. I had a great time. So who's next?"

Kim, a woman who'd never slept with anyone but her husband, quickly pointed out that everyone had had her turn already. Everyone, that was, but me.

June leaned toward me conspiratorially, "C'mon, Mel, you're not getting out of it that easily. We want details. Was it a he or a she?"

I knew it.

"How old were you? Did you already know you were a lesbian? Was it hot?"

The questions were cascading out of June, the most outspoken of the bunch. But as everyone sat staring, I realized she was speaking for the group.

I didn't really want to share my one perfect sexual experience, the thing that played like a movie in my head, only to have other people judge it and think it far less exciting than I always had. I didn't want other people's reactions to dull the gold of summer fields, the sounds of lung-emptying laughter, or the pungent green smell of the lake. Could I lie and come up with another story? I'm the worst liar on the planet. Maybe I could just substitute another fling.

June cocked an eyebrow. "Don't even think about it, sister. We want the scoop. And now you've taken so long stalling that it's got to be good. Dish, honey."

How'd she do that? God, June can be creepily intuitive sometimes. Regardless, I'm not going to let her bully me. No one had taken so much as a sip of wine.

"Okay, okay," I relented, with the full knowledge that I have absolutely no backbone to speak of. "But it's not even that great a story."

"Details," Kim chimed in as she reached for a cookie. The entire group responded with an emphatic whoop of agreement.

"You girls really need to get out more," I tell them, trying to sound smug, but now I'm nervous. I'm actually going to tell these horny straight women my story.

Pauli's parents moved from Philadelphia to my hometown of Santa Rosa, California, the summer I turned fifteen. I never expected anything out of the ordinary to happen since nothing really ever did in Santa Rosa.

I was at a party with my best friend, Gary, when I saw her. We were passing by this raven-haired girl holding court. She was bouncing among religion and politics and art and love. The seven or eight people listening seemed entranced.

"That's the new girl. She seems pompous if you ask me," Gary said snobbishly.

"Oh, yeah," I responded, never taking my eyes off her. For a split second she looked up and caught me staring at her, never skipping a beat, as she waxed poetic on the virtues of modern art.

Later on, we bumped into each other at the keg in the kitchen. Our arms brushed as we moved past each other, and I felt my skin grow hot. There was patch of fiery skin where we touched, and much to my surprise, when I went home that night, I couldn't get her out of my mind. As I brushed my teeth I found myself trying to remember every detail of her finely boned face and shaggy black hair. Then I began making my way down her body, the slope of her neck, her pert, small breasts, and the exposed navel.

I rinsed my mouth quickly, turning off my electric toothbrush and placing it on the porcelain sink. Before I let go of the toothbrush I slid to the floor, my hand under my shirt. And my toothbrush came crashing down, making a fantastic noise, just feet from my parents' bedroom. I stopped, stock still, waiting, but no one else was up.

I pinched my nipple hard, gasping. I was now lying flat on the floor and turned my head as I flicked my nipples, causing pleasurable pain. It was then that I caught sight of my toothbrush. My shorts were off in an instant, and I grabbed the one token I had from my last dentist appointment and pushed the soft rubber button. The head began whirring and vibrating. I looked around feeling a little foolish. I'd never used my toothbrush to masturbate, but the second I ran the head between my legs and over my cotton panties, I knew I'd be doing it again. Within seconds I was grasping the side of the tub, willing myself to be silent as the delicious warm waves of an orgasm began washing over me.

The next day when I ran into Pauli I immediately blushed, convinced she could somehow tell she was the picture in my head as I writhed on the cold tile floor. We stood in line at the Beanery, downtown's one and only true coffeehouse at the time.

"Hey," she said. "You were at the party last night. I never really got to meet you. I'm Pauli." She put out a hand.

I shook it, immediately feeling as if I would melt from her touch.

"Hi, I'm Mel. So you're new in town. How do you like it so far?" The words tumbled out of me much faster than I'd meant them to, but I was trying desperately not to notice that she was braless as her erect nipples pointed right at me from beneath her tank top.

"Okay, I guess," she replied as I concentrated on the drink menu with ferocious intensity, "but I don't really know my way around. This is my first little excursion by myself."

Trying to sound casual I said, "Oh, well, you know I've lived here my whole life. I could take you around. I mean, if you'd like. If you're not busy."

We left the Beanery, sipping our coffees, and headed toward her junker of a car. Any car, though, was a precious jewel of a thing, given that most of my friends didn't have licenses let alone their own cars.

"Where to?" she asked.

"Want to go hiking? We could hike up to the lake and go swimming," I suggested trying not to sound too hopeful.

She shrugged and smiled, "Why not?"

It was early June and the meadows and hillsides had already turned golden with heat, though wildflowers were still scattered here and there. While Pauli was in her element at the party, now I was in my element. I noticed her watching me, stepping where I stepped, as I moved around ruts made by horses and mountain bikers. She stopped when I stopped but never asked me to slow down. I could hear her struggling for breath, as the incline of the trail got steeper.

When we reached the lake our clothes clung to us, wet with perspiration. Normally I stripped down to my underwear and ran in the lake without a second thought, but I suddenly felt self-conscious.

"Want to cool off?" I asked while staring at the lake, not daring to look at her for fear of giving myself away.

"Sure," she responded kicking off her shoes. I didn't waste any time and quickly shed my shorts and shirt. I gingerly entered the lake, crossing over the slippery, algae-covered rocks, then plunged into the cool water. I turned just in time to watch Pauli take off her blue tank top revealing a second white tank top cut in half and acting as a bra. The underside of her breasts peeked out from the ragged shorn edge.

I said a little prayer then, suddenly becoming more religious than I'd ever been, "Dear God, please let Pauli come in past her waist."

She took a step onto the slippery rocks and her arms flew into the air grasping for balance. Her shirt lifted with the effort. I quickly hid my pleasure at having glimpsed more of her breasts by voicing my concern for her safety. It was then that I noticed the little striped bikini panties and how they hugged her perfectly lean frame. I wanted to run my fingers over the points of her hipbones and caress her almost nonexistent ass.

She didn't waste any time making her way to my side. And suddenly I couldn't wait to get out so I could see that white half tank top glued to her. Then I noticed that it kept rising up, exposing her small, teardrop breasts.

"Ugh," she groaned. "Do you mind if I just take this off? It's driving me insane. I may as well not have it on."

I looked up to the clouds in gratitude. "Oh, yeah, go ahead, people skinny-dip all the time."

"So why do you still have clothes on?" she asked with an eye-brow raised. Still treading water with one hand she hooked her index finger through my bra strap and gave it a tug. The straps had already expanded from being waterlogged and now the one drooped over my shoulder into the water, revealing the top of my very round, very large breast.

Before I could explain that I found my own voluptuousness embarrassing, Pauli shrieked in fear.

"Oh, my God, something just touched me," she cried. Curling herself around me she yelled, "It's biting me."

It was hard to keep both of us afloat with her legs locked around my middle and her breasts pushed against my collarbone.

"It's just the fish. Just keep moving. You just weren't moving enough," I reassured her.

"That's it, I'm getting out."

We got out, baking our half naked bodies in the sun, the entire afternoon becoming one long tease that would lead me to another evening spent with my beloved toothbrush.

Many more afternoons passed by in much the same way until I felt I might go insane. Gary and I tried to determine if she was a flirty lesbian or just a straight girl who was *very* comfortable in her own skin.

"Just put the moves on her if you want her so bad," Gary commanded.

"It's just that we've become really good friends. We've seen each other every day for the last month. I guess I just don't want to jeopardize that," I pouted.

"No, you just don't want to risk ruining this fantasy you've concocted. It's that simple," he added, sounding entirely too superior for his own good.

The next time I saw Pauli, I could hear Gary's voice in my head. So as we hiked through Annadel State Park once again, I decided it was now or never. I took her off trail to a small clearing hidden among the alder trees. I was nervous, sweating even though sunset was approaching and a cool evening breeze was offering relief.

She watched me quietly. I kept trying to find words, but would stop myself before I could get more than a syllable out. I thought of kissing her, but the image of her pushing me away, her touch casting me off rather than welcoming me, was too much.

I looked her straight in the face, locking eyes, and then lifted my T-shirt over my head. She continued to watch me, her eyes fixed on mine. My hands met at the front clasp of my bra. Now unfastened, it sprang apart, leaving me exposed. Before I could worry that I'd done the wrong thing, her mouth was pressed to mine and I was gasping for air, more from the shock and relief I was feeling than anything else.

She was tearing at my shorts, and soon I stood naked in front of her. She took a step back and looked at me from head to toe. Surprisingly, instead of feeling embarrassed I felt beautiful. The look on her face told me she'd been thinking about this as much and as long as I had. She reached both hands toward me, and holding my face, she kissed me hard and long.

My hands dove under her shirt, sliding it off, and I lowered my mouth to her breasts. We sank to our knees, cushioned by a bed of leaves. I kissed, licked and sucked the breasts that I'd studied at every opportunity, and I played out my every desire. I ran my tongue in concentric circles, passing closer and closer to her nipple, teasing it with quick butterfly strokes.

Her hands were on me, and her palms glided over my shoulders, down my arms, down my torso and thighs. She moved her lips over my neck, her teeth giving little nips that sent electric shocks throughout my body. One of her hands moved slowly, deliberately between my breasts, over my tummy, and plunged between my legs.

Her other hand moved around me, moving something on the ground, but I didn't care because her left hand was still rubbing the wet warmth between my legs. She gently stroked, beginning at my clitoris and stopping just short of my ass.

"Lie down," she whispered, her hot breath sending shivers down my spine. I promptly obeyed, and found that our clothes had been laid out behind me, creating a makeshift blanket. She began kissing me with feather-light pressure, covering my face and leisurely moving down until her hands gently pushed my legs apart. She looped an arm under one of my legs and reached up, pinching and tickling my nipple. Her other hand stroked my hip as her tongue traced my swollen, wet lips.

I ran my fingers through her hair and she peeked up long enough to give me a sly smile. Then the hand that had been stroking my hip moved and pulled up the skin at the base of my clitoris, exposing the raw cluster of nerves I'd never explored myself. The feeling was so intense that my whole body shook, my legs uncontrollably jumping with every stroke of her tongue.

She released me only for a moment, relinquishing her hold only to begin moving her fingers inside me, her thumb slipping between my cheeks slick with my own excitement. Her thumb pressed and rubbed yet another area I'd never explored or had ever contemplated as a source of pleasure. Reading my delighted surprise she moved her other hand between my legs. Her fingers and tongue, felt as though they were everywhere all at once. Each delicious inch between my legs was being explored. I was being licked, stroked and tickled by a tongue and two hands whose precise locations were a mystery because just then the most intense waves of pleasure were drowning me, leaving me breathless. I was gasping for air, pulling myself up. It was too much.

I pulled her up, determined to return every moment of bliss she had just given me. I threw her down on the clothes, pushing her back, demanding she lie down. Her breathing was heavy and her chest heaved with the anticipation of what was to come. But she remained propped on her elbows, watching me. I laid on top of her, rubbing my own moisture onto her, moving so quickly she let out a little gasp of excitement. Finally, she collapsed flat on her back, giving in to the moment.

I sat, my legs folded beneath me, and grabbed her hips, pulling her so that her ass rested on my thighs. I took her right leg and placed it carefully over my shoulder. I rubbed and stroked her as she had me, but I wanted to cast another sort of spell. Once I felt she was as wet as I was, I began to move inside her soft pink folds of flesh. First with one finger, then another. She was groaning and writhing with pleasure. She arched her back offering all of herself to me, and I welcomed the invitation.

Twilight was stretching out above us. Frogs in the marsh were chirping and a kind of stillness was settling over the park. I leaned down, sweetly kissing the inside of her thighs, moving my fingers inside her then pulling out. A whine of disappointment followed but I shook my head, scolding her. I wasn't done. I curled my hand into a tight, long cup and softly pushed inside her. My fingers immediately found the spot they'd searched out all along and began sending tiny throbs of pressure until she rhythmically began closing in around my hand. Her voice pierced the night just as a pack of coyotes began singing to the moon.

I'd become so aroused by my own story I almost forgot anyone was listening. I looked up and eight mouths hung agape.

Kim, mopping her brow with a cocktail napkin, was the first to speak. "So what happened after that?" she asked.

Shaking myself loose of the memory, I attempted a concise answer. "We fooled around for another few weeks and then her dad got offered a bigger, better job in New York. I never saw her again. We tried to keep in touch, but we were teenagers and time just slipped away."

"What a tragedy," June whispered. Seeming lost in another thought.

"Wishing you'd tried out for the other team, June?" I taunted.

Coming out of her fog, June smiled slyly and said, "Um, no. I know what I like, and it's not pussy, but you know I did just hire this writer that I'm pretty sure fancies it. Her screenplay focuses on a character named Melody."

I felt there was something more I was supposed to take away from her comment, but didn't understand just what.

"Hmm, Melody, just like me...coincidence," I offered a little confused.

"Okay, Mel, so ask me what the writer's name is."

"Okay, June, so what's the writer's name?" I shot back.

"Pauli."

Cherries Jubilee

BRANDY CHASE

Several months ago, my friend Cyndy came by my apartment to help me plan out the snack menu for a mutual friend's bachelorette party. I was going to be holding the party there the following Friday.

We were sitting at my kitchen table talking about the party, the food, and the upcoming wedding. We were relaxing on a hot June evening in shorts and halter tops, drinking Long Island iced tea in an attempt to cool off. Empty dishes with the residue of chocolate ice cream littered the table. Those, along with a nearby can of whipped cream and jar of maraschino cherries, were evidence of an earlier attempt to beat the heat. Still feeling oppressed by the weather, we turned to a more grown-up treat. We sat telling each other how beautiful we thought the other was going to look in her bridesmaid dress. We were both in the wedding party.

"The dress is going to look a lot better on you then it will on me," I said.

"The dresses are all the same. Why would it look any better on me?" Cyndy asked.

"Because you have those big bodacious boobs to fill up the top half," I giggled. I guess the Long Island iced tea was starting to get to me a bit.

"Sometimes you act just like a man, always thinking about someone else's tits," she laughed. "You sure you're not gay?"

"Cyndy, you know me better than that. Maybe it's just because I don't have any," I replied.

"You have plenty. Besides, aren't guys always saying that any more than a mouthful is a waste?" Cyndy asked.

"Are you honestly trying to tell me that you've heard a man say that?" I asked.

"Well, no, not personally," she grinned. "But, I have heard of it."

"No man has ever said that. And with a set like that on you, a mouthful is the last thing on a guy's mind," I giggled.

"They can have all they want on their little pea-sized minds, but they're not getting anywhere near my breasts," Cyndy replied.

"You expect me to believe that you don't let any of your dates get in your shirt?" I asked in mock horror.

"I didn't say that," she replied. "I said no *guys* ever get inside my blouse."

"I know I've had a little too much of this iced tea, but that doesn't make any sense," I said.

"Actually, it does, if you think about it for a minute," she replied.

"Okay, I've thought about it and I'm still lost. I guess I'm just having a blond moment."

"How long have you known me?" she asked.

"I don't know…a little more than a year," I answered.

"And have you ever seen me with a man?" she asked.

I thought the question over for several moments. "Well, now that you mention it, I can't actually think of any. But you talk about going out every once in a while."

"And who is it that I go out with?" she asked.

"Well, there was…um-m-m. You know what? I don't think you ever mentioned anyone by name."

"Exactly," she replied.

"You're trying to tell me you go out all by yourself?"

"Oh, brother, you really are having a blond moment! You really don't get it?"

"I guess not," I replied. "You know, you could just tell me what you're talking about."

I could tell that Cyndy was carefully considering whatever it was she was going to say next. I could also see that it must be very important, and that's why it was so difficult.

Suddenly, it hit me like an anvil. "Oh, my God, Cyndy! You're a lesbian," I exclaimed.

"Bingo! Does that change anything for you?" she asked. "I mean, as far as being my friend?"

"I don't know why it would," I replied. "Should it?"

"It does for a lot of people. That's why I don't tell too many people. The reaction you get for not sticking to society's rules is rarely pleasant," she replied.

"Well, it doesn't bother me one bit. It's your choice, not anyone else's," I said. "Okay, now you have to dish. What's it like to make love to another woman? I've always wondered about that."

"I guess that means you've never had a lesbian experience then. This should be interesting," Cyndy said.

"I don't mean I've ever wanted to, I was just curious about it, that's all," I said.

"It's not the kind of thing you can explain. I mean, why don't you tell me what it's like to make love to a man?" she said.

She cut me off when I attempted to describe making love with a man. "I didn't actually mean for you to describe it. Hell, I've been with men before. I just meant to think about it," she replied. "Now, just make all of that a lot sweeter, softer, more caring, more sharing, and usually greatly prolonged. *That's* what making love with another woman is like."

"Hmm. Have you been with lots of other women?" I asked.

"No, only a few I really liked. Just because I'm a lesbian doesn't mean I'm a slut," she replied.

"I didn't mean that the way it came out. No pun intended," I quickly apologized, picking up the whipped cream and spraying a small puff onto my finger and then eating it. I did so repeatedly, keeping myself distracted while asking potentially uncomfortable questions. "What kind of girls do you go for?"

"I don't know. Nothing in particular, I guess. They have to be sweet, good-hearted, fun, considerate," she replied. "A lot like you, actually."

As what Cyndy had said registered, I jumped, accidentally covering her in the topping.

"Well, that certainly seemed to make a difference to you," she laughed, whipped cream sliding down her chest and directly into her halter top.

"Oh, my God! I'm so sorry." I grabbed a towel from the counter. "I didn't mean...I just....oh, God...," I babbled, mindlessly dabbing the towel over her chest.

"What a waste," she giggled.

"We won't waste it," I said, running a finger through the creamy mess sliding down her chest. Holding my finger up to her mouth, I joked, "Here, we can salvage it."

Her lips wrapped around my finger and she slowly sucked the whipped cream from it. "Mmm, definitely too good to waste," she said, suddenly looking at me quite differently.

I just stood there, unsure of what to say or do. In fact, I was in total shock. I would have never expected my body to react the way it was to her mouth. I liked it. It felt absolutely delightful.

Finally, I regained my composure, "Ah, we, um, should probably get this stuff washed," I said pointing to her shirt and shorts, each having been sprayed with the cream. "I hope I didn't ruin them. I'll grab something for you to put on. Be right back," I said and rushed from the room.

A few minutes later I returned with a bathrobe for her. She was standing in the middle of my kitchen, her shorts in one hand, halter top in the other. There was nothing covering her except a skimpy red thong and the residue of whipped cream still clinging to her chest.

I dropped the bathrobe to the floor. The vision before me was just too beautiful for words. Her breasts were full, but still remained pert. Her dark-brown nipples stood taut, wanting attention. They had mine, every ounce of it. Feeling almost hypnotized, I walked toward her, my eyes unable to leave her beautiful breasts.

She set her clothes on the table and placed her hands on my flushed cheeks and gently pulled my face closer to her breasts. "Are you still curious what it would be like?" she cooed.

I couldn't speak; I just shook my head, yes. My tongue timidly edged its way between my lips, finding its way to the trail of cream still evident on her body. It was sweet, and the texture of her skin— soft and smooth against my tongue—was heavenly.

My tongue continued working its way down, nestling into her cleavage. I could feel the soft mounds of her breasts pressing against my cheeks. This sensation was setting me on fire. I didn't want it to stop.

I licked until there was no hint of whipped cream left. Looking down at me, she said with a hint of disappointment, "Looks like you got it all."

She wasn't nearly as disappointed as I was. I wanted more; I *needed* more. I grabbed the can from the table and quickly squirted a little dollop on each of her nipples. "No, not yet," I replied, not exactly sure why I had done such a thing.

Her smile grew intense. "Yeah, it seems I was mistaken. I trust you'll take care of it."

My tongue resumed its duties, but this time at the peaks of the mountains instead down in the valley.

"Mmm…are you sure you've never done this before?" she moaned.

I shook my head, yes, sucking one of her nipples into my mouth. A groan slipped from her throat as I nibbled the swollen morsel.

Suddenly, grabbing the sides of my halter top, she peeled it down around my hips in one nimble movement. My breath caught at the feel of her hands against my breasts. She pushed me backward until I dropped into one of the chairs.

Grabbing the whipped-cream can, she announced, "Now it's my turn." I was soon covered with a generous portion of whipped cream.

I thought my nipples had gotten hard when her hands had touched my breasts, and I thought they had gotten as hard as possible when the cool cream hit them. But the second her hot tongue swept over them, I thought they were going to burst.

After a minute or so, Cyndy had removed all of the whipped

cream. She bit down on one of my nipples, sending fingers of delightful fire through my body. I squealed with pleasure.

She sucked one of my breasts as far into her hungry mouth as possible and then released it. "See, there's a lot more than a mouthful there," she said with a smile. But this time the smile was different—it was a smile of conquest.

She rose and slowly backed away from me. "Are you okay?" she asked.

I just shook my head, yes. I couldn't utter a coherent word. My mind was racing.

"I mean, are you okay with what just happened?" she asked.

Again, I just shook my head, yes.

"Please, honey, say something, you're scaring me a little," she begged. "Are you really all right?"

I finally got my mouth into gear and said the only thing I could think to say, "I'm finer than a frog's fur right now. I'm just afraid you're really going to get fat."

"What do you mean?" she giggled as she asked.

"Well, it's just this stuff can be really fattening, and I have no intention of this being over any time soon."

Cyndy's giggle became a full throaty laugh, and she grabbed the can from my hand. After squirting a small dab between my breasts, she placed a Maraschino Cherry on top of it. In one long slow lick, she slurped up both. "I guess you're my little Cherries Jubilee now. What do you think of that?" she purred.

I didn't say a word. I just got up from the chair, took her by the hand, helped her off the floor, and led her to my bedroom, whipped cream and cherries in hand.

***

Cyndy stood quietly behind me while I turned the bed down. I felt her long slender arms snake around my waist as I stood up. Her kiss was soft and warm on the nape of my neck. My nipples pressed tight against the warm palms of her hands as she captured a breast with each.

Her breasts pressed against my shoulders as I leaned back into her embrace. I slid my hands slowly up and down her long, tapering thighs, enjoying the silky texture of her skin.

My breath caught in my throat when I felt her nimble fingers dancing over the button and zipper of my shorts. It rushed back into my lungs at the feel of her fingers sliding inside my panties and over the patch of hair crowning my womanhood.

I turned my head over my shoulder in search of the soft lips that had been whispering little kisses all up and down my neck. Her mouth quickly covered mine with the most tender kiss I'd ever experienced.

Her tongue played gently over my waiting lips and darted between them when they parted slightly. I felt my halter top, shorts, and panties being slid over my hips and dropped to my ankles. I turned toward her, our tongues still locked as if in mortal combat. She drew me closer, her hands cradling my behind.

I sucked hard on her tongue, wanting to keep it captive as Cyndy pulled back from our kiss.

"Careful there, you hungry little monster, you don't want to damage that. Let's just say it has a little ballet to perform for you this evening, and I promise, you *will* enjoy it," she smiled down at me.

I didn't reply. I just kept reaching for her lips with my own. As I lay there straining my neck, she gently pushed me backward onto the edge of the bed. I was sitting up, my legs dangling toward the floor.

I had no choice except to lie back and enjoy; my body literally collapsed at the sensation created by her velvety tongue gliding up my inner thigh, en route to the entrance of my sexuality.

As my mouth had so freely opened only moments earlier to receive her tongue, so opened my womanhood in anticipation of that same tongue's gracious attention.

My breathing seized up and my clitoris immediately shot to full readiness as a cool blast of air encompassed it. No, not air, icy cold whipped cream. I then felt slight pressure against it.

"Mustn't forget the cherry," Cyndy giggled. "It wouldn't be Cherries Jubilee without it."

If her tongue was going to dance the wonderful ballet she had promised, it was going to be a sugar-charged performance.

Within seconds, her talented tongue had declared war against the pearl of my womanhood. Like a rampaging crusader, her exquisite tongue held my clit under siege with a relentless barrage of magnificent assaults.

Almost immediately, my body was racked in the euphoric throes of female ecstasy. Surge after surge of womanly joy raged through me.

Cyndy's persistent tongue finally ceased its mind-numbing assault against my enraged clitoris, only to delve deep into the source of the lady-juices flowing from my very soul.

I grabbed a pillow and pulled it tight over my face in an attempt to stifle the impending scream. The muffled cry only served to encourage deeper and faster marauding by the pillaging tongue plundering so savagely within me.

I lay, unable to move, after the cessation of Cyndy's beautiful onslaught. "You said your tongue was going to do a ballet. You didn't say anything about a war dance," I mumbled.

"Are you complaining?" she asked, her eyebrows raised.

"Not in this lifetime. Ballet, rain dance, slow dance, war dance; I think they're all the same to that tongue of yours," I tried to smile, but I simply didn't have the strength left.

"I'm ready for some dessert, how about you?" Cyndy grinned, picking up the whipped-cream can.

"Keep that stuff away from me," I mumbled, crawling up the bed and under the covers for protection. "It makes you crazy."

"It makes you even more delicious than you already are," she teased, pulling the covers back down and acting like she was going to cover me with whipped cream again.

I grabbed the can from her hand. "Now get yourself between these sheets. I feel a second wind coming on."

"Oh, really? And just what do you have in mind?" she asked as she slid the skimpy red thong to the floor.

I smacked my hand on the bed. "Less talk and more movement toward the bed, please." I was taken aback by my own boldness.

I had never wanted to touch another woman before, but at that moment it was the only thing on my mind. I wanted to experience the giving side of the same pleasures she had just given me. The thought of seeing her squirming under my control as I had done under hers was threatening to drive me over the edge again, and she wasn't even touching me at the moment.

Cyndy slipped between the sheets and snuggled close to me. The feel of her flesh against me was a sensation I shall long treasure. She felt so tender and so yielding to my touch. Never before had I known such a sensuous feeling. The sweet gentle scent of her nearness was almost overpowering. I think, at that moment, I actually understood why most men always seem to have women and sex on their minds. How could they not? Once they had experienced such tenderness and such sweetness, how could anything else possibly occupy their minds? I felt I had just joined the ranks of the males of the world in desiring a lady—at least this particular lady.

I had thought I would be a bit apprehensive about touching and tasting another woman, but that was far from the case. I was being driven by the most intense desires I had ever known. Tasting her womanhood and the fruit of her passion was the only thing on my mind. The wrecks in my head were over, the highway was clear, and I was about to drive every ounce of love I possessed straight to her center. I didn't even want the whipped cream, I only wanted to taste her.

Gently making my way in between her thighs, I heard her gasp as I planted my hungry mouth tightly against her waiting womanhood. She jerked and squealed a bit as I shook my head back and forth, forcing her open to me and wiggling my tongue as deep inside of her as I could.

"Oh, my God," she exclaimed, as she came and filled my mouth.

I continued to drink deeply as her body trembled with waves of pleasure. The flow of her juices became too intense for me to keep up with; I escaped to her clitoris. When I sucked the tiny swollen pearl into my mouth, she raised her hips off the bed and grabbed for my head with both hands, accidentally pulling my hair a bit too hard. Still pressed tight against her, her engorged clit still in my hungry mouth, the pain of her pulling my hair caused a scream to soar from deep within me. The vibration of the scream against her already over-taxed body was more than she could handle. She seemed to be coming unglued. The heavy tremors of an immense orgasm quaked through her.

"Baby, please stop," I heard her weak voice. "I can't handle any more."

I stopped for a few moments. Using her beautiful patch of red hair as a pillow, I rested the side of my face against her. I heard one last little moan from her and then her body went completely limp. She was breathing in shallow little breaths and wore a contented smile on her face.

I crawled up beside her, snuggled into her arms, and went to sleep wearing that smile.

Blessed Art Thou

D. Alexandria

Every Thursday afternoon I take a trip back to the one time in my life I felt completely safe, whole, and accepted. Every Thursday, I park my car in the small, quiet parking lot on Viscera Boulevard and close my eyes, letting my head fall back, knowing what I'm about to do. I give myself the normal pep talk, telling myself that I am okay for doing this, and that I truly need it. As routine I then reach into my glove compartment and carefully take out the antique pearl rosary that I received from my grandmother on my Confirmation.

I hold the rosary tight in my hand and bring the golden crucifix to my lips, kissing it gently before I make the sign of the cross. I take a deep breath before I pray, asking for forgiveness for the act I cannot stop committing. As soon as I've finished, I kiss it again, before placing the rosary back in the glove compartment, then get out of the car, feeding the meter enough quarters for an hour.

The walk to Faith's is just around the corner from the parking lot. I press the buzzer for her apartment at exactly two o'clock. After a moment, I hear the buzzing of the door being unlocked and I walk through. My ascent up the stairs to her third-floor apartment is nerve-racking since I can hear the clicking of my heels on the stairs echoing through the quiet hallway. It always reminds me of the time in my life that I'm there to revisit. I can feel the knot forming in my stomach before I reach her apartment door.

I knock twice and wait for her to tell me to enter. When her voice comes, I take a deep breath, slowly open the door, and walk inside. As soon as the door is closed I look to the right, and there she stands, causing my breath to catch.

"Come here, child." Her voice is full of sympathy and warmth, and I begin to feel at ease. I move toward her, stopping just a foot away, the feeling of being too close to her is sacrilegious to me. But she smiles, raising her arms, and the chestnut color of her hands standing out against the black robes beckons me.

I let my eyes close as I step into her arms, allowing her to envelop me in her false sacredness. With a heavy sigh, I utter, "Sister."

She holds me for a moment, and I feel the sweetness of her lips against my forehead. "You've come for acceptance."

I keep my eyes tightly closed afraid to look at her, but I nod, "Yes, Sister."

"Then take it, child." She says softly.

My chest is swelling with apprehension, but I descend to my knees, as I lift the hem of her of robes. Finally, I look up at her caring face. As my eyes travel downward, I catch sight of the large wooden cross that she wears around her neck, and I feel a mixture of guilt along with the tingling that has overtaken my sex. I push through it as my eyes take in her long brown legs, traveling up past her thighs to the trimmed black hair that is covering the acceptance I seek.

I hesitate for a moment, but feel her hand on the back of my head, guiding me to her center. My eyes close before my lips feel the soft hair, and I sigh with relief. I part my lips, my tongue pushing between her swollen folds, and as soon as I taste her everything feels right again. It reminds me of why I came and why I needed this. For the next thirty minutes, I lose myself in the her wetness, always feeling as though I'm searching the depths of her for some kind of liberation. She is the closest link I have to the one moment of my life I truly felt free.

I have been seeing Faith for almost two years. I answered her ad in an adult personals section looking for submissive women with open minds. It took me about a month to talk myself into calling her, and as soon as I heard her voice, sensing the confident authority, I knew I had done the right thing. She was a beautiful black woman in her fifties, tall, average build, with piercing light brown eyes that seemed to know everything about me at first glance. The first time we met for coffee, her motherly nature was obvious, making me wonder if she indeed was the dominating woman she claimed to be. But she silenced my doubts as she gently fired questions, wanting me to give her all the basics of what I was looking for, assuring me that everything else would come out in due time. But I knew what I needed without a doubt. As I told her, she simply nodded, telling me that I was safe with her.

So every Thursday, on my lunch hour, I'd enter her apartment and face the woman she agreed to emulate. I'd kneel before her, and when I looked at her I saw the face that dominated my dreams and fantasies. I'd part her thighs and the hand on my head would guide me to what I needed most; remembrance of the woman I was forbidden to love yet still did.

March 24 is the date that my entire existence was altered. I was eighteen, in my senior year at Saint Agnes, and was facing possible detention for skipping two classes the previous day. It was the first time I'd ever done anything like that and had gotten caught. So that day I sat in the office, waiting to see the headmistress, Mother Superior, when the door opened and someone walked in. I hardly gave a look, preoccupied by my own thoughts, but an intriguing scent had filled my nostrils, causing me to look up.

Standing at the secretary's desk was a nun I recognized as Sister Mary Elaine, who had recently arrived at Saint Agnes's to teach. She was quite the center of talk among the students since we weren't faced with many black nuns. She taught the junior class, so I hadn't actually met her. She was much younger than the other nuns, only in her thirties, but she didn't have the contemporary air about her that I knew younger nuns sometimes had. My math teacher, Sister Virginia, for instance, only wore a veil with her daily gray skirt set. But Sister Mary Elaine dressed like the older nuns in a full black habit.

Her scent. Not many nuns wore cologne, and I wasn't sure that she did, but she had an earthy, somewhat spicy aroma, and I found it pleasurable. As I watched her, I could tell that she had a full figure, and I caught myself wondering what she'd look like naked.

As soon as the thought crossed my mind, I forced my eyes away, guilt immediately rising. I closed my eyes, silently hoping God had not heard my thoughts, but knowing that He had. He also knew they were the kind of thoughts I'd had for the past two years and that almost nightly I've prayed for them to go away. It was sinful to look at another female in a lustful way, but I was finding it harder and harder to ignore. And regardless of how loving God could be, I seriously doubted He'd be as loving and forgiving if I was having lustful thoughts about a nun.

But my eyes lifted again, this time meeting with dark, kind eyes, and I froze. Sister Mary Elaine smiled at me and nodded, and I forced myself to smile back. She turned to the secretary and thanked her before making her way over to the bench where I was sitting.

"You are Anna, correct?" She asked.

I nodded, "Yes, Sister."

"And why are you sitting here and not in class?"

Embarrassment flushed in my face and I looked away. "I have to see Mother Superior because I skipped classes yesterday."

She shook her head in slight disappointment, but her smile remained. Her smile was so beautiful and inviting, seeming to light up the room. "Sometimes it's too tempting to ignore the calling of recklessness during senior year, I understand that."

I didn't know how to respond, so I just smiled shyly.

"Well, as long as you accept the consequences for what you've done, things shouldn't turn out too badly."

I nodded. "I know, Sister."

She nodded, then reached out and patted my hand. I swore I felt electricity as soon as her skin touched mine, causing me to pull my hand away.

"Anna, Mother Superior is ready to see you now." The secretary's voice interrupted my thoughts, and I broke the gaze, fumbling with my bag and sweater as I rose to my feet.

"It was nice to meet you, Sister," I said to Sister Mary Elaine.

She just nodded and I forced myself to walk away, my mind racing, silently chastising myself because the sinful thoughts I had were obviously getting worse. I told myself that I would just pray tonight and again beg God for help. And with that I opened the headmistress's door and faced my punishment.

Mother Superior was more forgiving than I had expected, taking into account my nearly spotless school record. She gave me a week's detention that would start that day. I returned to my classes, and after school ended, walked to the first floor classroom that was at the end of the hall.

As I walked into the room, I recognized the other students, all senior boys, which didn't surprise me since the boys were more willing to test the rules. But what did surprise me was that Sister Mary Elaine was the teacher who was supervising detention. She looked up and just smiled at me, telling me to work quietly for the next half hour, which I did.

But I found it difficult to concentrate on my homework. Every so often I'd let my eyes rise to take her in, and my body responded. I wasn't sure what it was about her that was affecting me that way, but it was happening. I found myself watching her lips as they moved silently as she read. They were small but full, and I wondered how it would feel to kiss them.

And again, as soon as the thought entered my consciousness I immediately abolished it, forcing my eyes back to my book, wondering why my mind insisted on this awful path. Before I completely settled into the pages in front of me, I stole one more look at her, and again I met those kind dark eyes. Sister Mary Elaine looked just as startled as I did, and she quickly looked away. I wondered what thoughts filled her mind.

That night I knelt at the side of my bed, my grandmother's antique rosary tight in my palm. I closed my eyes and made the sign of the cross, "In the name of the Father, and of the Son, and of the Holy Spirit. Amen." For the next hour I prayed; my voice soft yet earnest, my fingers slowly moving from bead to bead, in the back of my mind begging God and the Blessed Mother to give me some kind of guidance. By the time I finished, I felt renewed as I climbed into bed, knowing that They wouldn't overlook me as I had made this prayer nightly since the first sinful thought. I hoped that this time They'd grant it.

But as time went on, it was clear that nothing had changed. There would be various female students I'd come across, and I would get that fluttery feeling in the pit of my stomach, or I'd be in gym class, the very scent of some of the girls causing my pulse to race. But nothing could compare to the reaction I had whenever I'd run into Sister Mary Elaine. Weeks went by and I found myself knowing her schedule, so I'd be able to see her at least once a day. The idea of what I was doing would make me feel horrible until I saw her and she'd flash her smile, completely rejuvenating me.

As the weeks turned into months, I grew an uneasy comfort with the steps I was taking, especially as Sister Mary Elaine's attitude towards me grew warmer with each "accidental" meeting. What started out as just a smile and soft hellos grew into brief conversations inquiring about my future plans after graduation, my career goals, what I did for hobbies, or current events. Each conversation took only a few minutes, but I looked forward to them. No matter what I did, I could not tame my feelings, especially when I felt so exposed to her probing, affectionate eyes. Sometimes I felt as if I stood before her completely naked, and I enjoyed it. I memorized those moments for when I was alone in my bedroom, replaying her smiles, the sound of her voice, and the feel of her hand on mine, soon finding my fingers tracing paths on my body, imagining her touch and that she wanted me just as much as I wanted her. But I would always stop, lecturing myself on how irrationally I was behaving, and that Sister Mary Elaine in no way could have feelings of that nature toward me.

Eventually the guilt renewed itself to the point that I was unable to think of anything else. I was becoming distracted. I couldn't pay attention in class or when I socialized with my friends. One day, after my last class, I was feeling so overwhelmed I hurried to the chapel, hoping that this extra step would get me the guidance I so needed.

The chapel was empty except for one nun who knelt at the altar. I hesitated for a moment, not wanting to disturb her, but knowing that I had no choice because I couldn't go on this way. I quietly walked up the aisle, and made the sign of the cross as I approached the altar. I took a spot about two feet away from the nun and knelt, clasping my hands tightly before me as I silently prayed.

Part of me wanted to cry because I felt I was hallucinating. Even in the sanctity of the chapel, I was haunted by the smell of her. I suddenly felt a hand on my arm, and my eyes flew open, my head turning to face the eyes I dreamed about, now filled with concern.

"Anna," Sister Mary Elaine said softly. "What is wrong, child? You look distressed."

What could I say? I was taught to never lie to a nun, but there was no way I could tell her the truth. So I just opted for silence, my gaze falling to the floor in shame.

Her own silence was heavy. She was watching me earnestly, and before I knew it, she laced her fingers through mine, grasping my hand tightly and turned back to pray. For a few moments, I wasn't sure what to do, but I did the same. And there we knelt, holding hands, and silently prayed together.

After we prayed she told me that she always prayed at the chapel at that hour, and if I needed her I could find her there. My first thought was to stay away, but the very next day I found myself entering that chapel, and wordlessly we again held hands and prayed. It went on like that for weeks. To my relief, Sister Mary Elaine didn't asked questions, although I could see them in her eyes. She would simply tighten her hold on my hand, which comforted me more than she could ever know—as well as added to my torture.

Then one day, when my eyes opened after I finished praying, I looked to my side to find her watching me.

"What troubles you, Anna?" She asked softly. "I can see that you have not yet found the answer you are looking for."

Again I couldn't say anything and cast my eyes downward, but her free hand lifted my chin, forcing my eyes to meet hers. Before the thought even crossed my mind, I turned my face slightly and my lips kissed her open palm. The very feel of her skin was glorifying.

Not a second later my eyes widened in surprise, and I began to apologize, but she held her finger to my lips to silence me. Our eyes locked, our gaze so intense I couldn't breathe. Then I felt her hand gently caressing my cheek, and when she smiled at me I felt complete acceptance from her.

Sister Mary Elaine broke the gaze, looking around, and then she got to her feet. "Follow me," she said softly.

I followed her out a side door to an area of the building I had never been in. We walked quietly down a hall until she stopped at a door. She again looked around before she opened it and ushered me inside, quickly closing and locking the door behind us. We were in a supply room that was filled with boxes and cleaning supplies.

We stood facing each other in silence for a few seconds before she spread her arms. I quickly fell into them, relishing in the feel of her arms around me, holding me so close. I felt her lips on my forehead, her kisses soft and gentle, as I knew they would be. I was surprised when her lips left my forehead, but I turned my face upwards, feeling her kisses on my closed eyelids and nose before they traveled to my cheeks and then covering every inch of my face. I held my breath in anticipation, my heart thudding in my chest.

Her lips lingered on one cheek as she breathed, hesitating for a moment. And then I felt it. Her lips gently pressed against mine, and I felt as if I breathed for the first time. She held me tightly, her hands caressing my back, my own finding the courage to rest on her shoulders. I was afraid, so I just followed her lead.

Sister Mary Elaine broke the kiss, her lips traveling down to my neck, my head fell back and I let out a sigh, enjoying the tingling feeling that was spreading through my body. A sliver of panic pricked the back of my mind. Wasn't this wrong? I was taught that it was sinful to give in to the pleasures of the flesh, yet here I was kissing and groping—with a nun no less. What would God say?

I opened my mouth to speak, but Sister Mary Elaine's lips covered mine, this time the kiss was more aggressive, and I felt her tongue slipping between my lips and all the nagging thoughts diminished, my entire being basking in the sensation of being so openly loved.

Eventually we moved and sat on a nearby box, still embracing each other tightly as we continued petting. My body was completely alive and felt as if it were on fire. I had never in my life imagined that kissing another person would feel so rewarding. I could feel that she mirrored the hunger I felt for her, but hers seemed almost maternal. She was being so careful, so gentle with me, as if her lips didn't scald me with unabashed passion and need.

Eventually she pulled away, her dark eyes completely drinking me in. Her fingers rose to brush across my bruised lips.

"I love you." I said it so quickly I couldn't have stopped myself even if I wanted to. But the honesty gave me a freedom I hadn't expected.

Her eyes were so caring. She cupped my cheek, leaning forward to kiss the tip of my nose. "I love you too, Anna."

We shared a few more kisses before time forced us to part. Sister Mary Elaine walked with me back to the chapel. As I turned to look at her before walking out the chapel doors, I couldn't help but notice that she looked troubled. Nevertheless, she smiled at me before I finally left.

That night was the first night I didn't pray for forgiveness. I climbed into bed, my heart feeling warm over the experience, and I couldn't get to sleep fast enough for the next day to arrive so I could see Sister Mary Elaine again.

Home room dragged on as if time itself was napping. I must have checked my hair and makeup countless times in my pocket mirror, anticipating the look on Sister Mary Elaine's face when she'd notice. As I got ready, I had to remind myself that even though we were in love, we had a complicated situation on our hands and that we would have to talk it out. But I was sure that we'd find some kind of solution.

It was almost time for home room to end, and I was ready for the bell to ring, when there was a knock on the door and one of the student aides walked in, handing a note to our homeroom teacher, Sister Diane. She read the note, looking perplexed and saddened, before turning to us.

"Unfortunately, I have some sad news," she began. "But I've been told that Sister Mary Elaine has resigned from Saint Agnes, effective immediately, for personal reasons."

There was a low murmur among the students, but I sat there in complete shock. In less than a minute, everything had completely crumbled. The bright skies I'd looked forward to were suddenly overtaken by dark clouds. The bell rang, and everyone else got to their feet. One of my friends nudged my arm to get me moving.

The remainder of the day was a blur as I moved about on autopilot. I tried to make sense of what I had learned. How could she leave? How was it that just the day before she had kissed me and expressed her love for me, only to walk out of my life? She had finally given me the hope and acceptance I had needed for so long only to take it away.

It was a day I would never be able to forget.

I graduated high school with top honors, somehow able to move on with my life despite the emptiness I felt. Out of respect for Sister Mary Elaine, I never breathed a word to another soul. Even during confession, when in my heart of hearts I wanted to let out all the frustration, I kept it to myself, opting to just lock it away and deal with the guilt.

As the years passed, I realized that I could neither blame Sister Mary Elaine nor myself any longer. The desires we had were true and valid, but her vow to God wouldn't allow her to pursue whatever feelings she had for me. Though it saddened me, it did help me in a way to accept who I was.

But always in the back of my mind and in a small corner of my heart was Sister Mary Elaine. I would always wonder *what if*, knowing that she was the only person to ever validate who I was back then. And that is what spurred me to continue seeing Faith.

All of this crossed my mind, as it always did, as I felt Faith's hand run through my hair, pressing my face deep into her. For a moment I couldn't breathe anything but her, not able to hear anything as her thighs clamped around my head, her hips lifting as her orgasm approached. As soon as I felt her body begin to shake, my own peaked and my fingers dug into her hips as I drank from her.

When Faith's body was calm, I quietly pulled away, keeping my eyes down. Her hand cupped my cheek and gently caressed my skin until I finally felt brave enough to look up at her.

"You will always have my love, child." She said softly.

I nodded, a grateful smile on my face. I finally got to my feet and hugged her, relishing in the motherly embrace she has always been able to give. Then quietly I turned around, retrieved my purse, and walked out of the apartment.

Down in the Park

AIMEE NICHOLS

Living across the road from a popular park has its advantages. For one thing, trees, grass, and flowers aren't exactly in abundance in a big city, and being the country girl that I am I like to feel some connection to my roots. And so it has become my habit of a Saturday afternoon to take a newspaper or whatever novel I am reading to the park, stretch out in the sun, and enjoy a few peaceful hours outside the cramped confines of my small flat. It's an escape, albeit a small one, from the stresses and frustrations of my life. It also offers some occasional entertainment.

Today the park is pleasantly empty, with far fewer occupants than usual for a Saturday. I stretch out on the grass, which flattens beneath me, in a spot only a few yards away from the elaborate main fountain that is the centerpiece of the park—shaded and hidden by a sprawling ancient oak tree and some shrubbery. Comfortable on my stomach, in a position where my breasts thankfully don't get squashed as I lie, I rummage for my book, and finding it, begin to read.

Despite my engrossment in the novel, I eventually become aware of a splashing noise that doesn't seem to be coming from the fountain's pumps. I look up and see a young woman sitting alone on the edge of the pool, running her fingers violently through the water, occasionally splashing it onto the concrete surrounding the fountain in an act of unconscious rebellion against some formerly controlling parent—"Don't play in the fountain!"

She appears young, perhaps twenty. She is slim and dressed completely in black, her bleached off-white hair mostly obscured by a knitted hat. Her hair is chin-length, and the ends stick out wildly in all directions as if fighting the oppression of the beanie.

She gazes moodily into the water, completely oblivious to the silent voyeur who watches from a near distance. I alternate between reading my book and watching her, noting the way her face grows steadily stormier as the minutes tick on. She begins to make little pacing journeys, getting up to stamp around for a few seconds, then throwing herself back down on the edge of the fountain. I attempt to read her, my more traditional reading material forgotten in my fascination with her tense, jerky actions. I wonder what could be upsetting her so and ponder whether I should get up and try to offer some consolation. But what would I say?

After about ten minutes, she is joined by another young woman. She stands up to greet her companion, and they begin to speak rapidly. I can't make out any words, but the voices carry the sounds of disagreement on the wind—one soft and apologetic, one low and harsh. The newcomer is red-haired, the kind of bright fiery red that can only come from a bottle. Her skin is luminously pale, and she is dressed to flaunt her voluptuousness. Her curves threaten to explode from her clothes at any moment, and I can't help but notice how the plump backside that faces me looks good enough to eat.

They sit down together, close like confidantes, but still with the stiffness of conflict unresolved. I return to my novel, slightly ashamed of being so willing and eager to watch their emotional drama unfold. I'm itching with curiosity about the two women and how their disagreement will play itself out, and there's more than a little bit of car-crash fascination in watching a couple fight so publicly, but I force myself to concentrate on the words in front of me. Eventually, though, I give in to the temptation: The urge to see how the argument will turn out makes me think of somebody watching a soap opera. It's too hard to keep my eyes on my book.

When I glance up again they are kissing, the behind-schedule redhead running her hands passionately through the blond's short hair. The blond seems to want to devour her, kissing with forceful, unbridled lust, her tongue occasionally leaving the redhead's mouth to explore her face and her neck with licks and sucks and—

yes—a bite. I see the redhead move involuntarily as the blond sinks her teeth in, her head wrenching back, away, her body jerking into the blond, a hopeful offering. The blond withdraws, sitting back and licking her lips. I am convinced, even from this distance, that I see blood on the redhead's slender neck. Obviously that's what you get for being late for a meeting with Blondie.

Red strokes the blond's face with her fingertips, then with the back of her hand. They sit staring into each other's eyes for some time, lost in the way that only lovers are capable of losing themselves. I remember with a pang the way I used to do that with my girlfriend, the gentle feeling of acceptance that goes with such intimate, sensual contact.

I watch attentively as the redhead starts to unbutton the blond's blouse, exposing small breasts and creamy white skin that glows in the sun. She runs her fingers down the exposed flesh; the blond's nipples become hard, straining towards their tormentor. The redhead leans over to take a nipple in her mouth, taking in most of the small pert breast along with it. The blond gasps in pleasure—I can see the movement of her pretty mouth from here. Blondie lies back on the edge of the fountain, stretching her arms above her head as she luxuriates in the redhead's attentions. Red in response moves to dominate her, leaning over her (my clit throbs as her full, heavy bosom becomes visible—those breasts!) moving her crotch in a thrusting motion, playing at fucking her through her clothes. The blond loves it, writhing joyously between the soft, curvaceous body of her companion and the hard, cold concrete of the ledge. The redhead pauses to unzip the blond's pants and forces her hand inside. The blond looks like she doesn't know whether to continue writhing or lie still, so she alternates between the two.

I find myself responding to their lovemaking, grinding my pelvis against the grass, the seam of my jeans wedging itself into the crevice of my vulva. I wriggle around to increase the pressure on my clitoris, careful not to make too much noise with the expression of my mounting arousal.

Blondie's moans become distinctly more audible, and I look

around nervously, more worried than they about discovery. If they're discovered, my entertainment's gone for the day. If they're discovered, then the pervy little sleaze in the bushes is likely to be discovered too. But I'm sure anyone, venturing to discover the source of the strange noises, would have my reaction. How could they not?

Red removes her hand from the blond's pants and shoves her fingers roughly into Blondie's mouth to shut her up. The blond sucks them eagerly, and I lick my own lips, wondering how her juices would taste.

The redhead straddles the fountain ledge, which means that one leg gets soaked up to the knee, but she doesn't seem too concerned. If I were in her situation, I wouldn't care either. Her free hand tugs Blondie's pants further down and embraces her clit once again, and I feel the echo in my own cunt. Oh, God, I shouldn't be doing this. Those girls are in Utopia; they seem totally unaware of where they are physically. Surely I'm taking advantage of them by lying here enjoying the show rather than creating some kind of distraction that will snap them back to the real world without causing them too much embarrassment. Does this make me a bad person? I know if a man were to do what I'm doing now, I'd be the first to bay for his blood. So am I a hypocrite as well as a pervert?

The guilt goes straight to my cunt.

A loud, grunting moan snaps my attention back to the girls. The blond is coming, her limbs flailing, her left arm splashing in the fountain as she struggles for control against the sensations that tear through her body. Red is murmuring to her—I can see her lips move, and I imagine she's telling the blond how she's a naughty little slut for coming so hard, and she's going to be punished later. The thought makes my solo frottage pay off, and I come hard against the seam of my jeans, biting my forearm to stop myself from crying out and alerting the girls to my shameful voyeurism. I collapse into the earth and for a long moment feel totally organic, as much a part of the park as the grass and trees. Then I realize the girls might be doing something else worth watching, grin for a second at my unabashed lasciviousness, and look up.

They're gone. Panicked and bereft, I struggle to my knees to scan the small area of the park visible through the foliage. I think I see a flash of movement off in front of me and to the left, but I'm not sure. I shake my head, feel more than a little foolish, and glance down at my abandoned book. Somehow I don't feel like reading too much at the moment. I grab the book, stand up, and begin walking home, purposefully ignoring the curious looks the grass stains on my jeans attract.

Her

STEFKA

I had no idea how long she had been staring at me. I really didn't notice her until I was alone for a few minutes, my friends having moved onto the dance floor. I was left to guard the table. When I saw her I gave her a big smile, wondering to myself why I hadn't noticed her from the beginning. She wasn't beautiful in the conventional sense. She was more elegant, regal. Her gaze was frank and appraising. It took a few moments before she returned my smile. I got the feeling that the smile was a show of approval. Generally speaking, I would usually ignore such a frank stare and carry on with my night, but she was different somehow, though I couldn't put my finger on just how.

She was sitting next to the bar, her softly lit table giving me a perfect view. She wore a filmy spaghetti-strapped black dress that shimmered in the light. Her shawl had slid off her shoulders, showing a tantalizing view of her smooth pale skin. Her hair, a glorious, glossy black, was shaped in a bob. The tips caressed her high cheekbones. I could just see the bottom of her earrings. I appraised her as she had me, taking in her delicate hand caressing the stem of her wineglass, while the other toyed with a silver cigarette case. There was a shiny bracelet on one wrist. The other was bare. From this distance I couldn't tell whether or not she was wearing any rings. She was a well-put-together package.

I smiled at her again, showing my approval. Amazingly, she dipped her head in response. I found the whole encounter intriguing. Instead of going to her, I sat there, lit a smoke, and watched some more. Her smile dipped slightly, and mine broadened. I wasn't going to be easy prey for her and she knew it.

I finished two cigarettes as I sat there watching her. During that time three women, at different times, came up to her and whispered in her ear. In turn she would smile and shake her head no, her eyes never leaving me. I crushed out my smoke and grabbed my jacket, telling my friends I'd see them later. I stood up and with casual slowness slipped on my jacket. Slowly I made my way over to her, stopping every so often to say a few words to some people I knew along the way. I was constantly aware of her eyes on me. I was enjoying the feeling of anticipation and the excitement of pursuit. I had to steel myself not to hurry. I knew that if she hadn't left by now, she wasn't going to, not without me.

I reached her table. She gave me a sidelong glance, holding an unlit cigarette between her long, slim fingers. I reached into my pocket, pulled out my lighter, and flicked it. With slow deliberate moves I bent down close to her, inhaling her scent as I lit the cigarette. Her scent was as elegant as she was. I spied an empty seat next to her and sat down. She really was a lovely woman, her eyes large and framed by long dark lashes. Her lips were full and pulled apart in a wide smile. She liked what she saw too.

I bent a little closer and opened my mouth to whisper my name when a movement behind her caught my eye. Frowning, I looked up to see a darkly handsome man in a casual coat and slacks sit down next to her. He grinned at me as he placed an arm around the back of her chair. His actions claimed her as his own. It hit me why she was different from all the other ladies. Pissed at being played with, I moved to get up when her hand, unadorned by rings, gripped mine. I looked down at it, disgusted, before looking back at her.

"I don't get involved with couples, especially straight ones."

"Hear us out before you turn tail and run," his voice rumbled at me. More determined to leave, I glared at him as I tried to move, hating the asshole's smirk, but her hand gripped my arm even tighter.

"Please." She said in a soft, husky voice.

My head screamed at me to leave, but my heart tripped over her pleading gaze. I found myself sitting back down.

"I have a proposition that would be beneficial to all of us," he said, his smirk grating on my nerves.

I looked pointedly at him. "I don't do men."

He shrugged as if what I did or didn't do wasn't important. I disliked him intensely. His arrogance and gall made my hackles rise. What I couldn't understand was why I was still there. I felt immobile from her warm hand.

He leaned forward in a conspiratorial manner. "I want you to fuck my wife."

Her grip on my hand tightened at his tone and reference, but still she said nothing. He was serious, and by her silence so was she.

"Why? Do you need lessons?" I sneered at him.

His smirk dipped a little. I had struck a nerve. "The reason isn't important. I just want you to do it." He was the type of man who gave orders and expected them to be followed without question. He'd picked the wrong woman.

"I told you I don't do straights."

He raised an eyebrow, his smirk in full bloom. "Why? Isn't she attractive enough for you?"

I glanced over at her before looking back at him. "Beauty isn't everything."

He chuckled as he leaned back in his chair. "I thought you people enjoyed breaking in new women."

It took everything I had not to belt him a good one. "It isn't my style."

He laughed. "A dyke with morals."

"And you are a son of a bitch." Why did I sit and take his shit, I wondered.

"Ah, you want to play hardball. Fine. A thousand dollars, then."

My jaw ached as my body trembled with held-in anger. I couldn't understand why the woman was with this asshole. "No amount of money would make me do this."

His eyebrow rose again. "Oh? Why?"

I leaned forward, vaguely aware that the woman's grip tightened further. "Because you want it."

"Two thousand."

My vision grew red. He didn't know when to quit. "No."

"Three thousand."

"Jesus Christ man, is *no* not in your vocabulary?" I ground out between clenched teeth.

"Four thousand."

I turned to her. "Are you going to just sit there and let him sell you like that?"

Her eyes blinked at me. "What if I want it?" she whispered.

"Want what? To be pimped off?"

Her hair gently caressed her cheeks as she shook her head. "You. I want you."

"Me?" My anger slowly left me as I stared into her eyes. She didn't reply but her gaze spoke volumes. She actually wanted me. I stared at her a few moments longer, trying to convince myself that what I was about to do wasn't crazy. With a control I never knew I had, I turned to him and gave him a brief nod.

His chuckle nearly pushed me over the edge. "Money always wins over morals," he stated confidently. "And for the amount I'm paying, I'm going to be there for the event."

I was about to tell him to go fuck himself when she did the oddest thing. She released my hand and grabbed my face. She planted on me the deepest, most incredible kiss I had ever experienced. It left me fighting for breath. When she released me I looked over at him, breathless and flushed. He looked a little shocked. I decided that I was going to show the son of a bitch that he had picked the wrong dyke.

I grinned at him as I gave her warm cheek a soft caress. "I accept, but you touch me, or her, even once and I walk." Again there was a flash of something in his gaze, but it was gone before I could figure it out.

He cleared his throat and stood up, taking the woman's arm as he did so. "Fine. Let's go."

I took my time standing up. "I'm following you." I enjoyed his stunned look before turning away, making them follow me. My anger was still there, just below the surface, but instead of lashing out at him it turned into a plan to make him pay and with something more valuable than money. I may be crazy, but I was going to enjoy every minute of it.

***

I had no idea what came over me to kiss her as I had. Could it have been the vivid anger in her gray eyes, or was it the clenched fists? Whatever the case may have been, she agreed afterward. Why was he being such a monster? He never had been before. What have I allowed to happen? The whole idea of exploring different sexual possibilities was getting way out of hand and the sad part was that I had allowed it to get that way.

It had started out as a game to add spice to a stale sexual relationship, but now it was turning into a crusade. Was there something happening to him I didn't see? To me? Why did he insist, no plead, to continue finding new ways, when our relationship seemed better in the last few months? I'm almost ashamed to even think about the things we—no, I—have gone through to please him, and I'm getting tired of it. I only agreed to do this if he promised this would be the last time we did this type of thing. He did, but I still wondered.

Naturally it was his suggestion that I would make love to another woman. I agreed. But when he said that the other woman had to be a lesbian, I balked at first. It wasn't that I didn't like them; it was because, from what I understood, most didn't appreciate straight couples pursuing them. He was adamant about it. I finally backed down with the stipulation that I was to pick the woman. He agreed.

When we arrived at the bar, he found me a table before disappearing to watch as I sat to seek out my perspective partner. It felt odd sitting there in a predominantly female place with a few men scattered about. I felt as if I were on display, waiting to be picked out and purchased. Three glasses of wine finally calmed my nerves, and I stopped fidgeting. Once I was relaxed, I saw her. I never saw her enter, she was just suddenly there, surrounded by her friends. At first I thought she already had a girlfriend by the way she had been hugging one particular girl, but within minutes she repeated the process several times with others. She was just being friendly. They had gathered around one table across from me and I settled down to watch her, relaxed.

She was delightful to look at, with wavy blond hair that liked to fall over one eye. She was compactly built; her leather jacket hugged her form nicely. She had a wide-open smile that was always present. She seemed to have a touch for anyone who was near her. When she shrugged out of her jacket, I found to my surprise that she was dressed rather femininely. Her blouse, a pleasant soft purple, was opened at the neck to show off a silver chain. I could tell the women around her enjoyed her company by the way they laughed and touched her. I figured she wouldn't even look my way; she just didn't seem the type to be on the make. I was about to give up on her when suddenly she was left alone at the table, her friends deserting her to dance. She chose that moment to look in my direction.

Her stare was as frank as mine was. She smiled at me, and I tingled all over with its brilliance. I dipped my head in acknowledgment, and her smiled widened. Instead of coming over, as I thought she might, she simply sat there smoking and watching me. It had me perplexed. It took three women to hit on me before she decided to come over, and even then she took her time. I hated to admit it, but I grew impatient and excited as I watched her slowly make her way over to my table. I wanted to scream every time she stopped at a table greet someone she knew. I wondered why I was reacting this way towards a total stranger, but in my impatience I didn't pursue the thought. I just wanted her at my side. I played with my unlit cigarette as I watched her make her way around to me.

When she finally got there I gave her only a sidelong glance, holding up my cigarette. She lit it in the most sensual way I had ever seen. Her moves were slow and sure. I fought not to tremble when I felt her breath in my hair. She was adorable, perfect, and I found that I wanted her like nothing I had ever wanted before. She sat close to me and my fingers itched to gently brush the bangs away from her eyes. But instead I gripped my wineglass and smiled at her. She returned one of her own.

The mood was broken when he arrived. Instantly I sensed a changed in him that hadn't been there before. There was going to be trouble, and his words proved it.

I have to give her credit for not hitting him. He was so insulting. It made things worse when he insulted me twice, and I did nothing about it. I really didn't realize I had spoken until I grabbed her hand. I tried to convey everything with that simple gesture, praying that she wouldn't leave, and incredibly she didn't. The whole conversation stunned me, especially when he started offering money up front. I understood her shock at my silence. Under normal circumstances I wouldn't have stood for what he was doing, but I wanted her so badly it hurt, and I told her as much. She agreed at first, but when he made another crass comment I knew if I didn't do something she would get up and leave. I kissed her. I put everything I had into the kiss and I was startled at the deep wanting I felt as I did so. I could tell by her expression that she had felt it too. My heart fluttered when she added her own demand. It excited me beyond anything when she told him that if he touched her or me, she would walk. She had already taken his control away, something he had never allowed to happen in the past. She was going to be different than anyone I'd encountered since these little games began. As a final touch, she told him that she was going to follow us. His face showed his dislike, but she left before he could say anything about it. Again the control was yanked away from him. She was incredible.

On the way home, we argued. He demanded to know why I had kissed her, and I told him it was because he had been such a beast. He didn't like that too much either. He wouldn't answer me when I questioned him about the money offered either. He simply brooded, constantly checking the rear view mirror to see if she was behind us. His cheek jumped with his agitation when he saw that she was.

"We can call this off, you know," he told me, his tone calmer.

"Why, so you can choose a different scenario? I don't think so. You promised this would be the last if I did this. I'm going to make sure that you keep that promise."

After a quick glance at me he faced the road again. "I thought you liked these adventures."

"I did in the beginning. But now they seem pointless. Our sex life has never been better, yet you insist we still need these little games. Why?"

He shrugged. "I just thought you liked them."

I reached over and touched his arm. "We don't need them anymore."

He gave me a look I didn't understand, but before I could say anything about it he pulled into the driveway. There was still a chance to call it off, but I didn't want to, not when I didn't understand what was happening to our marriage. I had a feeling that by the end of the evening I would.

***

The minute I pulled up behind them I realized the guy wasn't pulling my leg about the money. Their place was huge. It was a small mansion. It reminded me of a picture I had seen once of the house of some celebrity. As I turned off my truck a thought hit me. This was their idea of entertainment. I almost turned the engine back on, but as soon as I saw her I knew I was going to see this thing through. I had no idea how it was going to turn out. They waited patiently beside their BMW as I got out of my truck. Immediately I noticed a difference in him. *Did he have a change of heart?* I wondered as I sauntered up to them. She gave me another soft smile. It told me she hadn't changed her mind.

He gave me a brief tour of the place, mentioning what he did for a living. It hit me: He was a well-known author. After the tour, we ended up back in the living room where he insisted we have a drink. He was stalling. I agreed. I needed to calm my nerves. She was watching me constantly. My usual confidence had deserted me. He handed me something dark to drink.

"Scotch." He said before heading back to the bar and pouring himself one. I didn't like scotch, but anything would do at this point.

"So, tell me, what do you do for a living?" he asked, fingering his glass.

Before I could reply, she spoke up. "We don't need to get personal." I just loved her voice, low and soothing.

"I'm just making conversation. We don't even know her name."

"Why? We haven't before," she replied, looking at him.

Uh-oh, trouble. It was time for me to make a break for it while they hashed it out. Although I had to admit, I liked to watch him squirm. I downed the drink, holding back a cough as the dark liquid burned its way down my throat.

"Uh, excuse me, but where is the washroom?"

He gave me a funny look. "Upstairs, three doors down and to your left."

"Thanks. Be right back." I muttered as I hurried away. As I climbed the stairs, their voices rose. Trouble in paradise. He was chickening out. He was afraid that I might show him a few things, I thought, chuckling to myself.

The washroom was as big as my apartment. I stood there in awe as I took it all in. There were two showers along one wall, a huge bathtub that could be used as a small swimming pool, a commode, and a large marble counter with three sinks in it. The wall above the sinks was covered in mirrors. Shaking myself, I hurried to the middle sink. I turned on the cold water and splashed some on my face, trying to shock some sense into myself. *What am I doing here?* I asked my reflection. I wasn't the type to play games. I splashed some more water on my face before turning it off. I saw her dark reflection in the mirror. I hadn't turned on the light but I knew it was her.

"I brought you a towel," she said.

As I turned around I noticed several towels placed around the room. Bringing a towel was just an excuse to be there. She moved further into the room. Her shawl was missing, as were her shoes. She held out the towel.

I went to her and took it, wiping my dripping face. She was two feet from me when I was finished.

"You can back out now if you want," she whispered.

"Is that what you want?" I asked, mildly surprised when I didn't take the out she offered.

The silence was long as she thought about it. Her eyes searched my face before she answered. "No."

I let the towel drop to the floor as I reached for her, not quite clear why I was doing it. I knew it wasn't the money, and I certainly wasn't desperate. There was something about her that I liked and wanted. I traced one finger across her lips, remembering the way they felt against mine. The desire to have them back was strong. There was a slight hesitation on her part before her mouth opened slightly and her tongue came out and licked the tip of my finger. I instantly grew wet. I must have made some sort of noise because she took my finger in her mouth and began to gently suck. Unable to take it anymore, I removed my finger and gathered her close, enjoying the way her trim figure fit my body.

I lowered my head and captured her lips with mine, determined to show her how much I wanted her. She responded with equal fervor, and together we explored each other's mouths. I pulled her closer still as everything else faded. Her pelvis pushed up against my knee, and I gently pressed my knee against it. She groaned in response. Her hands slid inside my jacket and pushed it off. I let it fall to the floor as my lips traveled down her chin to her neck. I bit gently as I pushed one hand into her hair and gripped it tightly. With a slight yank I bent her head back as I bit harder on her neck, my other hand occupying itself with one of her breasts. Her response was to grind her hips into my knee harder, her body shaking. I was dripping in my jeans. I wanted her, and I wanted her right away.

"Not here," came a rumbled order. Shit, I'd forgotten about him.

***

She was incredible. Her lips were like fine silk as they slid over mine. Her hands, gentle but firm, roamed over my body. She traced it as if it were a map to a treasure. She wasn't like any other woman I had ever been with before. There was no nervousness, no giggles or gasps. There wasn't any fumbling. She knew what she was doing and I found myself loving it. He never made me feel this way. He never made me feel appreciated. I wanted more from her—so much more. It felt real somehow. The muscles beneath her shirt felt firm yet different from his. Her contours were similar to mine, but different. Could it be that she did this as a choice, or was it simply because she loved doing it? It was both. I wanted her, needed her.

"Not here," penetrated my lust-filled mind, and I opened my eyes to find him staring strangely at me.

Her hand released my hair as she slowly straightened up. She gave me a calm, soothing glance before looking at him.

"Where, then?" Her voice carried a note of sarcasm.

He glared at her, his jaw jumping from him clenching his teeth. "In the bedroom."

"Fine. Lead the way." She took a hold of my hand and waited as he turned and stalked out. "I don't think he likes this after all," she said, smiling.

"Does that change things?"

Her grin widened. "Hell, no. I want to make him squirm."

"And me?" I was worried that it had become a game to her.

She simply reached up and caressed my lip with one finger. She gave her head a small shake before dropping her finger and tugging me after her.

I followed behind her, scrambling to understand what was happening to me in regards to my feelings for him and her. When had this stopped being a game to me, and why did I have such a strong need for her? I really didn't have much time to think about it as we entered the master bedroom. He waited with impatience. His jaw jumped more when he noticed our hands were linked together. His anger made me want to laugh. I wanted to ask him why he was so pissed when it was his idea to begin with, but I didn't. All I wanted was to be in her arms again, to be touched and loved like I never had been before. He walked behind us and sat down on a chair next to the vanity. She smiled at him before turning me to face her again. I shivered as I felt both of their eyes on me. She pulled me closer, and as her lips met mine he faded from my mind. All that was left was her touch.

As she peeled my dress off, she peeled away a part of me, leaving me utterly exposed. Her gaze loved me like her fingers, all over, gentle yet firm. I stood there as she kissed me all over, my moans echoing in my ears as her warm lips gave me the shakes. How long did the cleansing go on? I didn't know, but suddenly I found myself lying on the bed, and she was above me, her jeans rubbing across my sensitive skin. She made me groan and arch as her fingers tickled and teased me. My nipples felt like rocks as a waterfall cascaded down my legs. I was ready for her to send me over the edge, make me scream, to make him scream, when all of a sudden a thought pushed through. *What would really push him over the edge?* Certainly not seeing another woman make love to me. He's seen that too many times to let it really bother him. What would really push him was if I made love to her. I had done that one other time with a man, and he had nearly flipped. A shiver shook my body. I wanted it to happen again.

I gripped her shoulders and wedged my thigh and knee between her legs. She rocked her pelvis into it as she continued to kiss me and bite my neck. With determined strength, I flipped her over and held her hands above her head. Her eyes were wide with surprise, her mouth agape. I ground my hips into her as I took her lips with mine. Her body relaxed as she returned the kiss. It was as if she understood what I was about to do. After a few moments I broke off the kiss and trailed my lips to her ear. I whispered my name and made it personal. Her gasp thrilled me and she returned the favor by telling me hers. We were no longer strangers.

I loved on her like no other, and in the back of my mind I could hear his heavy breathing. It grew louder as I stripped her naked, kissing every part of her skin. When I placed my mouth on her wetness, enjoying the sweetness, I heard him whimper through her screams. I couldn't believe what I was doing, but I didn't want to stop either. I wanted to drown in the heaven where my face was buried. Just as she arched in orgasm, my head was cruelly pulled away and I found myself staring into his agonized face.

"Stop," he ordered, his eyes wet.

"No. This is what you wanted. Don't you like it?"

"No, not like this. I wanted her to fuck you, not the other way around."

"I warned you that one day you would go too far." I jerked my head away from his grip and sat up, not bothering to wipe my face. I liked it sticky with her juices.

"I have had enough," he said.

"Well, I haven't."

He rubbed his face, his hands shaking. "No more games, I promise."

"Why?" I asked, strangely numb toward him.

"I don't want to lose you."

I wanted to laugh. The bed shifted as she sat up. I looked at her as she stared at me and suddenly we both knew.

"You already have," we told him.

La Belle Starr

GENEVA KING

"Belle Starr. Classic example of what happens when outlaws are allowed to mingle with the good townspeople." Judge Isaac Parker wiped his mouth and tossed down his napkin. "I've been trying to convict her for years, but she's always been one step ahead of me."

"And she's the worst type. I'm sure the James gang taught her everything they knew." Jake turned to his wife. "Why don't you start clearing up and let me talk to the judge for a bit?"

Ginger complied, taking one last look at the WANTED poster on the table. Belle's face smirked up at her. Ginger shivered and went back to clearing the table, trying to linger long enough to hear the conversation. As long as she looked busy, Jake wouldn't say anything to her.

"I hear she's a bit of a temptress."

"Temptress!" the judge roared. "A modern day Jezebel, I tell you." He slammed his fist on the table so hard Ginger was afraid he'd break it. "Now, some lawmen might be influenced by her, but not me. I'm immune to her particular sort of charms. They might call me the Hanging Judge, but I'm the only one brave enough to bring these criminals to justice."

"What is she wanted for?" Jake queried. "Ginger, when you're done, bring us something to drink."

She nodded, waiting to hear the Judge's reply.

"Robbery, horse thieving, murder, you name it. The problem is, we can only get her on counts of harboring fugitives. That's the game with her new husband."

"I thought she was married to Jim Reed."

"Naw, he was shot. She's shacking up with that Indian, Sam Starr." The judge leaned forward conspiratorially. "That's another problem with society, allowing the Indians to mingle with regular people. Their clothes might say civilized, but you better believe they're still savages."

Ginger caught her husband's warning look and ran off to the kitchen. She dumped the dishes in the wash bin and filled two mugs with ale. She set them on the table and went back to clean up. She put on an apron and scrubbed until she heard the scraping of the table chairs an hour later. She heard her husband escort the Judge to the door and close it behind him. The floorboards creaked as he stomped around. Ginger made a mental note to ask Jake to fix them. He stuck his head into the kitchen.

"Don't forget the glasses on the table."

She sat back, looking up at him. "Can you bring them in here?"

He left the room and came back in, plunking glasses down on the counter. "I'm going to bed. How much longer are you going to be?"

Ginger looked around. The dishes were almost finished, but she still needed to wipe down all the counters and sweep the floors. Oh, she reminded her herself, and clean the table. There's no telling what kind of mess the men had made. "Well, I don't suppose you want to help me clean up?"

Jake frowned at her. "I don't ask you to help me with the horses do I? Just be quick, I have to wake up early in the morning." He turned to leave.

"Jake. Why is the Judge so keen on catching Belle? She's no different than some of the men running around."

"It's different when a woman goes bad. I'm just glad I don't have to worry about that." He rubbed her hair. "Come to bed. This can wait until morning."

***

The next morning Ginger walked back to her house after her Ladies Society Meeting. She'd wanted to skip it, but as Jake reminded her, it would be unseemly for the sheriff's wife not to appear. Lately it seemed like her husband never spoke unless it was to remind her of her duties. She missed the fun and independent man she had married, the man who never failed to make her smile. A man who'd been missing since he became the sheriff.

A few feet from her house, Ginger felt a prickling sensation go down her back. She entered the house carefully, setting her hat down on the chair. "Jake, are you home?"

Before she took another step, an arm flew around her neck and she struggled, digging her nails into a patch of exposed skin. Her assailant drew a deep breath, and she jabbed her elbow backwards. The second the arm loosened, she slipped loose and ran into the kitchen to find a weapon.

She spied a pan from the night before on the counter. *Thank you, God, for making Jake interrupt me last night*, she prayed. Just before she reached it, another figure stepped in front of her.

"Just where do you think you're going, Red?" The newcomer grabbed her before they collided.

Ginger steadied herself, and then stared up to face the intruder. The face looked so familiar. Where had she seen it before?

"You look like you've seen a spirit, Red." The woman laughed mockingly at her captive.

Then it clicked. The hard face, the sneering eyes… "You're Belle Starr!"

Belle laughed. "I see my reputation precedes me." She nodded to someone over Ginger's shoulder; Ginger assumed the first intruder had gotten his breath back.

She squared her shoulders, and in what she hoped was a menacing voice said, "This is my house. If you leave now, you'll have time to escape before the lawmen catch up to you."

Belle's eyes locked onto Ginger's. "We're not going anywhere. But I'll tell you what: Keep quiet and we might let you live." Without breaking eye contact, she pulled a knife out of the folds of her coat. "And if you don't cooperate, I'll have to kill you. And don't think that I'm bluffing—I've killed more important people than you before."

Ginger swallowed as Belle ran the knife down her throat to her chest. She tapped the blade on her breasts, and then deftly sliced the ribbons at the top of Ginger's blouse. Ginger's cheeks burned as she heard Belle's partner chuckle behind her. Belle grinned at Ginger. "Although I will say it would pain me to kill something as pretty as you." She grabbed her breast and squeezed it roughly. "I could use you."

Impulsively, Ginger spat in Belle's face. Belle flinched, and Ginger lunged for the pot. Too slow. Belle grabbed Ginger's blouse, yanked her around, and slapped her cheek. "One more time and I *will* kill you."

Ginger looked into Belle's eyes and realized she meant every word. She nodded mutely, struggling to keep her anger in control.

"Sam, go do what you came here for. Red and I will be fine in here."

The man said nothing, but seconds later Ginger heard the door close behind him.

"Don't move." Belle stalked out of the kitchen and Ginger stood rubbing her jaw. She went towards the icebox in hopes of finding something cold to sooth her face.

"What are you doing?" She felt the knifepoint prink into her back.

"Looking for ice," she replied, as reproachfully as she dared.

Belle jerked her backwards. "Not now." She thumped Ginger in a chair and began to tie her wrists behind her back. She took another chair and sat facing Ginger. "Let me look at it."

Ginger braced herself for another rough jerk, but instead, Belle's touch was gentle. She turned Ginger's face to the side, examining it intently. "Damn, Red, you bruise easily."

Ginger gritted her teeth. "Ginger."

"What?"

"Ginger. My name is Ginger. Not Red. Ginger."

Belle went over to the icebox and pulled out a slab of meat. She cut a small portion off then put it on Ginger's injury. "Here, this will ease the pain." She sat down and held it in place while she continued to examine her captive.

Ginger returned the stare, refusing to back down. Belle's appearance contradicted her reputation as an outlaw. Her hair was pulled tightly off her face in a neat bun, and she was clad in a simple brown shirt with matching pants. Her face was astounding—Ginger would have called her beautiful if her eyes weren't so chilling.

"Like what you see?"

"I'd be happier if you untied me and left my house."

The door creaked open and Ginger straightened, hoping Jake was home. To her disappointment, a tall Indian man came into the kitchen. He nodded curtly at her before turning to Belle. "We're ready. Get rid of the girl and come on before it gets too dark."

Belle turned towards Ginger, a malicious glint in her eye. "I don't know, Sam, she's kind of cute."

"We don't have time to indulge your tastes this time. She'll only slow us down."

Belle approached her husband and cuddled close to his chest. "She's a sheriff's wife. It'll give us leverage."

"Leverage to get hanged." Sam looked at his wife and sighed. "Fine, bring her with us. But she's your responsibility. Make sure she doesn't get in our way."

Belle turned back to Ginger and held out a knife. "I can use this to cut the rope, or your throat. The choice is yours."

"What do you want with me?"

Belle winked. "I could use some female company. Just don't make me regret this."

Ginger looked down. As much as she didn't want to go with Belle, it was infinitely better than death. "I'll go."

"Good choice, Red. I'll get a few things to take with us."

Belle left the room returning moments later with a packed sack. She deftly cut the ropes and led her outside to the stables. Sam and his men had already saddled and loaded Jake's prize stallions with goods. Belle took a quick look at the stock and chose Ginger's favorite mare.

"Mount her."

Ginger climbed up quickly, rubbing the horse's ears. She wasn't sure who she was trying to reassure more, the horse or herself. Belle swung up behind her. Sam took another bit of rope and retied Ginger's wrists in front of her. "No games," he warned her before stalking over to his own horse.

"What's going to happen to Jake?"

"He's fine. We were more concerned with his horses. Now be quiet, Red."

They rode in silence for the better part of the trip. Ginger wasn't used to riding for such a long distance. Her arms were numb and she was willing to bet her backside was turning a horrid purple. She tried to think of anything that would get her mind off of her pain; she even sang old childhood ditties in her head.

After a while her anger drained away, and she became acutely aware of Belle's body. Her breasts pressed firmly against her back, and her hands rested on Ginger's stomach. Every now and then she would move the reigns, sending a small shiver through Ginger.

"Cold?"

Ginger shook her head, refusing to let her captor know that she was being affected in any way.

"How long have you been married?"

"Four years."

"No children?"

Ginger shook her head.

"Why Jake?"

"Why not?" Ginger kept her head straight ahead.

Belle chuckled. "You're still mad, I see. If I loosen your bonds, will that help any?"

"Perhaps."

"Hold up your hands." Belle reached for her knife and sawed through the rope.

"There. Now let's talk." Her toned turned hard once more. "I kept you because I thought you would amuse me. Don't forget, I can still kill you any time I like."

Ginger turned her head until she could see Belle's face. "If I answer your questions, will you answer some of mine?"

"You're not exactly in a bargaining position, Red." Her face changed again, as abruptly as before, and she smiled. "We'll see. So, why Jake?"

"It just made sense. He's a hard-working man, and at the time he was set to inherit his father's ranch."

"What made him become a sheriff?"

"The ranch burned down. He decided to become a deputy until he had enough money to start a ranch of his own. Then they needed a sheriff, and the people chose him." Ginger shrugged. "My parents thought it was a good choice."

"So why not just stay single? You don't seem to be motivated by any great passion."

Ginger hesitated. How much did she want to reveal to the outlaw? "Well, the normal reasons, I guess. Money, protection, name—like I said, it just made sense. Besides, he made me laugh."

"There's something you aren't telling me, Red."

Ginger stayed silent, looking at the forest around them.

Belle tilted her head until her mouth was level with Ginger's ear. "I have ways of finding things out, you know." Her tongue snaked out and traced the outside of Ginger's earlobe.

Ginger jerked up, so shocked by the woman's boldness that she almost fell off the horse. Belle grabbed her and held her steady. "Whoa girl, you'll be no good to me if you get trampled to death."

Ginger looked up into Belle's face, searching for some sort of sign. Belle's mouth was set in a serious line, but her eyes blatantly shone with desire. Shaken, Ginger turned back around.

Belle let her arms fall back around Ginger's waist. "So you had some questions for me?"

Ginger thought for a moment, relieved to be on safer ground. The only thing more disconcerting than Belle's behavior was Ginger's reaction to her advances. She couldn't completely blame the throbbing between her legs on the long ride. "You speak very well. You look more like a lady than an outlaw."

"Some lessons are hard to forget. The ones I got at the Carthage Female Academy are lodged in my brain." She winced. "And my backside."

Ginger giggled; it was easy to imagine a recalcitrant Belle being disciplined by her teachers. "How did you go from a lady to an out-law?"

"After the war, Cole Younger came back to town. He used to work with Jesse James, and they would hide in our barn. After a while it just seemed natural." Belle peered ahead as the horses slowed down. "I think we're stopping here for the night. You'll bunk with me." She swept the hair from Ginger's neck and kissed it softly before dismounting.

Sam pulled Ginger off the horse and pointed towards the edge of the clearing. "There's a hot water spring beyond the trees. We'll have some food ready by the time you and Belle are finished." He gave her a knowing leer.

Ginger squared her shoulders, refusing to let the outlaw get to her. "Thank you, I'm sure it will be refreshing," she said, taking her bag from his hand.

He grinned wider. "Belle will see to it."

Ginger limped towards the spring, anxious to soak the soreness from her muscles. Belle was her secondary concern. There was no doubt in her mind that Belle would try to seduce her again; it was only a question of how difficult Ginger planned to be before she gave in.

Ginger spied Belle on the bank. She lit a lantern, then climbed into the water. Her mouth curved up into a smile. Oh, yes, she planned to turn the tables on Belle Starr.

She stripped off her clothes and stepped into the water, careful to stay directly across from the other woman. She sighed, enjoying the heat on her muscles. The ground curved into a natural ledge, and Ginger sat so that the water went up to her shoulders.

"Feels good, doesn't it? It's one of my favorite springs."

"You come here often?"

"It's close to several towns. Nice and secluded. We don't have to worry about people finding us. Soap?"

Ginger opened her eyes. Belle stood over her, soap in hand. "Need help?"

Ginger nodded, smiling up at Belle. "That would be lovely."

Surprise flashed across Belle's face, but she recovered quickly. "Stand over here." She ran the soap down Ginger's arms, raising them to get her sides.

"Belle?"

"What now, Red?"

Ginger grinned at the brusqueness in Belle's voice. She was obviously trying to regain control of herself. "You like women?"

Belle started cleaning her back. "Sometimes I want a man, sometimes I like the taste of a woman."

Ginger leaned over so Belle could clean her buttocks. She made sure to poke her hips out. "I know what you mean."

Belle stopped. "Well, well, well," she chuckled. "You're full of surprises, Red. Go on."

"I've only been with two women, a schoolmarm and a girl who worked in the saloon. My father caught me with Annie, the teacher. He insisted I get married right away." She turned, allowing Belle to get a good look at her breasts. The night air caressed her body, causing her nipples to stand on end.

As Belle looked, Ginger reached out and pinched one of her nipples, watching carefully to see how the woman would react to her forwardness.

She didn't have to wait long; Belle grasped her shoulders and kissed her roughly. Ginger returned the embrace eagerly, running her fingers down Belle's back and feeling the curves of her hips. Belle pulled her deeper into the water and Ginger wrapped her legs around her waist and arched her back. Belle followed her lead, lowering her head to take one of Ginger's nipples between her lips.

Ginger moaned, moving her hips frantically against Belle's body. Belle bit down, and Ginger dug her nails into her captor's back. An image of Jake popped in her mind and she repressed the guilt.

"You want me to continue?" It was more a statement than a question.

Ginger nodded breathlessly, trying to pull Belle back towards her. Her captor shook her off and pinned her hands over her head.

"Tell me you want me to continue."

Ginger frowned, thinking of a way to regain the upper hand. She shouldn't be doing this, she was a married woman, and in any case Belle was the wrong sort of woman to get involved with. Except she wasn't like any other person she'd ever met.

Anyhow, she reasoned with herself, she could always tell her husband she was forced. Although there was no doubt she wanted to continue as much as Belle did. The only thing left for her was to admit it.

"Belle? Everything's ready. Come and eat," Sam's voice rang out.

"Jealous bastard," Belle muttered, more to herself than to Ginger. She pulled her up. "Come on, Red, we mustn't keep the men waiting." She kissed Ginger once more on the mouth before hauling her towards camp.

***

They left early the next morning. Once again Ginger rode in front of Belle. The men kept staring at them and sniggering, but Ginger kept her eyes on the path ahead. She wasn't quite sure how to act; Belle hadn't said two words to her since they woke. Last night they were almost lovers, but today she seemed to be a captive again. Part of her was relieved that they were interrupted before she could answer Belle's question. The other part was off sulking that nothing more had occurred. Oh, well, at least her hands weren't bound.

"Did you love them?"

Ginger started, surprised and confused. "Love who?"

"The other women."

"The saloon girl was just a friend. Annie—I cared more about Annie than I've ever cared about anyone else. We used to dream of running the school together. But then my father caught us, and it was over." Ginger shrugged.

"My parents never wanted me to be involved in this sort of life. Hell, they sent me to a fancy academy. They wanted me to be a lady and marry well. But when Cole came back and introduced me to Jesse James.... I don't know.... It felt great to be a part of their gang. Like it was my true calling. I hated trying to be all prissy anyhow. I just decided to do what made me happy. I think that works out better for everyone in the end."

Ginger shifted, trying to massage her hip. "The point of this would be?"

"Maybe you should do the same thing, Red." Belle smacked Ginger's hand. "Stop moving before you fall off. We're stopping at a real inn tonight." She slipped her hand in between Ginger's legs. "Maybe what you need is a little more...attention."

Ginger grabbed Belle's hand and placed it behind her. "Tell that to your husband."

"You don't have to worry about the men tonight. They'll get drunk at the bar and fall asleep. It's just you and me tonight, Red."

***

"Oh, yes, Red, like that! Fuck me now. *Please!*" she begged.

"Don't you want me to return the favor?"

"I want it now," Belle implored.

The need in her voice almost broke Ginger's resolve, but she blocked her mind to Belle's pleas. She knelt down, spread her cheeks, and ran her tongue along Belle's crack. Ginger found her anus and licked slow circles around it. She plunged her tongue in and out several times, reveling in Belle's grunts of ecstasy.

"Turn over," Ginger ordered, thoroughly enjoying her new dominating role.

Belle's face was flushed, and she was breathing heavily. Ginger opened her legs and began to lick the juices from her moist cunt. She loved Belle's taste, so different from Jake's. She sucked her clit and slid a finger into her warm vagina. Sleep threatened to overwhelm her, but she pushed it aside to concentrate on pleasuring Belle. She felt so powerful watching her captor writhe and scream with joy.

Ginger sucked more intensely; her nose was filled with the scent of Belle's cunt. Belle's hands made their way to the top of Ginger's head and tugged her hair. Belle was at her breaking point; Ginger could sense her starting to shake.

"What's my name?" Ginger asked, out of the blue.

"What?" Belle yelped.

"You heard me. Say my name."

"Red! Stop playing."

Ginger blew over Belle's lips. "It's really easy, Belle, just say it. Ginger. Say Ginger." She started tracing slow circles around Belle's clit.

Belle pursed her mouth and glared at Ginger. "I hate you…oh, God, Ginger, please Ginger…"

Ginger grasped Belle's clit between her lips and shook her head, while gently humming. Belle screamed, yanking on Ginger's hair as she came. Belle's ejaculation flowed over her tongue, and she opened her mouth, trying to catch every drop.

Ginger sat back to enjoy her handiwork. Belle's hair stuck out at odd angles over her head. Her legs splayed open to reveal her swollen clit, and her arms lay limply at her sides. Her eyes locked with Ginger's, utterly drained from the force of her orgasm.

"That was a dirty trick, Red." She motioned to Ginger. "Come here."

Ginger curled up next to her, placing an arm over Belle's stomach. She listened until Belle's breathing became deep and even before drifting off to sleep herself.

***

Sam jerked them awake the next morning. "Get up, now! The sheriff is on his way here. We have to leave now!"

Belle hopped out of bed, throwing on her clothes, while Ginger sat dazed.

"I don't…what's happening?"

Belle tossed her the outfit she wore last night. "Put this on, we have to go."

"We don't have enough time, Belle, let her go!" Sam yelled.

"No!"

"I told you before—she'll only slow us down. Look, we're leaving. If she's coming, hurry. If not, leave her here."

Belle turned towards Ginger, who was struggling to get dressed. "Come with us. It'll be a new start."

Ginger looked into the corner, weighing her decision. "I do want a new life."

Belle smiled widely, crossing to help her dress. Ginger held her hand out to stop her. "But not this life."

Belle nodded, disappointment welling in her eyes. "It's not for everyone. Some people are meant to stay good." She picked up a length of rope. "Speaking of which, I better make you look that way before I go."

Thirty minutes later, Jake burst into the room, surrounded by local lawmen. They found Ginger sitting in a chair, bound and gagged. Her head drooped forward and a bruise was starting to form on her temple. Jake untied his wife and carried her out of the room. If he'd have looked carefully, he might have noticed a light sheen on his wife's forehead, in the shape of lips.

***

Belle and her gang were caught a week later. They were brought back to town and tried by the Hanging Judge himself. Since Ginger refused to testify against her captors, they were convicted on the sole charge on horse theft and sentenced to one year in jail. After the trial, Ginger left Jake and moved out of town in search of Annie.

Layover

CAELIN TAYLOR

She didn't know how it had come to this, as an aging man in a rumpled linen suit reached over her shoulder for an otherwise life-like purple dildo. Just four hours ago, standing on a curb at the departure terminal, her mother and little brother had kissed her on the cheek and waved goodbye. Now in some Las Vegas adult boutique, with her back against what appeared to be a massive dildo display, she prayed the man beside her was not about to try to strike up a conversation.

"Excuse me," the man says in a deeply masculine voice, tapping gently on Hayden's shoulder.

"Shit," she says under her breath, jumping slightly. She turns, coming face to face with not only the purple phallus but also a boxed, special edition Jeff Stryker vibrator held firmly in the man's large hands.

"Which one of these would you recommend?"

"What?" Hayden asks, glancing around for her girlfriend. The man shifts his weight and shakes the items lightly.

"Its just," he lowers his voice. "Well, I'm a little embarrassed to admit this." He pauses and looks at his feet. "I've never used one of these. Time was, your equipment was good enough as it was." He clears his throat, chuckling. "My boyfriend and I are here…our first vacation together in six years. I don't want to leave anything to chance."

Hayden flushes, puts her hand up to cover an involuntary grin and shakes her head. "I, uh, well," she touches the box corner of the Stryker unit and smiles. "I don't know. I don't actually work here." The man's face goes red, and he drops his arms to his sides.

"Oh, shit…oh." He tilts his head. "Sorry."

"That's okay," she says, tucking a strand of brown hair behind her ear. "It happens all the time."

"Well," the man stops her as she begins to turn. "Do you have an opinion? You know," he holds up the choices again. "Either way." There is a moment of quiet, broken by their shared nervous laughter. Hayden takes a deep breath and reluctantly takes the items from the man to examine both.

"Sure…well, let's see. Jeff Stryker, huh? The porn star?" She laughs silently. "That kind of sets the bar high, don't you think?" The man retracts the box, looks at it, and begins to nod. He sets it down, disdainfully, on a nearby shelf.

"I never thought of that."

"This one, on the other hand," Hayden says, wiggling the purple model in her hand. "This one is nice, I guess. It's firm," she says, bending it. "Without loss of flexibility."

"Hayden?" A voice calls over a stack of adult movies. With a confused look on her face, Marli waves at her. Hayden hands the purple toy to the man and darts to her girlfriend. "What was that? Was that guy trying to mess with you?" Hayden pushes the short blond hair from Marli's forehead and grabs the lapels of her charcoal Donna Karan suit.

"No, no. He wasn't trying to mess with me."

"Then what did he want?"

"He wanted to buy me a dildo." Her face was serious as she shook Marli slightly.

"What?" She asks, swallowing hard.

"He wanted to buy me a ten-inch hard-as-rock purple cock," Hayden says slowly, carefully annunciating every syllable. As the two women continue to stare at one another, it is unclear who begins laughing first. With her arm slung around Hayden's slender waist, Marli leads her toward the back of the store.

"When's our flight?" She asks as Hayden takes a video from the shelf beside her.

"Six A.M., I think. I couldn't get a room…anywhere. There's some stupid convention in town." She turns the movie's case over and reads the brief synopsis. "Do you think we should buy something for Kris and Emily?" She laughs, holding up the movie.

"As if, Hayden. You know you'd be buying that for yourself," Marli says playfully pinching her arm.

"Not…necessarily," she laughs, replacing the movie. She turns and wraps her arms around Marli. "God, I'm just so glad to finally be alone with you. Don't get me wrong, but two weeks with my mom can be thirteen days too many." She pauses briefly as Marli shakes a fistful of something metallic in front of her. "Hey…what's that?" Hayden asks, grabbing for Marli's hand. Inside her grasp are at least a dozen pink tokens with embossed images of posed naked women.

"Well…we're laid over, right? In Las Vegas—the capitol of sin! No place to sleep in a town that doesn't, so, why not?" Marli stuffs the tokens into Hayden's light green shirt pocket, grabbing her breast quickly. When Hayden fails to respond, she adds, "Oh, for Christ's sake, Hayden! They're for the video arcade."

"Video arcade? What…you mean, like, video games?"

"Oh, my God, Hayden. It's for the adult movies in the back of the store."

"You're kidding," Hayden says, and grabs her mouth, snickering.

"Fuck, no, I'm not kidding. It'll be hilarious. Besides, if you could have thought of another way for us to be alone, you would have by now." She grabs Hayden's hand, slings her carry-on bag over her shoulder, and leads them through a threadbare red brocade, above which a sign reads PEEP SHOW.

Through the curtain, the two women stand at the head of a long hallway, beset on either side by numbered doors, some open, some closed. In the dim red light Hayden stifles a giggle and grabs Marli's ass.

Why not? She thinks to herself, following Marli down the corridor, past the muffled groans and nude dancers behind thick plexiglass windows. At the end of the hall, they enter room number 12. It was bigger than one might imagine, with a large, wall-inset monitor. The dark red walls were smooth, almost reflective. There was a wooden bench opposite the monitor, pushed against the wall.

"Look at this," Marli says in a light voice, holding up an engraved brass sign which reads TAKEN. She hangs the sign on the door and closes it. Hayden crosses and uncrosses her arms, smiling with nervous energy. Marli shrugs out of her coat and lays it down over the bench. She sits down, patting her knee invitingly. Tucking her hair behind her ears she sits delicately on Marli's leg, curving her left arm around her shoulder.

"Well," she says, extricating a token from Hayden's pocket. "What shall we watch?" She drops the token into the slot and reads aloud as the monitor flickers to life. "Let's see, we have *Dorm Room Blows 4, Locker Room Sluts, Shaved 6…*" Hayden holds up her hand, grinning, and points to a movie entitled *Strapped*.

"What about this one?" she asks tentatively. Her eyebrow arching, Marli shrugs and presses play.

There is no lead in, no title, no credits, only a brief moment in which a voluptuous redheaded woman tightens a strap fastened to a black leather harness. She runs her hand over the soft arc of her hip while the camera pans to her front, to a six-inch black dildo, slanting upward from her pelvis, ridged suggestively. A young woman lies on a sofa below, her right leg slung up over the sofa's top. She extends her left leg, curling it around the redhead's hip, pulling her down.

The redhead stops short, her hand on the shaft of the dildo, working it slowly up and down the woman's already swollen lips. The young woman is completely shaved. Her abnormally large breasts move like bowls of gelatin atop her extremely petite frame.

"Ew," Hayden says, pointing at the woman's artificial breasts, her nipples pointing in opposite directions. "So fake…watch how they jiggle." The redhead thrusts her pelvis forward, moving unhurriedly.

"Look, she's already acting like she's going to come," Marli giggles. The blond moves unrhythmically beneath the redhead, moaning loudly, her face turned toward the audience at all times.

The camera zooms in abruptly on the dildo, glistening, as it slides in and out of the blond. Marli laughs, but feels a familiar ache in her crotch as the redhead, her torso muscular and strong, flips over the blond, taking her from behind.

"Wow…okay. She's a dyke," Hayden remarks with a quiet voice, sucking absent-mindedly on her pinky. Fluidly, the redhead moves her body, her hands digging into the blond's small hips, pulling her back. Marli licks her suddenly dry lips. Out of the corner of her eye she sees a change coming over Hayden's face. She turns her attention to the monitor, to the blond's contorted face. The redhead stands then, moving their bodies without leaving the blond, repositioning them. Her hand reaches around the blond's ample hip and holds the woman's clit before she begins to move again. The black leather harness is so tightly fastened Marli wonders if it will leave marks.

The blond goes facedown into a cushion, her hands grabbing at the sofa's frame to balance herself. The camera pans to the side, focusing in on the dildo as the redhead slides herself almost all the way out of her, leaving just the very tip inside.

"You like that, don't you," she pants, sweat forming on her face and her back. "You like that, you little—" The monitor flickers off. The two women laugh quickly and Hayden holds out another token.

"Same one?" Marli asks, clearing her throat. Caressing the soft downy hairs at the base of Marli's neck, Hayden nods.

"Slut!" The redhead rolls her pelvis forward, panting hard, her body convulsing, before she collapses on top of the blond.

"Damn it!" Hayden slaps her knee, laughing. "She came."

The scene ends with a cheesy transition and jumps into the next, which finds the same redhead, now laying on her side, sandwiched between two women. The woman she faces is small, with short brown hair. Behind her is a tall, gorgeous black woman who is kissing her neck. Both women are wielding strap-ons. They all move as one, bucking and rocking slow, then fast. There is a mangle of hands, of legs, of breasts. The redhead rolls her head back, laying it against the woman behind her while the brunette kisses her roughly.

Hayden grabs at Marli's hair, holding the short tips between her fingers. Marli bends her head to kiss Hayden's neck below her ear, the sweet smell of her hair filling her. She touches Hayden's breast, softly rolling her fingertips over the woman's firm nipple.

The redhead sits on top of the brunette, her body golden and slightly damp with sweat. The redhead's legs are forward, her feet on either side of the brunette's head. Her hands grab at the bedsheet as the brunette raises her hips, her legs bent, pushing a thick pink dildo hard into the redhead. She moans, licking her lips, arching her body.

"That looks complicated," Hayden breathes as Marli begins to unbutton her blouse.

"What does?" Marli sighs, taking Hayden's nipple between her teeth. Hayden groans, pushing Marli's head to her breast with one hand as she puts in another token with the other.

There is a fast cut scene. A young woman with long flaxen hair, wearing a black suit, sits in a chair. She smokes a cigarette beneath a hanging lamp. A woman with shoulder-length black hair and wearing only a red thong enters the room and kneels before her. Her breasts touch the woman's knees as she leans forward, kissing her way down the woman's torso. Her fingers trailing behind, caressing the woman's beautiful breasts, bare underneath the suit coat. She puts her hands to the woman's crotch, smiling. There is a bulge. She unbuttons the woman's slacks and retracts a fleshy cream-colored dildo. As she puts it to her red lipsticked mouth, Marli unzips Hayden's jeans. Hayden wiggles out of them, pulling off her blouse, the T-shirt underneath. Marli's fingers trace the delicate lacy edge of her underwear, her breathing suddenly ragged.

"I want you," sighs Hayden. She looks down at Marli. "I want you inside me, now…"

She steps out of her red thong, letting it drop to the floor. She approaches the woman, standing completely naked before her. Gracefully she straddles the flaxen-haired beauty in the chair, pushing her suit open to reveal her smooth brown torso. As she guides the woman inside her and begins to move, their breasts sway, gliding against one another.

"That's it," groans the suited woman into her neck. "Fuck me."

Marli moves her fingers tentatively at first, shallowly, in and out of Hayden's pussy, loving the way it tightens around her as she begins to pull away and opens for her as she pounds herself inside. Marli puts her thumb to Hayden's full lower lip. Slowly, Hayden licks it before taking it into her mouth, sucking. Naked now, Hayden repositions herself to straddle Marli on the bench. Her underwear, pushed down, hang around her right ankle.

They kiss then, hungry. They bite at one another, their breath hot and quick. Marli tangles her fingers in Hayden's thick brown hair, pulling her head back, kissing her neck, her collarbone. Aching, her eyes closed, Hayden grinds her body down. She puts her hand to her clit, already swollen and hard, and begins to work it slowly. Marli grabs Hayden's hips, pulling her closer. Against her stomach she feels Hayden's arm moving, the muscles of her forearm hard as she pushes down, circles, holds, and sighs.

Roughly, Marli pushes her fingers into Hayden, the soft skin of their hands touching. She looks at her with her head thrown back, the arch of her neck, her chest as it rises and falls. They move together, awkwardly at first, but quickly finding a rhythm. She is so wet Marli's fingers move easily, deeply. Hayden's thighs tighten and she grabs for Marli's shoulders, her face.

"Right there," she moans, moving her hips. She thrusts her body down onto Marli's fingers, ramming them deeper inside her. "Oh, fuck…"

There is the sound of jagged breathing, the wood bench sliding back and forth across the tiled floor. The movie has stopped. There is sweat rolling down and over and in between Hayden's breasts. There is the throbbing of her body, the pain in her fingers, in her hand, the sound of her blood pounding in her ears. There is the soft string of profanity pouring from Hayden's lush, full lips. There is the frantic tightening of her grip and the moan that begins low, almost inaudibly. Then, Hayden opens her eyes to Marli. Everything is humming and she is moving without effort. There is a fire spreading inside her. It courses through every muscle, invading her tissue. She feels every curve, every inch, every ridge of Marli's fingers gliding in and out of her. She wants more, she wants this feeling to last, but she feels it, already half begun, risen to the pit of her stomach, stiffening her legs, her feet, her toes.

Nothing will stop it, not as Marli sees the sudden flash in her eyes, the subtle shift in her movements. Marli knows she is there, behind her wild gaze, waiting to be pushed over, to be taken. Marli puts her thumb to Hayden's clit again, circling it deftly, while she forcefully, hastily, roughly thrusts herself inside. They are looking at one another when she comes, violently. Everything, everywhere burning. She is saying her name, her hands clasping at Marli's open blouse.

When Hayden lifts her head from Marli's shoulder, she is unsure how much time has passed. There are faint bruises on her hips, on Marli's arms. They smile at one another and laugh quietly.

"Wow," Marli says, her voice deep. Hayden's eyes are heavy as Marli pushes the hair from her face.

"What, baby?"

"You're so beautiful," she smiles, caressing Hayden's face. "So beautiful, and so easy." They laugh, and Hayden punches her shoulder playfully.

"Fuck you," Hayden sighs, reaching between Marli's legs, feeling her, hot and damp.

"You wish," she chuckles, trying to ignore the subtle suggestion of Hayden's knowing touch.

"Mm-hmm," she breathes, her lips grazing Marli's ear. She presses a little harder against Marli's crotch. "Easy? You want easy?" Marli's eyes close, her hands, fisted, lay on either side of Hayden's thighs. "I bet I can make you come...just like this." She is barely touching her, but Marli feels her, her hand stroking her through her slacks, her underwear. She groans as Hayden pushes shallowly into her pussy, then moves back to her clit. "You're so ready...I can feel it. Your heart is pounding, isn't it? That feels good, doesn't it?"

"Yeah..." Marli says. "Yeah, just like that." She runs her hands along Hayden's bare legs to her ass, tiny goose bumps rising in her wake. Hayden's touch is delicate, precise, focused. She resists her own desire, the want to feel her, the need to taste her. Her pulse quickens. Marli's head falls back against the wall. As she strokes her, Hayden watches Marli's jugular throbbing just underneath her silken skin. Hayden leans forward until their mouths are only inches apart and Marli's hot breath covers her face.

"Fuck, Marli...you're so wet, baby...tell me what you need." Hayden touches her left hand to Marli's throat, tracing it to where it dips into her collarbone. "Talk to me."

"I want to feel you," it is a struggle to speak. Marli whispers, "I need to feel you...I need you, Hayden." Hayden strengthens her movements. "Oh...fuck. I need you to fuck me..."

"No," Hayden says. "Not yet...not yet." Marli moans, her fingers pulling Hayden's body closer until their torsos, their breasts, their stomachs wet with sweat, touch. She feels the hardness of Hayden's nipples against the smooth satin fabric of her bra. Marli knows Hayden will not give her what she wants until she asks for it, until she cannot wait any longer, until she is willing to do anything, say anything.

"Please, Hayden."

"Please, what?"

"Please...touch me." Hayden moves her hand from Marli's crotch. It takes only a moment for Marli to unzip her slacks, raise her hips and wiggle them slightly out of the way. "Please, Hayden...I need you."

Hayden looks at her, the way her stomach has tightened, the way her black panties hug her pelvis. Her gray slacks are open just enough now. She touches Marli's stomach, tan and smooth, running just a finger under the top elastic band of her underwear. They kiss, slowly, with tongues rolling over each other. Hayden pulls Marli's underwear to the side and enters her. She knows by the delicious wetness enveloping her fingers, from the way Marli has taken hold of her, that she will come soon. Hayden's own body twinges, tight again with want. She curves her fingers upward at the deepest point and feels the whole of Marli's body taking her in, as if to swallow her.

"Harder," she says, her hands, her fingers on Hayden's hips, her ass. Her white blouse, unbuttoned, lays bare her torso, which rises and falls quickly, almost matching Hayden's movements. Hayden pushes her hand into Marli, fast and hard, barely past her lips, barely into her pussy. "Oh, yeah…that's it…don't—don't stop…right there…" She thrusts fast, shallowly, her fingers covered with Marli, feeling as though she too is about to come.

It is as Hayden's fingers slide out of her, her breasts swaying with the movement, Hayden's thighs tight, breathing hard, that Marli comes. She puts her hand to Hayden's elbow and drives her fingers deep inside where everything is throbbing, aching for Hayden to fill her. Hayden pushes her hand in, as far as she can, and holds it there. Feeling, with eyes closed, Marli's body as it thumps with hard irregular contractions. Marli puts her hand to Hayden's crotch and presses hard against it. Hayden is surprised by the quickness of her body's response. She inhales sharply. They move their hands away, and Marli pulls her close until their pussies, their clits, touch. Hayden begins to move her hips, their bodies entwined, gliding against one another.

"Oh, my God," Hayden groans, her hands on the wall in an attempt to steady herself. "I'm going to come so hard…"

"I want you to," Marli gasps, her body still hot, vibrating. A phone rings, muffled. Marli's eyes glance about the room, knowing it must be her cell phone.

"Don't you…dare," Hayden says, kissing Marli's neck. Moving with force, she grinds her clit into Marli's. Biting her bottom lip, pulling Marli's short hair, she comes loudly without thought or inhibition, bucking wildly on Marli's lap.

After a few moments, she lifts her head from the slope of Marli's neck and smiles.

"What the fuck time is it?" She laughs, tucking the hair behind her ears and smoothing the hair from Marli's forehead. Flipping her watch over on her wrist, Marli sighs.

"It's late, baby. It's like two A.M."

"How long have we been in here?" Hayden stands and begins to pull up her underwear. On her knees, faint bruises have begun to appear. She finds her discarded T-shirt and draws it over her head.

"I don't know. Four hours, maybe." Marli laughs, slouching on the bench as she zips up her slacks.

"Shit," is all she manages until she pulls on her jeans. She stops, with a hand on Marli's shoulder. "Who the hell was calling us at two A.M.?"

"Let me check," Marli reaches for her bag, feeling around for her phone. Hayden puts on her boots and runs her fingers through her hair, wet with perspiration. "Kris and Emily...they're at Sea-Tac, wondering where the hell we are."

"Didn't you call them?" Hayden sits on the bench, laying her legs across Marli's lap, smiling. Marli shakes her head, wrapping her arms around Hayden.

"I forgot. I guess I was a little preoccupied." The two women kiss. "I'll call them on the way to the airport." Hayden begins unbuttoning Marli's blouse. She traces the exposed curve of her breast. "Are you hungry? Thirsty? Could you eat?"

"Mm-hmm...but it can wait," Hayden smiles.

"Oh, really?" Marli laughs, feeling the warmth of Hayden's hand as she cups her breast.

"Definitely."

Lotus

JULIEN LEE

Elena boarded the 5:20 P.M. eastbound metro train, like she did at the end of every workday. It had been a hard week, and all she could think about was a nice cool shower, a pint of ice cream, and a night of TV. Rather sad for a woman of her age, thirty-something and single. As usual, no seats were to be found and not a single gentlemen either. So she stood by the doors, ready for a quick escape when her stop came up. Her toned, creamy brown body hugged a pole for balance. Though her gray skirt was knee-length and her crisp white shirt was buttoned up, her natural curves were nowhere near as modest. She had the kind of body women envied and admirers fantasized about. Elena was simply a vision, especially when she straddled that pole like an exotic dancer.

As the train rocked slowly, lulling its passengers to sleep, Elena observed the world passing by her window. Gradually the graffiti crept into view and defined the cultural makeup of the neighborhood through images and words. The competing graffiti interested her. Every other day, one "artist's" work would be outdone or covered over by another's. *What a world this would be if this was the extent of their rivalry,* she thought. Occasionally, the train entered a tunnel and all would go black. Elena reveled in these moments of darkness because much excitement lay within. The deepest desires of the heart usually reveal themselves in the dark, away from eyes that would judge, criticize and shame. In a train full of strangers anything could happen, and the strangest thing finally did.

In the darkness Elena felt a gentle squeeze of her left breast. This stranger's fingers slowly glided over her breast, making the nipple harden with each pass. She was paralyzed with shock and at the same time aroused by the thought of someone so bold. When the light and her senses returned, Elena turned to identify her molester and found a rush of people storming their way toward the train doors. She scanned the crowd for any hint of a culprit and found only one who met her eyes. Padma was a striking Indian beauty, even with her raven hair pulled tightly in a bun. The train came to a stop and everyone herded out like cattle. Elena stood there a few moments more, unmoving, hoping the sweet sensation would linger a little longer.

Elena found Padma waiting for her on the platform. She thought it rather odd but gave up a smile and headed on her merry way.

"I've missed you," Padma said as she caught up with her.

"Sorry?" squeaked Elena, her mind racing to place who she was and how their paths could have crossed.

"I see you working out, but you don't ever come to class."

Elena realized she's the yoga instructor from her gym. In her defense, it was a painful class she took once and decided it wasn't worth revisiting. Now she wondered why she hadn't.

"I'm not very good at yoga," Elena shyly admitted. She noticed Padma's wedding ring (ah, that's why) and how perfectly her traditional India attire complimented her. The cloth was soft with hues of orange and red.

"Give me another chance. You will want more," Padma said playfully as she walked away.

"Promise?" Elena blurted out and hoped she was out of earshot.

She didn't know if Padma's last words were lost in translation, but all Elena could think about now was a hot, sudsy bath, a glass of wine, and a dirty magazine.

For the next few weeks Elena was Padma's eager student. Truly, she had no ulterior motive as Padma was married and mostly likely uninterested. However, she was nice to look at, and Elena enjoyed the hands-on instruction. As she held her poses, Padma would come by and adjust her body this way and that way. Her classmates were too focused on their own poses to notice her crush and how she blushed every time teacher touched her.

Elena usually took her time in the showers. Sometimes Padma made her so wet she couldn't resist pleasuring herself then and there, even if a thin plastic shower curtain was the only thing protecting her privacy. Elena quickly changed into her terry cloth robe and maneuvered her way to the private shower stalls. Padma gently soaped herself in the communal showers. Her areolas were far darker in color than the rest of her body, and the contrast made Elena suddenly crave milk and dark chocolate. The small pat of hair below just barely covered her delicate slit. Elena memorized every detail before Padma met her eyes. They exchanged smiles before Elena forced herself into a stall and pulled the curtain, mortified. She threw her robe over the curtain rod and turned on the water. It was cold at first, and then it warmed up. She hung her head underneath the stream. She was embarrassed, yes, but she couldn't let the mental picture go to waste. The fever grew within her again as she braced herself in a corner. She reached for the wetness between her legs and found it was thicker than the water flowing over her. Her eyes closed. In darkness she could imagine doing anything. Her middle finger pushed deep inside, then out, in and out. Her fingers rubbed against her tender meat. In. Out. Her other fingers strummed her nipple. Both her hands were in rhythm, coaxing her to a climax, when someone made them stop.

It was Padma. She held Elena's wrists away. A cruel thing to do, since all Elena wanted was to pull her drenched body against hers. Elena kissed her full on, persuading Padma to loosen her grip. Her hands worked quickly, one on the inward curves of her buttocks, the other laced in her hair. She slid down her neck and drained the wetness from her skin with harder kisses. She wanted to descend further, but Padma directed her back up. "Patience," she said. "You will have me, but not here." At this moment of weakness, Elena could not think and followed willingly.

Padma's house was just a few miles away. In their haste they both skipped toweling dry and now endured a car ride in their damp street clothes. Elena felt the stitching of her jeans rub against her sensitive spot—she skipped putting on her panties as well as her bra. They finally arrived. Padma took Elena's hand and led her in through the front door. "Help yourself to a drink. I'll be right back," said Padma as she headed down a dark corridor and disappeared around the corner. Elena wasn't thirsty for a drink, but her curiosity took her around the comfortably modern home. It was well-kept and tastefully furnished with expensive furniture, a professional kitchen, state-of-the-art electronics, and valuable Indian art—everything a power couple could afford. Pictures of Padma and her husband hung in the family room. Each depicted a different stage in their lives, together and apart. He was an attractive man, Indian, of course, with a metrosexual look about him. They were a handsome pair, and this made Elena wonder why the hell she was there.

Padma broke the silence, "Having second thoughts?"

"Are you?" Elena demanded to know. She partially dreaded the answer since they've come so far, but here was the out if she wanted it.

"No," Padma declared without a hint of anger or bitterness.

Elena was intrigued as to why. She decided to postpone her question when Padma stripped off her translucent T-shirt.

"He enjoys the company of men," she explained as she studied her nakedness, "and I enjoy yours." She cupped Elena's breast, brought her lips to it and swallowed her nipple whole. Elena's breathing came hard and heavy.

"I don't understand. Why stay married—" Padma shut her up with a kiss and unzipped Elena's jeans. Her hand dug inside. She was moist and ready. Elena slowly submitted to her, questions melting away.

"Later," Padma breathlessly whispered, "Answers will come later. I want you to come now."

They undressed, kissed, and groped each other as they made their way down the corridor. It was a heated dance that led them to the spacious meditation room. It was sparse yet inviting. There was a warm glow of jasmine-scented candles, smoky ribbons rising from the incense giving Elena the feeling of being in another

world. A large futon mattress lay on the floor in the center of the
room with a simple silk sheet draped over and numerous matching pillows. They fell into the bed, already entwined and fingering
the softness between each other's legs. Padma cupped Elena's wetness and lathered it on her lover's generous mounds. She sucked
hungrily and tugged her nipple to attention. Elena pressed her
head to her bosom, not wanting her to stop. She felt the double
pleasure overtaking her when suddenly Padma got to her knees
and climbed on top of her. She lowered her sex upon Elena's peak.
Its stiffness gave her the most gratifying ride. Elena stroked herself
as Padma heaved with each thrust of her hips and sighed when her
own fingers swept her nipples into a frenzy. Her moans grew
longer as motions came quicker. Elena willed her to come on her
breast, but Padma controlled herself. The night was young.

Padma turned herself around and presented her sex to Elena's
lips. Elena returned the welcome by parting her legs and allowed
Padma to explore her. She felt her forceful tongue penetrating her
soft walls and allowed herself to relish the rapture. She parted
Padma's sex with her fingertips and claimed the crest and reddened
ridges with her mouth. Two of her fingers sank into her valley and
was rewarded by sounds of delight. Padma mimicked her movements and soon she was moaning Padma's name. P-A-D-M-A. It
came out like a soothing mantra. Elena chanted it over and over.
Nirvana was close, and Padma could feel it. Again she broke away.
This drove Elena mad. She's been driven to the verge a few times
tonight and refused to be denied again.

Elena guided Padma back and saw the cloth-wrapped item she
was retrieving. It was long and drooped as she unraveled it with
one hand. The flesh-colored toy was eight inches in length with
almost two inches of girth. Elena hesitated. She didn't need that to
orgasm. She just needed her. Padma sat up, leaned back on one
hand and plunged the pliable rod into her body. Seeing Padma
pleasure herself, so openly and without inhibition, made Elena's
insides swell. Padma pulled it out and caressed Elena's sex with it.
The shaft was wet with Padma's honey. The thought of their juices

mingling made her want it. Elena nodded in approval. "Let me," Padma said politely as she slowly slipped it inside her.

It burrowed through her without resistance and found that deep spot Elena wanted conquered. She was never able to reach that place on her own, but Padma knew the way. She knew Elena's desires without her having to express them. In. Out. In. Out. Elena recognized the satisfaction in Padma's watchful eyes, seeing her hips buck and thighs shudder with every thrust, every twist. It was an extension of Padma and she wished it to probe deeper and deeper in her womb. Padma sensed Elena about to come. Elena pleaded with her eyes, "No, not this time."

Padma's lips curled into a smile as she drew the other end of the toy into her sex. She pushed forward until their pubic hairs met. Elena stifled her orgasm to wait for hers. They moved into comfortable positions and leveraged the angle to heighten the bliss. They enjoyed this erotic game of tug of war and twister until their bodies glistened with sweat and muscles cried for release. It felt so good neither could focus on anything else but that repetitive motion. They were in sync, moaning and thrusting and finally reached the paradise together. Their cries of ecstasy echoed through the house. It was so freeing.

Elena sunk down on the mattress, spent. Padma hovered over her, grabbed the middle of the shaft between their legs, and ever so slowly slid it in and out between their sexes. Within seconds, Elena reveled in her second orgasm and saw in Padma's face that she did too. She was not to be outdone. Padma came twice more before collapsing backwards on the mattress herself. They laid there in complete exhaustion and still connected.

The morning came and, as promised, Padma explained the arrangement with her husband. Elena spooned Padma as she told her story. "Sajan and I were childhood friends in India and knew early on our parents wanted a union. We married young, but it never felt right. We didn't find the opposite sex very appealing."

"Then why stay together?" Elena asked.

"We live our separate lives in the bedroom, but have all the benefits of a marriage: friendship, stability, a means to have a family."

Elena listened to the sincere optimism in Padma's voice and wondered if there would be room for her in Padma's future. Padma turned to face Elena. "So you see he is not a true husband. I don't want a husband." She caressed Elena's cheek and licked her lips. "I want you." She wanted Elena to understand, to say everything was okay. "You doubt my feelings for you." Elena silenced her paranoia with a kiss and began to pet her heavily until they began making love again.

Road Trip

LYNN COLE

"Your parents are going to hate me."

"You are brilliant, fabulous ,and I love you." I glanced at Laura, my girlfriend of six months and one week, and grinned. "They will tolerate you for my sake and then talk about you as soon as we're out of the house."

"Thanks, Jackie," she glared at me over the tops of her pink-tinted sunglasses. "You really know how to make me feel better."

I reached over and squeezed her hand. "It'll be okay. Promise."

We were making the pilgrimage from our apartment in Alexandria, Virginia, to my parents' house in Miami Beach because Laura had reached a milestone that few of my girlfriends ever had—the six-month mark. For whatever reason, despite my bitchy, moody nature, penchant for late-night junk food binges, obsession with the entire WNBA, and fondness for collecting animals (real ones, not stuffed), Laura had stuck with me. To reward her for her devotion to me, I was going to introduce her to Mr. and Mrs. Uptight, the wonderful couple who raised an intelligent, thoughtful, animal-loving lesbian and were still bewildered by the whole idea that I would not be settling down with the boy next door and popping out a few grandbabies for them to spoil. If this little get-together didn't send Laura running for the hills, grandchildren might still be a possibility.

"Tell me again why we're doing this," Laura said, staring out the window at the scenery, which consisted only of sunshine, scrub brush, flat land, and little old ladies crawling along at ten miles below the speed limit. Florida is a beautiful state, but interstate driving leaves much to be desired.

"As I recall, it was your idea." I moved into the left lane to avoid one of the blue-hairs who seemed more intent on staying between the lines than holding to any particular speed. "In fact, it was you who said, 'Take me to meet your parents.'"

"I think you'd just gotten me off for the fourth time in an hour. I was delirious."

"Exactly. Why else would you want to go see my parents?"

We'd bickered about this trip since I'd called my parents two weeks ago to tell them we were coming. Every time I was sure Laura had changed her mind I'd offer to call and cancel, only to have her change it back. I was starting to get a little annoyed.

"This is the longest drive ever."

I bit my lip and counted to ten before saying anything. "We could have flown, but I know you hate to fly."

"Sorry."

We rode in silence for a little bit. Then Laura started squirming again. "Is that as cold as the air conditioning gets?"

Another familiar argument. "The Mustang is sixteen years old. Yes, that's as cold as it gets. No, it doesn't bother me because I bought it for the convertible top."

Which, I didn't bother mentioning, I hadn't used much since meeting Laura because she was a natural redhead with the pale, easily burned skin to go with the hair.

"Sorry. I'm just bored."

"No kidding."

She let out a sigh that sounded like a slow leak. "I don't want to fight."

I gritted my teeth. "Okay."

She leaned over the center console and put her head on my shoulder. "Really, Jackie. I'm sorry. I'm just nervous."

"It'll be okay." I'd said it so many times, I felt like I should have it tattooed across my forehead. "You just need to relax."

"Stop telling me I need to relax." She was whining now. "I know I need to relax. I just don't know *how* to relax."

I decided we were never going to make it to my parents' house. We were going to have to pull off the side of the road and kill each other. "God, Laura, you're driving me nuts."

I didn't have to look at her to see she was flipping me the bird.

I reached over and smacked her bare thigh. "I saw that."

"Ouch! That hurt." She rubbed her thigh. "I should smack you back."

"Rule number 1: The driver is in charge." It was an old road trip joke, going back to when I was in high school. "Rule number 2: no hitting the driver."

"Very funny."

I spared her a sideways glance. "I'm serious. Now sit over there like a good girl and be quiet."

Something in my voice must have told her I really was serious because she sat back and stayed quiet.

I smirked just a little bit. "Since you need to relax, maybe you should start by loosening up your clothes. It's hard to relax when you're clothes are tight."

Laura stared at me as if I'd grown a second head. "What?"

"Undo your shorts."

"What?" she said, louder.

"I'm trying to help you relax. Undo your shorts."

She hesitated so long I didn't think she was going to do it. Then, slowly, I saw her hands moving at her waist. I heard her pull down the zipper on her khaki shorts. I couldn't keep from smiling now.

"Good girl. Now the tank top."

"What do you want me to do about it?" she asked, her voice just a little breathless.

"Take it off."

"Jackie! I can't!"

She was right, she really couldn't. That was just asking to be pulled over by a cop. "Fine. Pull it up."

That suited her better. She hiked her pink tank top up over her stomach, to just below her breasts. "Okay?"

"Higher."

"Jackie."

"I mean it, Laura. Higher."

She pulled it up, over her breasts. I stared so long I almost ran us off the road.

"Jackie! Shit! You're going to get us killed."

I focused on driving, the image of her perfect, hard, pink nipples ingrained on my brain. "God, you're hot. I just want to pull over and fuck you."

She laughed. "Then we'd never get to your parents' house."

"You'd like that, wouldn't you?"

"Just shut up and drive," she said.

I glanced over quickly and saw she had her hand down her pants. "What are you doing?"

"Jerking off."

I groaned. "Show me."

She didn't hesitate this time. She squirmed and wiggled until her shorts and underwear lay in a pile on the floor. Then she turned toward me and propped one foot on the dashboard. Her cunt glistened, covered with the same beautiful red hair as on her head.

"Damn, girl, I think you want me to get us killed."

"That would keep me from having to meet your parents," she said with a wicked grin.

"You're going to have to do more than flash your coochie, doll." I turned my attention back to the highway. Thankfully, traffic wasn't too heavy. "We'll be there in less than an hour."

I heard a soft whimper and looked over to see that she had two fingers buried inside her. I bit my lip. Hard. The girl was going to be the death of me yet. For once I wished I had cruise control; that would be one less thing for me to concentrate on. As it was, it took all my willpower to stay on the road.

"Mmm," Laura moaned. "Too bad you're driving."

She was finger fucking herself quickly, shoving her fingers in deep and then drawing them out and over her engorged clit. I knew how she would taste if I licked her right then, her clit swollen between my lips, her juices sweet and salty, the skin of her thighs silky soft against my cheeks.

"Go on, baby," I whispered hoarsely. "Fuck yourself."

She did. She twisted in the seat so that her back was against the car door, one foot propped on my headrest, the other wedged up on the dashboard. She was spread wide open and I couldn't do one damn thing except watch. I loved it.

"God, I'm soaked," she said. She slipped her fingers from her cunt and leaned toward me. "Here, taste."

I sucked her fingers between my lips. She was delicious. I kept looking for somewhere I could pull off, throw her in the back seat and fuck her senseless, but there was nowhere to stop on I-95 on a sunny afternoon. I groaned.

"This was your idea," she teased, reading my mind. "Now you just have to watch."

I knew by the change in her voice that her fingers were back inside her cunt. I glanced over, staring so long that I drifted into the next lane. The blare of a horn jerked me back into reality and made Laura gasp.

"Stop that. You're freaking me out."

I had a thought. "Fine, I'll keep my eyes on the road, but you have to let me touch you."

"Sounds dangerous."

"It's safer than teasing me like this," I argued. I didn't know if it was safer, but I knew I couldn't wait another minute to touch her. "Let me get you off."

She didn't say any more as I nudged her hand aside and slid a finger, then two, inside her. She was warm, wet. So wet. She scooted lower in the seat, sliding closer to me. Her left leg was now draped over the car seat, her right leg braced against the dashboard. I pushed a third finger into her and twisted my hand, feeling her G-spot swollen and spongy against my fingertips.

"Oh, there, right there," she gasped as I stroked that sensitive spot. "God, that feels so good."

I kept fucking her, keeping my eyes on the road. I didn't need to see her to fuck her. I could feel her thigh muscles tremble, her cunt clench against my fingers, hear the sweet sounds she made as I angled my hand up and stroked her clit with my thumb. I held the steering wheel in a white-knuckle grip with my left hand and fucked her slowly and steadily with my right.

"Fuck me, fuck me," she muttered, raising her ass off the car seat to thrust her cunt against my hand. "Harder. Please."

I braided my fingers together and drove them into her, fucking her hard and deep, her cunt slick and hot around my hand.

She started to pant, breathing through her mouth like a woman in labor, only she was sucking my fingers into her instead of pushing them out. I was fucking her as hard as I ever had, staring at the highway in front of me and seeing only her cunt in my mind, nearly swallowing my hand.

"That's it. Come for me, baby."

"Yes, yes, yes," she moaned, then screamed. "I'm going to come!"

I looked over then, I couldn't help it. She sounded too fucking amazing to not at least get a glimpse. Her hands were on her breasts, pinching and squeezing her nipples as if she couldn't help but touch herself. Her head was against the window, her back arched, her thighs straining as she thrust her cunt up to my hand. Her whole body was taut, humming with pent-up energy. And then she was coming, her juices soaking my hand, trickling down to wet the seat underneath her. Her cunt felt like a glove around my hand, so hot I could barely stand it.

She gripped my wrist tightly, as if afraid I was going to take my fingers away. I let her guide me, hold me, as her orgasm wrung her out and left her limp.

"Oh, God, oh, God, oh, God," she panted, still holding my wrist and keeping my fingers inside her. "I'm still coming."

I could feel it too. Her cunt rippled around my fingers like an exotic sea creature, clinging to me, wet and swollen. "Oh, baby," I whispered. "God, you're so hot."

She grinned at me, her eyes half closed. She looked like a cat, undulating in the car seat, stretching her limbs in the sunshine. "Thanks. That was amazing."

I withdrew my fingers slowly, hearing her groan of disappointment. My hand throbbed, hot and wet and feeling bruised. I licked my fingers, tasting her clean, salty taste and aching for the moment when I could bury my head between her legs and drink from the source.

She nudged my thigh with her foot. "I'll take care of you later."

"Oh, shit," I said, smacking the steering wheel with my still wet hand. "Shit, shit, shit."

Laura sat up, jerking down her tank top even while she swiveled around in the seat. "What? Cop? What?"

"No," I sighed. "I missed the exit."

M

AUNT FANNY

The heart was tattooed on her right breast. Only the women she fucked ever saw it.

It was empty, outlined in vermillion with a sexy little tail tickling the curve of her. Inside was the single letter M painted the same deep red. Up close a person could just make out the words I'LL KNOW HER WHEN I FIND HER in light pink ink running along the plump left side of the heart. It was quite an artistic valentine, almost three inches in diameter, and she kept the colors bright. Unusual for anyone, it was incongruously out of place on the rock-hard butch.

Ram never explained it, no matter who asked her or how tender the moment. "I did it when I was young," was all she'd offer. "I got drunk and wound up with this."

"Is the *M* for mother?" asked Mary.

"It's a woman's name, isn't it?" inquired Miranda.

"Don't you know her already?" questioned Misty.

"Did you have a vision or something? How do you know her name will begin with an M?" begged Marigold. "Is it me?"

Ram never talked about it and had in fact perfected a technique guaranteed to switch the topic in a hurry. Since she was invariably naked when the subject arose, and it was a given that her partner was too. Naked flesh can be a persuasive thing, and Ram's was decorated with dozens of tattooed images. By undulating the colorful hills and valleys of her body's skillful designs, she would use her tongue to effectively silence her partner. It would be a day or so later before her lover's head cleared enough to realize she still didn't know who the mysterious M was.

At thirty-five Ram was comfortable with her life. She spent her days bagging and running stock for the local superstore, her evenings singing in karaoke competitions at bars throughout seven counties. Her truck was the most expensive thing she owned, the pride of her life. At twenty she'd promised herself when she made twice as much singing as she did working, she'd quit her day job. Fifteen years later she still wasn't close, but it had become a way of life and both incomes kept her comfortable in what little time off she allowed herself. Standing six feet plus, she was tall, muscular, and sturdy. If she didn't work out every day she grew plump.

The blond-haired, blue-eyed giant's appetites were legendary. She was voracious in everything she did. Her passion for life was a fixed part of her personality. Ram took big juicy bites out of life, and everyone who met her soon knew it. She maintained her chis- eled physique with the same iron will she turned on any object of her desire.

Women lucky enough to draw special attention from her soon knew what it meant to be thoroughly romanced. Intimacy would be established gradually, sensually, growing normally in the natu- ral expression of playful fun. Thoughtful gifts became suggestive ones. She was spontaneous and creative, so Ram's women were treated to weeks of classy restaurants, picnics in the park, elegant evenings, nights cuddled up in front of the TV, fabulous sporting events, and barefoot strolls along moonlit beaches. When they finally tumbled into bed together, it was always beyond fabulous, earth-shattering, and addictive as hell. And it only happened once.

Immediately after she bedded a woman Ram would move on. No one could complain, exactly, as she never promised anything except pleasure, but many a confused woman woke a week after finally succumbing to the handsome butch's seduction wondering where her perfect lover had gone. Two weeks after their fuck, a small brooch of a ram's head in profile, fashioned in gold with a single ruby eye, would be delivered in a black velvet box. It was months before Ram would start another courtship. For years she had found romance, she'd found lust, but love proved ever elusive.

Mimi Mimieux arrived with all the spectacular pomp and circumstance that accompanies a new high femme. The minute she passed through the door of the small upscale gay pub hosting the karaoke competition Ram was entering, a hush swept over the room. Breaths were unconsciously held as every female eye devoured the vision that had just entered, and every male eye measured, weighed, and critiqued to exacting standards until thoroughly impressed. A lady of her own making had arrived, and those who saw her sat up straighter.

Dressed in a tea-length sleeveless gown of midnight blue that set off her luscious figure to perfection, the beautiful woman crossed the room casually on elegant legs elongated by four-inch pumps. She was comfortable, as if accustomed to stares, and her hips swung unselfconsciously. The fluidity of her movements spoke eloquently of an athletic background, perhaps gymnastics or dance. Dark, sleek, glossy hair was swept up into a neat French twist, drawing the eye up a slender neck to a beautiful heart-shaped face. Her powder-blue eyes and pearly teeth flashed in easy smiles from side to side, royalty greeting her loyal subjects. Ram met those flashing eyes for a moment, and knew the game was on.

A small rope in her gut tied itself firmly into a knot as she watched the petite femme from across the room. When she saw the waitress take her order, Ram was up and off her seat in a second, quickly threading the room to intercept the waitress and pay for the drink. When she saw it arrive at the table and the waitress's explanation caused the mysterious woman to glance her way in acknowledgment, she raised her own glass in salute. The lady smiled encouragingly.

A few minutes later Ram made her way up to Herschel, the disc jockey in charge of the competition, and registered. The top prize money was a lucrative thousand dollars, which guaranteed some solid competition, and second place was a juicy five hundred. She took her entry slip receipt back to her seat and sipped her gin and tonic, watching the beauty surreptitiously, mentally preparing herself for competition. Both of them.

Ram was pleased to see the lovely lady step up to Herschel later and sign up for the competition. Good: That meant her name would be announced when she was introduced. Ram planned to be magnanimous in victory, generous with her praise. As she'd learned years ago, it never hurts to flatter a woman.

She was as accustomed to winning these karaoke contests as the beauty was to being watched. When Ram sang she usually won. Only once in her years of competition had she lost, when her throat closed suddenly after eating a mysterious spice in a new Thai restaurant. She expected to take home some prize money.

Herschel knew Ram by name and was glad to introduce her as his first contestant, comfortable with her abilities to open his show with a bang. The karaoke world was not a large one. Talent like hers was rare. He expected her to win too.

Hopping up on the stage, Ram took the mic from his hand and waited through the musical intro, tapping one well-shod foot and running her free hand through her hair as she stepped into character. Ram's long rangy body, clad easily in dress slacks, a black shirt, silver tie, and jacket, sleeves shoved casually up to the elbow, emulated the intricate dragon tattooed around her wrist. She swayed easily to the rhythm of "The Lady Is a Tramp." Her strong, mellifluous alto voice filled the small bar, chasing every nook and cranny free of stale whispers of love and tattered shadows of lust.

Her rich, profound sound was absorbed by her audience, stirring their passion for music along with her own. It was an old karaoke standard, but she performed it well and knew it intimately. Ram sang with a passion born of desire, her sexual interest directed through the darkness to the beautiful stranger yet resounding in everyone listening.

Halfway through, women who'd seen her perform before started coming forward to offer dollar bills, and as the song progressed even a few men came up. Ram stretched out her hand to accept the money, but never paused in the performance of her song. She was there to sing, not to pander. If they brought it forward and offered it politely, she accepted it. It nearly tore her eyes from their sockets to turn briskly away from the beautiful stranger when she suddenly appeared at the edge of the stage holding out a ten spot. Sweeping the bill up and continuing along the edge of the stage, Ram felt her stomach lurch out of her belly to remain at the feet of the gorgeous femme. Apparently the feeling was mutual. The woman stood rooted in place until the end of the song, her eyes following Ram's every move, and only then returned to her table.

Ram felt flushed with success as she crossed the dark room to retake her seat and listen to her fellow competitors. Long ago she'd learned to put a polite smile on her face no matter what sounds came from the microphones during competitions. She'd heard it all: screeches and squawks, whispers and husks, off-key and tone deaf. Sometimes people moved as awkwardly as they sang. It wasn't easy not to laugh, but Ram would never make fun of someone brave enough to get up on stage and put themselves out there. It cost her each time she did it, knowing her studied casualness to be a lie. She was always a nervous wreck for at least twenty minutes following a performance. A roar of white noise filled her ears as she internally critiqued herself. She was her own harshest critic.

Luckily, Mimi Mimieux did not perform until almost an hour later. By that time Ram had recovered enough to have a pen handy when she was introduced, scribbling her name on a cocktail napkin. The big blond settled back, crossed one lanky leg over the other, and fixed a pleasant smile on her face to listen to the woman upon whom she'd set her sights.

Mimi took the stage with a swirl of her midnight blue skirt. The shaped bodice of her dress was sleeveless and low cut, revealing the creamy skin of full breasts, plump and inviting. A long-fingered, elegant hand took hold of the microphone and Mimi began to sing.

Many women have sung "When You're Good to Mama" and some have come close to capturing its message of mutual self-interest. The good ones make its cynicism humorous. Mimi's clear, resonant tones pushed them all aside.

Her compelling vocals mastered the strains of harmony and drumming rhythm to create sunshine in an underworld, lightness in the dark. Matron Mama Morton walked that stage, lush hips swaying, breasts heaving, her body selling sex for favors expressively. A marriage of sound and physicality dawned on that stage, and the audience was totally enraptured by the magic of Mimi's talent.

Ram wasn't aware she'd stopped breathing until the last note faded away and she found herself gasping for air. Thunderous applause threw a spotlight on the slight femme as she strolled calmly back to her table, smiling from side to side. Ram sat at her table, watching the little lady receive her accolades while she sipped her drink and plotted. She needed a smooth move.

Waiting impatiently for the next singer to squeak his way through "It's Raining Men," she planned what to say. It would be easy to be generous with praise, it was the unvarnished truth. Just as Ram was rising to make her way through the thrust-out chairs and casually draped limbs between herself and her objective, she heard Herschel say with distinct pleasure, "We have a tie." She sank back into her seat, turning to stare at the man at the mic.

"The judges have decided we need a run off to determine the winner of tonight's prize money, so we're going to have a half-hour break now, and when we come back we'll hear Ram and Mimi both sing again. We'll all just have to wait awhile longer for the results of tonight's competition." Recorded music blared, and the usual noise of friendly conversation rose steadily. The clinking of glass sounded all around the pub as new rounds were ordered. No one wanted to leave until after the finale—both women were that good.

Ram turned back to face Mimi's table, but she was gone. Quickly scanning the room, she saw the beauty disappearing toward the ladies room, near the kitchen. Up and walking before she gave herself time to think, the lanky butch crossed the room in a few steps. She burst through the bathroom door, waited impatiently, and watched for Mimi as the stalls gradually emptied. She wasn't there.

Leaving the restroom, Ram scanned the small upscale pub quickly. A flash of midnight blue was disappearing out the back door. She hurried after it.

Outside in the parking lot Ram found no one, only shadows thrown by the glare of streetlights. Looking left, looking right, she couldn't see Mimi anywhere. The area was deserted.

"Over here, Rambo," came her voice from the dark. The tall blond looked around, still unable to place the sound. "In the flatbed of your truck."

Ram wheeled around and stared in the direction where she'd parked. Sure enough, there was Mimi sitting in the darkness of her truck bed.

"How'd you know which one was mine?" The butch ambled over, casual now. Time to reestablish a little control over the situation.

"Oh, c'mon. Your name is Ram. The way you look you're sure to drive a truck, and this was the only Dodge Ram in the parking lot. It's not rocket science. I'm good at figuring out riddles." Mimi sat back in the darkness and patted the area next to her. "Join me."

Ram clambered up to sit beside the pretty femme. Even though she was sitting next to the woman of her choice in her own truck, Ram felt anything but in control. An odd fluttering was teasing the knot in her belly.

"Would you like a breast?" asked the beauty, the non sequitur knocking the wind out of the butch. Mimi laughed at Ram's look of confusion, then whipped out a foil-wrapped plate of the pub's fried chicken. "Or are you a leg woman?"

Ram laughed heartily as she reached for a plump chicken breast and bit down, tearing the meat with her teeth. She grinned wolfishly around the delicious food filling her mouth. Chewing thoughtfully she asked, "So you know the way to a butch's heart is through her belly, eh?"

"Let's just say I know a woman of sensual pleasure when I see one," countered the petite beauty, helping herself to a chicken leg. She nibbled on it daintily, enjoying the butch's large bites. "Singing works up an appetite, doesn't it?"

"It sure does," answered Ram before looking quickly at her

watch. "We've only got twenty more minutes." She finished the piece of chicken she was eating and gratefully took the napkin offered by Mimi, wiping her lips and chin. "I haven't even thought about which song to sing next."

"I have," answered Mimi, replacing the foil around the plate of chicken and putting it aside. Turning back to Ram she wrapped both arms around the butch's neck and leaned in, pressing rich full breasts against smaller, restrained ones. "Kiss me," she demanded.

Ram thought briefly about pushing her back, following her life long pattern of restraint and courtship. She'd ask for a date, slow the whole thing down a little. Then she realized she had a beautiful, willing woman in her arms demanding to be kissed. She complied willingly.

Warm soft lips met, caressing. Ram lingered sensually on Mimi's plump bottom lip, nibbling on it for a long moment. The femme sighed in her arms and nestled impatiently down in the bed of the truck until she'd pulled Ram down alongside her. Ram responded by refusing to deepen the kiss, keeping it at her own pace. Her lips grazed Mimi's, tongue tantalizing until the femme's lips parted eagerly, but still she meandered. Mimi countered by grabbing Ram's hand and pulling it to her breast, kneading it firmly around her plump flesh.

Unbidden, Ram's tongue plunged deeply into Mimi's mouth. Her hand explored the weight and heft of Mimi's breasts through the fabric of her dress and bra. Large nipples jumped to attention under the ministrations of her thumb. The butch settled in for a nice long petting session.

Suddenly Mimi reached behind herself and unzipped her dress, then pulled the shoulders of both her dress and bra down to her waist, freeing her breasts, to Ram's delighted eyes.

"Oh, my God," breathed the butch, dazzled by the beauty spread before her and barely visible in the darkness of the parking lot. She half sat up and stared around the area intensely, making sure they were alone before lowering herself into the lush flesh offered her. "We shouldn't be doing this," she murmured before she nuzzled Mimi's cleavage, running her tongue back and forth between perfect mounds. Using her hands she cupped both large breasts and dove between them, inhaling deeply of the femme's scent. "It isn't safe."

"I'm willing to take my chances," answered Mimi as she threaded her fingers through the butch's blond hair. She rolled from side to side lightly as Ram played with her breasts, reveling in the freedom of the cool night air, the risk of exposure, the exhilaration of possible danger. Noise from traffic on the street swept over them as she gasped when the butch's firm lips captured one nipple, nibbling and pulling at the exposed skin. Ram's tongue snaked around it, sucked it deep within her mouth, then released it to the sudden chill of fresh air.

Her lips were zeroing in on the other exposed nipple when Mimi said, "Are you packing?" Feeling once again yanked off her feet, Ram pulled back enough to nod her head.

"Fuck me," demanded Mimi. The dark tender skin of her nipples wrinkled in the cool night air, making it very difficult for Ram to wrench her attention to the task of rising to her knees, unzipping her fly, and releasing her cock from packing briefs and trousers. By the time she sank back on her knees Mimi had worked her way out of her shoes, hose, and panties, tossing them casually aside. Their eyes met and lust flared forcefully between them. Mimi opened her arms invitingly.

"Love me," commanded the femme. She spread her legs and pulled her skirt up over her waist, exposing herself completely to Ram's hungry view. Then she flipped herself over onto all four and once again tossed her skirt up over her waist, now exposing a perfect bottom. "Doggie style." She lowered her head and wriggled her upraised ass in the butch's direction.

That knotted rope deep in Ram's belly tugged her up behind the femme in an instant, both hands reaching out to caress the swelling curve of hips and ass. Her right hand slid between the soft skin of Mimi's thighs, spreading them wider. She presented the dildo's head to the dark-haired lips pouting just below the out thrust bottom. Nudging them apart, Ram firmly pushed the dildo in only an inch until she heard Mimi moan, then began milking her for moisture. She ran her free hand over the beautiful bottom before her, then reached around and down to grab two handfuls of breast, forcing another moan from the woman below.

As Mimi opened for her, Ram began a thrusting of her hips, increasing in steady rhythm as she piled in deeper. Hands stroked the femme's skin along her pale back, past her narrow waist and along her white, sloped shoulders where she finally anchored herself. Ram steadied herself on her knees and began a strong thrusting of her hips, soon releasing Mimi's shoulders and reaching eagerly for her engorged clit. She found it pulsing in the cool night air5 and swallowed it with her thick fingers. She pulled the swollen flesh, rolling it between fingers moistened by Mimi's own juices.

Ram used her knees to spread Mimi's wider. She leaned over the smaller woman, running her free hand back and forth from breast to clit. Her hips rocked easily back and forth, the dildo plunging in and out. In front of Ram's entranced eyes Mimi's beautiful bottom undulated up and down, then circled around and around as she eagerly sucked in the pleasure Ram offered her. The big butch leaned close and nibbled her neck while her free fingers pushed in on her clit. With a long drawn shudder, Mimi exploded in orgasm, rocking the truck bed back and forth wildly with her bucking. Ram held on, enjoying the ride.

Pulling out then pushing the beautiful woman beneath her down onto her stomach, Ram rolled her over until she could capture her lips. They kissed as the night air cooled their raging skin. Mimi's fingers began fumbling with the silicone cock. Questing fingers dipped beneath the edges.

"What are you doing?" asked Ram, lazily.

"I'm going to return the favor," answered Mimi, pushing her fingers farther below the dildo, into the blond curls of Ram's sex. The femme let a knowing smile curve her sexy lips as she found the butch's own wetness, a testimony to her desire. "Just lie back and enjoy it."

Mimi's finger glided into and out of Ram as she forced herself to relax. It went against her nature to allow this kind of one-sided action, but it felt so good. The knot in her belly had that excited fluttering around it again, and the blond descended into the erotic arms of herself.

Completely clothed, her dildo exposed to the cool night air, Ram leaned back against the cab and spread her legs for the woman she desired. Mimi reached deep inside her trousers, inserting first one, then a second, and finally a third finger, stretching the butch as far as she could go. Ram let a deep growl escape as she watched the pretty femme switch back to her knees, again throwing her skirt up so the butch could enjoy her naked bottom. Ram reached out one long arm and grabbed a cheek. This time Mimi growled.

Mimi's head descended into Ram's lap but bypassed the dildo altogether, much to Ram's secret relief. After all, silicone has no nerve endings. Instead, the pretty femme's head nuzzled directly into her lap, urging her to lie down lower still. Finally, Mimi's searching lips found their objective, Ram's eagerly waiting clit. The butch's free hand pushed the femme's head down deeper, sighing luxuriously as she took the hint.

Mimi swallowed her, taking in all of her clit and tonguing it relentlessly while the three fingers inside began a thrusting all their own. Ram's hand tightened on Mimi's bottom cheek, squeezing enthusiastically. Her fucking finger started a search of it's own.

The luscious femme's talented mouth stopped sucking for only a breath of time as Ram's finger thrust into her asshole. Her small gasp delighted the butch, who kept an easy in and out motion going while the femme tormented her with tongue, teeth, lips and fingers. It wasn't long before the wave of inevitability took her, throwing her up and over the top, sliding down in smaller and smaller crescendos.

Mimi's flesh twitched beneath Ram's big hand after the butch climaxed, and she soon found the femme's naked bottom lying across her lap encouragingly. Ram rose up and obliged with two healthy spanks, one on each exposed bottom cheek, followed by six smarter slaps spread across both cheeks at once. Then she grabbed Mimi's bottom and pulled it wide, exposing her tender, hotly gasping asshole to the cool night air.

"Yes, please," urged Mimi, so Ram's fucking finger reinserted itself in Mimi's asshole. Then her thumb found her pussy, causing a hungry gasp to escape the upended femme. Soon both fingers were working in harmony, bringing the luscious woman over her lap to orgasm, not once but twice as Ram continued to spank her. Mimi let loose a howl of sheer animal lust into the deep streets of the night. She raised herself off Ram's lap, then lowered herself once more onto the dildo, riding the butch. Her breasts bounced lusciously in Ram's face as the erotically charged woman chased a third orgasm and found it.

They were still sitting that way when the back door of the bar opened. "Ram? Mimi? Either of you out here?" they heard Herschel call. Mimi grabbed Ram's wrist and twisted it until she could read the watch.

"We're already ten minutes late getting back," she giggled, hurriedly rearranging her bra, then dress. She looked at her stockings and panties, then shrugged and handed them to Ram, who shoved them in her pocket.

The butch clambered over the side of the truck first, then turned and offered her hand to the barefooted femme, clearing her throat, determined to ask. She wanted to see more of this fascinating woman. "Mimi," she started as the femme steadied herself against Ram to slip her wicked pumps back on, "can I see you again?"

"Love to," answered the luscious femme firmly as she tugged on the big butch's hand and pulled, "but we'll talk later. We're late." They hurried across the parking lot.

"We're here!" she called to Herschel, after they made a quick trip to the bathroom. Relieved, he nevertheless took the time to point to his watch. Ram waved laconically at him as she took her seat once more, leaving Mimi to take the stage. At least she'd thought of a song to sing.

Ram watched, unable to tear her eyes away from Mimi as she whispered her song to Herschel. It seemed impossible to her that she had been enjoying that gorgeous woman only moments before. With a shock she realized that for once the knot in her belly had not untied. An insatiable hunger shook her as she watched Mimi wait through her musical intro on the stage. She wanted to see the beautiful femme under her again, writhing with pleasure.

Mimi began the gay anthem "I Will Survive," and the line, "Did you think I'd lay down and die? / Oh, no, not I!" caused Ram and the enthusiastic audience to leap to their feet with her encouragement, soon singing along with her. This was a technical violation of the competition, but it felt right and the place rocked. As the song ended the audience erupted into ecstatic applause. Mimi bowed twice, then left the stage to Ram.

Thinking quickly, Ram stepped up and whispered, " 'Lay, Lady, Lay,' please, Herschel." She tried to find Mimi in the group still crowding the stage, but couldn't locate her. Knowing she was listening in there somewhere Ram let her heart lead as she sang, "Lay, lady, lay / Lay across my big brass bed / Stay, lady, stay…"

Enthusiastic faces watched and listened from every direction, but still she couldn't see the object of her affection. Too many people were crowding around, and she couldn't see a scrap of midnight blue anywhere. Mimi was nowhere to be seen.

Pouring her soul into her song, Ram willed the beautiful femme to appear. Never before had she known such a fascinating woman, one who kept her so delightedly off-center. Every note rang with her wonder, desire, intrigue, and the passion that swelled in her breast at the thought of her new love. She sang for Mimi alone, finally opening her heart and offering it up. "Stay, lady, stay," she begged.

The last note died away. Ram searched the audience frantically as once again they exploded into wild applause. Vainly she looked, even when the applause died down and they returned to their seats, waiting for Mimi to rejoin her on stage. Instead, Herschel stepped up.

"Oddly enough," he began, "the competition has been decided by one of the participants herself. Mimi Mimieux has withdrawn from tonight's contest, with her regrets." A stunned gasp rose from the audience while the knot in Ram's belly twisted cruelly. "Which means the one-thousand-dollar prize goes to Ram!"

White noise crashed down all around her. She accepted the prize envelope and the congratulations of those around her numbly. Reaching Herschel, she asked about Mimi. He shrugged. "She left you something. It's with the check."

Staggering to her seat she ripped open the envelope, pushed aside the pub's check impatiently, and studied the small brooch that tumbled into her open palm. It was a gold ram's head in profile with a single ruby eye. Pulling out a folded note, she read:

Dear Miriam,

Yes, I know your real name. You whispered it to me once in a game of Truth or Dare.

We met five years ago at a competition much like this one. I was a blond then, fifty pounds heavier, rather bookish and shy. You courted me well, then fucked me better, but when I woke up the next morning you were gone. Two weeks later this cold token of your esteem arrived.

You helped me face things about myself I did not like. I learned how to love myself. I hope I've returned that favor, with this, tonight.

I've deciphered your tattoo. The "M" stands for "Miriam" or "Me". Your empty valentine is the metaphor of your life. You lock yourself in an empty heart so you cannot love others.

When you want to rejoin the human race, use this prize money to have your tattoo filled in. Only with a full heart can you offer yourself to a woman.

Never forget me.

The letter was signed simply, "—*M.*"

There Really Is a Kalamazoo

THERESE SZYMANSKI

The strobe lighting of the dance floor played across her lustrous dark hair, making highlights appear where there were none. Her dark eyes met mine across the table while a sultry grin lit her full lips.

We had first met online a year before. We had tried to hook up then, but things kept standing in the way, and in the meantime we had each met someone else. But still, sometimes things just must happen.

"You are even more beautiful than your pictures," I said, leaning forward so she could hear me over the music. My lips could almost brush her ear. But I behaved.

She leaned back just enough so her eyes could easily wander over me, sizing me up. "And you're everything I knew you would be." It had been a long time since we last spoke. I had been on a business trip to Oregon, and we had incredibly hot phone sex, started by my reading a scene from my latest book to her.

Her new girlfriend, Paula, didn't dance and apparently didn't know our history, so I was allowed to partner Leslie on the dance floor. The friends I was visiting in Kalamazoo, Michigan, obligingly kept Paula's attention so Leslie and I could dance more closely during the sexier songs.

Leslie pulled away from me and went to our table. She picked up her drink, a Sloe Comfortable Screw, and took a long, deep sip, watching me all the while. I picked up my Miller longneck and killed it, keeping my eyes on her.

She leaned down and deliberately kissed Paula on the lips, then walked away. I nonchalantly lifted my empty bottle and asked loudly, "Anyone need a refill?" I waited only a moment and started toward the bar, switching direction en route to go to the ladies room instead. Inside, I walked up behind her and laid a hand on her shoulder.

She turned to face me. "It's nice to find a butch who can take a hint. But can you be trained as well?" She grabbed my leather vest in one hand and drew me close, wrapping both arms around my neck and drawing me in for a long deep kiss. Our bodies melded together perfectly, her arms and one leg enveloping me as I pushed her back against the wall. "God, I had to know," she moaned when my hands grabbed her hips and pulled them against my leg. I ran my lips down her soft neck and then bit.

"Hey, you going, or are you just going to get a room?" a woman behind us asked, indicating the stall that had just been vacated.

I pulled away from Leslie and laid a glare on the woman. Leslie headed for the stall. Just before the door shut, I pushed it open and stepped in, latching it behind me.

"Like I said, you can take a hint, but can you be trained?"

"I can be anything you'd like me to be," I replied, pushing her against the door and claiming her mouth again for my own. I ran my hands down to her hips, enjoying the gentle swell, and kissed her neck. Then I grabbed her ass and pulled it toward me with one hand while the other hand yanked the zipper on her tight jeans down.

"Paula's just outside."

"But aren't there other things you have to know as well?" I quickly undid the buttons on her blouse and slipped the front clasp on her bra, exposing her velvety white breasts. "God, you are so beautiful," I whispered, caressing the naked flesh and quickly working the pink nipples into hardened buds.

She ground her crotch against my thigh and I lowered myself, first licking her nipples, one at a time, then biting them and rolling them between my teeth one at a time. She entwined her hands in my hair, yanking my head upward. Our lips found each other's again in a fevered kiss, then I dropped to my knees in one swift movement and pulled her jeans and underwear all the way down.

I didn't have time to strip her so I made do by kissing her inner thighs while I caressed her stomach, torso, and breasts.

"Please," she moaned, her hands still tightly wound in my hair, pulling my head toward her cunt.

I stopped, my hands on her hips, and looked up at her. "I always let my femme tell me what to do—except during sex." I deliberately lifted my head to run my tongue up her stomach and over her breasts.

"Please…now!" she whispered in fevered readiness.

"Patience, gorgeous." I nibbled again at a nipple, and then, when she was reaching desperation, I dropped one hand down to very briefly caress her wetness before plunging two fingers up into her. She gasped and her knees nearly buckled. I stood and wrapped one hand around her waist while I continued to fuck her with the other. Our breath was hot on each other's face.

I put my thumb to use on her clit, my fingers still inside her. I played her back and forth, working faster and faster, till I dropped to my knees in front of her. I held her hips in my hands. "Open yourself for me," I ordered. Knees trembling, breath coming in gasps, she reached down and used her thumbs to open her lips.

I kept my hands on her hips, supporting her, and buried my face between her long legs. She tasted as good as I thought she would. And I let her know it.

She lowered herself slightly, pushing herself harder and further into my mouth. I raised my hands to cup her breasts, squeezing the nipples hard between my thumbs and forefingers. Then I released her left nipple so I could use those fingers to fuck her. This time I started with three fingers, lubricating them first in her juices, sliding my fingers across her wetness even as I ran my tongue over her swollen clit.

When she came, my entire fist was inside of her, my head buried between her thighs. She collapsed down onto me, and when she was down, I stood, pulling her into my arms. I kissed her. Deeply. "We had to know."

She ran a finger over my mouth, wet with her. "Give your girlfriend a kiss for me."

Product Shoot

MICHELLE SINCLAIR

Chloe was on the verge of being officially late; bad form considering this was her first chance to work with Allison Chevier, currently the biggest name in commercial photography. Chloe had been recommended to Ms. Chevier by one of her favorite professors in photography school, the same school Ms. Chevier attended seven years earlier. She had just finished an M.S. in photography, but even with the glowing recommendation she received from her professor, Chloe was picked for the shoot only after Ms. Chevier's regular assistant had phoned in, unable to work because of a death in the family. The shoot involved photographing a line of holistic body therapy products created by a small, well-funded company based in Bern, Switzerland. The owner had specifically hired Allison Chevier to do the shoot, agreeing to ship out a full collection of products totaling fifty samples to be photographed in six days; the company was launching a major advertising campaign within the month.

Ms. Chevier had a private studio in Santa Barbara, located in an area of town know as the Funk Zone. Santa Barbara has a reputation of being home to "the newly wed or nearly dead" but if one is to take a closer look there is culture and a small budding arts community buzzing just below the surface, centered within the Funk Zone.

Chloe pulled into a parking space a block from Ms. Chevier's studio. She quickly gathered her equipment and walked towards the entrance of a tall, nondescript one-story building—flat gray in color with a corrugated steel awning protruding just beyond the wall facing the street. A light coating of perspiration cooled her arms and the back of her neck, reflecting a low luminescence as she walked away from the sun towards the studio. As she approached the entrance, the only discernable marking identifying the studio was a small sign depicting the numbers 345. As Chloe moved closer she noticed the 345 was actually an 8-by-10 black-and-white framed print, a nice detail, she thought, for a photography studio. She reached the door and made a motion to turn the handle but to her surprise the door was locked. To the right was a doorbell, and buzzing it she waited about thirty seconds before a young woman with short jet-black bobbed hair and bangs, black eyeliner, thick red painted lips, wearing a fifties-style full-length mauve dress and ankle-high black boots opened the door.

"Hi, my name is Chloe Patterson. I'm here to assist Ms. Allison Chevier."

"Yes, of course," said the girl, pausing a moment, her eyes brightening. "I'm Ashley, the studio manager. We've been expecting you. Please follow me."

Chloe recognized the look by the immediate rush of butterflies fluttering in her stomach. It was a familiar look, one she had been trying to ignore for so many years, ever since the time she was playing with a young friend. They were both in the second grade at the time. Little Christy was her very first best friend and the one to have the longest lasting impact on Chloe's life. As children they were inseparable. If one was playing at school the other was right there beside her. They had sleepovers, spent weekends and weekdays together, even played on the same dodgeball team together. One day in particular, while they were playing with their dolls, Christy began to relate a story she had heard from some older kids, how girls have something and boys have something else. Chloe's first thought was *What do you mean, something else?* She was perplexed by the thought of a difference, but even at such a young age her curiosity remained fixated on what it was the girls had. She knew, by the sheer fact that she was a girl, but this did not dissuade her true feelings. As Christy finished describing what she had heard, she asked Chloe if she wanted to compare. This excited Chloe, and led by innocence and curiosity she agreed to share. It was at the moment Chloe had shown hers and Christy looked down that Chloe felt a type of love, one she always wanted to share in. Because at that moment Christy smiled, sharing a "you are beautiful" kind of look, a look Chloe would recognize from that day forward. Over time, though, she grew to believe, as many do, that those feelings were to be reserved for the opposite sex, and Chloe in her desire to act appropriately, denied what she knew to be true.

She followed Ashley into the studio. The room opened up with tall ceilings, two desks facing the door, Macs set up on both desks, and various stacks of paperwork and other office products filling the bulk of each desk's surface. On the wall to the right of the door hung a series of three 20-by-24 black-and-white photographs comprising a triptych of urban landscape scenes. Odd characters filled the images, positioned between decrepit automobiles, standing on dirty sidewalks next to old grocery carts. One photograph showed two junkies, track marks visible, passed out on an old mattress lying against a chain link fence. Chloe could feel the stark, cold loneliness of each piece. It reminded her of the work of Robert Frank.

"Did Ms. Chevier shoot those images over there?"

Ashley laughed at the question. "Chloe, please address Allison by her first name. The public and her clients refer to her as Ms. Chevier, but the girls working in the studio refer to her simply as Allison. She prefers it that way."

Her cheeks flushed. "Yes, of course, Allison."

"And yes, Allison creates fine art as well as the commercial stuff."

Chloe felt her shoulders relax, a small wave of calm enveloping her body. *It's good to see work outside of the commercial realm,* she thought to herself. Her experience in graduate school had been strictly devoted to the technical aspect of photography, everything geared towards the commercial world, which was exactly what she was looking for to balance her undergraduate experience. She attended one class that feigned fine art, but in the end it was just a bunch of tech geeks, for the most part, pretending to work conceptually. The first "critique" for the class found her classmates mortified by the prospect of presenting work to be scrutinized, behavior that would have sent each of them to the door in her undergraduate fine arts program.

"I must admit I am relieved to see that Allison is involved in fine art."

"Believe me," Ashley said, "if Allison could make the same money doing that as she does for commercial, we wouldn't be shooting beauty products today."

Ashley continued to lead Chloe through the front office into the main studio. Even taller ceilings opened up into a space two to three times the size of the front office. Primer-gray walls, each supporting two windows apiece, broke the monotony, save for the thick black drapes covering them, impenetrable to the outside light. In the middle of the studio stood a wooden platform supporting a 4-by-8 piece of opaque white Plexiglas, sanded down to remove what was once a glossy surface, creating a matte finish. The Plexiglas lay flat for the first four feet and bent upward, eventually to a ninety-degree angle at the end to create a sweep. The effect produced a white background, and when lit properly the eye focused completely on the product, the background being virtually invisible. Three lights positioned relative to the four corners of the sweep provided all the illumination necessary for the shoot. A tripod with a digital camera stood just in front of the flat end of the sweep, a cable leading from the camera directly to a laptop. Each shot would be viewed on the computer as it was taken, testing exposure, and then it would be run through Photoshop as necessary. Chloe was so busy studying the layout she failed to notice the woman sitting at the computer, intently working on completing the final tasks before they could begin.

"Allison. *Allison*?"

Allison broke from her work to look up. "Ashley, what is it?"

"This," pointing to Chloe, "is Chloe."

Allison stood up and took a deep breath, trying to clear her head, mumbling to herself, "Okay, time to be social."

Chloe, fists clenched, standing completely erect, walked over to where Allison was standing and stuck out her hand. "Hi, I'm Chloe Patterson. I'll be your assistant for the next couple of days…" Her speech trailed off, her arm losing its rigidity, hand becoming limp.

Allison attempted to say something, but missed a beat as she looked at the beautiful woman standing before her—curly shoulder-length hair, soft lips, warm hazel eyes, breasts accentuated just enough by her slightly moist tank top to allow the imagination to roam. She fumbled her words for a moment, but regaining her composure she cleared her throat. "Hello, I'm Allison Chevier. Nice to meet you."

A pause ensued, both women intently watching each other, each trying in vain to maintain an air of professionalism. But for the life of her Chloe could not look away. Allison's eyes, colored with the vibrancy of a Van Gogh, invited her in and embraced her with a passion that in the end made her blush with embarrassment.

Without looking away Allison finally spoke up. "Okay, Ashley, thank you. We'll take it from here."

Ashley had witnessed Allison smitten with her assistants before, but never to this degree. "Okay," Ashley said, winking to herself as she walked towards the door. "I'll be out front taking care of business."

The sound of the studio door closing as Ashley made her exit snapped Allison back to focus. "So, Chloe, I see you made it here all right."

"Yeah, um, I mean yes, my boyfriend dropped me off."

"Your boyfriend, huh? What's his name?"

Chloe's hands were sweating, and goose bumps were raising the hairs on her arms. "His name?"

"Yes, your boyfriend. What's his name?"

Chloe furrowed her brow. "Yes, his name. Oh, his name—his name is Jonathan."

Chloe could feel an energy build inside. She could feel antici-

pation welling up, an overwhelming feeling of excitement beginning to take hold of her senses. She took a long, slow deep breath,
in through her nose out through her mouth. Waves were beginning
to seize her attention as if she were "coming on," the initial rush of
an ecstasy trip.

Allison looked at her new friend with wide eyes, taking deep
breaths. "Are you okay?"

The question brought Chloe back for a moment; embarrassed,
she composed herself as best she could. "Yes, I'm sorry. I'm just a
little nervous."

Allison could feel the energy as well. A definite spark was in the
air; but she wanted to get a handle on the situation. They had work
to do.

"Why don't we start with the camera? Have you used the 1DS
before?"

Chloe took another breath. "I had an orientation class, but honestly I haven't had the opportunity to really work with one."

"No problem. Why don't you come over, and I'll give you a
quick lesson." Chloe walked over and sat down behind the camera.
Allison positioned herself behind Chloe, pointing out different
functions but allowing Chloe to get the hands-on experience.

Chloe, fully intent to bring her focus back to the work at hand,
practiced with the focus, the aperture, and the battery case as
Allison watched.

"What is this button for?"

Allison came up behind Chloe and peered over her shoulder to
look at what she was curious about. The view of the button was
shadowed by Chloe's hand prompting Allison to reach over her
shoulder and direct it to the side. The first touch was simply too
much for Chloe to endure. It drove her to the brink, a lifetime of
denial refusing to be quelled for even a moment longer. She stood
up slowly, turned and drove her lips into the warm thick embrace
of Allison. There was no denying it for either of them. They kissed,
both experiencing a sense of being out of control, each of them
moving to create new positions, lips continually touching but at

varying angles and with a myriad of intensities. The natural flow and ease with which they danced was almost too much for Chloe. But she ran with it, taking the lead after a short while, gently biting Allison's upper lip and then her lower, kissing from the side of her mouth, tongue searching for ever more points of contact, the lips acting as a conduit of passion filling each woman with a sense of divine energy, immense passion, and anticipation of what was to come. Chloe could feel the wetness of her flower as it started to bloom; this was the first spring of a lifetime of seasons.

Allison paused for a moment, pushing Chloe to arms length. "You are so beautiful. Where did you come from?"

The momentary interruption brought Chloe back to her old self for a moment. "Oh, my God, I'm so sorry…"

"Stop. Don't even try denying what we're both feeling."

Chloe relaxed and melted into Allison's arms. Slowly they began to undress one another. Allison gently removing Chloe's light moist tank top, next ever-so-skillfully unhooking her bra to reveal firm breasts, erect nipples, and soft white skin. For Chloe a moment of self-consciousness disappeared as Allison removed her shirt, reaching out, pulling Chloe towards her to bring skin next to skin. Allison kissed her again, this time taking control as she moved down Chloe's neck, her warm tongue dancing across her skin, moving slowly down as she made her way towards a breast, the nipple so inviting. She pulled away ever so slightly to gently kiss it, fondle her nipple, watching as it grew ever harder. Quiet moans escaped Chloe's lips as Allison continued her exploration. She moved to the other breast, slowly moving away to admire the beauty of Chloe's body, and as the passion became irresistible she moved closer again, kissing between her breasts, making a delicate line with the tip of her tongue from the base of her neck to the indentation of her belly button. The moans became more audible. Chloe could feel herself getting wetter with each moment. The combination of lust and studio lights made for an almost tropical atmosphere, both women sweating, the heat of their skin flooding energy throughout the room. Slowly, with precision, Allison backed Chloe towards the sweep, moving the camera to the side and gently guiding Chloe to sit, all in one fluid motion. The madness of the moment had Chloe in full ecstasy. Allison directed Chloe with the touch of her hands to lay back, "Listen, love, I just want you to enjoy."

In the supine position Chloe stared into the tall ceiling during the fleeting moments she had her eyes open. Her feet dangled over the edge of the sweep as Allison gently untied and removed her black Adidas, moving to her pants to unbuckle Chloe's belt, release the button, and lower her zipper to gently remove her tan Dickies. Allison stepped back ever so slightly for a minute to admire the beauty of her new assistant; the sweat of her body, the glow of her skin, the upper regions of her strong shapely legs. Chloe had been able to release much of what she had been carrying all these years, finally succumbing to what her body and mind had long been yearning for.

Allison moved in again, biting the strap of Chloe's white G-string, pulling it down with her teeth to expose her cleanly shaven pubic region and her red engorged lips. Probing her navel, kissing her lower stomach, moving down the right leg, she left the imprint of her lips every few inches as she worked down the inner thigh. With a light touch she took her left hand to gently brush over Chloe's lips and clitoris. A passionate muted cry could be heard. Allison worked her way over to the left leg, following a similar line and applying equal passion to each kiss. Chloe's feet flexed back and forth, her upper body moved from side to side, her back arching at times as the energy became overwhelming. Allison made her way back to Chloe's naval, probing, tasting the salt of her sweat, inhaling the light scent of jasmine, the sweet smell of sex. She looked down. Chloe's lips were glistening, and not just from the sweat. She reached down with her hand and opened her lips, fully erect, flowing with the juice of lust. She got down on her knees, kissing and licking her clitoris, labia minora and majora. She reached around to place her hands underneath Chloe, penetrating her and grabbing her luscious round ass. Allison stood up for a moment to lift Chloe, moving her back just enough to get her feet on the table. She kissed her inner thigh, working her way down again. This time she started with the ass, making a line with her tongue and dragging it to her clit. Chloe was beside herself—she had never experienced such pleasure.

Time passed without notice. Allison continued, lust dancing through her mind and body, finding the zenith of joy in pleasuring Chloe. They continued their lovemaking, striking chords unknown before this day. Allison felt Chloe's thighs begin to close in; she was fondling her clitoris with her tongue, using two fingers to penetrate the vagina and dance with the g-spot, tempting her ass with her other hand. Chloe became quiet, her body began to quiver, and her thighs continued to close in. She reached down to hold Allison's head, absolutely beside herself with pleasure as her body quivered uncontrollably, the genius of her first true orgasm eliciting the excitement of every neuron in her body. Allison reached around with both hands to hold Chloe in her arms as her tongue released its grip. With her face pressed against her lower abdomen, the passion continued to flow. The orgasm continued its rush as smaller orgasms joined in forming a symphony, and Chloe let out a deep lustful cry. A few more minutes passed as the orgasm and its aftershocks began to subside. They both started to relax a bit, allowing the flow of energy to release and gather their senses. Chloe moved back onto the sweep to stretch out in a pool of sweat, exhausted from the experience. Allison stood up, removed what was left of her clothing, and joined Chloe on the sweep. They both relaxed into a light sleep under the warm glow; the shoot would begin later.

Reminding Her of the Cat

RAKELLE VALENCIA

Paula and Sue scurried out from behind their instruments, surrounding Juleen. "Tell us all about it before Carl gets back," Sue screeched, hopping up and down in anticipation.

"I don't kiss and tell," Juleen replied haughtily. She turned away to prop her guitar in its stand. The room felt smaller than usual. Carl's major equipment had been brought back in from a gig with his own band. That was it, she was sure.

Paula looked at Juleen through squinted eyes. "Since when?"

Sue asked, "So you kissed her? And?"

Juleen ignored Sue's giddy-girl probing for graphic details. She continued to direct her conversation to Paula. "I never have. And I definitely won't with this one. She's different."

"So 'the player' has finally fallen?" Sue asked.

"The ice queen? Get real. She's never in it for the relationship. Just for the thrill of the kill. And the sex." Paula was the cynical one. But reality and cynicism were nearly indistinguishable at times; it might have been hard to tell the difference.

"Carl seems to be taking it well. What's up with him?" Sue probed. "I'm sure it hurts his masculine pride. Or has he moved on to scoping out someone else?"

"He said he promised to do this gig with us and he'll uphold his end. I never expected he would. Guys can be so immature. I especially didn't expect he'd continue letting us use his rehearsal space too." Juleen shrugged. "I'll never figure men out."

"Maybe he thinks Darci will come back to her senses. You know, need a real man, some dick, and he'll be there when she does. And I don't blame him. Poor straight guy." Paula was empathetically fond of Carl. That irked Juleen.

"The show is tomorrow night, ladies. Then it's back to the garage for us, unless we can scrape together enough cash each month for our own studio space." Juleen changed the subject.

Carl walked into the room, hands filled with Jujubes. Sue and Paula pounced on him. He shared. They got back to rehearsing.

Juleen's mind wasn't focused on her immediate actions. She could play the guitar without much thought and sing by rote, so she allowed herself to reflect on the events of the previous night.

Darci's soft, firm lips had parted under her insistence. She ran her tongue along the inside of Darci's upper lip. Juleen felt the girl's body move, pressing against her with urgency.

They began to nibble on each other's lips, sucking each other's tongues, little slurping sounds echoing in the abandoned hall of the blond girl's apartment complex. The nuzzling grew fevered, Juleen sucking on Darci's earlobe, feeling the pulse in her own crotch strengthen to a dull throb.

Liberating a hand, Darci fumbled and managed to get the key into the lock, popping the door open. They stumbled in, still kissing. Juleen pushed the door shut with her elbow, dragging Darci's weight to her, leaning on the slammed door.

Aristophles wandered between their legs, rubbing his face against each one, following through with his arched back, gently purring, begging for some attention of his own. He didn't get any. The two women were engrossed. Aristophles's best move was to saunter off in a snit—dignified, martyred.

Juleen cupped either side of Darci's jaw, sucking the tipsy girl's tongue into her mouth, sliding her hands down her neck, along the collarbone and into Darci's denim jacket, pushing the garment from her shoulders. She followed it down Darci's arms, straightening the girl's elbows to drop it to the floor. Juleen took a firm hold of Darci's wrists, shoving them behind her back while jerking her body closer, mouths never parting.

She enclosed Darci's delicate wrists in one hand. The girl went limp, submitting in tremendous contradiction to her hungry, greedy mouth. Juleen deftly unbuttoned Darci's shirt until reaching her 501s. She hesitated for a moment, but Darci's uninhibited kissing urged her on. Juleen plucked each of the metal buttons from its buttonhole.

Juleen was wearing a crop top, her leather jacket, and loose-fitting Gap khakis. She unbuttoned her own pants, reaching for one of Darci's hands to shove it down inside the opening. Juleen slid into Darci's jeans at the same time, feeling cotton Jockey bikinis. She knew they were Jockeys—she had brushed past the little tag protruding from the left side at the front of the waistband.

Darci's hand stiffened in surprise. Juleen felt it, felt everything—she wasn't wearing underwear, and she was slick, shaven, soft as a prepubescent girl. That caught Darci by surprise. She hadn't been the first, and given a moment the shock usually became arousal.

There was no stopping now. Juleen pushed Darci back and yanked open her own fly, exposing her bare pussy. Darci stared, intrigued. Juleen placed Darci's hand back against her smooth skin and then drew their bodies together, reaching up to loosen Darci's bra. She murmured into Darci's ear about her own naked pussy, of the softness, the smoothness, and how she loved the way it felt to have Darci's hot palm against it—skin on skin, nothing between them.

In a lowered voice she told of how exquisitely wicked she felt wearing no underwear and knowing she was completely bare. Juleen whispered her desire to put her own hand against Darci just like this. She placed tiny, sensuous kisses from Darci's neck to her breasts. She licked at the erect nipples and the soft undersides of the round breasts, repeating the gist of her statement. "Feel the skin, as smooth as where my tongue is now."

A moan rumbled in Darci's throat and escaped her lips. Juleen led her by the hand to what she assumed was the bedroom. She stripped the beauty while they stood. Jockeys discarded, a bushy blond muff sprung forth, reminding her of the cat—longhaired and soft but definitely in the way for Juleen.

Tossed onto the bed, Darci was loosely blindfolded with her

own silk scarf. She giggled and turned her head to the side as if looking for something. Juleen glanced in that direction, eyeing only an open window with a view into another apartment complex across the alley. There was a chilly breeze titillating and taunting their bare flesh, but she didn't want to pull the shades.

Teasing Darci's body with her warm, moist tongue, Juleen licked her way up, from sucking on her toes to the nape of her neck, avoiding the muff. She laid her body lightly over Darci and felt the woman quivering beneath her. She breathed in Darci's ear about how she'd like to shave her. Would she let her?

Juleen could have suggested Chinese water torture, and Darci would have agreed. She rose slowly. "Be right back. Don't move." She further commanded Darci to keep her hands on her breasts while waiting. Juleen smiled wickedly as the blindfolded beauty cupped her small, perfectly round breast and kissed each one gently.

A quick search of the bathroom was successful. Juleen found everything she was looking for—scissors, facecloth, towel, razor, and shaving cream. All she needed was a pot of hot water. She realized the spell over the girl was fragile. She didn't want to give Darci a chance to think and put the brakes on. Maybe she didn't want to give the "straight girl" a chance to sober up.

"Juleen. Juleen!" Paula binged her off the head with a broken pick that had been discarded on the littered floor, shocking her back to the present, back to rehearsal.

"Huh?"

"You're all set, then? You don't need to bitch before we leave?"

"Don't tempt her," Sue said.

"Yeah, I'm with that. I'm out," Carl grumbled, stuffing his electric guitar in a hard case. "Nah. Nah, I'm good with it. Rehearsal was good. Super job, guys. I'll call you."

Juleen sat in her car outside her apartment, heat from the engine still warming the interior. She plucked her keys from the ignition, twirled them in the air on her index finger, silver and gold metal reflecting the glint of the streetlights. Mesmerized, she zoned out, thinking back to Darci, back to shaving the blond beauty's muff.

Her memories were vivid. Juleen had placed the pot of hot water and her scrounged bundle of necessities on the floor next to the bed. She gazed at Darci, still blindfolded, lying there, cupping her breasts in her hot palms as she had been instructed to do. Juleen had whispered in low tones about how beautiful Darci was, how smooth, how sexy. She remembered Darci responding with tiny gasps, incredulous panting. Juleen could hear those sounds echoing in her head even now as she sat alone, parked on the side of a busy neighborhood street.

She'd lain next to Darci, again running her hand along the blindfolded blond's far side, from her neck, slowing along her breast, to her belly, thigh, and back up. "Are you ready for me?" she asked.

Darci nodded assent, biting her lower lip.

As Juleen settled on the floor at the edge of the bed, she grabbed the towel, placing it under the girl. Juleen leaned between Darci's bent knees, lightly blowing hot breath onto her while spreading the nether lips with her fingers. Rewarded with a full-body shiver, Juleen dropped the facecloth in the pot of water, cooled to the perfect temperature.

Water trickled amongst the folds when she put the sodden cloth on Darci. She waited a moment, pressing her entire vagina with the palm of her hand, fingers curled over the mound. Darci squirmed and moaned. Juleen patted her as if quieting a restless child.

She removed the cloth and took the small scissors, trimming, using her fingers to hold the fuzzy hair aloft and to manipulate the lips for a better angle. Gasping, Darci wriggled on the towel, though she wasn't trying to escape. Her hands clutched at the bedsheets, and she continued to chew her lower lip.

Juleen slapped the soaking cloth on again, and Darci's hips

bucked in astonishment. She settled under Juleen's touch like a purring kitten, fingers caressing the skin on all sides of the cloth. "Oh. Oh." The complacent cries of wanting, needing, begging came steadily.

Lifting the corner of the facecloth, Juleen viewed the wetness dripping from Darci, a thick glistening moisture. She touched the girl, sliding her fingers in the slick slit, spreading the natural lubricant to the clit and circling it with her fingertips.

The shaving cream was almost a hindrance, the greater temptation to remain stroking the silky slit to fruition. Juleen started shaving from the bottom up, from Darci's anus to her crevice, to the outer lips, rinsing the razor with each stroke. She let warm water drip on Darci's belly before each stroke.

Darci grew wetter by the second. Low, quiet moans intermingled with gasps and short, quick breaths fighting for their turn in between.

Juleen watched Darci building toward orgasm. With the last swipe of the razor she grabbed the facecloth, wiping thin strips of shaving cream from the bare pussy. Juleen tugged Darci's clenched fist from the wrung sheets, placing it on the freshly shaved skin.

Darci caressed the smoothness of her outer lips, excited by the feel. Juleen leaned over, slid a finger in, and sucked her engorged clit. Darci's body tensed, muscles popping out on her arms and stomach. She clenched her jaw, puffing through closed teeth, squealing to orgasm. "Don't stop. Please don't quit." Darci thrust her own fingers into her wet slit, rubbing her clit shaft and encircling her protruding clit.

Sitting back on her heels to watch, Juleen pushed one more finger in, thrusting in time to Darci's ministrations, her writhing hips, and begging for more. Juleen gave it to her, stroking herself as she knelt there. She came with Darci that time, and the time after that, a flood in a night of multiple orgasms.

A horn blared, brakes screeched, an argument between two men ensued in the street not three car lengths from Juleen. "Damn." The visual snapped from Juleen's mind, and she took her hand away from her crotch and picked her car keys from the cup holder where they had fallen. She climbed out of her vehicle, beeped the alarm locking the doors, and hustled into her apartment.

School of Air

JODY EKERT

The sleek-nosed Cessna Titan descended quickly, bumping along the hard red dirt runway, jolting me awake. From the small windows I could see nothing but flat land, punctuated with the occasional stunted tree in muted greens and browns. The engines slowed to a standstill and the pilot turned.

"We're here," he said quickly. In the outback Australian desert this pilot was also a flying doctor, and he had house calls to make, babies to deliver, and lives to save.

I made my way down the stairs onto the runway, lugging my bag full of schoolbooks, and looked around. I was sweating right through my cut-off jeans and cotton shirt. In the distance I could see a cloud of dust rising, as a four-wheel drive sped toward me. Butterflies danced in my stomach, and I tried to calm myself. This was my first visit to an outback property as a teacher. I'd taken a job with the School of Air in Alice Springs only a few months before. I usually taught classes through radio contact with the children. Spread over an area of a million square kilometers, they were too isolated to travel to school. Each morning they would radio in, one by one, to commence classes from their properties, usually supervised by parents or home tutors. Once a year we would meet, and on this, my first visit, I was expecting to finally put faces to the names of a family of four young children.

The four-wheel drive stopped quickly, braking in the dust, and a bundle of blond children fell over each other in their hurry to greet me.

"Hello, hello, hello Ms. Ashley!" they squealed.

I looked down at their excited faces. "You must be Hannah…and Sarah…and Josh and Sam." I rattled off their names, glad I'd remembered them so easily.

"It's so good to finally meet you in person," I said, ruffling the hair of the nearest girl.

"Now, where is your father?" I asked.

"He's out rebuilding some fencing," came an unexpected voice.

I looked up to see a girl lazily pull herself out of the driver's seat.

"A mob of kangaroos knocked down some posts trying to get into the paddocks, and they scared the sheep. So he sent me instead," she explained.

I felt her eyes appraise my body, moving slowly up and down, without the least amount concern for discretion. I returned the look defiantly. She was about my height and slender, but with the look of strength that comes from hard labor. She had brown eyes, coffee-colored skin, and full lips. Well-toned biceps bulged out of her white singlet, and two perfectly round hips jutted over low-cut jeans that ended in Blundstone boots. Short black hair poked out from underneath her tightly pulled bandanna.

"Oh," I said, caught off guard by her raw sensuality.

"Well, I'm Ms. Ashley…eh…Andrea, I mean." I held out my hand, trying to sound confident.

"Well, hi, *Ms. Ashley*," she said with an amused smile, rolling my name around her mouth, as if trying to taste it. She wiped the dirt and sweat from her palms across her jeans and reached out to shake my hand.

"I'm Erin, one of the station's jillaroos. Welcome to Inglewood." She turned and picked up my bags, throwing them into the Land Rover. I watched in silent appreciation at the play of muscles rippling across her back.

The journey back to the homestead was enjoyably tense. Even with all the children screaming and laughing, I felt the heat rising between Erin and me. I glanced sideways, my mind racing. I only had one day at Inglewood, and I was determined to make it a memorable one.

The afternoon passed quickly, with lessons for the children and a tour of their schoolroom. I caught my mind drifting on several occasions to thoughts of Erin. After dropping us at the homestead she'd headed for the stables without a word, and I had watched her ride away. Back in Alice I had dated my fair share of girls, but in a small town it wasn't long before the excitement died. And now, hundreds of kilometers from the nearest nightclub, I had found something that made my heart race and my underwear grow damp.

With the children finally down for a rest before dinner I was free to roam around the property. I sat on the verandah and watched stockmen and jackaroos go about their business. It was a busy property, and judging by the long dining room table, had a sizeable staff. A few cattle dogs lay sleepily in the shade of the odd tree, close to old ice cream buckets filled with water, flies buzzing around.

I wandered toward the stables and entered the long, dark building. I was grateful for the slight breeze offered by the fans rotating above, struggling to keep the horses cool against the blistering heat. The smell of molasses and hay, leather and sweat filled the air. I idly fingered a rein, enjoying the feel of the old cracked leather. I smiled with the memories of a few wild nights when the beer flowed too easily back in Alice.

"So you like the feel of that?" The voice startled me, and I turned to see Erin leaning against a beam, smirking.

"Do you always sneak up on people like that?" I retorted.

"I asked a question first," she said, one eyebrow raised.

"Yes, as a matter of fact, I do."

Erin slowly approached me, and I took a slight step backward, bumping into a wall.

"Well, what else do you like?" she questioned, daring me.

Meeting her challenge I put a hand on her shoulder and pulled her close. My lips were almost on hers, and her nostrils flared in anticipation.

"This," and I kissed her hard, forcing her mouth open and meeting her tongue with mine.

Pausing for breath I noticed her hardened nipples, showing

through the thin, white cotton of her tank top. Wetness ran freely between my legs. I pulled the material down hard and with a rip her breast was exposed. Her small, round breasts met my hands and I twisted a nipple. Erin gasped.

"Do you always ride without a bra?" I asked, twisting once more.

"Only on days when school teachers are here, Andrea," she answered, breathing harder.

"That's Ms. Ashley to you," I commanded.

Erin reached up and grabbed both my hands, forcing them above my head. With one of her knees between my legs I could feel her hips on mine as she forced me against the wall, grinding. Continuing to hold my hands captive she reached and pulled the reins closer. Wrapping them around my wrists she tied them to a metal hoop in one corner of the stall. Enjoying the game, I waited for her to make the next move.

"Not so much in charge now then, are we, Ms. Ashley?"

And with her hands on my waist she unbuttoned my cut-offs and pushed them to my ankles.

"Step out of them," she instructed.

Obediently, I kicked my jeans away. I stood there, naked from the waist down.

"Oh, so now look who doesn't wear underwear," she laughed. Her fingers ran over my pubic hair, forcing apart my lips, and I gasped as she plunged them deep inside. She kissed my neck and the hair on my arms stood up. As she moved her fingers back and forth I began to groan and move with the rhythm, but she paused.

"What, what, don't stop!" I gasped, my face flushed and my wrists burning from the leather rein.

Without a word she turned and walked away from the stall. It seemed like an eternity before she returned with something in her hand. She held it up for me to see. It was a beautiful handmade dildo harness made from soft brown leather and polished to smoothness. Attached was a thick black dildo.

"It's not just you town girls that get to have all the fun," she said, as she stepped into the harness.

There were no more words. Her hips rubbed against mine as she rode me hard and I arched my back, straining to take all of her inside me. My mouth bent toward her nipples and I sucked and licked. The more excited she became the harder she pushed, until she owned me completely. She looked into my eyes and ran a hand slowly down my body.

"Come," she commanded, still watching my face.

I had no choice. With her eyes locked on mine I felt my clit swell, wanting more. With a hot rush my cunt contracted and released. She slowed her strokes as I surfed the waves of an orgasm until finally we were still. The only noises were the fans turning lazily overhead and the calls of the crickets as sunset approached. She withdrew and kissed me softly, as she undid the reins.

"See you next year, then," she said, and walked away.

Tea for Two

LISA BISHOP

When Sarah said that she had a special birthday surprise for me, she gave me an address, the name of an inn, and what time to be there. No other instructions, just to show up. When I found the small inn on the old country lane, I parked the car next to Sarah's and walked up to the white picket fence's gate and entered a rose garden. I couldn't help wondering what my best friend of twenty years was up to that day. Sarah was always filled with surprises, and birthdays were her specialty. Each year she found something better than the last, and after bungee jumping last year I wondered what she had planned this year for my thirtieth birthday. I walked through the garden on its stone path, then rang the brass bell that hung at the side of the inn's door.

A middle-aged woman opened it, and I told her my name and that I was here to meet Sarah Birch.

"Why, yes, we've been expecting you. Ms. Birch is in the parlor, if you'll follow me," flowed her English accent. I walked slowly behind the woman, taking in the scent of rose sachet, the ivory lace doilies beneath elaborate vases of tea roses on antique tables and buffets. Through the foyer she led me up the hardwood staircase and knocked on a door near the top of the stairs.

"Enter," I heard Sarah say from behind the door.

"Ms. Birch, your guest has arrived."

As I looked past her, I saw Sarah dressed in a mauve Victorian gown, her long brown hair pinned up as ringlet tendrils hung near her cheeks and watched as she pulled the other long white evening glove upon her hand and smoothed it up to her elbow.

"Gracie, happy birthday!"

"Thanks," I replied, still unable to believe how different my best friend appeared in that Victorian gown. I felt suddenly under-dressed.

"We must get you dressed, it's almost time for tea," said Sarah, taking me by the hand and pulling me to the closet where count-less other gowns hung.

"If that will be all, Ms. Birch, I shall attend to your tea. Please, ring the bell when you are ready to be served."

"Thank you, Jane."

Sarah rummaged through the closet until she found an emer-ald green taffeta gown and held it up to me.

"Interesting," she said, holding the gown up to me by its Juliet sleeves and turning the hanger so she could see the bustle on the rear. "What do you think?"

"It's nice," I replied, not sure what to do next.

"Don't just stand there, Gracie, get undressed."

I took off my clothes, donning a matching black bra and thong set. Sarah eyed me and smiled, making me blush as she carefully removed the gown from the hanger, and set it on the chaise longue near me. As I bent over to get it, I knew that Sarah's eyes were on me, especially since Sarah outed herself between my twenty-ninth and thirtieth birthday this year. The sky-blue brocaded fabric throughout the room and upholstery reminded me of the French colonial furniture in my aunt's house, the same furniture that has been covered with plastic for as long as I've known Sarah.

As I reached for the dress, Sarah removed another set of evening gloves from a bureau drawer. When I had slipped the dress over me, Sarah was there helping me into it, pulling my hands through the sleeves within her own gloved hands, entwining our fingers together. God, she was gorgeous. Always a beauty queen, no one expected her to announce that she preferred girls to boys, especially with the knockout fiancé she had acquired that year. I had to break the stare between us.

"So we're having tea today?"

"Yes, high tea, just for your birthday."

"This is interesting. I mean, the gown and all?"

"Where's your sense of adventure, Gracie? You loved playing dress-up when we were kids."

"We're a long way away from grade school, Sarah."

"You're feeling old about turning thirty, but I'm going to make you feel young again," she said, zipping up the back of the gown for me. I looked in the large round vanity mirror and peered at myself as Sarah handed me the gloves. While I slid them into place, she took a three-strand pearl choker and affixed it about my neck.

"You look incredible," she said, smoothing out the folds of my dress then pushing me down by the shoulders into the vanity chair that she had tucked beneath me. As Sarah picked up a silver brush, she released my black hair out of the ponytail that I had affixed before I left on this adventure. Pulling the hair high on my head, she twisted the hair about it, then pinned it under to make a lovely bun, and slid a beaded comb on the side for effect.

"I'd think we're ready for tea, what do you think?"

"Sure, I'm ready if you are."

Sarah went to the door and rang the bell near it. Immediately, we heard some chamber music come on in the suite, and Sarah led me to the set table, complete with a Royal Doulton service and brass napkin rings that held real roses between the folds of the linen napkin.

"This inn is beautiful," I said, "wherever did you find it?"

"A girl at work told me about it. I checked it out and thought it would be a lovely birthday surprise for you, especially after seeing *Sense and Sensibility* last month."

A knock on the door and Jane was there with a tea cart. She set the table, complete with a tiered platter of sandwiches and cookies, a Royal Doulton teapot, and a matching creamer and sugar set. When she finished serving and pouring our tea Jane left. Sarah quickly took the ivory linen napkin from the rose napkin holder and placed it in her lap, and I did likewise.

"Jane's walnut bread and cream cheese sandwiches are simply divine," Sarah said, adopting an almost separate persona. I raised my eyebrow, and she giggled.

"C'mon, Gracie, have a good time. This is supposed to make you feel young again."

"As if that's going to really happen by playing dress-up and tea party."

"Okay, I need to ask you something. If you could do one thing, just one thing that you've never done before in your entire life, for your birthday, what would it be?"

"God, I don't know."

"Yes, you do," she replied with a coy smile that showed off her dimples. I loved it when she did that—it extended the cupid's bow of her lips, those lips that I had spent nights fantasizing over.

"No, I don't."

"What's the one thing you fantasize about?" she asked as my face flushed red with embarrassment. She read my mind. After twenty years together she knew everything about me. Well, at least she thought she did.

I laughed at her, knowing better than to answer that question outright. Sarah raised an eyebrow at me before picking up her tea cup from its saucer and putting it to her full luscious lips.

"Tell me."

"No."

"Then I'll guess."

"Go ahead. You'll only embarrass yourself," I replied, as the loose-fitting shoulder of her gown fell down her forearm, exposing the top of her breast a bit more than it should have. Slowly, one of her gloved hands moved up her arms to push it back into place, disappointing me.

"Why can't you tell me? I thought I was your bestest friend in the whole world," she said as I took a bite of a cucumber finger sandwich.

"Sair, I love you, you know that."

"You love me more than as a friend."

"Look, just because you outed yourself this year doesn't mean I have to follow suit."

"Who says you have to out yourself? C'mon, Gracie, I know you want me."

I put the sandwich down on the plate before me then pushed my chair out from the table. I reached for my clothes and Sarah got up and rushed over to me.

"Gracie, don't go."

"You're making me feel uncomfortable."

"No, I'm not. Why can't you admit that you want me?"

"Look, I just ended it with Mickey, and I don't think that I'm in a good place right now. Emotionally, that is."

"Who says you have to be emotionally one hundred percent? Don't you remember when we were kids, when we would have sleepovers?"

"Yeah, pretending to be married and all that. Please, Sarah, I don't want to discuss it."

Sarah reached for my hand. I wanted to pull away, yet at the same time I wanted her to draw me against her. I really wanted her; Sarah knew that. She must have. When she reached up with her other gloved hand, she drew my face to hers. While her lipstick smothered my lips, her tongue invaded my mouth, dancing with mine. As if it had always wanted to do that, I relaxed and enjoyed the sensation of her kiss and the taste of more than just her mouth.

"I want you, Sarah," I whispered, "I…I just can't admit it to my folks—"

"They're not here. We are. Forget them. It's just us right now."

Her hand reached about my waist and pulled me against hers, crushing the crinoline between my legs, tickling the skin barely covered by the thong I wore.

We stood there kissing for what felt like hours, and I wanted her so badly that my hands searched her back, finding buttons where a zipper should have been. With these gloves there would be no hurrying. Sensing my frustration, Sarah took my hands and set each upon her perky breasts, whose nipples were like rocks peering through the satin dress. I wanted to drop them to my sides, but my hands were compelled to gently squeeze until I couldn't stand to have the satin and the gloves keeping our skin apart. As I pushed the sleeves down her bodice to her waist, Sarah stopped and watched me view her there, exposed to me. I had seen her naked plenty of times before in dressing rooms at department stores, but never alone like this. Well, not since we were kids. When she pulled me against her again, my mouth moved from hers to her shoulders, devouring them as her breasts were squashed against my taffeta gown. I wasn't letting her go now.

I tasted where she had sprayed perfume between her neck and shoulders, the bitter taste and sensuous scent that teased my senses as her tongue attacked my earlobe, poking through the hoop of my earring. As her hand reached beneath my ass, Sarah held me tightly against her. When she stepped back she took my hand and led me to the chaise longue against the wall.

She placed me in the corner of its arm before directing my legs and pivoting my body so that I was fully across the chaise. With my gown trapped beneath her so that I couldn't move my legs, Sarah straddled my body. Again our lips met in a fury of passionate kisses. No words were spoken—none were necessary as she removed each pin and comb from my hair until it all fell about my shoulders.

"Have I ever told you how sexy you look with your hair down? If you were my woman, you'd wear it down all the time."

"Really?" I asked, before she attacked my mouth again. Pinned into the corner of the brocaded chaise, the taffeta and brocade upholstery were more slippery than an icy sidewalk. Slowly I began to lose my grip and slid down the chaise until my back was on the seat and my head was on the roll pillow there on the chaise arm. Sarah was relentless, and my hands held her breasts, which were hanging in front of me. For the first time in my life I tasted one and found it delicious. No hair to get in the way like a man's, Sarah's skin was soft and smooth. Her nipple was taut and inviting to my teeth and tongue. I suckled her, and she moaned, a deep sweet sound that communicated her instant satisfaction.

"Oh, Gracie," she sighed as I moved to the other one. Her fingers went to the wet nipple and kneaded it between velvet fingertips as she moaned and bit her lower lip. I nibbled on her nipple and kneaded the other breast with my gloved hand. She moved off me a moment later, then put my feet flat on the seat of the chaise so that my knees were in the air before moving the gown and crinoline over my knees, exposing my legs to her. Sarah parted my legs as if I was a patient in the gynecological office where she worked as a nurse. Her gloved fingertips teased my inner thighs, going from the knee to my moist, thong-covered pussy, which had already wet its fabric thoroughly.

"Are you ready for your birthday present?" she asked as her eyes met mine. Pushing aside the thong with her gloved fingers, Sarah slipped them between the folds of my swollen lips. I nodded, and she bent down to kiss me while her fingertips found the delta of my sex. She pressed down on its pier and flicked it with a plush finger until I moaned through the kiss. Slowly, she left my side for the end of the chaise. With my knees up and the taffeta gown and tulle crinoline blocking my view of her actions, Sarah's touches excited me all the more as I wondered what she was doing to me. I felt her hands but not her skin, just the sheathed fabric of those gloves, moving in and out of my sex now, teasing the crack of my ass as her mouth and teeth teased my inner thighs.

"You're so deliciously wet, Gracie. I can't wait to taste you, to eat you. It's what I've dreamed about for years now. Happy birthday," she said as I felt her tongue invade me. I gasped, feeling it there, and her hands wrapped under me to pull my torso closer to the edge of the couch, like a teenager at the gynecologist's for the first time. My hands wrung the taffeta gown as I moaned with the deep pleasure I was experiencing. For years I too had wanted Sarah, and she had known that all along. My hands went to my breasts, kneading them while she attacked my wet pussy. I was so close to the edge of climax my heart raced and my hands squeezed the blood from my breasts, wanting satisfaction, wanting to fall over that orgasmic cliff.

I wanted Sarah for what seemed like forever. I always had. Now she was there, between my legs, her tongue satisfying the deepest of my orifices, her hands and mouth teasing me, sucking me until I could tolerate no more. My head bobbed from side to side, I felt dizzy and so close to orgasm when her tongue moved away so her fingers could plunge into me. At first there was one, then two velvety fingers, faster and deeper before three entered me, making me moan louder and louder until I could stand it no longer and released. Sarah moved the gown up my belly and teased me with wet kisses and her breath until I playfully batted her away and took her hand. She entwined her hand with mine and moved up to my face.

"I love you, Gracie. Be my lover."

"Yes, always," I replied between breaths, promising away my life to her and feeling right about it. After all, Sarah and I had been together for almost twenty years now. We were inseparable; why should sex be any different? I pulled her face down to mine and attacked her mouth, tasting my nectar for the first time.

We changed into our casual clothes and hung the nineteenth century garb in the closet.

"So what else do you have planned for today?"

"Depends. Your place or mine?"

"Mine. I have so much more to teach you," she said, picking up her purse and heading for the door.

"Sair," I said, and she stopped in her tracks. Sarah turned to me and tossed her hair from her back to her shoulder.

"Thanks for a great birthday."

The Second Time I Saw Her

METTE BACH

The first I time saw k.d. lang I was sixteen. She was on the cover of a magazine. I was in a grocery store line in my small town, and I thought she was a totally hot guy. When I met Cass, in my first year of university, the attraction was the same. Cass's sexuality made me question my own. We took English together. Not together, but I sat behind her in every lecture, casually dropping pens so I could pick them up and inhale her cologne or lightly brush against her shoulder. I didn't gather the nerve to speak to her until years later when bizarre circumstances pulled us together again.

It was December. I had been working overtime at my office job. My live-in girlfriend had been laid off some months before. To the rest of the world it appeared as though I took the extra hours to nobly help Laura with her portion of the rent and bills and to make sure we had a little extra something this time of year. We were struggling to get through the holidays without killing each other. Two years of living together had killed the meager spark there once had been between us. We cared about each other, much the way roommates do, and neither of us wanted to initiate the inevitable breakup, so things simply continued.

Laura worked on her graduate thesis, researching working conditions of women miners in Nova Scotia at the turn of the century. We'd met in the women's studies department five years ago. Even after our whole circle of friends had graduated, we still socialized with them regularly. I had become the ravenous outsider since last year when I took a corporate job downtown and started wearing suits. The winter solstice party that Laura wanted us to host was the last straw. My boss offered a trip to our regional district headquarters in Calgary, and because I wanted to be absolved of my domestic obligations and making ornaments and jam and cookies I agreed to go.

"Not many employees would go a week before Christmas," my boss said. "You're showing good initiative."

"Our house doesn't celebrate Christmas," I told her, thinking of how, years ago, when we rejected the tradition for political reasons, we would have wholeheartedly argued with anyone who made assumptions to the opposite by saying "Merry Christmas" instead of "Happy Holidays" or another less racist, less Western patriarchal greeting. I started to lose that edge when Laura became Wiccan and she and our friends started celebrating exclusively pagan holidays that weren't open to Christians, or straight people, or my coworkers, the corporate enemies.

My corporation, for what it was worth, is less damaging than most. It's a cosmetics company owned and operated mostly by gay men. Our major clientele is a mixture of drag queens and femme women. We donate profits from an entire line to HIV research. We landed RuPaul as spokeswoman and model. We don't test on animals; we recycle. Laura doesn't believe that gay men and lesbians are capable of sharing the same agenda. When she gets too politically wound up I like to remind her that lesbian, tranny, heterosexual, or gay, everyone looks better with great skin. It's not much, but as far as company visions go I can get behind mine.

The conference I was sent to was held outside Calgary at our manufacturing plant in a tiny industrial town, of which there are many. When I first arrived I was surprised at how small and friendly the feel was. I had never been in a factory warehouse with conference rooms and giant steel vats and barrels and tubes everywhere. The smell was frightening, and our billboard of RuPaul looked out of place on the wall behind the heavy-duty machinery.

At the presentation the team was mostly men. We were supplied with coffee and muffins and bottled water and expected to sit through a day of PowerPoint presentations, speeches about our previous fiscal year, and projections for the future. Bored, I browsed the itinerary. The most exciting event that would happen on this trip seemed to be a lip-gloss demonstration—our new spring line. It would happen at three.

By noon I was having difficulty staying awake. The fluorescent lights created a timelessness in the boardroom, and since there were no windows I repeatedly helped myself to coffee just to keep up appearances.

At three o'clock the CEO gave a little introduction to the new gloss we'd be launching in a few months and turned the floor over to Cass Johnson, project supervisor and technological guru. The room applauded, and my heart skipped a beat. She hadn't changed at all, and clearly my attraction hadn't either.

The room, thank God, was darkened almost immediately for Cass to do a slide-show presentation. I felt my cheeks flush and sank deeper into my chair, smiling girlishly in spite of my embarrassment. How do you face years of awkward unspoken attraction?

The lights came on. I jolted back to my well-formulated conservative composure. Cass went on with her presentation. She asked for a volunteer to demonstrate the new lip gloss. Asking was clearly just a formality, as she was staring into my eyes the whole time. All eyes in the room turned to look at me as I walked to the front. Cass seated me in a high metal chair facing the group. The chill from the steel was almost unbearable. Nervous and titillated, I was afraid of revealing my inner longings, afraid of giggling idiotically, afraid of smelling Cass's alluring scent.

"Close your eyes and tilt your head back slightly," she instructed loudly. Then she leaned in, adjusting the chair, and whispered, "like I'm going to kiss you."

I did as she said. The room disappeared. Onlookers became irrelevant. *Kiss me,* I thought as I felt her left hand cup my face. With her right hand she brushed a gloss onto my lips. It was so soft, so delicate. She had an amazing capacity to render me amorphously soft deep inside. No touch had ever felt this thorough, and I wondered what I had missed during all of those years. I opened my eyes to the room. The strangers' eyes were suddenly invasive, as though Cass and I had been alone together the entire time. I was afraid of having revealed too much. Back in my seat at the back of the room I could barely make out the main points of Cass's presentation.

Later that night some colleagues met at the town's only gay bar. I had taken care not to spend too much time getting ready. After all, I had no intention of cheating on my girlfriend. I wore a simple outfit—jeans with a black top and matching boots. The only element of the ensemble that made me irresistible was wearing my hair down. That part I couldn't help. Hair is seductive, and everyone compliments me on mine.

Inside the smoky, crowded place, I thought I would casually wait for an opportunity to spy Cass from afar. No such luck. She was loud and boisterous and entertaining a small entourage up by the bar. I walked up to order my drink. That wouldn't be too obvious. She saw me, acknowledged me, and smiled. I almost melted. I haven't felt butterflies like this since I used to fantasize about her back in first year.

Her group subsided for a while. The bar played British pop and the energy of the place shifted from drinking to dancing. This conveniently left Cass sitting by herself on one of the bar stools. I had the feeling she was waiting for me to approach her. How could I be so arrogant? Her comfort told me she would have liked to have danced. Her focus on avoiding eye contact with me told me she was nervous. Maybe I was reading too much into this. I had to find out.

"That was some application today," I told her. "My lips were shiny for hours." I smiled.

"You liked it? It's all in the application," she said stoically, single-handedly swinging a barstool around to face hers and offering me a seat. I climbed up. "I know I shouldn't say that because we're in the business of marketing specific products, but the truth is that any gloss can do what I did with yours. It's the brush," Cass continued.

I was awed by her shyness. Moments earlier she had been laughing and shouting her stories to her femme fans, and now she seemed to be having difficulty holding a simple conversation. I couldn't help myself. I had to level with her.

"I know this'll sound weird, but you were pretty instrumental in helping me come out," I confessed to her, wondering if she would remember me, and if she did whether she would admit it— or care.

She took a sip of her beer, puzzled. Her forehead glistened slightly as she stared intently at me. I was afraid I had said too much, afraid of sounding forward.

"Is that right?" Her concentration and severity turned to a friendly expression. "And how exactly did I do that?" She smiled coyly.

"Well," I started, feeling a lump in my throat as I was suddenly eighteen again, hands clammy, confused about myself, my body, boys, girls, the lecture hall crush. "I really liked you, and I was deathly scared of admitting it."

She leaned in. She wasn't going to let on whether she remembered me or not. Her body radiated heat, and although it was different I could smell her cologne again. I felt a shiver run down my spine. "Are you still scared?" she asked flirtatiously, smiling at me not with a grin but with longing bedroom eyes. My legs could barely hold me. My jeans were wet, and I liked it. I had waited a decade for this moment.

"No," I said, even though I was. I thought about Laura briefly, About how utterly wrong it was to be standing here with Cass inches from me. It would be even more wrong to invite her back to my hotel. It would be even more wrong to kiss her or fuck her, but I couldn't help thinking about it now, just as I couldn't have stopped my thoughts when I was younger.

I leaned into her. Her lips barely had to move toward me and we locked our mouths together. The bar was loud, and we were outside of the crowd. She had put her beer down without me noticing, on the bar behind me. I was sandwiched between her strong presence and the tall wooden bar, in a corner, against the wall. With her right hand she held the nape of my neck, enveloping my long hair with her palm. Her left hand came up and squeezed gently on my firm nipples. I was gushing, holding onto her leather belt and the waist of her tattered jeans for support.

A table of gay men got up and started dancing. In a quick swoop she lifted one of their high metal-legged barstools over to where we were. She picked me up and planted me firmly on the chair. I spread my legs enough that she could stand between them.

I felt the bulge of her crotch and she felt the wetness of mine. There was no way for me to hide my utter hunger for her.

"How badly did you like me then?"

"Pretty badly."

"That's good. I should have no trouble making you come, then," she said, sliding her right hand down across my breast, along my side, around my waist, and landing on my thigh. I jumped with anticipation. I couldn't believe what was happening. She was going to touch me right here, in the middle of a noisy and busy bar, and I hadn't even told her I have a girlfriend. This wasn't supposed to be happening. I was in over my head and loving every second.

Cass pushed my boundaries. I should have objected to her controlling way right there in the bar, but I didn't. I only encouraged her, and with that I brought out more of her dragonlike tendencies. I could tell she didn't give a damn who I was, only that she could have her way because conveniently I had approached her and told her this was something I wanted.

Her hand slid easily to my crotch. My teen angst had raised her onto a pedestal back then. I obeyed her now because of what I thought I wanted then. I had been raised a good girl, and good girls don't fuck in crowded gay bars. She pushed her fingers against me.

"Here?" I said shyly.

With that she unzipped my jeans, slid my underwear to one side, inserted at least one finger, and silenced me with one flowing movement of her arm. She answered my question and didn't care that it wasn't the answer I wanted. She faced me, and her back sheltered us, but her pumping arm would have been obvious to anyone who cared to look. I was scared. Aroused beyond my means, I had never done this kind of thing before. All the lesbians I know are pacifist hippie types who believe in love and goddesses. I tried to remember whether Cass even knew my name as her fingers slid deep inside me. My Southern belle clit was being roughly man-handled by this tough rogue, and there was nothing I could do about it. I tucked my head into her shoulder and felt protected by her in my vaguely fetal position.

"Good," she said, "I want to hear you moan."

I was about to cheat, I realized, as blood rushed through me. I was already cheating. And it wasn't the consensual safe sex that I was accustomed to either. I had never had rough sex. My only experience had been loving, nurturing, slow sensual sex with women I cared about. Cass clearly neither cared nor had time to consider any possible ramifications or feelings.

I started to moan as she violently agitated my clit. "Don't you want to get out of here? Maybe we can go back to my hotel room," I suggested. It would at least be a fraction more moral.

"Yes, definitely. But first I'm going to make you come right here."

"It's really crowded," I objected, "I'm not sure I can." I looked around. It was too foreign, too crazy. There were too many eyes.

"Daddy knows when he's dealing with a bad girl. Your panties were soaked before I even came near you. I know you can come. I know you want to."

Cass's voice cut through layers of social conditioning deep into the root of my sexuality. I wanted to be a little girl made to come against her own will. My memory drifted back to an incident when I was twelve, masturbating at my parents' friends' cocktail party in the downstairs bathroom, feeling guilty and ashamed that I could-n't wait. How I scrubbed my hands afterward and prayed that no one had noticed I had disappeared by myself for so long.

I looked up at Cass's stern eyes. There was urgency in her expression. She was determined in a way I have never seen any woman express. I couldn't disappoint her, and I needed release. I could feel a massive orgasm build inside me. The heavy beat of the music pounded in my ears as Cass incessantly rubbed against me in time to the music. To the half drunk we might have appeared as though we were dancing, the way I held onto her shoulders and neck. Although still somewhat cradled on the stool, I was almost standing, my thighs clamping hard around the circular seat. Waves of excitement rushed through me. My vision blurred, and nothing in the room mattered anymore. I was pulsing and gasping for air.

"That's my girl," Cass whispered in a new, almost tender voice. My panting subsided, and Cass held me tight as I sat down on the stool again to catch my breath. She let go, stepped to reach for her beer, took a sip, and smirked at me with one eyebrow raised. I was in heaven. I hadn't known what it was like to feel taken until that moment. When she came back close to me, I grabbed her, pulled her in to where she had been before. This time, I clung to her shoulders and wrapped my legs tightly around her waist. Her palms came down around me, caressing me as I was supported by the stool, and then, as I had wanted, grasped firmly onto the roundness of my ass as she hoisted me up with one move and carried me out of the loud place.

In the coldness of the street, still cradling me, she asked the only question that mattered: "Where's your hotel?"

On the way, in the chill of the night air and the warmth of our touching bodies, I felt a heightened sense of awareness of my body and Cass's. It was undeniable and primal: my postorgasmic bliss and the bulge I could feel in Cass's jeans as she carried me to our destination. Laura was a world away. Besides, she had never packed. The few times we fooled around with strap-ons were only playful and ended with her not wanting to perpetuate patriarchal norms of sexuality. I told her then that that kind of thinking is bullshit, but I couldn't convince her.

Once at the hotel we started tearing at each other's clothes. I couldn't help myself. I needed to touch her cock, to stroke it, ride it. I needed to come again…and again. I wasn't hungry; I was ravenous. She stopped me when I tried to unzip her jeans.

"Who's in charge here?" she asked rather sternly.

"You are." I played along, figuring she would let me have my way in a moment.

"And who am I to you?"

I knew the answer she was looking for, and although it would have felt awkward with anyone else, my soaked cunt attested to my utter love of saying it: "Daddy."

"You've been such a naughty girl this evening. Let's see if Daddy can straighten you out," Cass said. "Everyone knows that good girls don't let their cunts get fucked at crowded bars."

"Yes."

"Yes, what?"

"Yes, Daddy, you're right. I'll never do it again."

"That's where you're wrong. You will do it again. And soon. You'll do anything I want." Cass's tone was determined.

Memory is deceptive, particularly when circumstances are new. I had never been with a man before, so I had no training for what came next. I knew when we were in first year and she wore her biker jacket to class and carried her wallet on a chain that she was out of my league—more experienced, more uninhibited, and more rough. More, more, more.

"Daddy's got a plan for his little sweetness," Cass said as she stroked the bulge of her pants with her right hand. I had tried to unzip her before. I was hoping that she was going to undress, but somehow I knew that would have been far too simple—and not her style. She unfastened her leather belt. Carefully, slowly, while I sat cross-legged on the bed and stared anxiously, she unthreaded the belt from the loops in her jeans. I thought about how I had clung to that belt at the bar, how it had served as an anchor in this wealthy ocean of sexual knowledge. Cass held the belt in front of her in both of her hands, like an offering. She approached me, sat down next to me. Our eyes, which had locked in intensive stare minutes before, were attuned with each other. I followed the sternness of her expression and her outstretched hand and instinctively gave her mine. I should have known she didn't want to hold hands. In a swoop she had me cradled palm to palm between her fingers as she encircled my wrists with her belt. She completed her project and fastened the buckle, instantly showing me she was in control. Everything until now had felt good. I had gone against my better judgment but not against my will. I would have been able to stop her or myself at any point before, but with my wrists tied I was starting to lose that ability.

My eyes must have been as round as teacups. A loud gulp sounded in my throat. We had barely spoken to each other. What could I say now? She had penetrated my public image and shaken the little bad girl in my core. Did I trust her? I wasn't sure. Did I trust myself and the decades of conditioning that had yielded supposedly healthy sexual experiences with supposedly healthy women? What did I know? At that moment Cass reached into her back pocket and pulled out a black bandanna. I knew I didn't know anything. She puckered her lips boyishly and pseudo-smiled at me, sending chills throughout my body. Kneeling in front of me on the bed, Cass held the bandanna in her right hand and ran it up my arm and around my neck. She grabbed the cloth together with my hair in her fist and jerked me forward. Her eyes, which hadn't left mine, closed and she leaned in and kissed me deeply, wrapping her tongue around mine, mimicking the magnetism her eyes had had. I closed my eyes. In the darkness I felt safe and beautiful, and also felt the augmented sensation of the wetness we created together. I could feel her left hand meeting her right and the bandanna squeezing tightly around the circumference of my head. Another knot. Cass had successfully removed my ability to see or move.

I could hear the zipper of her jeans.

"I know you've been wanting this all night."

"Mmm," I moaned. I could imagine what she was doing, what she looked like underneath her jeans, but I wanted so badly to see for myself. I wanted so badly to not be in the state she had put me in, where my curiosity would have to wait and could potentially remain unappeased forever. Oh, God, how I needed to see her, touch her, feel her touching me. Nothing was happening. I felt alone in the dark, with my imagination running wild. It was like those times as a child, touching myself in seclusion and risking the absolute devastation that someone could find out. I was doing this, being more vulnerable than I would have imagined myself capable of, in front of Cass. My God. I was shaking with self-doubt and arousal, and just when I reached the limit of what I could take, I felt it.

Cass's cock caressed my lips, and hungrily I opened my mouth. Her hands caressed my head as I intuitively engulfed her strap-on. She moaned and stroked the back of my head and I felt the strangest freedom of utter desire. It consumed me. Nothing mattered in that moment more than pleasing Cass and hearing proof of that pleasure. Her hands guided my head back and forth on the firm shaft, and I lost myself entirely. All I could think about was her cock and the possibility that she might fuck me. I was still a virgin in the official way. I probably should have been scared, but I wasn't. Cass stopped. She slid the dildo out of my mouth and I heard her step back.

"You like that, don't you? You dirty little slut."

"I do, Cass. I really like it. I mean, yes, Daddy, I do. I love it."

"You want it again."

"Yes."

"Then beg."

My mind exploded. This would be the impossible. It was one thing that she had so brutally taken me and tied me against my will; that I had consented didn't matter. But to ask me to beg, to ask me to admit how deeply desirous and ravenous and filthy I was. I didn't think I was capable.

"Well?" Cass was becoming impatient. I was scared. I didn't know how to do this. I didn't know what to say. I didn't want her to stop what we had been doing. I needed her back. I needed more of her.

"Please," I urged quietly.

"What was that?" Cass insisted. "I can barely hear you."

"Please," I said louder.

"Please, what?"

"Please, Daddy?"

"Please, Daddy what?"

"Please, Daddy, may I suck your cock?" I said, and shed a lifetime of shame and angst. I was capable of asking for what I wanted. I could articulate my desires, and I could trust myself. I was liberated. I was on fire. "Daddy, I need your cock. Please, may I have it?"

"That's better," Cass said as she came back and let me continue. Ferociously, I devoured her. I wanted to show her how good I could be. I moved my body rhythmically and found a momentum that worked. We both moaned and swayed together, and even though I couldn't see her I could feel her and hear her. She was caressing my back and making me feel so good. The silicone dildo slid easily over my tongue and along the roof of my mouth. She moaned and stared down at me, caressing my head, holding it firmly in her hands, refusing to let me stop. I have always been pragmatic and therefore never believed in things that weren't real. And that is how I know that that evening, her cock was more than silicone. I don't know if it was she who breathed life into it or me who sucked life out of it, but it was alive.

She stopped me and turned me around. All she said was, "Daddy wants to fuck." I wasn't used to taking direction, and Cass was a woman of few words, the fewest I'd ever experienced. Her stoicism worked, though. I wouldn't have dared to ask her any questions—either about herself or about her decisions. She took control of the situation and gave me no power to strive for. I knew that all I had was my trust that she would do what was best, and I believed in it. Her firm hands gripped my side, and she positioned me on my hands and knees, facing away from her. My mind was exploding with anticipation of what this would feel like. My first time ever with a cock, and I was to be on my knees. I'd only ever seen women do this in porn. Even during our wildest nights, Laura and I would have been nicely cradled at each other's sides. I was preparing to be pounded and couldn't believe how completely turned on I was at the idea of it. Political correctness was far away.

I didn't want anything more than to please Daddy.

Behind me, also resting on her bent knees, I could feel Cass finding the right grasp of my ass and hips. I knew I was wet, but she touched me and felt for herself, as she was entitled to do. Her fingers slid inside of me with ease, and I let out a gasp. The feeling was surreal. Part of my pleasure was from her touch, but mostly it was her invasion of my freedom and my awareness of it. I was able to watch myself submit to her, crumble beneath the weight of her, give her everything she could possibly want. I went from virgin to slut in a matter of hours in the capsule of a hotel room.

Cass's cock entered me without grace or care. She knew what she wanted, and her cock knew as well. Everything I had been scared of as a virgin for the entirety of my life to that point had been false. It didn't hurt. I didn't need someone to be gentle my first time. I didn't even need her to know. I wanted to have my brains fucked out, and that was what I got. Cass gripped me by the waist. She used my hips as her steering wheel, driving herself deeper and deeper. I moaned in pleasure and sighed with relief that it felt like this.

"Daddy's going to come inside you," Cass said. She bellowed, and I felt her throbbing invasion come to a massive halt. She held me poised in that position for what seemed like forever. I held my breath and listened to her moans.

She stopped, turned me around, and found me with her tongue. As she licked my clit intensely, her moans sent wild tintinnabulations through my body. In a giant shudder I released with orchestra-like elegance, the biggest concerto of a climax I have ever experienced.

After that a sense of bliss set in. I couldn't possibly come down from this high to the gentle sleepiness I was used to. I was shocked at myself, delighted by her and my body's capacity to feel such thorough pleasure. Waves of postclimax shudders came over me and paralleled my disbelief. I didn't know what would happen tomorrow, how I would deal with the aftermath, how she would treat me in the morning. I guessed I would have to move out when

I got home. Those speculations weren't important. For what I had that night with Cass I would have given up everything that was comfortable and safe. And I did.

We lay side by side. She smoked. I listened to her pulse slow down to its usual tempo. There weren't words to describe it, no niceties to be exchanged. After what seemed like hours, Cass turned on her side and faced me, our bodies intertwined in our sheets and excess clothing.

"I have a confession to make," Cass said as I lay on her arm in the messiness of the hotel sheets. "I remember you too. You were brunette then and a bit of a hippie. You wore long skirts, little makeup, and smelled like sandalwood. You sat in the fourth row. That's why I always sat in the third."

Spring Cleaning

Rachel Kramer Bussel

During my week off in April, one I take every year to approximate my memories of spring break, I decided that instead of going away to some tropical paradise I needed to stick a little closer to home. Like my bedroom. The time had come to tackle the truly horrendous catastrophe that my collection of clothes, books, magazines, papers, knickknacks, cards, gifts, clothes, and just plain, well, stuff, had become. I'd tried everything. Like the best dieter, who can reel off the calories in almost every food item and has tried them all, from Atkins to the Zone, I have tried almost everything I can think of or have ever heard about in order to manage the belongings I have accumulated over the past twenty-five years. Yet somehow even if it looks like it will last, it never does, and within days I'm back to the drawing board. So I made the decision to call in the big guns—Let Us Do the Dirty Work. They are a personal organizing firm that I'd heard about from well-intentioned friends who just didn't seem to understand that deep down inside me lurked the heart of a clean, neat, tidy woman. Finally I'd gotten a decent job and had enough money to invest in getting the job done right. I figured I'd fork over a hefty sum of cash and they'd literally do my dirty work for me. I'd go out, run some errands, and a few hours later my place would be spick-and-span, and I'd never have to hunt around for my keys, cell phone, or missing black miniskirt again. Boy, was I wrong.

They assigned me to a woman named Charlene, who sounded pleasant enough on the phone—kind and warm with a hint of a Southern accent. Charlene didn't look like a taskmaster or mistress. In fact, she looked very much like her name suggested she might: Her appearance was soft, sweet, pink. She dressed in an efficient yet elegant pink silk suit along with simple nude stockings and pink pumps. She was perky and cheerful as she surveyed the abyss that was my room.

"I'm so glad that you chose to work with my company. We really have the special touch, and we'll get all this mess taken care of in no time." She paused, beaming at me. "So you can use your bedroom for more creative endeavors," she said, and her words here took on the spark of something else—teasing, sass, flirtation. But just as soon as I thought I caught a gleam in her eye, she had moved on. The warmth in her voice quickly vanished as she set about giving me tasks. "You sit here," she commanded, firmly pushing me down into a chair, and proceeding to pile things in my lap, telling me to sort them into "keep" and "give away" piles. I thought I was doing pretty well while she was busy working her way around the room. However, when she returned half an hour later and my lap was still covered in clothes, she looked down at me reprovingly.

"You're not really into this. You're just going through the motions. Why bother with someone like me if you're not going to do it right?" she demanded, glaring down at me. "Where I come from, insolence like this just isn't tolerated. Good thing I found something amidst the rubble here that will help drill that lesson into your head, or at least your ass," she said. I looked up to find her wielding a riding crop, the one that had been a gift from my ex, Sarah. The one I'd thrown on the ground ages ago and hadn't seen since. It was gorgeous, studded with purple crystals, short but sweet, and it packed a satisfying wallop. It looked quite menacing now, the way Charlene was gripping it, running her fingers up and down the skinny rod, then tapping it against her palm, like a schoolteacher, belaying a calm that did little to forestall the impending storm. With one carefully manicured hand, she swept the clutter from my lap onto the floor. She took a step closer until she and her heaving breasts were staring down at me. I wanted to laugh, but something on her face told me she didn't find this at all amusing. She took my chin between her thumb and forefinger and forced me to look up at her.

"Listen to me, sweetie. We're going to whip this room into shape whether you like it or not. You're not allowed to be a spoiled brat as long as I'm around. I think maybe you need a little added incentive, a special something to keep you on track. Get up," she said, shooing me out of the chair, before sitting down on it herself. "Strip," she said, as if she were demanding I take out the trash or stack magazines neatly in the corner. I stared at her, my body beginning to tingle as I realized she was absolutely serious. The sneaky Southern belle thought she could just order me around; she was right. I suddenly wanted to do everything she said, wanted to move at warp speed around my room and throw out every last piece of paper, errant receipt, crumpled shirt, and forgotten pair of stockings. I wanted to take all of it and throw it out the window, wanted to show her that I could be the poster child for tidiness. But before that I definitely wanted to see what she would do with that riding crop. Sarah and I had only played with it jokingly, mostly teasing or threatening each other, neither of us having the gumption to actually bring it down through the air so it whistled and landed with a sting. I had a feeling Charlene would have no such trouble.

I fumbled with my buttons, my fingers suddenly forgetting how to perform the simplest of tasks. When I'd misjudged for the third time, Charlene stepped toward me and pushed my hands down by my sides. "I'll do it. Just like I have to do everything around here, clearly," she huffed, and made quick work of the buttons. She pulled down the zipper of my jeans and in just a few efficient motions had me completely naked. "Now, where are we going to put you? Clearly, there's not much room in this junk heap." She shoved everything off the chair and planted herself in it. "Get over here, and lay down across my lap." I stood there for a moment, hovering. "I know there's not that much room, but who's fault is that? Find a way to make it work, or you'll be in for something even worse," she said, her voice quickly losing any semblance of patience. I did as I was told, somehow precariously balancing so that my feet skimmed the surface of my desk, my fingertips brushed the floor, and my ass was right in Charlene's line of vision.

"Now this is what I like to see: a ripe, curvy ass like yours just waiting to be spanked. I know what you need, my dear. I saw this coming a mile away. I wanted to give you a chance to surprise me, but I knew you wouldn't. I've been in this business for enough years to know that the most severe cases like you need prodding of a different sort to finally work on their clutter. And that's exactly what you're going to get," she said, her voice rising in sadistic glee as her hand came slamming down on my ass. It hurt! And yet, right beneath the sting of her palm connecting with my bare cheek was a warmth that traveled throughout my skin. She must have been ambidextrous, because she used her other hand to land just as forceful a blow to my other cheek. Soon she was spanking away, and just when I thought I'd gotten used to the pain, I heard the crop whistling through the air. Sarah would certainly never have hit me like that. The shock of it stilled me for a moment, my heart the only part of me that still seemed to be moving. It felt like a jolt of electricity had just traveled straight from that one spot on my ass deep into my cunt. I realized that I must be dripping wet. Surely Charlene had to notice. Even though she was the one who'd forced me to strip, who'd ordered me across her lap and began spanking me, I was embarrassed to be so turned on by this. What must she think of me? Would she think I had led her on, had hired her firm just so I could get off? But I hadn't, right? How could I have? I couldn't think about it anymore, because Charlene let loose with a series of blows that left me bracing for the next one, my body simply a vessel of heat and arousal.

"That's right. You take all that I have to give you, and I know you like it. I know what kind of brat you are, and I'm here to tell you that this kind of slovenliness will no longer be tolerated. You are going to get this room in tip-top shape, or else you'll face much worse punishments, believe you me, missy.

I'm going to smack the slob right out of you." Charlene punctuated her words with harsh blows, ones that seemed especially powerful for a tiny woman like her. Her accent had become more prominent too, and she dug her red talon-like nails into the curvy flesh of my ass to emphasize her point before raking them up along my already reddened skin. I broke down and whimpered, not sure whether I wanted her to stop or continue. No one had ever touched me like that, had dared to shock me or take any such risk, let alone talk to me like that. Perhaps I'd been begging for punishment all along and had simply never found the person to give it to me right.

Just when I thought I couldn't take any more and the heat and pain were collapsing in on themselves, she stopped. She pressed her palms against my lower back, and I felt their heat. She let her hand glide along my wet opening, teasing me when I moaned. She slid one finger inside me, and I clutched it greedily, needing it to complete the promise of my orgasm. Maybe I'd been turned on ever since she came in the room. I wasn't sure. She didn't say a word as her hand softly probed, lightly stroking me until I came, a burst of hot white light filling my closed eyes, an explosion of lava as she petted my back. I felt like I'd been traveling, orbiting in some far off solar system, and was suddenly spiraling back to earth, back to reality. My eyes had been clenched shut since I first lowered myself across her lap, and when I opened them everything looked slightly off. Was this really my home? This grandiose mess of items that now looked so foreign—I couldn't remember ever acquiring them. I peeked behind me, seeing her hand resting on my ass, the hints of red still lingering on my pale skin. She didn't smile at me, but her eyes told me that she trusted me to fulfill her mandate.

I saw Charlene again a few months later. We were both out at the same club. She beckoned me to her, arching her finger in that come hither movement that usually looks so cheesy, but I was still under her spell. This time she kissed me intensely before her hand went to my ass. We didn't say a word as we danced song after song, winding together like two snakes. When I got her home we practically floated across the perfectly clear, clean wooden floors. And when we landed on my pristine new queen-size bed, free of everything except sheets, pillows, and a comforter, this time I got on top of her.

My Mistress Awaits

JULIEN LEE

Anne was at an age when horny brothers would forget themselves and their blood ties. Simple, innocent things like bathing became a risky pleasure as lustful eyes would always keep her company. She was not a Venus or anything near to beauty, not in her current state anyway. Her hair was dark as rosewood and tangled like briars. Her eyes were a mix of blue, green, and brown. A coveted combination, you may think, but to her the blend was not as enchanting as its parts. Daily she labored in the fields and tended the stock, and yet the sun refused to reward her with the golden hue of a goddess. She felt unmemorable in every way, but this humble nature made her more beautiful to keen eyes.

It was a fortunate day when Isabelle fixed her eyes upon Anne. On a whim, like most of her decision-making, Isabelle convinced herself she could ride and tame a wild horse. As the daughter of wealthy and well-respected family, she could do whatever her heart desired as long as her family name was never tarnished. Her father had recently acquired a white-gray horse and intended to break the fiery animal himself. It refused to be mastered by anyone, and its capture required the strength of six men. Isabelle asked the stable boy to distract the horse as it bucked in its wood-fenced pen. She patiently waited, balancing atop the fence, and then mounted the wild horse when the opportunity came. She held tightly to its mane, which only spurred it to jump the fence and charge through the countryside.

It mercilessly trampled the blossoming fields nearby, and it was a difficult ride for Isabelle—riding bareback bruised her delicate inner thighs. In a desperate moment Isabelle leapt off the mad beast and landed in a trough of rainwater. Anne rushed to calm the horse before it caused any more damage. She had always had a way with animals. Isabelle gave a joyful laugh, which charmed Anne.

"Are you all right?" Anne yelled as she placated the horse with gentle pats and soothing words.

"Are you talking to me or the horse?" Isabelle joked.

"You, of course," Anne retorted as she led the horse toward the water trough.

The golden-haired woman rose from her bath with her clothes clinging tightly to her skin. Her breasts, coy and enviable, revealed their full shape under the dampness of the cloth. Pale pink nipples beckoned to be kissed and warmed by an eager mouth. "I'll live," replied Isabelle. For a moment, Anne was so lost in the feelings that stirred within that she did not hear Isabelle's reply. What she felt went beyond anything she'd ever known, triggering the most primal reaction. Now she understood the satisfaction that came from looking at another's nakedness. And though they were but a breath away, Anne resigned herself to believing Isabelle was beyond her reach.

A small cavalry of horsemen, including the stable boy, came to escort their Mistress home. "Thank you…" Isabelle began to say when she realized she didn't know to whom she should address her appreciation.

"Anne," the farm girl replied. Isabelle mounted a horse while the stable boy held its reins. This was goodbye, and Anne was helpless to stop it. The wild horse resisted as the stable boy tried to rope its neck. "Would you help us return the horse to the stable?" Isabelle pleaded. "I will have one of my servants return you safely by nightfall." This was her chance to be with Isabelle, even if it was for just a few hours longer. She had everything to gain and nothing to lose. Anne smiled, climbed onto the white-gray horse, and rode alongside Isabelle all the way.

Anne did not return to her farm by nightfall. In fact, she never returned. A new life opened to Anne when Isabelle's father rewarded her kindness to his daughter with a job working as a servant of the family with occasional duties in the stable. For most, this would seem an insult. Anne saw it differently. She loved living in a grand estate, being paid for her hard work, and being free from unwanted attention. What she loved most of all was being with Isabelle. Anne enjoyed doing things for her—serving her breakfast in bed, dressing her, brushing her hair, drawing her bath, being the first to see her in the morning and the last to see her at night. She grew to love Isabelle and wanted desperately to be loved by her. Many nights Anne would lie in bed fantasizing Isabelle was beside her, stroking the sensual areas of her body only she had ever touched. She enjoyed dreams in which she and Isabelle made love, and in reality she would orgasm.

Another night alone became too much for Anne to bear. She rallied her courage and entered Isabelle's bed chamber unnoticed. The candles were unexpectedly lit, casting large shadows on the walls. Anne hid in a dark corner and spied silently. Isabelle lay naked in the middle of her plush bed, the soft white sheets kicked down to her ankles. She writhed in utter pleasure, caressing her breast with one hand as the other playfully massaged her pubic curls. Her eyes were closed, her mind imagining more than what was in the room. The wet, rhythmic sounds from her loins would crescendo and decrescendo as her fingers slid in and out in waves. The titillating scene made Anne breathless and hot. Her heart was not the only organ palpitating. She was content as a voyeur, standing silent and pacifying her own arousal when she heard Isabelle softly moan her name. Anne stopped breathing. Did she really hear it? Isabelle moaned her name again and confirmed her hopes. "Isabelle," Anne whispered back. Isabelle opened her eyes and turned towards Anne, who emerged from the shadows. She did not move to cover herself or scream for Anne's dismissal. Instead, Isabelle's hands remained on her body, poised in mid motion. Her smile signaled Anne to come closer.

Anne's limbs tingled with excitement as she crawled onto the bed. Isabelle sat up and touched Anne's flushed cheek and traced her trembling lips with her thumb. Anne could taste her honeyed finger and sucked it deeply. Isabelle untied Anne's nightgown with her free hand and peeled the cloth down to her waist. Anne's breasts were soft and supple. Nipples curved slightly upwards awaiting Isabelle's lips. She bent and welcomed it with a tongued kiss. She could feel the resonance between her legs as she tasted the sweetness of Anne's skin. The smooth nipple grew hard in her mouth—as her tongue sparred, her lips would kiss it in truce. Her teeth gently brushed the sensitive area and made Anne cry out. Her other breast peaked on its own in anticipation.

Anne pulled Isabelle up to her lips and engulfed her in a deep kiss. They fell back onto the bed, fondling the other's breast. Their legs laced together tightly. Anne would thrust her pelvis against Isabelle, spreading the wetness over her smooth leg. Hungry for the taste, Isabelle kissed her way down to the source. Anne became weak and spread her legs in surrender, feeling the cool tongue against her feverish, swollen sex. It circled and licked and teased her into madness. Anne moaned as Isabelle reached up to squeeze her breast. She moaned again when Isabelle's tongue penetrated the center of her soft flesh, savoring what she found within. Anne began to salivate, thirsting for that honey once more.

Anne pulled Isabelle's face up to hers. She could taste herself in Isabelle's wet kiss. She pressed her onto her back. Anne inverted her body over Isabelle, parting Isabelle's delicate legs. She lingered on her tender apex and found pleasure in hearing Isabelle wail. She delved hungrily into her, swallowing the warm juice her sex released. Isabelle drank Anne in too; her hands pulled Anne's buttocks apart, allowing her tongue to fully taste the length of her hot flesh. They alternated taking breaths, keeping the pleasure continuous. Their bodies pulsated and burned, straining to hold back the sweet release. But their lips below stiffened, demanded it now, now, now. Isabelle cried out first. Anne felt Isabelle throbbing in her mouth but refused to stop. She let up only when Isabelle tongued her in return, harder, deeper, faster. She sought the sweet spot that would make her lover come. Anne could not expect from which direction it would swoop next, and this excited her into orgasm. She pressed herself more firmly onto Isabelle's mouth as she came and came again. The beating inside them finally subsided, and they released each other. Isabelle spun herself around, slid into Anne's arms and fell asleep.

Isabelle awoke to the bright morning sun and found that Anne was no longer beside her. Somehow she knew Anne would not return and did not want to be found. As feelings of abandonment crept in, Isabelle tightly clutched the pillow beside her and inhaled the fading scent of her first love.

Anne loved Isabelle but believed familial and societal obligations would one day tear them apart. Anne accepted this and thought it better to swim in dreams and memories than brave the torrents of a broken heart. She would remember every detail of that night for the rest of her days.

Heating Up

TINA SIMMONS

Ninety-one degrees. That's what the thermostat said. Ninety-fuck-ing-one degrees.

I needed my air conditioner fixed and I didn't much care who did the job. But when I answered the door to a hot looking dyke in a wife beater, low-slung jeans, and brown work boots, the prospect of getting my air conditioning fixed took on a whole new meaning.

"I'm Tamara, from Atlanta Heating and Cooling," she said, with just a trace of that Southern belle accent that drives me wild.

"Thank God."

She grinned wryly. "Y'know, sometimes I think I'm in this business because of all the adulation and worship I get."

"Sorry, but next to a naked Tori Amos, I can't think of anyone I'd rather see." I knew I sounded desperate, but damn, I was sweating my ass off.

She ran a hand through her short mop of blondish-brown curls and hitched a battered tool bag higher on her shoulder. "Honey, that's probably the best compliment I've gotten all week."

I gestured her into my town house. When I'd been able to save enough to put a down payment on my own little bit of heaven, Atlanta—home to sweet tea, peach pie, and Scarlett O'Hara—had seemed like an ideal location to this Midwestern girl. Now in the August heat I wanted to be in the frozen tundra, not surrounded by swimming pools and asphalt.

"Thanks, I think." She looked around, appraising my sparsely decorated place, which consisted mostly of second-hand furniture, a bunch of photographic equipment, and a dozen or so black-and-white photographs and prints in various sizes on the walls. "Are you a photographer?"

I nodded. "Yeah."

She studied one of my favorites—a black and white nude of my ex-girlfriend Kylie—with an appreciative nod. "I love this."

"Thanks."

She looked at me. "How long has your air conditioning been out?"

"A week and a half," I said, trying not to sound annoyed. It wasn't her fault her company had been booked solid since my air conditioner went on the fritz. "I'm about ready to go stay in a hotel."

"That's a bitch. Can I check your thermostat?"

I led her to the thermostat on the wall between the kitchen and my bedroom. We were standing shoulder to shoulder in the narrow hall. She smelled like sweat and coconut shampoo.

She put her tool bag on the floor and popped the cover off the thermostat. I was utterly mesmerized watching her fiddle with the wires and dig tools out of her tool bag. Her hands were small and deeply tanned like the rest of her, with short, neat nails. I decided those hands could work me over any day of the week.

"Must be the heat," I muttered.

"Excuse me?"

"Nothing," I said, feeling the temperature rising as I stood there. "So, what's the problem?"

"I don't think it's the thermostat," she said finally, looking up at me with wide, green eyes.

I realized I was too close to her and took two steps back. Something about this girl was making me hotter than being without air conditioning in August. Maybe I was suffering from heatstroke. Or maybe it was just the ridiculously long dry spell I'd been experiencing lately. Whatever it was, Tamara had me creaming my shorts. I could practically smell my cunt getting juicy.

"I'll have to check the unit. It's out back?"

I wanted to tell her I had a unit she could check, but I only nodded.

She cocked her head to the side and stared at me. "You all right?"

"Sure," I said. "Just hot."

In more ways than one.

"Right." She hefted the tool bag up on her shoulder and headed for the front door. "I'll check back with you when I figure out what's wrong. Shouldn't take too long."

I watched her leave and decided her ass was as delicious as the rest of her.

I wanted to go outside and drool over Tamara, but I didn't want her to think I was some sort of wacko. Instead I walked through to the kitchen and peeked in the fridge, even though I wasn't hungry. The cool blast of air felt wonderful, but it didn't take the edge off my lust for the air conditioning repair babe. I hooked a finger in my tank top and pulled it from my sweat-soaked body, feeling my nipples go rigid from the cold.

I wandered into my bedroom, contemplating a shower. I'd have to wait until Tamara took off though. As soon as I jumped in the shower, she'd be back. I flung myself across my bed and tried to think cool thoughts. Instead all I could think about was the sexy little thing working on my air conditioner.

I could hear banging noises coming from out back. I wanted to be the one getting banged. One minute I was laying there, sprawled across the bed with my arms over my head, the next minute I had one hand down the front of my baggy shorts, my fingers digging into my hungry cunt.

Between salacious thoughts of Tamara and the overwhelming heat in my apartment, I was slick and swollen. I thrust two fingers inside my cunt and fucked myself hard, strumming my clit with my thumb on the down stroke.

It was one of those orgasms that didn't need coaxing. Quick and dirty—or at least sweaty—I came hard, my quivering cunt clenching around my fingers as I writhed on the bed. I lay there, feeling the ripples subside as I gently stroked my clit. It had felt good to get off, but it hadn't come close to satisfying me.

My breathing was still a little ragged, and I guess that's why I hadn't heard her. It wasn't until I opened my eyes that I saw

Tamara standing in my bedroom door, her tool bag on the floor beside her.

"I knocked, but I guess you didn't hear me." She didn't look the least bit embarrassed. "I think I found your problem."

If it hadn't been so damn hot and I hadn't just jerked myself off, I probably would have blushed. As it was I yanked my hand from my pants and sat up.

"Uh, what's that?" I said, looking anywhere but at Tamara.

"You need to get laid."

"Hmm?" I had suddenly lost all capability of coherent speech. Not that I'd been doing a very good job of it before.

Tamara came toward me, stripping off her wife beater. Her tight, white sports bra hugged her tits but couldn't hide her plump, hard nipples. By the time she was standing at the end of the bed, working her belt loose, I was up on my knees, nearly eye level with her.

"That was the hottest thing I've ever seen," she murmured against my mouth as I reached for her zipper.

I wasn't going to give her a chance to change her mind. I stripped my own sweat-soaked T-shirt over my bed, my bare tits swaying as I flung the shirt away. She cupped them in her hands, up and towards her mouth where she greedily devoured first one nipple, then the other. I moaned and pulled her down by her mane of unruly curls.

I lost my balance on the bed and we tumbled backward, her mouth still attached to my tit. She bit down, a little harder than I like, and I tugged her head back by her hair.

"Easy there," I said, fumbling with her jeans. She was as sweaty as I was and her jeans clung to her body like a wet suit. I got them, along with her white cotton underwear, down around her hips through sheer determination and a lot of tugging.

I gave up on stripping her naked and slid one hand up between her thighs, still pinned close together by her jeans. She was already soaked when I touched her. I moaned, knowing it had been my little masturbatory show that had gotten her so wet. I pushed two fingers into her, hard. She whimpered. I started stroking her G spot like it was a worry stone, and she nearly came off the bed.

I pushed her head back down to my tits, and she latched onto my nipple like she would never let go—which was just fine by me. I drove my fingers into her, listening to her whimper around my swollen nipple. My cunt twitched in response as she sucked to the rhythm of my fingers fucking her.

I wrapped my thighs around her hip and pressed against her, the rough fabric of my shorts rubbing against my engorged clit. "God, you're hot."

She moaned in response and arched against me, driving her jean-clad hipbone against my crotch. "I'm gonna come."

"Yeah, babe," I panted, by way of encouragement. "Yeah."

Her breath caught, and then she came with a long breathy sigh and a gush of wetness. She clutched at my wrist, drawing my fingers deeper until my entire hand was wedged between the lips of her cunt, plump and ripe as a Georgia peach. She was almost too hot to touch, but I kept fucking her until her nails dug into my wrist and she dragged me away.

I was so focused on getting her off, I hadn't realized how close I was to coming again. I thrust against her hip until I was sure I must be bruising the hell out of her, but she never complained. I came, riding her hip like she was a bucking bronco and ignoring the roughness of my shorts on my sensitive cunt. Despite my earlier orgasm this one was longer and harder, and I held her head between my sweaty tits until my orgasm subsided.

Reluctantly, I pulled away from her. My chest glistened with sweat and I felt like I was wearing a diaper, the fabric of my shorts damp and bunched up in my crotch. Despite the discomfort, I grinned like a fool.

Tamara let out a deep sigh. "Oh, honey. Talk about perks of the job."

We lay there for several silent minutes, inches apart because it was just too damn hot to be touching now that we'd fucked ourselves silly. Finally, I laughed.

"What's so funny?" she asked, flinging her arms over her head. She was still wearing her sports bra and hadn't bothered to pull her jeans up yet, and her hair was a sweaty matted mess. She looked silly and sexy at the same time.

I leaned over and teased her nipple through her bra with my teeth. "I was contemplating sabotaging my air conditioner to get you back over here again."

"You don't have to worry about that."

Her tone suggested I wasn't going to like the reason, but I asked anyway. "Why?"

"The bad news is, I have to replace the air handler," she said. "The part won't be in for a week."

The thought of another week without air conditioning made me whimper, and not in a good way. "What's the good news?"

She rolled on her side toward me and grinned. "I live alone and have a king-sized bed."

"Yeah," I said, as seriously as I could. "But do you have air conditioning?"

A Bowl of Cherries

ANNIE GAUGER

I

Lucy had parted her legs, her calves tangling in the flannel sheets.

"Go ahead," she said, leaning against the pillows. "I'm ready."

Lucy stroked Sarah's face and waited for the moment Sarah would rub the tip of her penis against Lucy's clitoris. Lucy sighed and looked at the moon.

Oh, the moon, splashing its reflection across the water. Oh, the little town across the bay, its silhouette a black cutout against the sky. Oh, the wind, billowing the red-and-green striped curtains overhead. Oh, the moan of Nina Simone spinning a ballad out of the boom box.

"Just a little rub around the mound of Venus. A little rub before you dip into the honey pot."

Lucy felt the delicious circling, the wet that Sarah streaked out of her. Lucy waited. The circling turned to a pulse until the only thing she thought of was the easy plunge to come. Wet begot wet, and still Lucy waited. She wondered if she would have to beg. She hated to beg—begging meant she was out of control. But begging was worth it if she had to.

"Please," said Lucy.

But no plunge came. Instead Sarah in the moonlight held up a cherry on its stem.

"Do you remember?" said Sarah.

"It's how you won me over," Lucy said. Sarah had unusual talents. She could tie a knot in a cherry stem with her tongue. Lucy thought back to their first date. When she counted up twenty-seven tongue-tied cherry stems laid out on the bar at the end of the night, she knew she had found a woman she wanted to spend some time with.

"Please?" said Lucy. She spread her legs further, wondering if they should start over, and if she should affect the role of a prude. Cat and mouse. Cat and mouse in the pink beach house.

Sarah dangled the cherry. In silhouette against the moonlight, Sarah kissed it as she would a penis, her lips encircling the tip. A sweet penis, belonging to someone Lucy imagined. Yet a penis disembodied. Sarah's lips puckered around it. Then, as requested, the cherry circled around Lucy's clitoris like a penis—the wet being drawn up through the folds of her vulva, the clitoris becoming like an erect nipple, waiting.

"Very nice," said Lucy. "Almost like the real thing. But where is our little friend?" Lucy thought of the boomerang-shaped double-headed dildo, and spread her labia.

Sarah plunged the cherry up inside Lucy who drew a sharp breath. She was speechless for a moment.

"I wanted to try something different," whispered Sarah. She leaned back and reached for the bowl. She kissed a cherry. Wet in the dark, Sarah pushed it inside of Lucy.

"But where's?"

"Shh."

Sarah sucked a new cherry—a double headed cherry. Lucy arched her back in anticipation. Sarah bit it.

"How could you?"

Sarah slipped the broken cherry between Lucy's lips. The tart juice burst in Lucy's mouth. Her tongue soon held two pits. The tide was up. Waves broke on the dock outside the window.

"Shh."

"I want—"

Sarah kissed her and moved her hips between Lucy's legs. Lucy wrapped around Sarah, then she pressed her knees into her lover's side. They were a perfect fit, their breasts barely kissing in the moonlight.

"Where's our little friend? I want to spit out the cherries now."

But Sarah kissed her, then loosened an arm. She took a bottle of Candy Joy Edible Lubricant, flicked open its lid, and dribbled it on the cherries. She reclicked the cap and left the half-full bottle in the bowl. Then one by one by one, Sarah pushed handfuls of cherries into Lucy.

As the bowl of cherries filled her, Lucy forgot about Sarah's penis. She spread her knees to her ears, as though she were a perfect vase waiting to spill, a cornucopia to overflow.

"Please," she said.

Sarah slid down the length of the bed and sucked Lucy's clitoris until one by one by one the warmed fruit involuntarily popped out again.

"I don't want to come," said Lucy. "I want to come when you come. So come on."

Lucy wanted Sarah. She wanted Sarah to fuck her and lose control. She wanted a magic wand to reach up inside her to rub her cervix, that cherry with its stemless dent within. First she wanted Sarah's middle finger, then the dildo, or the handle of a certain pink hairbrush. She needed Sarah's hand because it knew the exact amount of pressure and when to apply it. Sometimes as Sarah pressed her breasts against Lucy, as Sarah thrust her penis inside Lucy—the other end of the penis thrusting up into Sarah—Lucy thought they had been lovers for centuries. That in another life, Sarah had fathered a dozen children, that she, Lucy, had birthed them so easily. That she, Lucy, had fathered a few children, herself. Lucky they didn't have to be boy/girl this life around.

II

The moon was setting, and each time Lucy giggled, cherries popped into the flannel sheets. Sarah tickled her until she had refilled the bowl, burying the bottle of Candy Joy Edible Lubricant at the bottom. Sarah set the bowl of still-wet cherries on top of the dresser for later. They gleamed in the morning light, pretty enough to be painted into a still life.

Lucy and Sarah rarely slept in the big bedroom that looked out over the sea because the room belonged to Lucy's mother. When they had arrived the night before, they dropped their suitcases in the living room and went their separate ways. Lucy went to the grocery store for fresh produce while Sarah went outside to plant a row of topiaries in the shape of twisted ice-cream cones. When they came together after dark, they fell into each other's arms in the bedroom overlooking the sea.

The curtains billowed in the breeze, and Lucy wrapped the flannel sheets around them as Sarah got back into bed.

"But your penis?" said Lucy. "I'm ready to moan your name."

"Well, dear, I have some bad news," said Sarah. "Scout got it."

Lucy sat up. "Scoutie? How?" She looked out the bedroom door of the beach house. In the morning light she saw a dozen pet toys strewn across the braided rug. What could the dog possibly need with their dildo?

"Well, darling," said Sarah, "Scout is upset. She's doesn't like to leave home. I let her sleep in your suitcase while I was outside planting the bushes. You know, so she could smell us. To reassure her. When I came back inside, well, she had the dildo on the rug. And, well, it was a really good chew. A great chew. You should have seen her eyes. She was wild."

"It smelled like us," said Lucy, remembering how the latex was imbued with a decade's worth of spice.

"Ten years," said Sarah. "I was still with Eva when I got that dildo. It's been a great dildo—I had to chase Scoutie for quite some time—when I got it back she had chewed off a crucial four inches."

"A fifteen-pound dog outsmarted you?"

"I'm not proud."

"Did you yell at her?"

"I did." Sarah was sheepish.

They leaned over the side of the bed to look at Scout. The dog was curled up as tightly as a doughnut. Her back was to Lucy and Sarah, and her dark-brown ears rested on a stuffed rabbit with its head chewed off. The dog moaned in her sleep.

"How loud did you yell?"

"Too loud."

"Look at her—she's pouting. You know she's going to mope all day."

"Darling, don't be mad." She straddled Lucy, kissed her, and then twirled a curl on the middle of her forehead. "Are you sure it's going to be okay for Eva to throw her sex-toy party here tonight?"

Lucy sighed. That evening, Sarah's ex lover, Eva, was officially launching her Web site business by selling samples of sex toys to two dozen of their closest friends. Sarah had tried to convince Lucy that it was going to be like a Tupperware Party. Lucy still wasn't sure that she completely approved of Eva or the party.

Eva was a free spirit. She was an ex-bodybuilder who ran marathons. After she left Sarah, Eva had made a bundle by making porn videos. Not that she needed more money; Eva had won $20,000 from a lottery scratch ticket. Instead of investing the cash in an IRA or the stock market, she decided to develop and sell sex toys with adventurous lesbians in mind. Lucy was jealous of Eva's luck. While she and Sarah were commuting in and out of Boston like dutiful worker bees, Eva had successfully evaded working a nine-to-five job her entire adult life.

Despite her reservations, Lucy had to like Eva because Scout *adored* Eva, and Lucy always trusted her dog's judgement. Scout had psychic powers. In one glance Scout would tail up or tail down a stranger, and Lucy would instinctively know what kind of person she was dealing with. Lucy was obliged to like Eva because Scout knew something she didn't. Whenever Eva visited, Scout charged and leapt into Eva's arms. And much to Lucy's chagrin, Scout cuddled up and slept with Eva whenever she stayed over.

"I know this is your mother's house," said Sarah.

"Yes, but we've seen to it that mother is away," said Lucy. "You yourself put her on an airplane yesterday. By now she should be in Tucson."

Every year Lucy's mother, Phyllis, went to an AA square dance roundup in the Southwest. They had planned the party for the same weekend Phyllis would be on her trip. Lucy got out of bed and walked towards her mother's painting studio. "I wonder if mother cleaned up like she promised," she said.

"Oh, give your mom a break," said Sarah. "We have all day to get ready."

"Now we *need* that party," mumbled Lucy. She hated not being in control. Lucy had arrived at middle age as a respectable editor of children's picture books at Greene & Company on Beacon Hill in Boston. From her fine corner office she made deals via speaker-phone. Artists and writers were hired and fired as she looked out over the Common, the ruler of her roost. She thought of herself as reserved. She passed as modest, demure, decorous, and behaved. Remaining honorably bored through editorial meetings, where she flipped through the printers books of color chips to pass the time. She wore black pinstripes, and on casual Fridays donned starched blue jeans. She was the mother to one small brown dog—adopted, of course, and because she worked in a business that catered to the whims of children, Lucy, naturally, secretly hated them. She had no maternal instincts per se; it was her own juvenile sensibilities that she loved. Children were hazardous to the things she loved most: well-made books, antique windup toys, vacations in Tuscany, Scout's tail, and a clean house.

Lucy stood in the doorway of the studio, tying the belt of her robe. The fumes of dissipating turpentine wound around the scent of hardening oil paint. Honeysuckle wafted in from the bushes outside, along with a sea breeze and the hot smell of beach pine. The smell was home to Lucy. Her mother's recent canvases were stacked neatly in the corner. Squeezed-out tubes of paint, brushes, and pallets had all been put on shelves under the table. Clear of debris, the floor shone with over forty years' worth of smears and paint splatters. Lucy stepped down into the studio. The walls were white, changing hue where the second floor had been removed to accommodate the larger canvases Phyllis worked on in the seven-ties. Light spilled in from the second-floor windows, and Lucy noticed the stains from where the south window still leaked. She shook her head. She really ought to hire someone, she thought. She ought to hire someone to plug the house before its goes down in a blow. Now that her dad was dead she could get it done without imposing on his manly incompetence. Phyllis wouldn't care if Lucy hired a carpenter to repair the window frame. So long as Phyllis was uninterrupted she wouldn't care who came or went from the house or what was worked on. Lucy shook her head and turned to face a painting that had caught the corner of her eye. It hung over the fireplace. She started when she saw it.

"I was worried that it might be too strange for you to buy a dildo from my ex-lover," Sarah called from the next room.

"*We* are buying a dildo," said Lucy.

"Yes, we," said Sarah. "How bad is the studio?" She appeared in the doorway with a cup of coffee in each hand. "Wow, not bad at all. I don't think I've ever seen it so picked up. What are you looking at?"

Lucy pointed. Sarah stepped into the room and turned to face the painting.

"Whoa. Where did that come from?"

"Mom painted it twenty years ago."

The painting was six feet tall by three feet wide.

"Are you sure your mother is straight?" said Sarah.

"Why do you ask?"

"Because those are scrumptious breasts," said Sarah. "Right down to the melting freeze pop."

"Mother tends to embellish reality," said Lucy. She shook her head. The painting was called "Belinda With an Orange Popsicle," and she hadn't seen it since her mother sold it in August 1979. Belinda was an artists model. In the painting she was wearing a mauve square dancer's dress that was unbuttoned around the waist. Her legs straddled a hammock and the tulle of the full skirt was pulled up around her thighs, barely covering her pantyless crotch. Or what looked like a pantyless crotch. Lucy stared at the crotch. The shadow was made with a dab of brown and gray paint in the very center of the composition.

"Hello, old friend," she said to the dab.

Yet there was the white dot next to the brown. At a distance, the white looked like it could be cotton panties. Carter's Girl's, size 12, she supposed. The pink paint of the skirt looked alive and wet—as if it were still swinging with the motion of the hammock, twenty years after Phyllis had put down her brush. Above the splash of pink, Belinda leaned against the weave of the hammock, forever waiting, sucking on a Popsicle, her other hand buried in the pink tulle. *Oh, the hammock,* thought Lucy, remembering the August night when, lying head to foot, she first discovered how legs could be entangled around another girl's torso, how wrists could be clasped to pull until vaginas locked together. How surprised she had been to discover the magnetic pull as she pushed up the billowy fabrics of Belinda's vintage skirt—their skin prevented from touching by the two-inch-wide membrane of their panties. How shocked she had been when she felt the warmth of Belinda. As a star shot across the sky, Lucy began to throb, a wet spot absorbed by the cotton between them. Pulling away would have been the right thing to do, and as Lucy thought of it she gripped Belinda's wrists all the more and struggled to find the right motion. Belinda's butt touching her own proved irresistible. Momentum sent the hammock in a gentle swing, and the swing almost disguised the fact that Lucy was humping Belinda. As they rocked, Belinda humped her in return, her legs pushing away the skirt to clutch Lucy's ass and abdomen between her knees. She should have stopped. She meant to stop, but how could she? Were they really doing anything at all? They hadn't named it with a kiss, so did any of it count? Or were they just two girls in a hammock, watching a meteor shower, their heads facing away from each other like a pair of Jacks on a playing card?

"I'm sorry," said Lucy. "Finding this painting comes as a surprise."

"Why? Your mother's prolific."

"Because she promised me that this was the one painting I could keep. But no sooner had she promised than she showed it, sold it, packed it up, and sent it to Zurich. Something like that."

"What's it doing here?"

"Beats me."

"Then it will be the centerpiece of the party," said Sarah. "Look, she's giving head to her Popsicle. Very sexy. I'll bet Eva will have a run on any orange strap-ons. By the way, darling, do you have any idea what kind of dildo you would like?"

"One that will inspire you."

"Any particular color?"

"Slippery," said Lucy. "Slippery is the best color."

Sarah patted Lucy's knee with affection.

"And once we get rid of all the guests we'll have the house to ourselves," said Lucy.

Sarah kissed her. "Size does matter. I still say we buy a few. New dildos are like having an affair: you get to fuck around with someone new without all the cheating or the guilt."

III

"Hey, hi there," said Eva, digging boxes out of her car. Lucy's eyes rested on Eva's ass hanging out of her shorts. Despite Eva's advanced age of forty-eight, her display of flesh actually looked good. Her butt was terra firma because Eva was also an aerobics instructor. She taught a class called "Fat Dyke Aerobics" during the spring and summer—a class Lucy was too proud to attend. Nevertheless, Sarah occasionally donned a warm-up suit with racing stripes down the legs and jumped around with the fat dykes, who, in Lucy's opinion, were not really fat at all, just dressed slovenly. A bottle of Super Sun-in stuck out from the side pocket of Eva's cutoffs. It was barely May. Eva was tan all over, and what gray hair she might have had was bleached white.

"Are you ready?" Eva said, tromping into the house with a box under each arm.

Lucy grinned and blushed.

"Oh, don't worry, Love," said Eva. "I'm sure I have plenty of G-spotting devices to interest you."

Eva set the two boxes of sex toys on the dining room table, put her fingers in her mouth and whistled. "Scout?" she said. "Scoutie? Look what I have!" Eva held up a deluxe anal plug made of red and yellow swirls of silicone.

"I hope that's new," said Sarah.

"Of course, darling," said Eva. "Here, girl!"

Yet the dog didn't budge from her corner where she had sat for most of the day.

"What's wrong with Scout?" said Eva.

"She's grounded," said Sarah.

"Grounded?"

"Sarah yelled at her," said Lucy.

"Oh, dear!" said Eva. "How could you?" Eva scooped up the dog, and Lucy noticed how Scout began to sniff. The dog's eyes grew wider. Her tail wagged and then she began to lick Eva's neck.

"I daresay," said Sarah. "I think she likes you because you smell of latex. Scout goes mad for the scent like a kitty high on catnip."

Revived, Scout proceeded to go on a tear through the house, butt plug clamped in her jaws, until exhausted, she collapsed in Eva's arms and stayed there until the house was ready for the guests. By the time the small blue penis Christmas lights were hung on the deck facing the ocean, Scout was set down amid the flurry of activity. The caterers delivered fruit and cheese platters, which were set out amongst tubed orchids on the buffet. Samples of dildos with price tags were set up on the worktable in Phyllis's studio and throughout the shining house. The guests were a half hour short of arriving when Lucy's mother pulled into the drive.

"Oh, hell," said Sarah.

Lucy was frozen for a second. She saw her mother get out of the car.

"Well, hello, Phyllis," said Sarah, ambling out onto the front porch. "What a surprise."

Lucy's mother took off her sunglasses and got out her cigarettes. "You'll never believe what happened," said Phyllis. "I got to Tucson and blah, blah, blah. Then I had an epiphany—can you believe it? An epiphany."

"Really?"

"There I was baring my soul to a group of strange old Republicans—all dressed in crinolines, mind you, when it hits me: I don't have a drinking problem; Bob had a drinking problem. Then I realized—I never really liked square dancing, just the dresses, and usually on someone else—so I thought, what the hell am I doing here? Just what the hell is someone my age with my shape doing dressing like a Barbie Doll? Then you'll never believe what dawned on me."

"I can't guess," said Sarah.

"It dawned on me that I was dying for a Bloody Mary. I don't know what I've been thinking all these years. I've missed having cocktails, and by God now that Bob's dead I really ought to have a few. So I says to myself: *Phyllis, girl, call your old buddy Doloris, tell her to meet you at the Crown and Anchor, fly home from Tucson, drive on down to the Cape, park your cars, stay with the girls, and go!* Time's a-wasting. Ha! So I thought: *What am I doing in Arizona?* I should be with you kids."

"Oh, my," mumbled Sarah.

"So blah, blah, blah, booked a flight home, got in the car, and here I am. Enough about me. What are you girls up to?"

"Oh, a dinner party with a few friends," said Sarah. Lucy came to the door and stood behind Sarah with her hands on her hips.

"Sorry I'm going to miss it," said Phyllis. "Did you find the painting? I left it out for you my last trip."

"Did I find the painting?" said Lucy. "Oh, I found the painting."

"Good. Keep it," said Phyllis. "Drag it back to Boston if you like. It's yours." Phyllis looked at her watch. "Crap on a crumpet, I'm late. I'm supposed to meet Doloris at six o'clock. But I'll be back."

"When?" said Lucy. She came down the front steps and noticed that her mother was wearing crushed velvet stretch pants that clung all the way down to her skinny ankles. On her top was a purple oversized sweatshirt with sequined teddy bears appliquéd on the front and back.

Phyllis mirrored Lucy by putting her fists on her hips. "Now that I'm single, do I have a curfew?"

"No," said Lucy. "I'm just wondering when to throw out all the guests."

"Oh, don't mind me," said Phyllis. "I'll be back whenever. I'll just sneak in like you girls used to when you were young and bad."

"Here," said Sarah. "Take my cell phone. Call me when you're ready to come home, and I'll come get you."

"Would you?"

"Of course," said Sarah.

"That's great," said Phyllis. "Just great. You know I can't stand spending money on cabs, and I'm just too fat and tired to be out walking that time of night."

Phyllis fired up a cigarette. "You girls be good," she said. The cigarette waggled in her mouth, flipping ash as she spoke. "Don't talk to strangers unless they offer you candy." She slung her handbag over her shoulder. The contents rattled as they shifted. Phyllis grinned. "Free shampoo bottles and an ashtray that says TUCSON BEST WESTERN."

Lucy rolled her eyes.

"You need it for the party? It's got a cactus and a howling dog on it. You'll love it. I guess not. All right," said Phyllis. "I'm off."

Sarah and Lucy watched Phyllis amble down the street.

"I say we throw the party," said Sarah. "We're too old for orgies. We do sex toys and finger food and wrap it up by nine."

IV

Someone arrived in a stretch limousine, while another blocked traffic with a horse and carriage. Car horns beeped until the carriage pulled away. The gay press had arrived—a small army in black polyester and Doc Martin boots with their specific golden threads that always seemed to say "I'm in the life." People sat in the pink Adirondack chairs scattered around the lawn, and on the front porch a mystery guest had parked a vintage bicycle. Lucy's eyes widened when she saw it—she imagined herself riding, riding,

riding up and down all the little hills in the dunes. A dildo rose out of the buffed chrome where the seat should have been. Who rode it there? Or was it walked? Or was it humped? *I bet it was Stella,* thought Lucy. Sexy Stella who dressed in yella and never kissed a fella. Where was she? Lucy needed to get an eyeful. Blue clouds blew onto the bay. The scent of beach pine wafted over the grass and the sand turned tawny orange in the fading sun. A glass dropped somewhere in the house, followed by a high pitched laugh. Someone bellowed "Darling!" every thirty seconds or so.

Lucy was looking for Scout. The last time she saw the dog, Scout was at the top of the stairs looking down on the crowd, her nose between her paws, her tail half-mast and undecided. Lucy walked around the outside of the studio and looked in.

"NFS," said a guest. He nursed his martini in front of the painting of Belinda.

"Not for sale, Bear," said the boyfriend.

"Anything can be bought for a price," said martini guy.

Lucy glared at them through the window. Martini guy was wearing a retro olive-green suit, and slip-on shoes with elastic and no laces. The other guy was just another guy—she'd seen him race to the gym in his midlife crisis–red Saab with a vanity license plate that said SNAAB. He was as thin as a queen, buff as a queen, and so concerned with how he looked that he probably packed a scale when he went on vacation. *Poor creature,* thought Lucy. Gay boys were worse than a fussy single woman on a husband hunt.

"What do you want with a picture of a cunt?" said the beauty queen.

"Good art. Good investment. I could sell it later if I got tired of it."

"I'm already tired of it."

Lucy entered the studio from outside just as the fashionable couple wandered off. She had to stifle her impulse to track them down and pop them on their heads. But she looked at the painting again. It reminded her of listening to the Talking Heads twenty years before. Once upon a time, when she had first studied the painting, she realized, *Oh, my gawd, I must be one of* those *girls after all. Maybe this isn't a phase because I adore the womanly curve just below Belinda's breasts. I'd like to stick my head under the chiaroscuro of all that tulle to see what's there. What would happen if I got into the hammock with this girl? I want to keep this painting in my room. How did my mother get my girl friend to pose like this? And why is she barely covered with my mother's dress? What were they doing? They were locked alone in the studio all afternoon—the artist and the model. Did Belinda sit nude in the same position, legs parted, leaving nothing to the imagination?*

The sounds of hilarity poured in the studio door. A glass broke. A blender started up. "Darling!" Lucy heard a sneeze.

She turned around. "Scout," she said.

The dog was sitting under the worktable, her tail down. She'd been guarding the studio. She sneezed again, and Lucy scooped her up to comfort her. As Lucy stepped into the main part of the house, a drag queen with eight-inch platform shoes got up onto her mother's dining-room table and started ringing a cowbell. The drag queen, in her silver spandex Speedo, couldn't help but dance. "Oh, my favorite song," she cried. "Crank it up!"

Scout leapt from Lucy's arms onto the table as the drag queen started to swing her golden dreadlocks. The dog waited for the perfect moment, then caught hold of a braid and swung to the floor.

"Hey!" The drag queen pitched forward and was caught by a mosh pit of pilgrims making their way to the living room for Eva's presentation.

"Hey! My hair," she cried.

But the screen door slammed and Scout was out the door, dragging the wig up the beach with Lucy in close pursuit.

The living room was packed with friends and stockholders when they returned. Eva was almost finished showing some of her best selling items.

"For the guys," said Eva. "No, girls, we can't forget the guys. They're big spenders. For the guys I have silicone anal plugs in a plethora of pleasurable shapes. Try these nonvibrating insertable toys to create a pleasurable sense of fullness. For your anal adventures to proceed smoothly, don't forget to use plenty of lubricant. I have three sizes—the loner, the groaners, and orgy size, with a handy press-pump dispenser.

"For the girls we've developed this new G spot stimulator." Eva held up a Lucite wand shaped like an S. "Climb aboard, girls, and ride! The stimulator can be used by you yourself or with a friend. And it's beautiful when wet.

"For all you single gals on the go, I have the battery-operated Pocket Rocket. Fits nicely in its own fancy travel purse that can be used as a cosmetic box if you leave home without it. The Pocket Rocket is for everyone. It's perfect for the newly divorced, steady eddies, single girls on the go, or widows. It easily adapts to a strap-on holster or can be used all by its lonesome." Eva flicked a switch and the vibrator began to hum. "It uses four rechargeable batteries and comes in six colors: *Bing* cherry red, har*vest* gold, blue *balls* blue, sea-*foam* green, lavender *spar*kle, and *rain*bow twist.

"For you girls who like to ride bareback we have developed the new Janus doubleheader. The innovative V shape will leave your hands free! No fussy straps. Take the double-headed dildo plunge and go, go, go, girls! Available in blue-pearl swirl and lavender sparkle.

"Having trouble with arrhythmia? Is your partner finding it difficult staying steady long enough to get the job done? Well—one of my newest products is the combination fuck sling that doubles as a hammock. It can be hung virtually anywhere, and no one has to know its intended purpose." Eva held up the macramé hammock. "The fuck sling gives new meaning to the idea of waving a big stick. Imagine that! Have a great slam in the back yard under the moonlight. No one has to know. Sunday morning the fuck sling becomes the perfect place to read the paper and siesta."

Eva held up a tiny strap with a rubber lavender moth in the middle. "Set your lover's senses aflutter with this battery remote-operated flutter-by. Slip into the elastic straps, get dressed, and then let your partner turn you on from the other room! At only $89.95 you're bound to give someone a bang at a distance. One size fits most. And that concludes my presentation of *fab*ulous products."

V

Sarah was holding up the lavender moth vibrator when the phone rang. Lucy answered it. "Yes? Of course, mother. I'll come. Give me ten. Okay, buh-bye." She hung up and rolled her eyes. "Just when things were starting to cook." Sexy Stella dressed in yella was dancing topless on the table, swinging her ass in short shorts and fishnets to the synthesized wah-wah-pedal beat. Stella was smooth, every so often tossing five cherries up in the air, catching the last to fall in her mouth. It was painful for Lucy to look away. The bowl of cherries—Lucy's new perishable toy of choice—was at Stella's feet. *Eat me*, Lucy thought with guilty pleasure.

Sarah dangled the remote battery-operated moth vibrator in front of Lucy. "Put it on," said Sarah. "When I've thrown out Eva and the guests I'll give you a buzz and you can come home."

"But what about—"

"I'll have to pick one. What do you want?"

"Surprise me."

VI

Phyllis was flushed. "I thought my pants would never dry! Oh, it's been so long since I had cocktails. I didn't know what I was missing." She leaned back in her chair, pulling on a pair of fluffy bedroom slippers. The bowl of cherries sat in front of her.

"So what is that portrait of Belinda doing here?" said Lucy. "Did some dealer sell it back to you?"

"Not exactly," said Phyllis. She shrugged, then chuckled again. "I got it out of storage."

"How'd it get there?"

"I always had it," said Phyllis.

"Had it? You told me you sold it. That the gallery packed it and shipped it to Zurich. I saw the crate."

"A painting got shipped, but not exactly that one," Phyllis said.

Lucy was exasperated. "You told me I could have that painting over twenty years ago," she said. "Then you said you sold it."

"Something like that," said Phyllis, dismissing her. "I'm finally giving it to you, why are you so mad?"

"You lied to me."

"I did not," said Phyllis. "I said you could have the painting, but I didn't say when. So now you can have it. It's yours. Don't you want it?"

"Of course I want it, mother. I've always wanted it."

"Then don't belly ache. Say thank you."

"Thank you," said Lucy. "Would you still let me keep it if someone offered you ten grand?"

"Does someone want it?" said Phyllis.

"I'm just asking."

Phyllis picked up a cherry and touched it to her lips.

"Here, Mother, let me rinse those for you," said Lucy.

"That's okay," said Phyllis. She sniffed the cherry and furrowed her brow.

"I insist," said Lucy. "You never know where anything's been these days."

"Nope, nope, nope, I won't let you. I want to be reckless." Phyllis claimed the bowl, hunched over it, and swatted away her daughter's hand.

"I wouldn't want you to get sick or anything."

"When you're as old as me, bitterness makes you immune to everything. Why are there footprints on my good table?"

Lucy put her head in her hands. "Oh, mother. What the hell are you doing here? I told you we were having a special party."

"So special your old mom can't come?"

"Yes, in fact, you really were not invited."

"But this is my house."

"I know that. But really, mother, I did tell you there was one weekend—one weekend when we needed the house—but you came anyway."

"Well, I didn't wake up in Tucson and think, *Gee, I'm bored, I think I'll go home and torture the children.*"

"But that's exactly what you did."

"I'm sorry I'm such a bother. I thought you'd understand. Shoot. I thought you'd be happy to see me, especially since I came home to make amends."

"Amends?"

"Yes, amends. I got that damn painting out for you so you'd forgive me. I haven't been sitting through AA meetings listening to strangers blather on all these years for nothing."

"Amends," said Lucy. "Amends…"

"Don't snap your cap. I got out of the way so you could throw your secret party, whatever the hell it was. The least you could do was keep people from dancing on the furniture. Look at the scuff marks here," she said, rubbing the surface of the table.

"That's not the point," said Lucy.

"The point is I've missed you," said Phyllis.

"Really?"

"I did. I do. Since your dad died I've had a lot of things to think over, and I've come to realize I'm sorry."

"What for?"

"The summer of 1979, for starters."

"I'm not following you."

Phyllis reached for the cherries. "These are pretty. Like little apples. Yellow and red. Yellow and red. These aren't Bing cherries. What are they?"

"Bang cherries," said Sarah.

"I'm going to have to get us some more," she said, "because I intend to eat them all." She turned one in her fingers. "So perfect and no stems and so big. Oh, my." She ate one. "I've never had bang cherries. These are delicious." Phyllis reached for a handful.

"All right. You've come to make amends. Hit me."

"Okay, I am. Here goes: I'm sorry for the time you made friends with that girl, Belinda, and I said you couldn't sleep in the same bed because you weren't married like your brothers. It was silly of me. Of course you weren't married."

Lucy was silent. Phyllis grabbed her purse and hunched over it. "There. I said it. I'm sorry. Do you want some little travel bottles of shampoo from the hotel? Do you forgive your old mom?"

"I'm rather shocked," said Lucy. "Shocked."

"Why?"

"That you came all the way back here to apologize for something I barely remember."

"Really?" said Phyllis. "How could you forget?"

"Except that we ended up sleeping on the dock."

Sarah stood up. "Look at Lucy blush," she said. "My guess is you didn't do much sleeping."

Lucy's face was like the *Mona Lisa*.

"You got that right," said Phyllis. "I came outside to smoke because Bob didn't like it in the house—always whining about the proximity of ashes and turpentine—I wanted to see what they were giggling about. They laughed all night. I felt so helplessly left out. They were so gay. I followed the laughter under the moonlight, thinking about how we used to read *Good Night Moon* together every night."

"And?" said Sarah.

"I was picturing my baby girl, and wouldn't you know it surprised me to see her suddenly so grown up. I mean, there it was, three in the morning, I can't sleep because I'm going through the change, and suddenly the girls aren't laughing anymore because they are kissing. That's what I mean."

"Belinda? Belinda?" said Sarah. "Before that painting turned up you never mentioned anyone named Belinda."

Lucy blushed. She remembered Belinda well. How on August 24, 1979, during a hot spell, they laid out in the hammock until everyone finally went to bed. After the stereo had quit Lucy went down to the dock in the moonlight and sat watching the flickering reflections in the water. Belinda sat beside her, then kissed her. Lucy was afraid she'd be seen so she took off her skirt and slipped off the dock into water as warm as a bath. She gave in to her longing and let Belinda kiss her. Barnacles scratched her back as Belinda and the tide pressed her to the post of the dock. Lucy planned to kiss her and then mention her boyfriend. But Belinda pressed her breasts into Lucy until Lucy was weak. A quick hour passed and the tide subsided around them as she gave in, letting Belinda caress her waist, reaching up to her breasts. She'd taken a dance class that year, and she pretended her legs were in a second position as the girl pulled her panties away from her ass. Lucy had brought her legs together just enough for Belinda to take them and let them drift away with the tide. Then she stood again in the pretense of second position, nervously digging her toes into the sand. Belinda was on her knees. She reached up, caressed the tops of Lucy's thighs, and said, "Let me see." And Lucy, ashamed, couldn't resist lowering herself into Belinda's palms. Belinda squeezed her ass—the place like two breasts below the slit of her vulva—and Lucy found that she couldn't stop herself once Belinda spread her labia and slipped her tongue into her cunt. Without realizing what she was doing, Lucy was losing her virginity. Wasn't it supposed to hurt? Wasn't she supposed to worry about pregnancy? No. She was on a ride with an unstoppable momentum. When Belinda laid her on the beach, her mouth suctioned on her cunt, Lucy felt as though her legs were in the way. She couldn't open them wide enough, nor could her knees press up as far as they should. Belinda stopped suddenly and lay back on the sand. She motioned for Lucy to sit on her face. So Lucy straddled her. The sea was silver in the moonlight, a full-bodied animal lapping all that it touched. When Lucy looked down and saw Belinda's breasts, the curve of her waist and the rock of her hips, she leaned forward and kissed her above the pubic bone. Her elbows rested in the sand, and she knew that she should stop. *What's-his-name,* she thought. *I must date What's-his-name.* She wanted to stop. She insisted to herself that she should stop, but just as she meant to, Belinda's tongue would discover a new fold in Lucy's vagina, and she would lose herself. *Enough,* she thought. But then she caressed Belinda's vulva and felt how swollen she was. The two Twinkies she'd seen in Belinda's swim suit all August were now engorged under the white cotton panties. Lucy reached a finger under the elastic. Belinda's labia peeked out like petals, sweet and wet like egg white, begged to be massaged. Surprise. Belinda groaned, her tongue plunging up into Lucy, who received her gratefully. To distract herself, Lucy forgot to stop, pulled the crotch of the panties aside, and dipped into Belinda's cunt. She stroked until Belinda started to spread her legs and thrust. Lucy tore the panties and pushed her finger inside, reaching for that place she knew so well on herself. She had planned to stop, yet she found herself bending over Belinda and wrapping her lips around her clitoris. She was disgusted, a salt smell covered her lips, but then a sweet salt surprised her: Belinda squirmed in pleasure, which made Lucy seem to flood. Belinda not only tasted like scallops but also like herself. Her clit grew in Lucy's mouth. Her vulva opened and every time Lucy told herself to stop, she found herself stroking Belinda's face with her vagina like a wet paintbrush slapping a wall. *How does this happen?* she wondered, going over the edge. Wasn't she supposed to want a penis? Wasn't it a surprise to discover a starfish hand? she thought as she opened her mouth in a silent cry one more time. Lucy opened her eyes. The sky was pinkening. Somewhere a door slammed.

"I think Lucy was a bit of a hussy," said Phyllis, stirring her cup of tea.

"Mother."

"Well, you were, dear."

"She was?" said Sarah. "My prim little Lucy?"

"Yes, a hussy," said Phyllis. "And if the truth be known, she got the most action of all my children, and she gave me the least worries. And then there was that Belinda, running around the yard and onto the beach with her top off. In and out of the house without a second thought about Bob. I finally had to buy her a bus ticket and send her away."

"Mother."

"I did. That California nudist colony crap does not go over in Massachusetts. And every time she got arrested for being topless on the beach she told the ranger she lived here! And every time the ranger came to the door with a summons, Bob quietly wrote a check. Your father had a boner for weeks, darling. You have no idea. Then he was drunk all the time and saying crass things he just couldn't help. So I put that damn painting away because, frankly, I was sick of it, and of her, and of him. Sick of you, sick of everything."

"You were jealous," said Lucy.

"Jealous? Me? Of whom?"

"Of Belinda."

Phyllis shrugged.

"You were," said Lucy. "A girl's mother expects a son-in-law, not another woman to come and take her place."

Phyllis was silent for a moment. "I don't know about that," she finally said. "But if you had a husband and kids and the whole package, you'd know."

"There, see? You were jealous. And what in the hell were you doing painting Belinda topless?"

"She was always naked," said Phyllis.

"Then how did you get her to put on your square-dance dress?"

"I don't remember."

"Was she wearing underwear?"

"She always had the decency to wear cheerleader's trunks," said Phyllis.

"See, you remember a lot more than you should."

"When did you get so puritanical? You, of all people."

"You weren't supposed to flirt with my girlfriend, mother."

"She was my model long before she was your girlfriend."

"And what does that mean?"

"Oh, hell," said Phyllis. "Oh, screw. You wonder why I wanted to get rid of the painting? Maybe I should cut it from the canvas and throw it out. All it does is remind me of a particularly confusing summer."

"You'll do no such thing," said Lucy. "I'm taking it to Boston. Belinda was my first lover. There, I said it. That painting is the only picture I have of her." Lucy turned to Sarah, who had been standing in the doorway with her hands hanging in her pockets. "Do you have any problem with hanging that painting in our apartment?"

Sarah shook her head.

Phyllis sighed and ate another handful of cherries, one by one.

"Used to be you either loved my girlfriends and invaded our

space, or you snubbed them," said Lucy. "I could never read you until I figured out the more I loved someone, the more you hated her. You were delighted with Belinda before she became my lover. What happened?"

"She must've overstayed her welcome," said Phyllis. "Look, please forgive me. I came all the way home to say I'm sorry."

They remained silent until Scout started to bark in the other room. Then the dog shot out of the bedroom, her tail pushed between her legs as she ran. She streaked by, leapt onto a stuffed chair, rebounded to the sofa, then banked the length of the living room. Scout then ran up the stairs, jumped from bed to bed, and returned to the braided rug where she paused, rump in the air, a wild look in her eyes.

"I guess Scout has recovered from being yelled at," said Lucy.

"Moodiness can be a habit," said Phyllis. "Just you remember that, missy."

As they spoke, Scout retrieved her toys from the bedroom, spread them across the rug, and barked at them. Phyllis ate a cherry, threw back her head and laughed. After her romp Scout darted in the bedroom and came out dancing with a new toy. She shook it and growled.

"Isn't that cute," said Phyllis. "Scout wants to play tug. What do you have there, missy? Let old grandma put on her glasses and see. If you'd hold still, I could have a better look."

Phyllis put on her bifocals and took hold of the other end of a new double-headed dildo and tugged back. "Come on, girl. Come on!"

The little dog growled fiercely.

"Well, aren't you tough," said Phyllis. "Ruff, tough."

"Oh, no," said Lucy.

Phyllis gripped the glittered dildo then dropped it. "Oh, my." said Phyllis. "Is that what I think that is?"

"Yes, mother."

"Oh, my. Oh, my. A marital aid. Just what have you girls been up to? Let me have a closer look."

"Quick—get it!"

But Scout scooped it and pranced off with the dildo bouncing out of either side of her mouth. The dog growled, shook it, and shot upstairs with Lucy in hot pursuit.

Sarah scratched her head.

Phyllis fanned her blushing face. "Well, what was that about? Aye, yi, yi."

They both listened to the thundering on the floorboards above.

"I've never told you," said Phyllis, "but I think Lucy is lucky to have found you."

"Why do you say that?"

"Because you're a nice girl. I see you've hung a new hammock for her out in the yard. It's in the same place as the old one."

Sarah smiled and shoved her hands in her pockets. "Oh, it's just a little something in the side yard."

"It will be a nice private place to read," said Phyllis. "Yes, lucky."

"I think we work at our luck," said Sarah.

"Hmm. I chose the name Lucy because it's one letter short of *lucky.*"

The foghorn sounded in the distance. The tide was coming up again.

"You know, I hear a buzz," said Phyllis. "I've been hearing it all night. Do you hear a buzz?"

"I don't hear a buzz," said Sarah.

"Maybe I'm slipping into Alzheimer's."

"Hah!" said Lucy. "Got it." She came in the room with the dildo in one hand and Scout in the other.

Phyllis's eyes fixed on the length and width of the dildo Lucy held in her hand.

"Looks like a boomerang," said Phyllis.

"You always get back whatever you give," said Sarah.

"How do you get one of those?"

"Here, darling," said Lucy. "Let me pass the baton. You explain to mother what we've been up to."

Lucy went into the bedroom to tuck Scout in her bed.

"We we're having a sex-toy party," said Sarah. "Our friend Eva was selling her samples."

"You were?" said Phyllis. "And you didn't want me around?"

Lucy returned to the dining room table. "Mother," she said.

"Did it ever occur to you that maybe I'd be interested?"

"I was going to send you a vibrator for Mother's Day," said Sarah.

Phyllis's mouth hung open. Her face was frozen half in delight, half in horror.

Sarah went into the bedroom and came back with a purple pocket rocket in its handy case. "But I think I'll give you one instead. I've bought a few things."

"Oh, my," said Phyllis, taking the vibrator out of its case.

"I had planned to send it to you anonymously," said Sarah.

"Good thing you didn't. I'd have thought it came from a perverted secret admirer. There's that buzzing again. Listen."

They were silent.

"Is it coming from Lucy?" said Phyllis. "Are you all right, dear?"

"Perfectly fine."

"Well, I don't know about you," said Sarah. "But I'm going to leave Phyllis with her new date, go sit in the hammock, and watch the moon rise. Good night, girls."

VII

"I thought you'd never get the hint," said Sarah. She slowed the swing of the hammock and made room for Lucy, who climbed in next to her. Gravity pushed them together as Sarah started to rock. "Is this hammock a—?"

"Of course, but a much improved edition."

"My Pleasure Moth works all the way out at Herring Cove."

"I thought it might."

With the rocking of the hammock, the moon rose, the moon set, the moon rose. The air off the sea was close to perfume. A star shot across the sky, turning from red to orange to green to blue as it faded into a trail.

"Do you hear a buzzing?" said Sarah.

Lucy pried the remote from Sarah's hand and kissed her. She wrapped her leg over Sarah, trying to pull her closer.

"Want to get lucky?" whispered Sarah.

Lucy kissed her, felt the wide set of Sarah's breasts, and reached for the front of her Levi's. Lucy was startled by Sarah's supposed erection.

"I am lucky," she said, wondering what color, what shape it might be. She started at the zipper to find out.

Contributor Biographies

Janet Williams has embraced her creative muse. As a writer she has been published in newspapers and magazines. Her work as a graphic artist and illustrator appears in numerous printed pieces and texts. Her fine artwork has been represented in galleries across Southern California, where she resides.

Rachel Kramer Bussel (www.rachelkramerbussel.com) is senior editor at *Penthouse Variations*. Her books include *The Lesbian Sex Book (Second Edition)*; *Up All Night: Adventures in Lesbian Sex*; *Glamour Girls: Femme/Femme Erotica*; and *Naughty Spanking Stories from A to Z*. Her erotica has appeared in more than forty anthologies—including *Best American Erotica 2004* and *Best Lesbian Erotica 2001* and *2004*—and she contributes to *Bust, On Our Backs, Velvetpark, The Village Voice*, and other publications.

Diana Chase is a twenty-two-year-old dyke from San Diego, currently living and teaching high school English in the Los Angeles area. She earned her B.A. in writing at the University of California, San Diego, and has been reveling in writer's block since. Her hobbies include cooking, watching porn, and being a merciless tease.

Tara Alton (www.taraalton.com) has published erotica in *The Mammoth Book of Best New Erotica, Best Lesbian Erotica 2005, Best Women's Erotica, Hot Women's Erotica, Clean Sheets*, and *Scarlet Letters*. She writes erotica because that is what is in her head and it needs to come out.

Wendy Caster wrote *The Lesbian Sex Book* (Alyson Books). Her one-act play, *You Look Just Like Him*, was presented at the Estrogenius Festival in New York City. She is currently working on a full-length play. Wendy lives in the East Village in New York City. She has no girlfriend or cats, yet her life is full.

Amie M. Evans is a confirmed femme bottom who lives life like a spontaneously choreographed performance. She is a well-published creative nonfiction and literary erotica writer, workshop provider, and a burlesque and high femme drag performer. She has her B.A. in Literature and is currently working on her MLA at Harvard.

Catherine Lundoff lives in Minneapolis with her fabulous partner and is a professional computer geek. She is the author of the collection *Night's Kiss: Lesbian Erotica* (Torquere Press). In her free time she is a columnist for the Erotica Readers and Writer's Association (www.erotica readers.com) and teaches erotic writing workshops at Writing-World.com.

Crystal Sincoff (erotikryter@yahoo.com) is a photographer and reporter for a California newspaper. Her short stories are featured in the anthologies *Rode Hard, Put Away Wet: Lesbian Cowboy Erotica,* and *Call of the Dark: Erotic Lesbian Tales of the Supernatural.*

Kristina Wright (www.kristinawright.com) has published her fiction in over twenty anthologies, including *Ultimate Lesbian Erotica 2005; Best Lesbian Erotica 2002, 2004,* and *2005; Show and Tell: True Stories of Lesbian Lust* and *Ultimate Gay Erotica.* She lives in Virginia and is pursuing a masters degree in humanities.

Jean Roberta lives on the Canadian prairie, teaches English at a local university, and writes sex stories, rants, reviews, and articles. She has a monthly column, "In My Jeans," on the Web site *Blue*

Food. Her true coming-out story is in *Up All Night: Adventures in Lesbian Sex* (Alyson Books).

Paige Griffin, originally from the East Coast, is now a California girl. She lives with her family and their exotic menagerie in Los Angeles. She's a full-time mother, writer, and lover. She wishes that everyone could be as happy with their sex lives as she is after twelve years of monogamy and two children.

Brandy Chase was born in Washington, D.C., in the middle of the twentieth century. Growing up outside of Alexandria, Virginia, in Fairfax County, she graduated from Thomas A. Edison High School in 1968. She still lives within a hundred miles of her childhood home with the husband she married while still in high school. She's the mother of two and the grandmother of six.

D. Alexandria, a Gemini child and Jamaican descendant, hails from Boston. A self-proclaimed "Boughetto princess," she has been published in *Best Lesbian Erotica 2005*, and under the pseudonym "Glitter" published *Queer Ramblings Magazine*, *GBF Magazine*. She is a regular contributor to Kuma2.net. She is currently penning her first novel and a collection of black lesbian erotica.

Aimee Nichols is a student and freelance writer, which means she spends a lot of time sitting in front of a computer with her head in her hands. Her work has appeared internationally in anthologies, magazines, and online. Further information can be cobbled together from www.intergalactic-hussy.net.

Stefka has been writing for as long as she can remember, and can't think of a better way to entertain people. This is her fourth short story published by Alyson. Her work will appear in the upcoming anthology *Show and Tell*. Without the inspiration of her partner, Rebekah, and the antics of her six cats, she wouldn't be able to express herself as she does.

Geneva King, a member of the Erotic Readers and Writers Association, has been published in *Erotic Fantasy: Tales of the Paranormal* and *Who's Your Daddy*. She intends to publish a collection of her stories if her professors ever give her enough time to do so. You can visit her website at www.angelfire.com/empire2/gking/index.html.

Caelin Taylor lives in Seattle, where she enjoys drinking cheap beer with good friends at a roadhouse called Bubba's. She loves the Mojave, independent film, and Pink's chili dogs.

Julien Lee found her calling at the tender age of fifteen after winning accolades for her short stories. *My Mistress Awaits* was her first foray into the world of erotica with *Lotus* shortly following. She lives in Los Angeles with her pug, Zoe.

Lynn Cole is an American expatriate living in London. When she's not writing in a café or entertaining tourists on a walking tour of the city, she is making music with her band, Bubba Chryst. Her story *Minding the Gap* appeared in *Ultimate Lesbian Erotica 2005*.

Aunt Fanny was born during a flying carpet ride back in the dark ages (a bumpy start at best), and has traveled the world, seen everything, and eaten most of it. Having no parents, siblings, or children of her own, she's family to no one, and Aunt to everyone—especially you.

Therese Szymanski is the Lammy finalist author of the *Brett Higgins MotorCity Thrillers*; editor of *Back to Basics*, *Call of the Dark*, and *A Perfect Valentine*; part of the team that created *Once Upon a Dyke* and *Bell, Book, and Dyke*; and a contributor to a few dozen other anthologies.

Michelle Sinclair is a writer currently living and drawing much of her inspiration in San Francisco. The cornucopia of female delicacies residing within the city limits continue to infuse Michelle's work with a spice and fervor that she delights in the prospect of to no end.

Rakelle Valencia has jumped into the smut-writing business with both booted feet. Besides coediting the anthologies *Rode Hard, Put Away Wet,* and *Dykes on Bikes,* she has recently been published in *Ultimate Lesbian Erotica 2005, On Our Backs, Best Lesbian Erotica 2004* and *2005, Best of the Best Lesbian Erotica 2, Naughty Spanking Stories A-Z,* and *Best Lesbian Love Stories.*

Jody Ekert lives in Sydney. Attempts at entering the workforce have seen her working everywhere from camp counseling at "Fat Camp" to night management of a backpackers hotel, a cruise ship videographer, and even a phone sex operator. Above all she writes and performs.

Lisa Bishop has had her erotic fiction published in *Playgirl, Girlphoria, Cyber-Mistress, Pink Flamingo,* and *Satin Slippers.* She lives in northwestern Pennsylvania with her spouse, four children, and two cats—her four-legged editors in chief.

Mette Bach lives, works, and plays in Vancouver, Canada. Her stories have been published across North America. She writes a regular column called "Not That Kind of Girl" and is proof that you don't need a cock to be an arrogant prick.

Tina Simmons followed in the footsteps of many great writers and moved to Key West, Florida, to pursue her creative passions. She doesn't have a telephone or a Web site, but she can be found every night at sunset in Mallory Square. If you run into her, she just might tell you a story.

Annie Gauger attended the University of Massachusetts and

Boston University, and currently works full-time at the Dana Farber Cancer Institute in Boston. Her former thesis, *The Annotated Wind in the Willows*, is forthcoming from W.W. Norton in 2008. On May 20, 2004, she married her bride of fifteen years.